DEATH AND TRANSFIGURATION

ALSO BY GERALD ELIAS

Devil's Trill

Danse Macabre

Death and the Maiden

DEATH AND TRANSFIGURATION

GERALD ELIAS

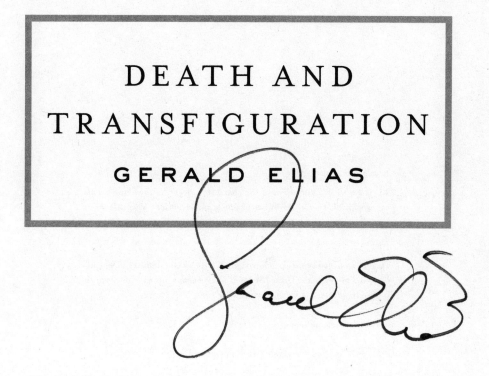

Minotaur Books

New York

This is a work of fiction. All of the characters, organizations, and events portrayed in this novel are either products of the author's imagination or are used fictitiously.

DEATH AND TRANSFIGURATION. Copyright © 2012 by Gerald Elias. All rights reserved. Printed in the United States of America. For information, address St. Martin's Press, 175 Fifth Avenue, New York, N.Y. 10010.

www.minotaurbooks.com

Library of Congress Cataloging-in-Publication Data

Elias, Gerald.
    Death and transfiguration : a Daniel Jacobus novel / Gerald Elias. — 1st ed.
        p. cm.
    ISBN 978-0-312-67835-7 (hardcover)
    ISBN 978-1-250-01480-1 (e-book)
    1. Violin teachers—Fiction.   2. Conductors (Music)—Fiction.   I. Title.
    PS3605.L389D44 2012
    813'.6—dc23

                                                            2012005488

First Edition: June 2012

10 9 8 7 6 5 4 3 2 1

Dedicated to orchestral musicians,

without whose three centuries of determined efforts

the Three B's would have been hard-pressed for employment

AUTHOR'S NOTE

Few sounds in the universe elicit a greater visceral thrill than that of an orchestra, a hundred musicians strong, performing a symphonic masterpiece by Beethoven or Tchaikovsky. The unique combination of strings, winds, brass, and percussion that comprises the symphony orchestra is one of the great cultural achievements of mankind. It is the very power of the music, though, and the apparent passion with which the musicians perform it, that spawns a slew of illusions and misconceptions among concertgoers and the public regarding the true nature of the relationship between concert organizers and performers.

For example, because the musical rewards are so enriching, there's the notion that since musicians love what they do, they don't need to be paid. Even assuming that the first part of that is true (and it isn't always, by any means), it suggests, absurdly, that the less one enjoys what one does for a living, the more one should be compensated.

I've often heard a variation of this: "You play music so beautifully, but what do you do for a living?" not taking into account that there really isn't much time left over when one is rehearsing for and performing more than a hundred concerts a year.

There's also the illusion—created by the musicians' uniform formal attire and intricate synchronicity—that they all get along as well as Masons on a picnic. In reality, there are as many different, and often conflicting, personalities and points of view among orchestral musicians as in the General Assembly of the United Nations. Indeed, when musicians walk off the stage after a concert, you'll hear as many of them lambasting the performance they've just completed as praising it.

There, too, is the notion that the musicians select the music they perform. While some orchestras do have artistic advisory committees that suggest repertoire, this task is relegated primarily to the music director (the principal conductor) and a staff of artistic administrators. Many are the times when the musicians would rather be playing anything *but* the music thrust in front of them.

Playing in a symphony orchestra is not only an artistic endeavor, it also is a job. The musicians have an employer, receive a biweekly paycheck with which they pay for things like houses and their kids' education, and like any other workers with an employer, there is a relationship defined by compensation, schedule, and working conditions. In the symphonic field this often leads to prolonged, contentious negotiations. On a personal note, some of the most creative work I did as a member of both the Boston Symphony and Utah Symphony was to negotiate and pen contracts on behalf of the musicians. It was certainly more fun than playing Bruckner's Eighth Symphony.

Perhaps the biggest illusion of all, though, is in regard to the conductor. What in fact does he really do? (For the record, these days there are a growing number of shes on the podium.) During the concert, it appears as if he derives spontaneous inspiration from the sounds he hears, and by conjuring up some mystical telepathy imparts that inspiration to the musicians by waving his arms and appearing impassioned. How else to account for the airborne Leonard Bernstein, the balletlike magic of Seiji Ozawa, or the rapture of Klaus Tennstedt?

The reality, though, is that all great conductors spend their lives studying the music down to its most infinitesimal detail, from which they determine their interpretation. They then do the heavy lifting with the musicians during the rehearsals in which every physical gesture imparts specific information, and that process (not necessarily the interpretation) can range from enlightening to deadly boring. The performance itself is essentially a reenactment. When the stars are properly aligned, it sometimes comes off in unexpectedly exciting fashion. More often than not, though, everyone on stage can readily predict the outcome.

This means the relationship between the conductor and the musicians is crucial, because it's his interpretation that is imposed upon the musicians. For a meeting of the minds to occur, not only must the conductor be the best musician on the stage, he also needs to have the rehearsal skills and personality (which can come in many forms), and most of all an unflinching level of conviction, to get the musicians to buy into his vision. This single-minded pursuit of a musical vision is both necessary and a source of friction. In an apparent paradox, some musicians yearn for a conductor who takes control of the orchestra while others chafe at the same conductor for "telling me how to play my instrument."

Last summer I was playing doubles tennis with some of my retired former Boston Symphony colleagues. As usual, we spent much of the time retrieving balls hit into the woods, providing ample opportunity to reminisce about our years as orchestral musicians. At one point one of my friends commented, "When there's a great performance the conductor always gets the credit, but when there's a bad concert the orchestra always gets the blame. The reality of it should be the other way around." A debatable point, perhaps, but it does help explain why traditionally there's often a love-hate relationship between a maestro and the musicians. Sometimes it's hate-hate; rarely is it love-love, except perhaps when the conductor throws a good party.

Though all the characters in *Death and Transfiguration* are fictional, the situations—from the auditions to the rehearsals to the contract negotiations—are all as real as the high price of gasoline. In fact, many of the insults emanating from the mouth of mythical maestro Vaclav Herza are actual quotes from conductors. Like a ship's captain, the person on the podium with the little stick in his hand, even the least competent, has almost irrationally unfettered authority. On the sea, that unquestioned chain of command can mean the difference between survival and a sinking ship; on stage, it might not be actual life or death, but it can certainly feel that way when a concert begins to run aground. For sure, a strong hand at the helm may be necessary to steady the ship, but just as you have your occasional Captain Bligh who exceeds the bounds of authority on the high seas, you have your maestro who does the same on the high C's.

When I began writing the Daniel Jacobus mystery series that takes place in the seamier corners of the classical music world, the very first question that burst forth from the lips of many of my colleagues was, "How are you going to kill the conductor?" Note, please, the question was not "whether" but "how."

It's a funny thing, Alice,

dying is just the way I composed it in "Death and Transfiguration."

—Richard Strauss to his daughter-in-law
as he lay on his deathbed in 1949

DEATH AND TRANSFIGURATION

In the necessitous little room, dimly lighted by only a candle-end, lies the sick man on his bed. But just now he has wrestled despairingly with Death. Now he has sunk exhausted into sleep, and thou hearest only the soft ticking of the clock on the wall in the room, whose awful silence gives a foreboding of the nearness of death. Over the sick man's pale features plays a sad smile. Dreams he, on the boundary of life, of the golden time of childhood?

But Death does not grant sleep and dreams to his victim. Cruelly he shakes him awake, and the fight begins afresh. Will to live and power of Death! What frightful wrestling! Neither bears off the victory, and all is silent once more!

Sunk back tired of battle, sleepless, as in fever-frenzy the sick man now sees his life pass before his inner eye, trait by trait and scene by scene. First the morning red of childhood, shining bright in pure innocence! Then the youth's saucier play—exerting and trying his strength—till he ripens to the man's fight, and now burns with hot lust after the higher prizes of life. The one high purpose that has led him through life was to shape all he saw transfigured into a still more transfigured form. Cold and sneering, the world sets barrier upon barrier in the way of his achievement. If he thinks himself near his goal, a "Halt!" thunders in his ear. "Make the barrier thy stirrup! Ever higher and onward go!" And so he pushes forward, so he climbs, desists not from his sacred purpose. That he has ever sought with his heart's deepest yearning, he still seeks in his death-sweat. Seeks—alas! And finds it never. Whether he comprehends it more clearly or that it grows upon him gradually, he can yet never exhaust it, cannot complete it in his spirit. Then clangs the last stroke of Death's iron hammer, breaks the earthly body in twain, covers the eye with the night of death.

But from the heavenly spaces sounds mightily to greet him what he yearningly sought for here: deliverance from the world, transfiguration of the world.

—Poem by Alexander Ritter, a friend of Richard Strauss, describing the music of *Death and Transfiguration* and included with the consent of the composer as a preface to the score. Prose translation by W. F. Apthorp.

PROLOGUE

"You shouldn't have pushed him over the edge."

"What a metaphorical way to die."

"It's not funny."

"He was ready to jump. I only shortened his misery. I did him a favor."

"You didn't have to push him."

"Look, he was an over-the-hill alcoholic."

"And a Communist."

"That, too. You have nothing to worry about."

"Where's your driver?"

"At the end of the bridge. Waiting in the car."

"In the dark?"

"Again you speak metaphorically?"

"Yes and no."

"Don't worry. He knows nothing other than to wipe my ass when I tell him to."

"Never contact me again. Never."

"As I said, you have nothing to worry about."

DEATH

ONE

THURSDAY

It even felt like a Thursday. Days of the week, mused Jacobus, are like keys in music, each possessing a distinct personality. Thursday. Thursday, he considered, that would be B-flat major. Not brilliant like A major, not friendly like G major, not even the nestled warmth of F major. Certainly not morbid, like G minor, the key of the *Devil's Trill Sonata, Danse Macabre,* and the slow movement of *Death and the Maiden.* What day would G minor be? Not Thursday. Thursday didn't feel like death, at least not any more than usual. Jacobus didn't know it for a fact, but he would have bet the Spanish Inquisition did not start on a Thursday. Thursday. Just . . . B-flat. It didn't matter whether the summer heat was melting the tar on Route 41 or you were freezing your ass off going outside for firewood on a frigid February night, you can always tell when it's a Thursday. Today's steamy, mildew-inducing drizzle had been no exception. At least until the phone call.

The summer morning had started out the same as the others for the past week. Jacobus, sweat dripping down his back, twiddled the pawn between his thumb and fingers. It was the one piece on the board that hadn't started to gather dust, because every day since Nathaniel had left for Europe, Jacobus had been twiddling that insignificant chunk of wood as if that action alone might somehow divulge how it was he had managed to snatch defeat from the jaws of victory.

To be brought down by a lowly pawn! Once again Jacobus felt its pedestrian curves and grooves, no different from any other pawn. To have allowed Nathaniel to queen a pawn, exposing his own king, rendering it helpless and defenseless! In a breathtaking turn of events he had resigned in ignominy. Yeah, he thought, I could have taken the pawn with my queen, but then she would have been captured by his knight, and the game would be over in three more moves. Four at the most. It wasn't that Jacobus minded losing—actually, he did mind, terribly—it was the humiliation of so precipitous a demise that Nathaniel had even refrained from gloating—at least verbally, but who knew if he was silently smirking?—no easy task for someone who had oft been the object of Jacobus's unrestrained victory celebrations.

Jacobus refused to use his blindness as an excuse for not "seeing" the impending disaster. Though they used black and white pieces for Nathaniel's benefit, they used pieces from separate sets of different size so that Jacobus could always tell which were his when feeling the board. They never bothered with the chess player's rarefied vocabulary, "black Q4 to white K5," or whatever terminology it was they used. Rather, Nathaniel would say, "Just moved my bishop three spaces toward the kitchen," which was a lot easier for Jacobus to remember. Nevertheless, Nathaniel's minuscule white pawn had leveled his oversized black king. An ironic twist here, thought Jacobus, considering their respective skin colors and sizes.

Jacobus mentally reenacted each move, trying to ascertain what he could have done differently. Every one had seemed so well reasoned, so well calculated, taking into account his overall strategy amid the local skirmishes, the majority of which he had won. Yet somehow, unbelievably, Nathaniel had managed to navigate his pawn all the way through to his end of the board. Though consumed with self-loathing for his failure, Jacobus mused upon the miraculous metamorphosis of the pawn: A dispensable, almost worthless foot soldier, finding itself in the right spot at the right time, becomes, by some mysterious alchemy, a queen, the ultimate power broker. It made no sense. What anonymous medieval chess master had come up with that rule? It was stupid, Jacobus concluded, because it simply never happens in reality. GIs don't become Jackie Kennedy, and she wasn't even a real queen. It was the only rule in chess he could think of, in fact, that didn't have its reflection in the real world.

The brittle ring of Jacobus's ancient black rotary phone shocked him out of his petulant reflections. He hadn't gotten a call in days, and that last one was a wrong number asking for the Williamsville Inn. When Nathaniel left for Europe, Jacobus pulled the plug on the answering machine that his friend had imposed upon him. He had told Nathaniel that an answering machine was worthless because even if he received any messages he wouldn't answer them, but just to humor him he let Nathaniel install it. Now it was uninstalled.

Jacobus reached for the phone. "Yeah?" he said, annoyed at being disturbed in the middle of self-flagellation.

"Dr. Jacobus?"

"There's no Dr. Jacobus here," he said and hung up.

Bored with flogging himself over the pawn-cum-queen, with his right foot he located his cane on the floor beside his chair, retrieved it, and poked his way into the kitchen. The path was so familiar from the pattern of grudging creaks in the worn pine floorboards that he could easily have navigated with his ears alone. Jacobus needed the cane, however, for other purposes.

Sitting on the kitchen counter next to his empty mug, the twenty-four-ounce one with the Caffiends logo that Yumi had given him, was a single-burner electric hot plate. He turned the dial, listening for the click to know it was on, until he could feel the little pointer positioned at two o'clock. If he turned it to three o'clock it would boil the water faster, but it would short out his antediluvian fuse in the basement, and that was a pain in the ass to replace. Next he turned on the faucet and filled the mug, sticking his finger in it to know when the water had reached the top. Then he poured the water into a teakettle that he had owned longer than he could remember, and set it on the hot plate. He opened the cupboard above the counter, and using the point of his cane, felt for the two-pound can of Folger's instant coffee among the other cans, all of which he could identify by their shape and/or size. He would have preferred to keep the cans on the counter so he wouldn't have to reach for them, but they attracted mice, even with their lids on. The mice scared his gargantuan bull-dog, Trotsky, which Jacobus couldn't care less about, but he did care that they would shit all over his kitchen. He used to keep peanut butter–baited traps on the floor, but the dog had found the treat irresistible, and with a brain capacity inversely proportional to his stomach's, was unable to make the cause-and-effect connection between licking the peanut butter and the intense pain on his tongue that inevitably followed immediately thereafter. So now Jacobus kept the cans in the cupboards.

He maneuvered the can with his cane, and when it was an inch over the edge of the shelf, deftly flicked it off and caught it in his left hand. He did the same exercise with a plastic jar of sugar. By the time he had emptied three teaspoons of coffee and one of sugar in his mug with the spoon he kept in the can, the water was boiling, which he could tell from the foghornlike moan the kettle gave off. He touched the spout of the kettle to the lip of the mug so it wouldn't spill, and poured.

While the coffee cooled enough so he wouldn't burn his tongue off, he yanked open the recalcitrant door of the refrigerator—perhaps the last of its species, which needed defrosting, though he never bothered—and inhaled deeply. The sound of the door opening was followed by the predictable clattering of Trotsky's claws as he skidded around the corner into the kitchen.

Slim pickings. Jacobus fondled a half-empty bag of Lit'l Smokies smoked sausages and put that back. He felt an onion whose soft spot had grown alarmingly since yesterday, and backed away from an open can of sardines. He took one sniff of a prehistoric chunk of liverwurst and with heavy ambivalence let it drop from his hand, assured that before it hit the ground Trotsky would catch it in his gaping maw, swallow it, and beg for more. All that remained were condiments of an undefined nature and an open bottle of Rolling Rock. Unbidden came Jacobus's recollection of the few days he had spent at the home of Yumi's grandmother, Cato Hashimoto, aka Kate Padgett, in her mountain home in Japan, and of the profusion of delicacies that had been assembled before him, one after another, for his alimentary consideration.

Jacobus brusquely banished that thought from his mind, and, supplanting it with serious consideration of the Rolling Rock, calculated whether it was the appropriate time of day for a beer.

The phone rang again. He pulled his handkerchief out of his back pocket and wiped the sweat off his head. After the fifteenth ring he decided that his sanity was worth more than his privacy.

"Yeah?"

"*Mister* Jacobus?"

"Yeah."

"This is Sherry O'Brien."

"So?"

"I'm the acting concertmaster of Harmonium."

"As opposed to the juggling concertmaster?"

"I was wondering if I could come play for you."

"Why?"

"I'm auditioning for the permanent concertmaster position in a few days, and you've come highly recommended. The orchestra's here at Tanglewood for the week and since you're nearby I thought, well, I thought I'd give you a try. I'm happy to pay whatever your fee is."

Jacobus considered his schedule. In the afternoon, his former student and surrogate daughter, Yumi Shinagawa, was going to play for him in preparation for the same audition. When was the last time he had seen Yumi? He couldn't remember. Almost a year? Tomorrow he had nothing. The day after that he had nothing. The day after that . . . Actually, his calendar was clear for the rest of his life, however long or short that would last.

"I'm very busy," he said.

"I'm sure you are," she pursued, "but I was really hoping . . ."

He didn't hang up but let the silence linger.

"Maybe tomorrow afternoon?" she continued, picking up her own thread.

"When?" he asked.

"Today and tomorrow we have morning rehearsals at ten. Would one o'clock be okay?"

"You know how to get here?"

"I've got GPS."

"Then maybe you should have that treated first."

"And your fee?"

"Incalculable."

Jacobus hung up.

From what O'Brien said, Jacobus figured it must now be about 9:30 A.M. He removed the Rolling Rock from the fridge, chugged it, and took his coffee to the rusty iron lawn chair that had once been painted green that sat in front of his house, wondering along the way why the acting concertmaster of the world's most famous orchestra would ask for a lesson from a total stranger three days before an audition. And why Thursday suddenly felt like G minor.

TWO

He met Yumi in front of his house.

"I brought you a care package from the city," she announced, emerging from her car. "Carnegie Deli pastrami, corned beef, chopped liver—"

"Beware of grease-bearing gifts," he said, unable to quell his sense of foreboding from O'Brien's call.

"Jake, I think you're getting overly suspicious in your old age," Yumi said, pretending to sound hurt. "Maybe you've been involved in one too many murders."

"Then what gives, may I ask?"

"It's been almost a year since I saw you in New York, and I figured you might be getting a little tired of the local organic kale you love so much here in the Berkshires. I also brought some tongue, Swiss cheese, and mustard, and rye bread, and half-sour and sour pickles, and pickled tomatoes."

"Have I ever told you you were the best student I ever had?"

"No."

"Good. You shouldn't have a swelled head."

"I'll just put it all in the fridge. Is it still running?"

"Hobbling is more like it. Ol' Bessie is a designated Superfund site." Jacobus hollered in the direction of Yumi's footsteps. "And don't let Trotsky eat any of it!"

"Worry not. I brought him a doggy treat from Bone Appétit."

It struck Jacobus that Yumi's Japanese accent and manner of speaking, tinged with her English grandmother's inflection and grammar, had over the years become almost thoroughly Americanized. A reflection of her responsive ear, no doubt. But he also observed that whatever she might be losing of her childhood speech patterns was being replenished with Granny's maturity, becoming more like her by the day. Her talent, her perceptiveness, kindness, tenacity. Her sense of humor. Her general brilliance. Yet Jacobus had shunned Kate when the promise of a happy future presented itself. Why had he done that? he asked himself, and though he knew the answer, he denied knowing it. He would prefer living and dying miserable and unloved than admit the source of his pain.

Jacobus followed Yumi back into the house. He jerked at the door a few times to try closing it behind him, its hinges bent askew by Trotsky's joyfully misguided efforts to greet visitors by running through the screen. A few miles down the road, the Condos at Elk Meadow had been built for summer hordes of New Yorkers. That it was neither a meadow nor had there been an elk spotted in the area since before Cotton Mather preached to the Puritans hadn't diminished the demand for the homes, which had resulted in a property tax increase on Jacobus's humble cottage, magically now worth substantially more than the sum of its mildewed parts. The town tax assessor had summarily dismissed his reasoned argument that naming his house the Hovel at Slug Haven should result in a tax reduction. By lifting the handle and leaning against the screen door, Jacobus closed it as well as he could, hoping to keep the flies and mosquitoes out. While Yumi was in the kitchen, voicing expressions of revulsion in both English and Japanese as she exhumed the malodorous contents of his shuddering refrigerator, he took his seat in the dilapidated Naugahyde swivel chair in the living room that also served as his teaching studio. The room had changed little in aspect over the years, except that the dust, which had settled over a surreal landscape of music, books, and recordings strewn in disheveled piles on the floor and every other horizontal surface, had grown into uniform three-dimensional fuzz.

"So you're sure you want to play in an orchestra?" Jacobus asked Yumi after she had finished unpacking the food and then her violin. "You know, you won't have any artistic autonomy. You play a lot of crap by de-composers that would have been better unwritten, and have no choice in the matter. You've got a bunch of bored colleagues sitting behind you waiting to stab you in the back. It's an endless grind that never pays as much as it's worth. Everyone ends up with aches and pains, if not chronic injuries, from overplaying. You have to deal with managements that are usually trying to screw the musicians out of this or that in their contract. And last but not least, you've got guys like Vaclav Herza who can be bastards even if they're geniuses, which they're usually not."

"Thanks for painting such a sunny picture, Jake," said Yumi, tuning her violin. "You've really given me motivation."

"Hey, look before you leap, honey. Buyer beware. Say you win the job and then hate it. I don't want you to come crying that I hadn't told you so."

"Well, I have to admit that if I still had a steady job I wouldn't be doing this, but since the nightmare with my quartet last year it's been tough trying to cobble together enough freelancing and teaching and also afford my apartment, so the idea of a guaranteed paycheck, with paid vacation, pension, and health care, sounds pretty appealing at the moment—even though the rest of it might not be so alluring. I've never played in an orchestra—at least not since I was in public school in Japan—so this is kind of challenging. And exciting."

"What's on the repertoire list for the audition?" Jacobus asked. He pulled a pack of Camels out of his flannel shirt pocket, congratulating himself that he had refrained from smoking until noon—well, almost noon.

"They want one Romantic concerto and one Mozart, so I'm doing Brahms and Mozart Five. Then there're Mozart symphonies Thirty-nine and Forty-one, Schubert Two, Beethoven Three and Nine, Brahms Four, the Mendelssohn Scherzo from *Midsummer Night's Dream,* the Scherzo from Schumann Two, Berlioz *Symphonie Fantastique,* Prokofiev Five, and the solos from Bach's *St. Matthew Passion,* Brahms One, Rimsky-Korsakov's *Scheherazade,* Strauss's *Ein Heldenleben,* Mahler Four, and Shosta-kovich Five. I think that's it. I might have left out a couple things."

"How long's the audition? A week?" Jacobus asked, lighting up.

"Ten to fifteen minutes for the semifinals is my guess. They're let-ting me skip the preliminaries—my performing experience with the Magini Quartet must have looked good on the résumé. The finals—if I make it that far—I guess will be longer."

"How many in the preliminaries?"

"About eighty applied is what I heard."

"Eighty," mulled Jacobus, blowing what he hoped would look like smoke rings. "Why so few?"

"I think because it's a concertmaster audition they tried to sepa-rate the wheat from the chaff and discouraged a lot of less experi-enced people from attending. Still, the audition committee will be listening to preliminaries at least all day Monday."

"Will Herza be there for all of that?"

"Just for the finals is what I was told."

"That's par for the course. In the old days the conductor could hire anyone he wanted, especially concertmaster, because he's his right-hand man. Now you're lucky they show up at all, but Herza's reputation is that he wants the best, and over the years he's gotten what he wants."

"I'm getting nervous just talking about it. Maybe I should do some playing before I get cold feet."

For the next three hours, Jacobus drilled Yumi on the repertoire, admonishing her again and again that the artistic license that made for a great string quartet player was not the stuff of winning an orchestra audition. She had to learn to perform more like a *tutti* player, a musical term originating from the eighteenth century for a musician within the string section, as opposed to a principal player. In recent history, being called a *tutti* player had taken on the disparaging, almost insulting connotation of lacking musical personality, but in Jacobus's eyes, being a good *tutti* player was the height of professionalism because it combined the highest level of skill and artistry within the strict confines of being one among up to sixty string players in the orchestra.

"What I'm trying to say, Yumi," Jacobus concluded with the extinguishing of the last Camel of the pack, "is that this isn't the kind of audition where you have to play double harmonics and fart the 'Carnival of Venice' at the same time in order to make an impression."

The fact that Yumi had never played professionally in an orchestra was undoubtedly a deficit. There are certain unwritten traditions in every significant piece of the symphonic repertoire regarding particular changes in tempo, certain bow strokes, and even which string to play on, that orchestral veterans know but for which Jacobus had been compelled to give Yumi a crash course. Even if Yumi were to play an otherwise perfect audition, if she slipped up in this regard, the committee would disqualify her without hesitation because they would know she was not ready to be the leader of the world's greatest orchestra.

"I'm schvitzin' and exhausted," Yumi said after they had tackled the last movement of Brahms Four.

"Yeah. Me too," Jacobus lied. He found that the marathon lesson had invigorated him as he relived his own all-too-brief career as an orchestral player. It had come crashing down on the day of the

concertmaster audition for the Boston Symphony so many years ago—
the audition that he won even though he had been stricken with the
sudden blindness that forced him to relinquish the position and that
changed his life.

"I think I've got the hang of it," Yumi said, packing her violin
away. "Just one question. What happens if I make a mistake at the
audition? It probably means I've lost, right?"

"That's two questions, Yumi."

"Okay, just two questions, then."

"I'll answer the second one first. If you make one mistake it might
well mean you lost because it's always possible someone will play as
well as you and make no mistakes."

"So I give up?"

"Hell, no. Did it sound like I was suggesting that? You never give
up. Here's the answer to the first question. If you make a mistake,
forget about it. By the time you've played a note out of tune or made a
clumsy shift it's already in the past and there's nothing you can do to
retrieve it and make it better. Music's not like a painting, where you
can dabble at it until you've reshaped the boob to your satisfaction.
With music, especially an audition, you have to stay focused entirely
on the present, so if you make an error, put it out of your mind and
just play as beautifully as you know how. Don't go out of your way to
impress them to make up for a mistake, either, because that's when
people really fuck up.

"You know," Jacobus continued, "I used to be an admirer of
Turner."

"Ted Turner, the media mogul?"

"No, he's a stomach turner. I mean J.M.W. Turner, the nineteenth-
century English romantic artist. Mentioning painting reminded me
there's an exhibit of his stuff up at the Clark Art Institute in Williamstown."

"Yes, I read about it in a Berkshire tourist guide. Turner and Gainsborough. Why do you mention it?"

"You should go. Then you tell me why."

"If I have time, then."

"It'll help with your audition."

"Okay, if you say so. I'll try to." Yumi gathered her violin case.

Jacobus shifted uncomfortably in his seat. He reached for another cigarette but finding the pack empty, tossed it on the floor.

"O'Brien's playing for me tomorrow," he said. It sounded almost like a confession. As soon as he said the words, he was aware that Yumi's actions came to a halt.

To compensate for the lack of visual stimuli, Jacobus had developed an acute sensitivity to subtle nuances, shades of inflection, of the human voice, but even a deaf person could have heard the frost in Yumi's one-word response.

"Really?" she said.

"Yeah. She called me this morning, out of the blue, and asked," said Jacobus, hoping that the explanation would make it acceptable.

"You usually say no to last-minute requests for lessons," said Yumi.

"It's not really a lesson."

"Coming from you, Jake, that's pretty lame. Might there be some reason you'd rather I not win?"

"Of course not." Then why, he asked himself, had he agreed to hear O'Brien? "It's just," he improvised, "so I can gauge the competition for you."

"Keep working on it," said Yumi. "But thank you for the lesson. Really."

THREE

FRIDAY

O'Brien's lesson was a different story altogether. When she arrived, he beckoned to her from his living room chair.

"Is this where you teach?" O'Brien asked upon entering.

"Yeah, why?"

"It's just that you've got all this . . . paraphernalia."

"Paraphernalia? You mean like a dope addict?"

"No, no. Just all the music, all the records and books scattered around. It all seems so . . . dusty. But in a comforting way . . . I suppose."

"You have an issue with that? Are you allergic to dust or something?"

"Not at all. And I like the ivy," she said as she searched for a flat surface on which to put her violin case.

"What ivy?"

"The ivy that's grown over your windows."

"What the hell should windows mean to me?"

"Seriously, I like it. Personally. It gives your studio a real cozy feel. But what about your visitors?"

"What visitors?"

Jacobus heard O'Brien tuning her violin. "So what are you going to play first?" he asked. " 'Tiptoe Through the Tulips'?"

"*Heldenleben*?"

"Be my guest."

The day had begun with Jacobus engaging in his daily exercise of listening to silence, hoping in the process to relieve his ennui.

Though he had never feared death—more often than not he welcomed the possibility of its imminent arrival—or his blindness, what did petrify him was the prospect he could lose another of his senses as the clutches of old age ensnared him. Even the thought of a mild diminution of his finely honed sense of hearing, the tether that connected him to the world, sent him into fits of dread followed by episodes of despondence. So every day he practiced listening to silence, the same way he had been trained to listen to music: not passive, not for enjoyment, but disciplined, rigorous, active. Work. To hear everything, not just the two or three things that were most blatantly evident. He told his students, all of them, that if he succeeded in training them how to listen, they would have no further need for him as a teacher, and that would make everyone happier.

So on this morning, when the remnants of dawn's tree-shaded coolness had not yet completely surrendered to the encroaching sun, a morning on which any other person would exclaim, "My, how quiet things are!" Jacobus opened his ears to the cacophony.

But today he had trouble concentrating and forced himself into the structure of listening to the sounds that were closest and gradually expanding his range. First, a fly—was it a horsefly or a deerfly? Hope it's not a deerfly—those mothers bite like a bitch. More like a horsefly—deeper whir. From the basement, the click of the water heater switching on. From in front of him a bird, maybe, rummaging in the brush? Now it's going up a tree. Not a bird but a rodent. Squirrel? Chipmunk? Too much ruckus for a chipmunk. Brown or gray squirrel? Who the hell knows? Or cares? Which tree? Sounds like rough bark. Must be the black walnut, not the ash.

Birds calling in the trees. Thrushes, warblers. A phoebe darting by, wings flapping like there's no tomorrow. Sociable buggers, those phoebes—nesting in the eaves and keeping me up all night. Going after that horsefly, maybe. A low-grade hum of swarming gnats, like flying tumbleweed, almost inaudible. Do phoebes eat gnats?

From his right to his left high up in the treetops, leaves suddenly fluttered with a sound remarkably similar to the water birds, alarmed by his approach, lifting off from the rice paddy next to Kate Padgett's Nishiyama home. It was a sound well etched in his memory; it was the moment he had first met Kate.

A gentle northerly breeze, said the leaves, as Jacobus reflected upon the past. The breeze flowed first through the maples and ash, and then through the pine trees. No, not northerly, more westerly. Thunderstorms later, maybe, and the change in the air revived the sense of amorphous dread that he had first felt with O'Brien's phone call and that now seemed to envelop him like the sound of the gnats.

"Dammit!" Jacobus said, unable to concentrate. "You've come highly recommended," is what O'Brien had said over the phone. "You've come highly recommended." What kind of ass-backward sentence was that, especially considering that everything else she said was ass-forward? Anyone else would have said, always *had* said, "Mr. Shitzenburger recommended you," or at least, "Mr. Shitzenburger suggested I call you." So cool and collected was she. Too collected. What's she hiding? What does she want from me?

Something dropped next to Jacobus, from the treetop. Tree limbs shaking, way up. That damn squirrel, bombarding me with acorns.

In an effort to dispel his foreboding, Jacobus poked around with his cane and found one of the offending acorns. He leaned over and picked it up, and gauged its density and size in his left hand. It was early in the season and the acorn still had most of its moisture content, so it retained most of its weight. He pried off its cap to create aerodynamic equilibrium, and holding the cane in his right hand like a baseball bat, with careful calculation, Jacobus prepared to toss the acorn into the air.

At first Jacobus had resented the cane; for him it symbolized weakness and disability, even though he used it more to ease his incipient arthritis and less for his blindness. Little by little, though, he began to realize the cane's potential, and it became almost a new appendage, a sensory device. He had discarded his first cane, the standard newfangled, automatically retractable metal variety, and replaced it with one made of pernambuco wood, out of which the finest violin bows are made. He had the cane designed to his explicit specifications regarding density, hardness, dimensions, and calibration, by one of his old Boston Symphony cronies, a percussion player who manufactured his own drumsticks. Like his bow, the cane became an extension of his personality.

Now, imagining the arc of the acorn's flight in his mind's eye, Jacobus tossed it in the air and waited until it descended to what he determined would be chest level. In his best Willie Mays pose, he took a controlled home run swing—and missed the acorn entirely. He heard it land by his left foot, whereupon he cursed and stomped on it with his heel until he heard its shell crack.

No longer in the mood to continue his listening exercise, he hastily concluded there had been nothing to indicate the day was not what people with sight would call "pleasant." Never certainty, though, always doubt. This was what his life was—a series of inferences, guesses, assumptions. This was Jacobus's reality. This was his despair. His prison. He went inside for no particular reason and waited for Sherry O'Brien.

She had arrived from the just completed orchestra rehearsal, so requiring no warming up dove into the extravagant concertmaster solo from Richard Strauss's vast tone poem *Ein Heldenleben,* A Hero's Life. The musical story portrays an idealistic, far-seeing hero besieged by, and finally overcoming, the world's sniping, mundane forces, from critics to the hero's mercurial wife, who is at times flirtatious or nagging, sensuous or enraged. The wife is depicted by a violin solo, one of the most challenging in the entire literature. Strauss, who claimed that he couldn't compose unless he had a story to provide the inspiration, gave imaginative instructions in the music for the violinist to make his intent clear: *heuchlerisch schmachtend* (hypocritically pining), *zart, etwas sentimental* (gentle, a little sentimental), *übermütig* (high-spirited), *getragen* (hesitating), *liebenswürdig* (amiable, charming), *rasender* (furious), *lustig* (merry), *immer heftiger* (more and more violent). It was no secret that the hero in this musical saga was none other than Strauss himself, no shrinking violet when it came to ego, but Jacobus always wondered if Strauss had ever told his wife what the music was all about.

"Okay, honey," said Jacobus, when O'Brien finished. "What gives? Why are you here? Really."

"What do you mean? To get some pointers for the audition. I just know that Herza will want to hear this."

"No one's going to play better than that at the audition," said Jacobus.

"What about Yumi, your former student?"

"Is that it, then? You're here to case the competition? Why? You know this stuff inside out. You've been there. You've got a leg up and you know that, too, so don't jerk me around, please. You played that *Heldenleben* solo like it was written for you, and that's yet one more thing you know. You need pointers like Job needed bad luck. So what gives?"

There are many kinds of silences. Jacobus had studied them all. He could feel in the ether the essence of any given one. This particular hiatus was the time-to-fess-up silence combined with the tell-the-truth-but-tell-as-little-of-it-as-possible silence. So he waited, not sure what the words would be but knowing it wouldn't be all of them.

"You're right, Mr. Jacobus. I have a problem. It does have to do with the audition, and you're the only one left who can help me."

"Me, huh. Then you really do have a problem. Go ahead, spit it out."

"All right. This audition, this concertmaster position, means everything to me. I have to win."

"I don't see that as a problem. That's the mind-set anyone should have for an audition. None of this 'I'm just doing it for the experience' crap. Then, afterward, if you're one of the ninety-nine percent who don't win, you move on to the next audition that means everything to you."

"I know that what I said sounds like everyone else. But I'm different. I've spent my whole life getting ready to be the concertmaster of the greatest orchestra in the world, and this is my chance. If I don't win, I don't know what I'll do. I know that sounds melodramatic, but it's the truth."

"You have a family? I mean a husband, kids?"

"No. Not that I don't want children, but I've been holding off until I reach my goal. It wouldn't be fair to anyone if I had babies, because of my practicing."

"How old are you?"

"Forty-one. I'll be forty-two in November."

"How long have you been acting concertmaster?"

"Two years, almost."

"Why so long? Didn't they have an audition last year?"

"They did."

"And?"

"I won. And I lost."

"Hey, are you in the fortune cookie business or something? I'm going to die of overexposure to obfuscation."

"Let me explain. When I was first hired two years ago, it was in the middle of the season, and the idea was for me to temporarily replace Myron Moskowitz while he was on leave."

"Why didn't they just have the associate concertmaster move up?"

"Lawrence? I don't know. I never asked. Maybe it's because I'm one of Myron's former students, and Maestro Herza hired me at his suggestion. But then Myron decided to retire so they gave me a one-year contract. At the audition, a majority of the committee voted for me. No one else was close, but Herza refused to accept their recommendation, and he's got the final say."

"Music directors *always* have the final say, especially for a concertmaster. He's got to have total confidence in his concertmaster."

"I know that, and I've done everything he's asked for and I've kept a positive attitude. But in return all he does is insult me, more even since the audition."

"So what makes you think there will be anything different at this one?"

"I *have* to think things will be different. I played well last time. My goal is to play perfectly this time, to play so well that the vote will be unanimous and Herza won't have any option but to hire me. It's been a difficult road, but I truly believe it was meant to be."

"Nothing was meant to be, honey, except heartburn, but for the sake of argument, let's say you do win. Are you willing to endure the way he treats you for the rest of your career?"

"He's tough on everyone. As long as it's professional criticism, I'm willing to put up with it because of the end result."

"Well, Pollyanna, if all this is meant to be, what's your problem and why do you need my help?"

"I'm going to file a grievance against Maestro Herza to stop harassing me."

"*Oy gevalt!* You don't need a teacher to solve your problems, sweetheart. You need a psychiatrist."

"That's what my psychiatrist says. But I have to, Mr. Jacobus. It isn't right, the kind of abuse I've gotten from him. He calls me 'my little girl' and 'you blondes' and 'cutie.' Once at a rehearsal of Ravel's 'Mother Goose Suite,' I was playing the violin solo in 'Beauty and the Beast,' where the Beast is being transformed, and he stopped me and said, 'You know what you need, my little girl?' I asked him what, and he made this obscene gesture with his baton. It was disgusting. He demeans me in front of my colleagues, and if I'm going to be concertmaster, that kind of treatment is unacceptable."

"It might or might not be unacceptable, but haven't you considered what it means to your chances of winning the audition? Maybe you're Beauty and Herza's the Beast, but a fairy tale's a fairy tale. Auditions are real life."

"I've come to the conclusion the only things Maestro Herza respects are music and power. I think if, besides playing perfectly, I won't buckle under his authority, it'll prove to him that I'm strong enough for the position. I actually think the grievance will help me. In any event, I can't stop from doing what's right, regardless."

"Maybe Herza doesn't like you because you're short and feisty and it has nothing to do with being female."

"How do you know those things?" O'Brien asked, alarm suddenly in her voice. "Have you been checking up on me?"

"Don't flatter yourself. I never heard of you until you called me."

"Then how?"

Jacobus took a deep breath. He hated being quizzed on things that seemed so obvious and resented the implication that blind people were idiots.

"It's evident from the fingerings you chose for *Heldenleben* that you have small hands. Specifically, you prefer shifting positions and crossing strings to staying on one string and reaching up with your fourth finger or back with your first. That means you have small hands. With your right hand, you're clearly more comfortable in the lower half of the bow near the frog than the upper half toward the point. As a result, you play with a sound that could obliterate the Marine Corps marching band. Conclusion: short, powerful arms.

"I also could tell the size of your hand from your handshake and your height from the angle at which you grasped my hand when you arrived. Then there was the tempo of your stride as you entered the living room. Too fast for anyone with long legs. I'd say five two. Five three at most."

"Five one. But what about feisty?"

"Again, the handshake and the stride. Not the demure type. All business. But mainly from your playing. You dare the listeners to tell you they've heard better. But they haven't. Need I go on? About the way you drove down the winding driveway without hesitation even though this was your first time here and how you slammed on the brake, and—"

"Thank you. That's enough."

"Good, because playing Twenty Questions bores me. Getting back to the issue at hand, have you consulted the union about the grievance? Or the symphony administration? Isn't there an orchestra committee you can go to?"

"May I sit down?"

"If you can find something to sit on."

Another silence. The cursory, reconnoitering kind. There was the couch, yes, but that was Trotsky's self-appointed lair.

"I'll just stand.

"The symphony's position is that I'm technically a glorified substitute, not even up to the level of a nontenured member of the orchestra. They claim I don't have the right to file a grievance. They won't even acknowledge it. That protects them, because if I were to win a settlement would come out of their pockets, so they're not real big fans of mine."

"Maybe it's not so much a settlement they're worried about."

"What do you mean?"

"First of all, if it got into the press that Herza was nailed for harassment, think of what it would do to Harmonium's marketing. You know who buys symphony tickets? Women. The husbands just go along for the ride and have a snooze until they can go home and watch the football highlights on ESPN. But second, and this is the biggie, sexual harassment is against the law. Harmonium could be forced to fire Herza, and he could even be brought up on criminal charges. How do you think they'd feel about that?"

O'Brien didn't respond.

"What did the union have to say?"

"The union says that because Maestro Herza never actually touched me and because the criticisms were not innately sexual, even though they clearly were as far as I'm concerned, then it's hard to prove harassment. They didn't think there was enough evidence to warrant paying a lawyer to represent me. The attorney they have on retainer is involved in contract negotiations for the musicians, and the orchestra committee says they don't want him sidetracked. Plus they said they're at a critical point in negotiations with management and don't want to rock the boat with side issues, at least until afterward. I get the feeling that they just don't want the hassle."

"Why not hire a lawyer on your own?"

"Do you know a good one?"

"That's an oxymoron if I ever heard one. There's one guy I've grappled with before, Cy Rosenthal, who's worked with musicians. I wouldn't go as far as saying he's honest, but deep down inside, there seems to be a glimmer of a conscience."

"I don't think that will work. Rosenthal happens to be the union's labor lawyer."

"So much for that idea, then. Let me go back to my first question, which I will now ask for the third time. What do you need my help for?"

Another silence. The come-on-baby-just-let-it-spill-out kind. Jacobus took the opportunity to extract a cigarette from a new pack, light it, and take the first deep draft.

"I've heard about your reputation for figuring things out and for solving problems," she said finally. "Maybe after I win the audition, Maestro Herza and I can sit down and work things out. Maybe I'll never have to file that grievance. But if I lose, it will only be because I've been cheated, and if I've been cheated I'm going to do everything in my power to make sure he pays for it. What I'd like to ask you is to find out about Maestro Herza's past. Whether he's ever done anything that I can use to support my grievance."

Jacobus spit out his cigarette, not caring where it fell. He heard O'Brien quickly stomp on it before it threatened to re-create the immolation scene from *Götterdämmerung*.

"You want me to dig up dirt on Vaclav Herza?" he asked. He knew he shouldn't have agreed to this "lesson." "What does this look like, a detective agency? The only shingle out front is the one that slid off the roof."

"If I can establish that over the years Herza has a pattern of harassing women," O'Brien persisted, "then I'm sure I'll have a strong case."

"Do you know the Berkshires well, Miss O'Brien?"

"First time. It's beautiful. Why?"

"Because if you need some straws to grasp at, I know the manager of the Agway in Great Barrington who can help you to a whole bale of it a lot cheaper than hiring a lawyer. Herza's the world's greatest conductor. He's untouchable. And as you well know, the unique history of Harmonium is that it's almost exclusively a touring orchestra. I'm not going to go traipsing all over the world to find out if Vaclav Herza ever copped a feel."

"I should have guessed. You're a man. You wouldn't know what it's like to be harassed. You don't understand humiliation."

Jacobus froze. No one could interpret this silence, not even he, except that he knew that a large component of it was rage. She could stand there until hell froze over, for all he cared. He had nothing more to say.

"So you're not going to help me then?" she asked finally.

"That's correct."

"Then I'm sorry I've wasted your time."

"Apology not accepted."

FOUR
SATURDAY

As he has done every morning for many years, Lubomir Butkus positions one hand under the soft forearm of Vaclav Herza and with his other clasps the great maestro's hand, gently delivering him from the shower with loving care. Lubomir gingerly dabs Maestro's ravaged body dry with a thick white Turkish towel embossed with a florid maroon *VH*. Herza sits facing a gilt-framed Baroque mirror as Lubomir administers Herza's daily shoulder massage and shave, the latter starting from the top of his mottled head down to the base of his neck, using an old-fashioned straight razor honed impeccably by its Japanese manufacturer. In all these years, Lubomir has not once nicked his master's soft skin, though the fire that nearly claimed the maestro's life has left swaths of scar tissue as a permanent souvenir. With the wild mane that helped stamp his early fame thus impossible to restore, Herza has opted for total baldness. Unlike the shorn Samson, however, his power remains undiminished. Next, Lubomir applies the assortment of unguents and lotions that the doctors recommended as a salve for the burns that Maestro can still feel under his skin, that extend in angry pink patches from his head to parts of his face, left arm, torso, back, and legs.

Lubomir swathes Herza in the silk kimono, gold with embroidered blue irises, a gift to the maestro from Hideo Saito, the legendary director of the Toho Gakuen Music School in Tokyo in gratitude for his performance of Beethoven's Ninth Symphony with the student orchestra twenty-five years before, which had cemented the unabated reverence the musicians of Japan have for him, culminating in the Order of the Sacred Treasure bestowed upon him by the Japanese government. With one hand on Lubomir's arm and the other on the time-polished oak banister, Herza is judiciously escorted down the chandeliered staircase, the withered left side of his body never having recovered full strength and coordination after his stroke in 1968.

Lubomir seats Herza at the breakfast table, opens the *New York Times* to the Arts and Leisure section and places it next to Herza's Wedgwood place setting, then silently glides to the kitchen to prepare a pot of first flush Makaibari Estate Darjeeling tea, a one-and-one-half-minute boiled egg, and one slice of unbuttered wheat toast that is Herza's unchanging morning meal. Lubomir slices open the pointed end of the egg, poised in its porcelain cup, exposing partially coagulated albumen and liquid yolk.

After breakfast, Lubomir escorts Herza back upstairs into the bathroom, and while Herza relieves himself, Lubomir removes Herza's outfit from the closet and polishes Herza's black shoes. When the maestro emerges from the toilet, Lubomir dresses him in his dark blue suit (with white linen handkerchief carefully folded in the breast pocket), white shirt, and maroon cravat that he wears en route to every rehearsal. Finally, Lubomir places a black wool beret on Herza's head, always at the same jaunty angle.

Lubomir fetches Herza's valise containing his rehearsal outfit, retrieves the alligator-skin briefcase containing his scores and baton from the study, and helps Herza down the stairs a second time, passing the breakfast room on their way out the door. Lubomir runs ahead to buzz for the elevator, which is opened by Manny the elevator operator. "Good morning, Maestro," Manny says every day when Herza arrives. Manny has been instructed by his employer to greet all of the building's eight residents with equal courtesy. He also bows curtly, though neither part of the greeting has ever elicited a response from the maestro.

The elevator stops in the marbled lobby. Manny opens the door for Herza, with Lubomir in tow, and gives a heads-up to the familiar triumvirate huddled by the front desk. Their conversation abruptly terminated, they quickly disperse to their appointed positions. From behind the front desk, Raul, the concierge, secretes his *Daily News* and wishes Herza a good day on this beautiful, sunny summer morning, and is ignored in customary fashion. Oscar, the doorman, standing at attention, opens the front door of the apartment building and tips his cap. Herza, his eyes straight ahead, gives what someone who sees the best in people would call a nod as he passes by.

The chauffeur, uniformed Paddy Donaghue, stands in soldierly fashion next to the gleaming black Lincoln Town Car, leased by Harmonium, parked close to the curb of the narrow one-way street. Because the curb is high, Donaghue is situated by the back right door on the street side. Grinding his heel on his half-finished cigarette, he opens the door when Herza emerges from his residence.

With painstaking care, Lubomir eases the maestro into the backseat and hands him the briefcase, then takes his own place in front next to

Donaghue, who starts the engine. At that signal, Manny, Raul, and Oscar resume their discussion of the Yankees' prospects of making the playoffs.

Everything according to the daily script except, however, today the maestro's entourage is not making the forty-minute commute downtown to Carnegie or Avery Fischer Hall. Rather, after a series of turns, they head north, in which direction they will drive for three hours, to the Tanglewood Music Festival.

FIVE

Yumi answered after the first ring.

"You want to go to the open rehearsal?" Jacobus asked without pre-amble. "It starts in an hour."

"Are you asking me on a date?" Yumi asked, teasing. "Did Sherry O'Brien turn you down?"

"I don't give a fig for a date." *Maybe if I were forty years younger,* he thought. *And if your name was Kate.*

"Well, I appreciate the offer, Jake, but I was just on my way up to the Clark in Williamstown like you suggested. Nine hours a day on those excerpts is all the music I can bear. It's almost as boring as playing eight *Phantoms* a week on Broadway. I need a little diversion to keep my sanity. How about you keep me company?"

"A blind man at an art exhibit? And you talk about sanity. I think I'll pass on that. Maybe if you were going to MASS MoCA in North Adams, I'd take you up on it, but not the Clark."

"Why's that?"

"Because at MASS MoCA I'd have the satisfaction of not being able to see all that modern shit."

"Jake, I think your opinions about art are getting calcified in your old age."

"Old age has nothing to do with it. They were calcified when I was still young, but back then it was called good taste."

"Well, in that case I'll definitely go to MASS MoCA, too, but if you need a ride, I'd be happy to drive you to Tanglewood. I'm staying at the Red Lion Inn, so I can be there in ten minutes."

"All right," he said and hung up.

Jacobus left Trotsky sleeping on the threadbare couch in the living room—the one that Jacobus had always liked to snooze on until Trotsky usurped it for his own—and waited outside.

He began his daily listening exercise, but habitual impatience overtook him. Where was Yumi already? he asked himself after about thirty seconds.

"Let's go," he said when her car pulled up shortly thereafter. "We'll be late."

"Good morning, Jake," said Yumi.

Once they were on their way, Yumi asked, "So what's your interest in the rehearsal? You usually don't care for open rehearsals. What is it that you call them? Half-fast performances?"

"Yeah, but after all these years, I've never heard Herza in the flesh and he's the last of the great old-school maestros, so I want to get to him before one of us kicks off."

"Don't say that, please," said Yumi, "even in jest."

"Sorry," said Jacobus. It had been less than a year since the other three members of the New Magini String Quartet had been slain, and Yumi had almost been the fourth. The pain was still raw, and the prospect of a new life as concertmaster of Harmonium would help put that agonizing chapter behind her.

Yumi made a right turn onto Lenox Road, a quiet lane that wound downhill through the woods and emerged at Tanglewood's doorstep.

Today, however, they encountered heavy traffic, all going to hear Harmonium and the great Vaclav Herza.

"Can't you go any faster?" asked Jacobus, who viewed traffic jams as an infringement on his life's ticking clock.

"Yes, of course," said Yumi.

"Then why don't you?"

"Because I would hit the car in front of me that's going fifteen miles an hour."

"You think you've got your grandmother's sense of humor, huh?"

"No, I think I've got yours. Don't worry, we'll get there."

"That's what Moses said," he replied. "Assuming we do arrive by the time they play the last note, I also thought I'd get the lay of the land for you. See if there's anything I can pick up from the rehearsal that might help you with your audition."

"Thanks," said Yumi. "I appreciate that. When I played for you on Thursday, I think I was more nervous than I'll be at the audition. Since then, I finished memorizing all the excerpts, like you did when you won the audition for the Boston Symphony."

"Don't say that, please," said Jacobus, "even in jest."

"Sorry," she said. "We're even."

That day, many years ago, when Jacobus won the BSO concertmaster position, he was stricken by sudden blindness, a condition called foveomacular dystrophy. Miraculously, he not only managed his way through the audition, he won it, because he had memorized the music. It was a hollow victory, of course; an orchestral musician needs to see the music and the conductor. Though Jacobus argued that he would be able to take on the challenge, the administration of the BSO disagreed and hired the runner-up.

"Whatever," said Jacobus.

Yumi stopped the car.

"What's the problem now?" Jacobus asked.

"No problem. We're at the main gate. Right on cue."

Yumi reached over him and opened the door.

"Enjoy the rehearsal," she said and drove off.

Fifty yards away, the Lincoln is waved through the tree-lined Authorized Personnel Only gate, coming to a stop at the Guest Artist parking area behind the Tanglewood Shed, that most venerable of outdoor symphonic concert halls.

Lubomir removes the valise containing Herza's rehearsal clothes from the trunk. Donaghue opens the car door for Herza, who hands Lubomir the briefcase of scores that he has cradled protectively to his bosom. Lubomir assists him up the concrete steps—which Herza, like a toddler learning to walk, has to mount by hoisting his left foot to meet up with his right, step by step—through the backstage area and into the dressing room reserved for guest conductors. Herza stands in the middle of the room, arms outstretched like the Messiah on the cross, as Lubomir removes his cravat and white shirt, replacing them with a white linen rehearsal tunic that he buttons all the way to Herza's throat. Herza sits at the desk while Lubomir brews a second cup of the Darjeeling tea he has brought from New York. He hands it to Herza along with his daily dose of Coumadin. After Maestro has swallowed the pills, Lubomir places the scores of the music to be rehearsed and Herza's baton directly in front of him on the desk. Lubomir then exits the room, closes the door behind him, and stands guard.

Herza closes his eyes and proceeds with his daily ritual of spreading his fingers and placing his hands on the unopened scores, by psychic osmosis silently absorbing inspiration, power, and love from the composer. Several minutes later, when it is time for the rehearsal to begin, Lubomir knocks on the door, waits twenty seconds, then opens it. He picks up the scores and baton from the desk.

With his hand on Lubomir's arm, Herza limps along the quiet corridor to the offstage area on the viola side of the stage. They pass a group of quietly conversing midlevel staff members whom Herza does not recognize. They say, "Good day, Maestro," "Bravo, Maestro," to which Herza shows no indication of hearing. The musicians are already onstage. A Tanglewood stagehand sets out Herza's stool on the podium, specially designed to accommodate his physical disabilities. His left, stroke-withered leg is several inches shorter than his right, and if he stands for extended periods, his back revolts with incapacitating spasm. Lubomir hands the scores and baton to Randall Brimley, the orchestra librarian, who hands Lubomir a large blue mug of water. Lubomir leaves Herza's side in order to place the mug on a stand next to the conductor's podium. Brimley, following Lubomir, places the scores, unopened, on the maestro's music stand, then sets the baton, placed diagonally, knob side at the bottom right, over the scores. Herza conducts everything from memory—indeed, he rarely opens his eyes when he conducts—but having the scores in front of him connects him to the source of his strength. Years ago, an impudent fool of a student accosted him backstage after a concert and asked him about his prodigious memory. He repeated Pierre Monteux's famous aphorism: "I don't memorize the score. I *know* the score."

On a packed clay floor hardened by the footsteps of countless musical pilgrims, Jacobus had eagerly navigated down the aisle toward the stage of the open-sided Tanglewood Shed, his cane extended like the pole of a slalom racer, tapping its point against the chair back at the end of each row. From time to time he had to alter his course around obstructions in the form of other rehearsalgoers, but he managed to trace a path to the empty front row, and he slid toward its middle.

Jacobus was long familiar with Herza's recordings, especially those of Strauss and the Czech composers, for which he was considered the premier interpreter, but he had never "seen" Herza live. Jacobus didn't have enough fingers and toes, and certainly not a good enough memory, to count all the conductors he had heard who pay infinite attention to the most minute details of the music but who are clueless how to synthesize those details into an overall conception of the music, an exercise akin to a non–English speaker memorizing Shakespeare with phonetic antiseptic perfection. Jacobus would bitch that the result was superficial, academic nitpicking, notable for its correctness but lacking essence, its ability to move the listeners' emotions as compelling as the dissection of a formaldehyde-saturated frog on a high school biology workbench. Herza was one of the handful who had been able to see the forest *and* the trees, giving the music transparency of detail plus sweep, power, and depth, like a Turner sea.

That Herza had overcome so many personal obstacles provided Jacobus with a sense of kinship, a sense of shared sacrifice perhaps, though the two had never met. Everyone knew the political part. How in 1956 Herza had fled Prague in the face of seemingly imminent invasion by the Soviets, who had just crushed the Hungarians; to his support—though from afar—of Alexander Dubček during the Prague Spring in 1968; and then his collaboration with the playwright turned political leader Václav Havel for the final liberation of Czechoslovakia from the Soviet bloc.

But it was Herza's determination after the fire, and then the stroke years later, that evoked Jacobus's intense admiration. Severely burned in a car accident, there was a question whether Herza would even survive. That brash, handsome youthfulness, that famous mane, and that reckless arrogance, all of which evoked the image of the young Beethoven, was transformed in an instant into that ghoulishly scarred face and patchily tufted scalp. How could he appear again in public? How could he look at himself in the mirror?

But he had. Undaunted, Herza returned to the concert stage, and the audiences, blinded by Herza's personal power and musicianship, seemed not to notice his disfiguration in the least. Then, in 1968, the disabling stroke that prevented Herza's triumphant return to Prague during the short-lived Dubček regime, a return that might have turned the tide of the world's political history, left him almost unable to walk and slurred his speech. Yet again, Herza persevered. His music making became even more powerful, as if nourished, like Antaeus thrown to the earth, by adversity.

"Excuse me, sir," said a voice that Jacobus immediately identified as a representative of that nemesis species, the usher. "Do you have authorization to sit in this section?"

"Yes."

"May I see it, please?"

"I left it at home."

"I'm sorry, but you'll have to get permission from the personnel manager to sit here."

"Look, honey, if you can't tell, I'm blind. I need to sit up front so I can hear what the maestro has to say. Otherwise I might as well stay home and listen to the record."

"I'm sorry, sir, but we have our rules and—"

"Excuse me, madam," interrupted another voice, one that Jacobus had not heard for some time but also recognized instantly, "this gentleman is with me. Here's my press pass."

"In that case," said the usher, still grasping tenaciously to sovereign authority over her domain, "all right, but you have to take responsibility for him."

"With greatest respect for the import of the task you have bestowed upon me, you may be sure."

When she had left, Jacobus said, "Lilburn, I thought the *Times* had finally put you out to pasture."

"Alas, Mr. Jacobus, forgotten but not gone. I am technically retired, but my former employer calls upon me for the occasional freelance feature when the new critic, who shall remain nameless, is too busy pontificating from on high. I'm here to interview the maestro and finish a story on the opening of Harmonium Hall next week."

Lilburn led Jacobus to a seat immediately at the foot of the conductor's podium, unfolded it for him, and then sat beside him. The rest of the section was empty save for Harmonium staff and a few of the Tanglewood conducting Fellows. On this sunny summery Saturday in New England, thousands of Herzaphiles were congregating behind them to witness the open rehearsal, the first ever given by Herza and Harmonium, since until now Herza had throughout his career refused to allow the public to his rehearsals. A buzzy, festive atmosphere reigned as musicians trickled onto the stage to warm up.

"Comfy?" asked Lilburn.

"Yeah," said Jacobus, already fidgety. "When does the rehearsal start?"

"Still about ten, fifteen minutes to go."

"What's so interesting in the program?"

"Mr. Jacobus, you're still a constant source of amazement. How did you know I was reading the program book?"

"I'd need to be deaf not to hear you flipping pages back and forth like a parent looking for his kid's photo in the local newspaper. Hell, what else would you be reading ten minutes before a rehearsal? A Bible? First, you're an atheist, and second, Sunday isn't until tomorrow."

"You're right as usual. I find it fascinating the information these new-style program books contain. Even the ads. Here's one for a bank with a photo of some over-the-hill male model supposedly looking like a conductor. A very serious expression on his face. The only problem is he's holding the baton in his left hand. 'Conduct your financial affairs with class,' it says in elegant writing."

"I'm thrilled you're having such a fine time keeping yourself entertained," said Jacobus.

Lilburn ignored him. "In the old days, a program was one page, maybe two, listing the music that was going to be played that day. Later they started adding the roster of orchestra personnel, staff, and board, and maybe one or two ads from sponsors. Now you get a program book as thick as that Bible I'm not reading. It's got program notes for each piece, a bio of Herza and of all the composers whose music will be performed, all the guest artists, a history of Harmonium, photos all over the place, pages of contributors from million-dollar 'Beethoven' patrons to the ten-dollar 'Bruckner' donors. I could almost do my whole story just plagiarizing from this program."

"That's never stopped you," Jacobus cracked.

Lilburn laughed. "Time hasn't altered you a bit, Mr. Jacobus. It's a comfort to know some things never change."

"There's one thing that changes, according to you."

"What might that be?"

"Program books. What else have they got?"

"Here are five pages just on the building of the new hall, which will be the orchestra's first real home. Can you believe that, after forty years?"

"I thought they play at Carnegie and Avery Fischer," said Jacobus, more attracted to the Carnegie Deli than Carnegie Hall on the infrequent occasions he was dragged to New York City.

"Yes and no," said Lilburn. "They've been playing a handful of times every year at those halls for God knows how long, but the vast majority of their concerts have been on the road. 'The only orchestra in the world,' it says here, 'for which touring is their primary concert activity.'"

"Sounds like those nineteenth-century violinists," said Jacobus. "Like when Paganini left Italy for a six-year tour of Europe!"

"And that's before suitcases had wheels. It's hard to imagine an individual doing that, let alone an orchestra. Can you imagine the expense, the planning, the—"

"Fuck-ups? The complaining?" Jacobus added. "Taking a hundred musicians on the road is like putting a hundred cats in a shoe box."

"I can imagine it."

"No, actually you can't. Anything else interesting in the book?"

"Have you heard much about the new hall?" asked Lilburn.

"Not much. It's on landfill in New York Harbor, right?"

"In the Hudson, right at the base of Manhattan, with a view of the Statue of Liberty. That was Herza's idea. In fact, the whole brilliantly insane idea was his, like Wagner building Bayreuth. He designed it, named it, chose the location—"

"How do you get to it, if it's in the middle of the river?"

"The Freedom Bridge. Paid for by the Prague government as a gift to New York and the U.S. in gratitude for America's stance against communism, or so the canard goes. A monument like the Statue of Liberty, in a way. The design parallels its ancient sister bridge in Prague, the Charles Bridge, except it's updated, of course, and the colossal statues that line its sides are composers instead of saints."

"Sounds like Herza's a man on a mission."

"He's the last of the old-time maestros, in my humble opinion. These days, your typical jet-setting music directors spend ten, twelve, maybe fifteen weeks a year max with 'their' orchestras. The feathers in their cap accrue not with the quality of their musicianship but with the number of orchestras they conduct. In the golden age, a music director spent thirty to forty weeks with his band and the badge of honor was derived from the musical personality of the orchestra the maestro developed. The Philadelphia sound of Stokowski and Ormandy. The Cleveland sound of George Szell. Any serious concertgoer can conjure those sounds in his head. Herza has been and still is the only conductor that Harmonium plays for. Unprecedented. The New York Phil has had five different music directors during his reign, and that's why the Harmonium sound is so distinct and every other orchestra so faceless."

"I never heard you say that when you were the *Times* critic," said Jacobus.

"Well, perhaps not to that degree," Lilburn confessed. "Perhaps it was more nuanced."

"You mean you needed to keep your job," Jacobus added.

"Mr. Jacobus, do you insinuate—"

"Calm down, Lilburn. I was trying to unnuance your nuance."

Jacobus squirmed in his seat. The rehearsal still hadn't started, but the arthritic pain had.

"I've got a question," he said. "Don't the musicians get tired of seeing Herza's same ugly kisser day in, day out, if he's conducting them forty weeks a year?"

"I was at his first U.S. concert in '56—that dates me, doesn't it?—when he filled in for Stokowski at the last minute and did Mahler Nine. I wrote at the time that it was 'unsurpassed perfection,' which in hindsight is very poor writing, but in my view nothing has changed. So how can the musicians complain? Now and then there have been some rumors about illicit behavior—innuendo, no doubt, as is the case with a lot of conductors—that you would more likely find in the *National Enquirer* than the Harmonium program book, but in the end, it's the best orchestra, bar none, and they're also the highest paid.

They're negotiating a new contract right now—their old one expires the day before the hall opening, so things might get contentious, but I'll bet Herza's hold on the orchestra is secure."

"I assume they're a union orchestra."

"They were one of the last to unionize, maybe because they were already so well compensated and didn't feel they needed the AF of M, or maybe because Herza's grip on the orchestra is so firm. But considering his avowed history as a champion of the common man, it would have been hypocritical for him to deny the musicians their right to bargain collectively. There's no doubt, though, that Harmonium is an organizational anachronism, a throwback to Toscanini's NBC Symphony. Greatness with the despot, or run-of-the-mill without. Take your pick."

"But if the big event opening the hall is next week, why is Maestro and his merry band gracing the Shed with their presence?"

"Well, the reason is simple: construction delays. They're still putting the finishing touches on the hall, and I'm informed that the workers, in order to complete the project on time, have been at it nonstop, making it impossible to rehearse there. Too much noise and commotion. Since the Boston Symphony is on tour in Europe, Harmonium was able to hastily make a deal with BSO management to rehearse and play a concert up here. The BSO is good at planning on the fly. Not a summer goes by when a conductor or guest artist doesn't cancel at the last minute. But Herza has never done an open rehearsal—that was part of the deal because it'll make a splash and bring the BSO a welcome windfall—so it should be an interesting occasion, to say the least."

Jacobus asked Lilburn to read the personnel list in the program book, curious if there was anyone in the orchestra he knew from the old days. Lilburn started with the first violins, then the seconds. Halfway through the viola section, Jacobus interrupted him.

"You know, when I started playing professionally you heard a lot of guys speaking French or German or Hungarian," he said. "After the war, only NASA benefited more than orchestras from the European brain drain. Now, not only do I not recognize any of the names, I'm wondering whether the official language of this orchestra is Mandarin or Japanese!"

"There certainly has been an influx of Asian musicians in the past decade," said Lilburn, "not least among them your former student, Yumi Shinagawa."

"And to their credit," said Jacobus. "I'm no conspiracy theorist, but Harmonium seems to have a corner on the market. Any string players left on the program who might be from our hemisphere?"

"Mind if I join you gents?" interrupted a deep male voice with a Southern lilt.

"Only if you're authorized," said Jacobus.

"Authorized? I play in this band, sir."

"Why aren't you on stage, then?" asked Lilburn.

"Because Mozart was wise enough not to include trombones in the 'Jupiter' Symphony."

"So, a busman's holiday?" interrupted Jacobus. "Any self-respecting musician would be on the golf course when he didn't have to play."

"Who mentioned anything about self-respect? By the way, Parsley's the name. Junior Parsley."

"Well, Mr. Parsley, please join us in our little oasis," said Lilburn. "I suppose we too should introduce ourselves. I'm Martin Lilburn, occasionally of the *New York Times,* and this is my friend, Daniel Jacobus, eminent violin pedagogue."

Jacobus extended his hand into the air and Parsley shook it.

From the size of Parsley's hand, Jacobus guessed he was well over six feet tall, and when Parsley overflowed the seat next to him he gathered he was equally wide.

"Any trombone player who'll listen to Mozart when he doesn't have to is worth shaking hands with," Jacobus said.

"We were just discussing the preponderance of Asian musicians in Harmonium," Lilburn continued. "Perhaps you can shed some light."

"None of this is for the record. Right?" asked Parsley. "See, I also happen to be chair of the orchestra committee, and as you may know we're coming down to the wire with our contract negotiations."

"In the interest of full disclosure, I am assembling a story on the history of Herza and Harmonium. I hadn't intended to include anything about your orchestra's demographics—it was more Mr. Jacobus's curiosity than mine—but if I do, it will only be in the broad context of the profession as a whole, and you'll have no worries about attribution in either case. Fair enough?"

"Seems reasonable, Mr. Lilburn. Well, then, the orchestra business is still a pretty safe haven for good old red-blooded American trombonists such as myself, but string players from Asia have made some real inroads. They can certainly play, for sure, but I think Maestro has a special affinity for them—he's almost a cult figure there, particularly Japan. That's one of our primo touring destinations. Have you ever been to the Sapporo brewery up in Hokkaido? They have this lamb dish called the Genghis Khan that—"

"I can't say I have, but it sounds lovely. Why do you suppose this to be the case, that Herza and the East have such a relationship?"

Jacobus felt Parsley shift his weight. An uncomfortable question? Jacobus listened with curiosity to the answer with one ear. With his other he listened intently as more musicians arrived onstage, learning about the personality of the orchestra by the way they warmed up. In the back of his brain he made a mental note to find out more about the Genghis Khan.

"As you may already know," Parsley replied, "and will no doubt experience in a few minutes, Maestro Herza has a predilection for—how to say it nicely—exerting musical will over the musicians. We euphemistically call it his Old World charm, especially after we've downed a few beers. It can rub American guys the wrong way, but the Asian musicians, they almost seem to bask in it. As I say, he's almost a god in Japan."

This time it was Jacobus who squirmed. Disinclined to reverence of anyone other than Beethoven, as an orchestral musician he had been particularly cognizant of the narcissism that bloomed when that little white stick magically transformed a mortal into a "maestro." He also squirmed for another reason: From within the rising onstage cacophony, his ears lasered in on the sound of a particular violin. Emanating directly in front of him, he had no doubt it was Sherry O'Brien practicing a slow C major scale—plain old C major—carefully massaging the intonation and vibrato. What could he glean from that?

First, a musician a few days away from the most important audition of her career would more likely be frantically sawing away at her concertos and excerpts. Though that would annoy everyone within earshot it would do her little actual good, because when everyone's onstage warming up, you can barely hear yourself think. So that meant she displayed levelheaded, analytical judgment. Second, she wasn't even practicing the music for that morning's rehearsal. With a demanding conductor like Herza, you don't want to be caught with your bloomers down, especially the concertmaster, so she must have done her homework in advance. Conclusion: calm, prepared, and supremely confident. Maybe her grievance wouldn't backfire after all. The other side of the coin was that Yumi would be hard-pressed to win the audition.

Jacobus put those thoughts in his back pocket and returned to the conversation, changing its trajectory.

"And the old-timers?" he asked. "Do they prostrate themselves before the maestro?"

"Yes and no. There's always some bitching and moaning. But that's true of any orchestra, any music director."

"Just before you arrived," Lilburn said, "I was reading the personnel list for Mr. Jacobus to see if there were any veterans whom he might know."

"In the strings?"

"For starters," said Jacobus.

"There aren't too many left from your day. No offense, sir," said Parsley. "Try this pair on for size: Ebeneezer Frumkin and Casper Lulich."

"Beanie and Cappy!" Jacobus exclaimed. "Cappy the Whistler! They're still kickin'?"

"Kickin' each other's more like it. They've been sitting together for decades. Only difference is they used to be the first stand of the viola section; now they're in the back. We call it Beanie and Cappy's Last Stand. They've had what one would call a hate-hate relationship. The Mega-Herza versus the Killa-Herza, in a nutshell."

"You've lost me."

"This orchestra may play together like nobody's business, Mr. Jacobus, but it's divided right down the middle with how the guys feel about Maestro. Maestro's personality does not engender fence-sitting, so just about everyone's lined up either pro or con, and we've taken to calling each group the Mega-Herzas and Killa-Herzas. That's not for publication, Mr. Lilburn, by the way.

"Beanie, bless his heart, is self-absorbed in the minutiae of existence, the polar opposite of Cappy, and is a Mega. He takes a half hour to make sure his bow tie's on straight before a concert. He and Cappy, an ardent Killa, almost came to blows because Beanie pencils in fingerings over virtually every note of his music, or—"

"Excuse me, but is something wrong with that?" interrupted Lilburn, who had once been a pianist. "Wouldn't it be helpful to insert one's fingerings?"

"As a trombone player, it's all a nonissue as far as I'm concerned. But as chair of the orchestra committee, I've had to be a referee and forcibly separate combatants from time to time. I'll defer to Mr. Jacobus to explain the intricacies."

"The gist is," Jacobus said, "it's okay to write in your fingerings if you don't have to share music with anyone else, like if you're in a string quartet. But when you're sharing the same part with your stand partner, it can drive him to distraction, since everyone's hands are different and what makes sense for one musician could be totally useless for another. Also, some musicians come up with a good fingering and stick with it their whole lives, but others like using different fingerings every day depending on what they think is musically appropriate for the moment. Having someone else's fingering is like Chinese water torture; at first it's a mild irritant, but after a while you want to strangle someone, then yourself."

"Strangling myself," said Lilburn with a condescending chuckle. "Quite a trick."

"Try it sometime," said Jacobus. "You might like it."

"Most orchestra string players tacitly discourage writing fingerings in their parts," Jacobus continued. "Some orchestras ban it outright."

"I take it Mr. Lulich sees things differently from Mr. Frumkin," Lilburn commented.

"Cappy's a natural," said Jacobus. "It's like one day he picked up the viola and just started to play it and never needed a lesson or had to practice, but he's undisciplined in all ways, including music. Regardless of what's written on the page or whatever anyone else is doing, Cappy follows his own muse."

"Mr. Jacobus called him 'the Whistler.' Is that part of his muse as well?" Lilburn asked Parsley.

"You'll find that a lot of orchestral musicians have unique callings. Everything from fly tying to collecting antique Chinese porcelains. Cappy's is the knack of being able to whistle imitations of a piccolo or any birdcall in the universe. He's very proud of himself—he's even made up a few of his own."

"Quite a talent," said Lilburn.

"Charming," said Jacobus, "except it used to drive everyone, especially Beanie, nuts. I think the more Beanie wrote in the fingerings, the more Cappy would do his whistling thing. Until it became a compulsion. Then the guy just couldn't stop. You could hear him coming from a mile away."

"Providing enough of a heads-up for everyone to head for the hills," said Parsley. "Maybe after the rehearsal," he said to Jacobus, "you can mosey over to the personnel manager's office and see them."

"How do you know they'll be there?" asked Jacobus.

"Oh, they'll be there! If there's an issue, they'll find it. And if there isn't, they'll invent one. My brother tells me all about it when he needs to vent."

"Your brother?" asked Jacobus.

"Tyson Parsley. He's the orchestra personnel manager."

The clamorous warming-up onstage suddenly subsided.

"Aha!" said Junior. "Things seem to be getting under way. Here comes Lubomir."

"Lubomir?" asked Jacobus.

"Lubomir Butkus," Parsley said, now in a semiwhisper. "Herza's man Friday since God knows when. Some of the guys in the orchestra call him, uncharitably, I suppose, Herza's 'butt boy,' or Bupkis, or Buttkiss. Orchestra humor. Loyal to the core, though. One of his rituals before every rehearsal is to place a towel and a mug of something on a music stand for Maestro."

"You said you were chairman of the orchestra committee?" asked Jacobus.

"That's right."

"What can you tell me about Sherry O'Brien's grievance against Herza?"

"We process a million grievances. The rehearsal should begin any moment now."

SIX

When the orchestra completes its tuning, Lubomir intones his daily mantra, "Wishing you the joy of greatness," and Herza, under his own limited power, hobbles between the cellos and violas toward the podium, dragging his left leg behind him. Several thousand worshippers erupt into a thunderous ovation.

Herza stops in his tracks and glowers at the throng, silencing them.

"This behavior is disgraceful," he says in stroke-slurred speech. "This is a rehearsal, not a rock concert. You will be silent or you will leave."

The audience receives the admonition with shocked obedience, except for nervous laughter rippling through the tongue-tied hush from those few who can't quite believe it. Jacobus, within earshot, hears him mutter, "Filthy public."

Herza mounts the podium, grunting with effort. "Mozart," he commands. The musicians, more familiar than the audience with Herza's routine, lift their instruments, soldiers responding to the order to present arms.

The orchestra plays the first three notes of Symphony Forty-one, the "Jupiter." Herza screams.

"No!! No!! You play *bump! brrump! brrump!* I conducted *bump! brrump!! brrump!!!*" His eyes bulge. "You play like cattle! *Bump! brrump!! brrump!!!* Not *bump! brrump! brrump!* Again, the beginning."

The orchestra plays the first three notes a second time. Herza stops.

"What did I just say?" Herza rants. "What did I just say? Larsen, what did I just say? Are you deaf? Answer! Are you deaf?"

"No, Maestro," says Larsen, from the middle of the second-violin section.

"Then why do you play *bump! brrump! brrump!* when everyone else plays *bump! brrump!! brrump!!!*?"

"I'm sorry, Maestro."

"You are sorry, you say. You are sorry. Play it. Alone."

Larsen does not respond. In the silent standoff that ensues, Jacobus hears footsteps emerge from the wings.

"And that would be Tyson," Jacobus comments offhandedly.

"You're right!" says Parsley. "But how did you know?"

"Heavy but rapid footsteps. A large man, like you, and in a hurry. Who else but the personnel manager in a situation like this?"

"You got it," says Parsley. "Sometimes it slips Maestro's mind that crucifying a section player is no longer de rigueur. World's hardest position, personnel manager. Don't know how bro does it."

"Maestro," Jacobus hears Tyson Parsley say in similar soothing, Southern-inflected tones to his brother's, "it's not permitted to single out a string player to play alone."

"Permitted?" asks Herza, as if the word were an obscenity not to be uttered in polite society. "And tell me, who decides what is permitted? You?"

"No, not me, Maestro. It's in our contract. The collective-bargaining agreement between the musicians and the symphony. It's been there for twenty years."

Herza considers the situation and redirects his glower upon Larsen.

"I will speak to you at intermission, Larsen. About your future with this orchestra, perhaps. See me in my room. And for God's sake, stop shaking so. You make me nervous. Now we begin again."

The orchestra resumes and this time manages its way through the second phrase.

Herza yells, "Stop! Have you never heard this music before? Can it be? Even deaf people would know you were out of tune! Listen: The first phrase, *bump! brrump!! brrump!!!*, it is masculine. The second phrase, *lu-Lah, lu-Lah, lu-Lah-lah*, it is feminine. It fades away. That's why I drop my hands to my sides. Don't you see me drop my hands? Even a blind person could see that, like that vagrant in the front row behind me. Then it repeats: male-female, male-female. Play it this way, not like four homosexuals who can't decide what they are."

"Is he always this pleasant?" asks Jacobus.

"Nah. He's on good behavior because it's an open rehearsal. He'll spend a good hour on the first page tongue-lashing the orchestra. Somehow, in the end, it all gets done."

By the time intermission arrived, Jacobus was as exhausted as if he had been playing in the orchestra, and almost as disillusioned. Junior Parsley excused himself to go warm up for *Death and Transfiguration*.

"I guess Cappy and Beanie aren't the only ones with a hate-hate relationship," said Lilburn, as the musicians departed the stage for the sanctuary of the coffee machine. "Care to join me for a lemonade, Mr. Jacobus? Twenty minutes before the truce ends and combat resumes. No need to sit on our hands till then."

"Lemonade? I could use something stronger than that," Jacobus replied. "They have a liquor stand on the grounds?"

"A good idea, but unlikely. And I guess you didn't know. I've been on the wagon. Ten years."

"Me too."

"You? No alcohol?"

"No lemonade," said Jacobus.

The day was hot and sunny, and hundreds of blankets were strewn on the vast lawn surrounding the Shed, upon which picnicking music lovers consumed Camembert, cucumber, and quiche in copious quantity. Lilburn offered to assist Jacobus navigate through the umbrellaed labyrinth toward the lemonade stand, but Jacobus, using his ears and nose, had less difficulty avoiding the flowing Frascati and foie gras than did his clumsy companion.

"Lilburn," Jacobus asked, accidentally poking a picnicker with the end of his cane, "you know something about music, so tell me. On one hand, this great maestro Herza is one little son of a bitch. On the other, it's magic how he gets the orchestra to sound—you could hear it by the time they got done with the Mozart. But I can't see the guy. Is he doing something no one else can do?"

"Quite the opposite, Mr. Jacobus. It's remarkable how much control he has with such economy of movement. He sits there and barely moves a muscle, yet the orchestra responds like a racehorse that's been given the whip around the backstretch. It reminds me of William Steinberg, when he was old and infirm. At the bitter end, he too sat when he conducted, and all he had to do was waggle those elephantine ears of his and the musicians would go into a frenzy! Nowadays we've got these young Adonises who dance all over the podium like Bernstein on methamphetamine, yet they get no response from the orchestra except a sneer and a snicker."

"I heard a story," said Jacobus, "about Fritz Reiner when he conducted the Chicago Symphony. His beat was so small that at one rehearsal a string bass player took out a pair of binoculars to make the point that Reiner needed to give a more discernible beat."

"And what happened?"

"He got fired. Don't know if it's true, but it's a good story."

"Perhaps Maestro Herza has some of Reiner's genes. You know Herza studied with Wilhelm Furtwängler in Switzerland after the war."

"So maybe he has Nazi genes, too."

"Though Furtwängler was exonerated by the truth commission for complicity with the Nazis. We're here at the lemonade stand, by the way. Can I get you one? My treat."

"No, thanks," said Jacobus, revolted by the thought. "I'll just listen to you drink yours."

"It wasn't clear-cut, though, with Furtwängler. He said his goal was simply to keep the music alive and that he had no political motives."

"Just following ordure, eh? You go for that line?"

"Well, it was never proved otherwise," said Lilburn. "On one hand, there's no question he was a great and respected conductor. There's a story that after von Karajan took over the Berlin Philharmonic from him, when Furtwängler entered the room during a rehearsal the orchestra immediately sounded better. On the other, he did manage to stay in the party's good graces until the end of the war. I suppose Herza is trying to keep that tradition alive—the musical part, anyway—though his professional and personal adversity seems to have soured his disposition."

"You have a gift for understatement, Lilburn. That's never been one of my strengths. Herza also studied with Strauss, didn't he?"

"More that he basked in the glow of his idol than actual study. He spent a few summers with the Strauss family after the war and listened to the old man extemporize on his own greatness and the incompetence of everyone else. Strauss also had a spotty record with the Nazis, but his disdain for them, and his desire to be left alone to compose music, seems a more convincing narrative than Furtwängler's. It's no surprise that the young, impressionable Herza, with his skills, devoted himself to the music of Strauss and became his foremost interpreter."

"Well, fuck them both!" Jacobus exploded unexpectedly. "Both Furtwängler and Strauss. I don't give a shit if they were Mozart and Beethoven incarnate. Slightly Nazi's like slightly pregnant. They should've hanged the pair of them. We all have our excuses, don't we?"

"I seem to have caused an upset here," said Lilburn, surprise in his voice. "Have I said something?"

"Never mind," Jacobus muttered, pulling back from his personal abyss. It had not been Furtwängler and Strauss who had exterminated his family. They were silently complicit, perhaps, in a tangential way, but who wasn't? On this bright day, Jacobus's mood had turned black, and though he had become accustomed to the incendiary onset of his rage, the pain was always raw.

"Anyway," Jacobus forced himself to say, "Strauss composed *Death and Transfiguration* long before the war, before he became 'slightly' Nazi."

"Indeed," said Lilburn, attempting to mollify Jacobus, "it's a fine piece, and the second half of the rehearsal should be interesting."

The loud Tanglewood bell clanged, summoning the audience back to their seats.

"Time to fasten our seat belts," said Lilburn.

Jacobus muttered something unintelligible and allowed Lilburn to guide him by his arm back toward the Shed.

"I'm also curious," said Lilburn as they retraced their serpentine route, "about the new work they're rehearsing after the Strauss this morning."

"Haven't heard about that."

"I'm sure it's something you'll just love, knowing you."

"Try me."

"It's a minimalist piece called 'Life and Disfiguration'—"

"You can stop right there."

"By Ignaz Fouk."

"You mean the Christopher Rouse clone who's a John Adams clone who's a Philip Glass clone who's a Steve Reich clone who's—"

"I'm not certain of your genealogy, but yes, that Ignaz Fouk. To-morrow will be the world premiere, and according to Mr. Fouk it may be performed only alongside *Death and Transfiguration*. That together they create—and I'm quoting here—'the duality of existence that comprises the All.'"

"Send in the clones. I'm surprised Herza would fall for that," Jacobus commented.

"Perhaps because Fouk is Czech and was co-commissioned by the NEA and the Czech cultural ministry to compose something for the opening of the new hall. I take it you're not a minimalist fan."

"To put it bluntly," said Jacobus, "it's the greatest dumbing down of classical music ever conceived."

"Don't you think that statement is a bit simplistic? After all—"

"You take a few pleasant-sounding but otherwise unrelated chords, you overlap them at their edges creating what masquerades as cre-ative harmonies, then you doll them up with mathematically altered rhythms and repeat it until your mind is numb. As an afterthought you choose a few random tempos and dynamics, and there's your masterpiece."

"Powerfully stated, Mr. Jacobus," said Lilburn as they took their seats, "though I still believe your opinion uncomfortably severe. But have you ever given thought to composing, yourself?"

"Minimally."

Some of the musicians, returned to the stage, were rehashing last-second details before the rehearsal of *Death and Transfiguration*. Jacobus felt that the stories—and the music—of some of the later tone poems, *Alpine Symphony* and *Symphony Domestica*, for example, verged on the trivial; that Strauss had run out of inspiration and was running on fumes. But in *Death and Transfiguration*, written when the composer was still young, Jacobus felt Strauss had realized his most profound creation until the *Four Last Songs* that he composed on his deathbed and in which he quoted this earlier work. *Death and Transfiguration* is not so much a story as it is a dramatic scene in which a fatally ill man undergoes his final death throes and emerges into the light of a more beautiful world.

The orchestra tuned again, and Vaclav Herza again mounted the podium, this time sans applause, for *Death and Transfiguration*.

Herza's interpretation of the protagonist's feebly pulsating heart at the beginning of the piece, played first by the strings and then by solo timpani, was so convincing that Jacobus covertly placed his hand on his chest to make sure his own was still beating. Then the sudden stab of pain, the music rushing into a panic of anxiety—perfect, just perfect, thought Jacobus. Unlike the first half of the rehearsal, this time Vaclav Herza hardly stopped at all, a refreshing change for the audience and, Jacobus was certain, for the musicians as well. Perhaps, because it was one of Herza's signature pieces, the orchestra knew it so well that it needed no correction. Perhaps Herza was happy with the way things were going, unlikely as that might be. Or perhaps he was getting tired. Or bored. With conductors, one never knew. In any event, the tone poem proceeded like an opera without libretto. With music whose meaning was so clearly apparent, words would have been superfluous.

There are momentary oases in *Death and Transfiguration* during which the dying man, racked with physical and spiritual agony, glimpses an ephemeral ray of divine light through his torment. One of these visions is portrayed by a concertmaster solo. Though not on the scale, either in terms of technical challenge or length, of some of Strauss's concertmaster solos in other of his tone poems, it nevertheless requires a beautiful quality of sound and sense of line. Jacobus awaited the solo in order to gauge Sherry O'Brien's ability to play under pressure.

The moment arrived and O'Brien began. After just a few notes Herza stopped the orchestra. To Jacobus, capable of being critical of any violinist save Jascha Heifetz, it sounded fine. He could not think of anything he would have suggested for improvement, so perhaps it was some other instrument he had not been listening to that required Herza's attention.

There was commotion on the stage.

"What's going on?" Jacobus asked Lilburn.

"Maestro has stepped down from his podium, has gotten down on his knees, painfully so from all appearances, and has put his hands together in supplication to Ms. O'Brien."

Jacobus heard Maestro's next words, not because his hearing was so acute or because he was in the front row, but because Maestro made sure they were audible to the entire audience.

"How can such a pretty little girl," he said, "play so ugly?"

The audience, accustomed to respectful, if not always cordial, interaction between conductor and orchestra at Boston Symphony rehearsals, buzzed with as much shock as the decorum of a classical music audience would allow. Jacobus thought to himself, He's an even bigger prick than I am.

"Maestro," said the voice Jacobus recognized from the day before, "I'd be happy to play it however you want. In the meantime, can I help you up?"

There was laughter from the audience but none from the stage. The tension behind him may have broken, but so too had the flow of the rehearsal. Herza reverted to his first-half form, stopping every few seconds to dispense criticism, often, for no apparent reason, aimed at Junior Parsley. By the time they finished the piece, only a few minutes were left of the rehearsal, and they still needed to work on "Life and Disfiguration," which, like most premieres, especially of modern music, needed the most preparation.

Predictably, Herza announced, "Fouk. One hour overtime." What was a surprise, however, was that Tyson Parsley returned to the stage even faster than he had earlier. Herza said to him, "What do you want?" to which the personnel manager replied in his soft Southern drawl, "Sorry, Maestro, but overtime is not permitted today."

Herza was incredulous. "And why not?"

"Our collective-bargaining agreement prohibits overtime on tours."

"This is no tour! This is Tanglewood."

"Also, our contract between the Boston Symphony and Harmonium makes it explicit that there can't be overtime today because they have to clear the grounds to prepare for a James Taylor concert tonight. The musicians must be excused now."

"I have spent my entire career fighting against this kind of nonsense," said Herza, as the stage quickly emptied. "Strauss would not have permitted this."

"Strauss is not party to our contract, Maestro. At least the last time I checked."

"The parties to your contract may rot in hell. Tomorrow's concert is canceled."

SEVEN

Lilburn bounced up from his seat, quickly said his good-byes to Jacobus, and headed off with a severe case of ambivalence for his interview with Herza. This might not be the best time for it, Jacobus thought, but if Lilburn still has the balls to go after his story, I should have enough backbone to ask Tyson Parsley a few questions about Sherry O'Brien. His interest had been piqued by the inordinately harsh treatment Herza had doled out to her. Perhaps there was something more going on under the surface. Besides, when would he have another chance to see his old cronies, Beanie and Cappy?

Jacobus made his way to the backstage area of the Shed. For the few years he was a member of the Boston Symphony violin section, before the onset of the blindness that ended his performance career, that area was more like a summer camp cabin, with the smell of wood, sweat, and humidity permeating the rickety structure seemingly tacked on as an afterthought behind the dominating presence of the Shed auditorium. Since then, it had been torn down and had undergone a complete reconstruction, tripling its size. In addition to more spacious air-conditioned dressing rooms, there were designated rooms for the harps, percussion instruments, pianos; for practicing, guest artists, management, and even the orchestra's own credit union. Jacobus ended up wandering in circles, randomly knocking on doors.

"All you who enter, give up hope," said a buoyantly accommodating voice, the voice he had heard onstage holding its own again Herza. Big brother Tyson. This was the place. Finally.

As Jacobus opened the door to the overly air-conditioned room, someone brushed by him, hurriedly, mumbling a curt, "Pardon, sir," on the way out. Someone else jumped from a seat and rushed toward him. Alarmed, Jacobus put out his arm for protection and retreated a step. Then he felt a hand even bigger than Nathaniel's on his shoulder.

"Please let me help you to a seat," Tyson Parsley said.

Jacobus needed seven steps to get to where he was being led; his new acquaintance, only three.

"Didn't know there were any Irish in the orchestra," Jacobus commented, "except for Sherry O'Brien, and she doesn't have a baritone brogue like the guy who just passed by me."

"Ay, laddie, that would have been our esteemed symphony chauffeur, Mr. Paddy Donaghue. He just needed to finish his therapeutic rant before the quotidian polishing of the Batmobile for his nibs."

"So what was eating him?"

"Oh, this and that. And what can I do for you on this fine day, sir?" said Parsley.

"Your brother told me I could find you here."

"You met Junior."

"Yeah, Junior. What's his real name?"

"That's it: Junior. We're twins. He was born ninety-two seconds after me. So we're Tiny and Junior even though we're each three hundred pounds of sheer joy."

"Identical, I gather."

"They couldn't have cloned the Pillsbury Doughboy any better. Mama even had to put a bracelet on Junior to tell us apart."

"Junior told me I could find Beanie and Cappy here. They're old friends of mine."

"They'll show up. A day without a complaint from Beanie and Cappy is a day without sunshine. You'd think two gentlemen from the Midwest who wore white socks and plaid pants would occasionally be able to find common ground. And just how do you know Tweedledum and Tweedledee?"

"We went to Juilliard together. I played the violin and one semester we did the Mozart G-Minor Quintet and—"

"Hey, are you Daniel Jacobus? The legendary blind dude?"

"That would be Ray Charles. I am not nor have I ever been either legendary or a dude."

"Well, I am honored, sir. You are indeed a shining star in the orchestra galaxy." Jacobus felt his hand engulfed by Parsley's and shaken so briskly that his shoulder felt as if it would be dislodged any moment.

"Tiny Parsley, sir. At your service. Pleased to make your acquaintance. Can I get you something to drink? Water? Coffee? Bourbon?"

"Anything but lemonade. Coffee would be fine, thanks."

Jacobus heard Parsley pick up the phone and tell one of the gofer management interns to bring a fresh pot.

"I'd go myself but I have to sit tight for a while," he added to Jacobus after he hung up.

"And why's that?" asked Jacobus. "Maybe this isn't the best time for me to be here after what went on onstage."

"No, no, no. Part of the job. Maestro was just a mite peeved about not being able to have overtime. He's having one of his snit fits and is threatening to cancel the concert. Our beloved CEO, Adrianne Vickers, is trying to mollify him and talk him out of it, so I have to stand by. If we're on, no problem. If it's off, I have to contact all the musicians, make arrangements for getting them out of their hotels, figure out reimbursements for their per diem, arrange transportation for some of them back to New York, cancel the contracts of some of the subs. That kind of thing."

"Your brother mentioned the joys of personnel managing."

"Yes, one tends to get it from both ends in this position. Nary a day passes that I don't get a ridiculous complaint or request from a musician that is not offset by something even more absurd from up-stairs. It's boheca all the way."

"Boheca?"

" 'Bend over, here 'e comes again.' It's ugly, but someone has to do it."

"Why you? You enjoy bending over?"

Parsley laughed. "I've had my share. You see, you and I, we're more alike than you think."

"How's that?"

"You can't see with either eye. I can't see with my right eye. Lost it. My mama, she even prophesied it."

"How so?"

"One day, when I was still a little tyke, she says to her Tuesday-night bridge group, 'You know, from the moment I became pregnant, I knew Tyson would be the one-eyed bear.' "

"Did your mother really say that?"

"No, but she did play bridge."

"So how'd it happen, Tyson?"

"Call me Tiny. Everyone does. I used to play trombone in the or-chestra, like Junior, but then I popped one champagne cork too many."

"You were hit in the eye with a champagne cork?"

"Not quite. We'd just finished a run of *Elektra* and there was a pretty raucous cast party afterward. The bubbly had been flowing freely, and well, after all, you know trombone players. So after a while I started making untoward advances to some of the female members of the cast. One thing led to another and at one point, I guess—I don't even remember this, they just told me afterward—I guess I groped the Clytemnestra."

"That probably wasn't appreciated."

"You can say that again. Her partner snatched the champagne bottle right out of my hand and clobbered me on the head with it."

"Not the kind of snatch you were looking for. You have to watch out for the jealous guys, huh?"

"It was a gal."

"Hmm. So couldn't you play trombone anymore, with one eye?"

"Hell, yeah, I could play with no eyes. With some of these conductors, it would be an advantage! Thing was, I also got smacked in the lip and rent it asunder, as the good book would say. It wasn't a pretty sight. I knew my playing days were over."

"So you went into personnel management."

"They say I have people skills."

"I can tell."

Two young ladies, chatting in Chinese, walked into Parsley's chilled office.

"It's too hot onstage," said one of them. "Yang and I are too hot."

"That's because it's summer, Li Jian," said Parsley, "and we're playing outdoors. It gets hot outdoors in the summer."

"But it's no good for instruments. It's way too hot."

"You're telling me this now. The rehearsal is already over."

"But what about the concert?"

"That's tomorrow."

"So you're not going to do anything?" asked Yang.

"What is it you would like me to do?"

"I don't know. That's not my job. That's your job."

"Okay. Well, why don't we wait until tomorrow and see? Maybe I can think of something by then. Maybe the climate will change."

When the women had left, Jacobus said, "I see what you mean."

"You should see the outfits they're wearing. They look like they were sprayed on. No wonder they're hot. Hate to say it, but some of the musicians call those two 'Shanghai street corner.'"

"Pretty nasty."

"Yeah, but most of it is just talk. Anything more serious I keep on file.

"Sometimes I do wonder why I got into this profession—personnel managing, that is. You're always in the middle and someone's always getting pissed off. There's one young lady—I can't mention names—who's sick a lot. We have generous sick leave and some people think she takes advantage of it. Part of the provision requires a doctor's note stating the reason for the absence. The musicians balked at that and are trying to get it written out of the next contract, but since there are pretty frequent injuries as a result of overplaying, I figure they'd rather have the leave and give up some of their privacy."

"And the young lady in question?"

"Even some of her own colleagues were bitching about how much she had been out. And one day she comes into the office and asks for a week's leave—unpaid, of course—to take her family to Disneyland. I told her I'd have to turn that down, given how much she had been absent. She started hollering that one thing didn't have anything to do with the other, and she was going to file a grievance with the union, and so on and so on."

"What happened in the end?"

"She got sick that week."

"For real?"

"Well, she handed in a doctor's note."

"A doctor in Anaheim?"

"I hadn't thought of that. I should have checked."

"How does she play?"

"Terrific."

"Then I'd drop it."

"My thought exactly."

"But you get it from management too, you say?"

"Sometimes worse. Take a look at the Fouk we're doing. Harmonium's a big orchestra, but I still had to hire four saxophonists and a slide whistle player for that piece. Can you believe there's also a part for a bouncing basketball? There's no getting around it. I have to hire enough guys to fit the music.

"But week in, week out I get a memo from upstairs—we're big on memos here—telling me I've got to reduce my budget for extra players, that we're running a serious deficit as it is, and would I please try to control the costs. Yip yip yip yip yip. My response is—and this is just between you and me—what the fuck? I didn't decide we should commission a new work! I didn't ask Mr. Fouk to compose a piece that requires the services of the Harlem Globetrotters. I didn't—"

"You seem to handle it well, Tiny," said Jacobus, confident that if he had had that job, he would have killed many people.

"Thank you. I try to be organized and patient. There is no doubt being part of a symphony organization is a high-stress job for everyone, and I remind myself of that every time I'm inclined to strangle someone. I think of orchestra musicians as horses."

"Yes," said Jacobus. "It's hard to strangle a horse."

"Good observation, sir. My point, though, is that when musicians are young, still developing, they're trained to be thoroughbreds. Of course, they're taught all the mechanical skills, but the musicians who really thrive are those who acquire the greatest level of artistic expression, of creativity, of personality. Of individuality. Even on trombone, if you can believe that. And don't forget that most of that is achieved in isolation. All by oneself in a practice room, hour upon hour, day upon day, year upon year. Getting ready for that musical Kentucky Derby that will win fame and fortune.

"But what's the reality, Mr. Jacobus? The reality is, as soon as that budding young artist wins the big audition for his dream job in an orchestra, passing through that invisible starting gate from wannabe to elite, he's no longer a thoroughbred. He is a packhorse. A beast of burden. He is anonymous. If he's a string player, he cannot be heard. In fact, he can hardly hear himself. All that creativity he spent half a lifetime striving for is not only wasted, it's discouraged. He's got a load on his back and is being led down the trail right behind the ass in front of him, doing the maestro's bidding. When you do a hundred concerts a year and even more than that of rehearsals, and you add up the years, you'll find a lot of frustration, a lot of depression, and a lot of very unhappy, jaded people.

"So, yes, I try to be patient. Things generally work out."

"But still you have the files."

"You're a good listener, sir. No wonder you were a good musician. I've got a file for everyone in the orchestra."

"What's in them?"

"Mainly contracts, letters of commendation or reprimand as the case may be, keeping track of when people are absent and for what reason. Particular issues with management, difficulties with other musicians, records of the outside concerts they do, medical records when appropriate. That sort of thing."

"Even Beanie and Cappy?"

"Theirs are among the thicker files."

"You have a file on Sherry O'Brien?"

"Right in between Nyquist and Okeda. Scheherazade O'Brien."

"Scheherazade, is it?"

"Yes. Not a name you hear in daily intercourse. Rumor has it her parents wanted her to be a violinist, not a Persian princess. Why do you ask about Sherry? You know her?"

"She played for me a little, getting ready for the concertmaster audition. Told me a little bit about her grievance."

"Oo! That young lady certainly has a bee in her bonnet. Off the record I can't say I blame her. She's been in limbo here for two years now. So she's neither fish nor fowl, and if she manages to come out on top with this audition, she'll still have a year's probation, at least."

"That may be mildly irritating, but it doesn't sound like grounds for a grievance against a guy like Herza."

"Not in itself, but he really does get on her case, as you heard earlier. It's almost like he's stringing her along just so that he can torment her."

"But he also did that with the second violinist," countered Jacobus. "That guy Larsen."

"Poor Sigurd!" said Parsley. "Herza has an uncanny knack for picking vulnerable musicians. I can't tell you what's in his file, but believe me, if there's one person who needs to avoid stress, it's Sigurd. He's a year away from his full pension, and I just hope he's still fit to fiddle off into the sunset to enjoy it."

"So what's O'Brien's Achilles' heel?"

"That's the thousand-dollar question! Herza hasn't found it yet, and I think that's why he hounds her like he does. She's so strong willed that she's able to sit there and take it. Kind of like the *Thousand and One Nights*. She has to keep pleasing Grand Poobah Herza so he doesn't kill her. If he were to fire her, in a strange way it would almost be like she won the battle, and I don't think he's willing to lose face. So on it goes."

"Why, though, if she plays so well?"

Parsley took his time responding. "Mr. Jacobus, you used to play in orchestras. You know conductors. It's as much about power as it is about music."

"Yeah. Stupid question."

"I'll strike it from the record."

"How is it that everyone seems to tolerate Herza?" Jacobus pursued. "I thought these days conductors were supposed to be warm and fuzzy with the musicians."

"You got that right," said Parsley. "Where I grew up, in Lexington, Kentucky, you even called the garbageman 'sir.' You know the saying: 'I was bred in ol' Kentucky, but I'm just a crumb up here.' But it's different these days: With a lot of conductors, you can call them by their first names and they won't bat an eyelash—Seiji or Michael or Joey. Can you imagine if someone had called Toscanini 'Artie'? Toscanini would've had him skewered. With Herza, he's got a rule—no one's even allowed to talk to him unless he speaks to them first. Which is why I have what I call my own personal Talent/Asshole Continuum, or TAC, as it were."

"The better the conductor . . ."

"You've got the idea! The better the conductor, the bigger the asshole he can get away with being. The theoretical absolute greatest conductor would have the highest talent rating but be at the saintly bottom of the asshole index. That would make him a ten-zero. There have been very few ten-zeros throughout recorded history going back to the time of ancient Rome. The amazing thing is how many in my TAC are at the bottom of the talent index and high on the asshole index. It's like they think, 'Hey, maybe if I'm an asshole, that will turn me into a great conductor.' There's one guy, a music director in South America. I had him above middlin' on the talent index and he seemed to be a nice guy, about a six-five, but then he went ahead and fired his entire orchestra. It caused me to rethink his status."

"Why do you keep files on all the conductors?" asked Jacobus. "This is Herza's orchestra. There aren't any guest conductors."

"You're right, we do have a unique situation here. Some orchestras, like Boston, have a music director, a principal guest conductor, a conductor emeritus, a pops conductor, a couple of assistant conductors, at least a half dozen guest conductors during the winter season, and another truckload during Tanglewood. Hell, there are more conductors there than musicians! That might create the spice of life for the troops, but you don't get the same distinct, individualized sound that you got when it was Koussevitzky's Boston Symphony. Nowadays, all the orchestras are pretty much vitamin D homogenized. Except ours. No one can mistake any other orchestra for ours.

"But all good things—or if you're a Herza basher, bad things—must come to an end, and the man is clearly unwell. There will be a day when Harmonium will need a successor, or successors. He can barely make it to the podium some days."

"Yet if there's one thing you hear in his music," said Jacobus, "it's his power. I can't see what the hell he's doing. Give me some insight."

"That's the same thing, Mr. Jacobus, that all the talentless asshole conductors—"

"The zero-tens—"

"You've got it, have been trying to figure out. If you're watching Herza from the audience, sometimes you can't even see him move. He sits there and, yes, his hands move—a little. His gestures have never been very dramatic, and now in his dotage they're almost nonexistent. Yet when he raises his head and gives you that stare of his, it's like he's giving you not only all the information you need to play the way he wants, he's transferring power into your own gut. And then, when he actually does make a physical gesture, he can get the orchestra to blow the roof off. I remember one time in the Allegretto of Beethoven Seventh, he made that twenty-four-measure crescendo—you know the one I'm talking about—from pianissimo to fortissimo, and all he did was start with a closed fist in front of his face and gradually unclench his fingers. It was hair-raising. Most of the guys respond pretty damn quick, anyway, because if you don't, you've got hell to pay."

Jacobus wanted to get back to the subject of Sherry O'Brien's file, but the phone rang.

Parsley said, "You'll have to excuse me, Mr. Jacobus. Probably Adrianne about the cancellation. Shouldn't be long."

Jacobus, listening to one side of the conversation, gathered that Herza was true to his word; the concert was indeed going to be canceled. The greater part of the discussion, though, was to do with whether to pay the extras and substitutes for the concert, plus a day of per diem for everyone, even though there was no longer any orchestral service. That expense alone was well over $10,000.

Parsley made the case that Harmonium was obligated to pay them. A contract had been signed, and this was not a force majeur, a situation totally out of their hands to prevent. He was clearly getting resistance, however, from his superior at the other end. Though Jacobus admired Parsley's controlled, patient responses, he believed a few choice obscenities would at least have added some spice to the discussion.

One of the benefits, if it could be deemed that, of being blind was how miraculously easy it was to become invisible to others. Maybe, thought Jacobus, it was because in order for his ear to be closest to the sound he was listening to he turned his head away, giving the impression he wasn't paying attention. So as Jacobus sat there like a piece of furniture, Tyson Parsley had no qualms explaining the entire contract to his boss and, from there, urging reconsideration of the cancellation.

Jacobus tired of waiting, and though he was curious to find out more about O'Brien's situation, he was considering leaving when his thoughts were interrupted by a familiar birdlike whistle coming from the hall. The volume received a boost when the door to the office opened, then the whistling stopped abruptly.

"Hey, Beanie! Look what the cat drug in!" said the Whistler.

"Cappy! Beanie!" said Jacobus.

"I see the oaf of office is occupied," said Beanie. "Can you believe

I can't see a damn thing where I'm sitting on this ridiculous stage, and what's he doing? He's on the phone. As usual."

"It wouldn't help your playing, anyway," said Cappy. "Jake, come join us for lunch. We heard there's a new place in Lenox."

Jacobus thought about waiting for Parsley to finish his phone call and about all the Carnegie Deli cold cuts waiting for him at home, but since he didn't have a ride anyway . . .

EIGHT

Lilburn, having parted company with Jacobus after the abrupt termination of the rehearsal, found Herza's dressing room. What he hadn't expected to encounter was Lubomir Butkus barring his entrance.

"I regret to inform you that your interview with Maestro is canceled," said Lubomir, in an accent similar to Herza's but with feigned, rather than innate, authority.

Lilburn pleaded his case. "But I've come all the way from the city for this." He removed an already saturated handkerchief from the pocket of his snug sport jacket and wiped his brow yet again. "It was Harmonium staff, in fact, who proposed this specific time. The story has been in preparation for months and must run before the opening of Harmonium Hall next week."

"Maestro is very upset at the treatment he has received here. He has canceled tomorrow's concert."

"That is precisely one of the issues I would like to discuss with him," Lilburn dissembled. "The world needs to hear his point of view. If you would please inform Maestro Herza that—"

"I don't *inform* Maestro of anything."

"Please be kind enough to convey to Maestro Herza that if he consents to speak to me, I will be happy to listen to his opinion of how he has been treated here. And please inform . . . let him know that without his own words, my article will be lacking in the gravitas so crucial in exciting the public awareness of the historic opening of Harmonium Hall to the degree to which—"

"Maestro doesn't need PR from the *New York Times* to sell tickets to his concerts, if that's what you're implying."

"Could you just please ask him?"

"Very well."

Lubomir entered Herza's dressing room and closed the door behind him. Lilburn checked his watch three times before he emerged.

"Maestro will speak to you for five minutes. And remember, remain standing, do not shake his hand, and do not speak until you are spoken to."

Lilburn stood in front of Herza's desk and had the opportunity to examine all the framed photos of the picturesque Berkshire Mountains, twice, before the maestro looked up from his score.

"You wish to speak to me?" asked Herza.

"Thank you for your time, Maestro. I was at the rehearsal just now. I understand that you were not permitted to rehearse 'Life and Disfiguration.' What is your reaction to that?"

"That is none of your business. Is there anything else?"

"The opening of Harmonium Hall next week is perhaps the most important event in the history of your orchestra since its founding. It is the first time, after decades of being primarily a touring orchestra, that it will have a real home. Could you tell me what it means to you?"

"It is a place to play music."

"Would you care to elaborate on that?"

"No."

"Maestro, I understand that the musicians are now in contract negotiations with management over a new and substantially revised contract. The deadline is the night before the opening concert at Harmonium Hall."

"I have nothing to do with negotiations."

"But are you concerned at all that a strike or a lockout might prevent the opening from occurring?"

"My musicians are the highest paid in the world. They are expected to be in their seats for every concert. They will be there."

"Maestro," said Lilburn, "you have assembled a very interesting program for the opening of Harmonium Hall."

"I am not interested in 'interesting.' There is great music and there is shit music."

"Clearly. I say 'interesting' in that the program reflects the cooperation you've received from the governments of the Czech Republic and Prague, and is associated with your Czech past and your renown with the music of Strauss."

"It has nothing to do with any of those things."

"But certainly, there is no denying that *Don Giovanni,* of which you are performing the overture, was premiered in Prague, that *The Moldau* and 'New World' Symphony are two of the most iconic works of the entire Czech repertoire, and your interpretation of *Death and Transfiguration* is considered unparalleled."

"You critics miss the point entirely."

"Then you'll please enlighten me."

"First, I will say a word about overtures. Other conductors program overtures at the beginning of concerts partly because they are usually no more than ten minutes long. They feel this gives the audience something entertaining to listen to but also allows a chance for latecomers to get to their seats without missing 'the meat' of the program. Parking lot music, you may say, that usually results in polite, restless applause."

"I take it you do not subscribe to this way of thinking."

"I certainly do not. In *Don Giovanni* we have a hero for whom life is no struggle but who is nevertheless ultimately dragged into hell by the ghost of the man he has murdered, the father of the woman Giovanni ravished in the first scene. In *Death and Transfiguration*, we have a hero who struggles for his very breath in life but goes to heaven. A critical juxtaposition, wouldn't you say?

"Most people, including yourself, apparently, think *The Moldau* is about a river. It is not. It is a metaphor. It is about the progress of life, from its fragile beginnings through its joys and turbulence and on to its end, its magnificent end. I correct you in your reference to the piece you call the 'New World' Symphony, Dvořák's final symphony. That is not its name. It is titled the Symphony in E Minor, opus 95, 'Z nového světa,' or as you would say in English if you were accurate, '*From* the New World.' In your naïve arrogance you assume the reference is to America because Dvořák happened to be living here when he wrote it. I kindly refer you to the last note of the piece to suggest you don't know what you are talking about. After all the buildup to it, why does Dvořák hold the last note out, getting softer and softer, until it disappears into infinity? Why doesn't he just end it in the big-bang grand tradition of lesser composers? I don't suppose you have ever given that a moment of thought. I will tell you. He is saying that everything that came before it is insubstantial, a mirage, a figment of imagination. Life is a mirage. The 'New World,' in fact, is what exists *after* the last note.

"So here you have your connections, Mr. Lilburn. I am not so mundane as your limited imagination would have you believe."

"Maestro, I have only a few brief moments remaining. Your ascent to the pinnacle of the conducting world, from the time you were a student of Furtwängler and Strauss, to your departure from Prague in 1956, to your first fame in this country when you stepped in at the last moment for an ailing Leopold Stokowski, to your continued efforts on behalf of your native land with Alexander Dubček and Václav Havel, to the founding of your orchestra, Harmonium—all this has been well documented. Is there anything, Maestro, of a personal nature of which the public is unaware that you would care to add to this account?"

"No."

"What of your feelings when your country finally found true independence when the Iron Curtain fell?"

"As you say, it is well documented."

"Then I have only one final question. Were you or have you ever been troubled that your two idols and mentors, Wilhelm Furtwängler and Richard Strauss, had, though they sought to qualify their complicity, well-known associations with the Nazi Party?"

"Your five minutes are up."

NINE

"Welcome to K&J's Diner, 'a place for grub.' I'm Scott, and I'll be your server today," the waiter announced to no one's interest. "Our special today is pulled elk sliders with a Dr Pepper barbecue sauce. Do you gentlemen need a few moments to decide on your luncheon preference?"

"I'll have the meat loaf," said Jacobus.

"With or without raspberry tapenade?"

"Without. I'll have the Heinz 57 tapenade."

"Same for me," said Cappy.

"I need a few minutes," said Beanie.

"Certainly," said Scott the server. "And something to drink in the meantime?"

"You have Rolling Rock?" asked Jacobus.

"Excellent choice."

"Make that two," said Cappy.

"A pair of Rolling Rocks. Sounds good. And you, sir?"

"Still water, please," said Beanie. "No lemon. Ice on the side."

When Scott the server was out of earshot, Beanie whispered, "Why do they always put ice in water without asking? You'd think they would ask first before putting additives in your drinks."

"Interesting point," said Jacobus.

"Interesting as yesterday's weather," said Cappy.

Jacobus changed the subject. "Why do you suppose they call this place a diner? I thought diners had counters and Formica tables and smelled like grease."

"Time is passing us by, Jake," said Cappy. "Those days are long gone. They only call it a diner to evoke the nostalgia of a bygone era."

"That's not it at all," said Beanie. "There's no specific definition of 'diner.' Anyplace one eats could reasonably be called a diner."

"So how is it," Jacobus asked, trying a different subject, "after all this time, you guys are still together, and on the last stand?"

"Six years ago I went to Tiny and asked to be moved back," said Cappy. "I couldn't stand it anymore, with his fingerings over each note and marking up the part every time the conductor said something profound, like 'good morning.' It's like he was born with a pencil in his hand and the music said 'this space for doodling.'"

"I just so happen to believe," said Beanie, "that if you're going to play your best, it doesn't hurt to have all the information in front of you."

"So you say, O Prince of Digitation. I happen to be more the adventurous type," Cappy said to Jacobus.

"There's a fine line between adventurous and deadbeat," said Beanie.

"See what I mean, Jake?" said Cappy. "So I moved back, to get rid of Mr. IBM here, and, to tell you the truth, I don't mind not being in Herza's line of fire anymore."

Scott the server brought their drinks and asked Beanie if he had decided.

"I'll have the Cobb salad," he said. "Dressing on the side. And are the olives green or black?"

"Black, sir."

"Okay. Pitted?"

"Yes, sir."

"Well, that explains half the story," said Jacobus after Scott the server left, "but pardon me if I'm a little confused. Maybe I'm getting doddering in my old age. But explain to me, how did you end up together again after just one of you moved back? After all, don't orchestras these days have seating rotation in the string sections? I don't get it."

"That's an easy one," said Beanie. "I requested to be reseated next to Cappy."

"But why, if you can't stand each other?"

"Simple," Beanie continued. "I'm going to sit next to him until the day he dies."

"Well, I guess that explains it," said Jacobus. "There's a beautiful logic to that."

"If you had Cappy turning pages for you," said Beanie, "you'd know what I was talking about."

"Not that again," said Cappy.

"I never thought I would say this," said Beanie, "but I actually have learned one thing from Cappy. He has made the art of turning pages into a leisure activity. By the time he's put his viola down, made sure he's nice and comfy, perused the music he has just played, and deigned to turn the page, the rest of the orchestra's already halfway through it. It's enough to give you an ulcer."

Scott the server arrived with their lunches. "Will there be anything else?" he asked.

"You have some Rolaids for an ulcer?" Jacobus asked.

"I can check," said Scott.

"Never mind."

Scott left, but Cappy wouldn't let the argument go.

"Maybe if you'd let me get within fifty yards of the music," he said, "I wouldn't have to take so much time. Jake, it's like he's set up a police barricade around the music so that he can—"

"So that I can have enough room to bow freely, see the music, and see the conductor without getting a hernia," said Beanie. "Is that too much to ask?"

"It is if everyone else in the section has to sit in each other's lap!"

"Boys, boys!" interrupted Jacobus through a mouthful of meat loaf, in the rare role of conciliator. "Hey, did you hear the joke about the two violists in the back of the section?"

"I know a joke about one violist in the back of the section," said Cappy. "And the punch line is Ebeneezer Frumkin."

"That's not the one I had in mind. In this story, the last violist is also a conductor, and one night the music director gets sick right before the concert, so management, frantic for a replacement, asks the violist to conduct, which he does to great acclaim. The next morning at the rehearsal, he sits down in his customary seat, and his stand partner says, 'Where were you last night?' "

"I don't get it," said Beanie. With his fork, he carefully separated the yolk from the white of the hard-boiled egg in his Cobb salad, sprinkled some salt on it, dipped it in the salad dressing, cut it in half, and cautiously ate it.

"I heard an even better one," said Cappy. "One night, this violist goes back to his house. He finds that it's been burned down to the ground, and his dog is dead on the front lawn. He runs around crazy, calling to his wife, who appears in a total mess, all bruised up and so forth. He says to her, 'Oh, my God, what's happened?' She says, 'I've been beaten and raped, he killed the dog, and then he burned down the house.' The violist says, 'Who did this dastardly thing? It's unforgivable! Who?' She says, 'It was Maestro! Maestro did this!' at which point the violist's eyes open wide and he says, 'Maestro came to *our house*?'"

Jacobus guffawed at that one, but Beanie was silent.

"I don't know why you always have to take a dig at Herza," he said.

"What do you mean, 'a dig'? Did I say the word 'Herza'? It was a joke!"

"Every opportunity to degrade a great man. It never fails."

"Hey, the 'great man' is a vampire. He sucks the blood out of everyone. It's what keeps him alive."

"So why are you still in the orchestra, then, Mr. Zombie?"

"Because it pays great, the benefits are great, the pension is great—"

"And the music is great," added Beanie.

Before Cappy was able to argue even that point, Jacobus intervened.

"That was quite a display Maestro put on at the rehearsal."

"He's just having his period," said Cappy.

"Yes, he is strict," said Beanie, "but fair."

"Yeah, just like *old* Nazis," said Cappy.

"He's not a Nazi. He's a Commie."

"When I was in the BSO," Jacobus said, refereeing yet again, "we once had Kurt Sanderling conduct us."

"Is this another viola joke?" asked Beanie.

"No. This is a true story, and your comment just reminded me of it. I mention it because Sanderling fled Germany to escape the Nazis, but he made the mistake of going east instead of west and ended up in Russia."

"Where he had a great career."

"Indeed, because he was a great conductor. Anyway, we were in the middle of rehearsing Bruckner Seventh, and he makes a mistake, which someone of his caliber would almost never make. So he stops and tells the following story: 'Where I come from,' he says, 'they say only conductors and KGB never make mistakes. But of course they are wrong. Sometimes KGB make mistakes.' That one comment broke the ice, everyone had a good laugh, and the performance went better than if he had never made that mistake."

"And your point is?" asked Beanie.

"I guess my point is that you don't have to browbeat professionals to be a good conductor."

"Hear! Hear!" said Cappy, swallowing his last bite of meat loaf.

"I need some coffee," he added. The others concurred, finding at least one point of common ground. Cappy beckoned Scott and put in the order, declining the French press option.

"Except that Herza is a greater conductor than Sanderling ever was," said Beanie, continuing the argument.

"Give it up," said Cappy. "You sound like the Shanghai street corner."

"I noticed a lot of Asians on the roster," said Jacobus.

"Is something wrong with that?" asked Beanie. "They are highly capable."

"And compliant, and malleable, and 'well trained,'" said Cappy.

"Someone might say you're sounding a little racist," said Jacobus, perplexed but pleased with his newly discovered diplomatic skills. All it took was two people more pigheaded than he.

"I know it's a touchy subject," said Cappy. "I've got nothing against the Asian girls—"

"I'll say," said Beanie. "You should have a bucket for your drool."

"Except that they're all young and inexperienced. And they're all Megas. But did you also notice there are no longer any Europeans in the orchestra? Not even from Maestro's own homeland? There's something to be said for having the compositions we play performed by musicians from the same culture as the composer. The guys in the orchestra, they used to come from everywhere, and the orchestra benefited from having all that international flavor. Hell, at least the stories were a lot more interesting. Now, the only old farts left are has-beens like Beanie and me."

"Speak for yourself."

"What about O'Brien?" asked Jacobus. "She played for me. I haven't heard anyone better, Austrian or Asian, period."

"The Ice Maiden? Yeah, she's good. Real good," said Cappy. "But she's not a member."

"Ice Maiden?"

"Cold as a whitefish on a Green Bay winter morn. When she first joined the orchestra, some of the younger fellows tried to get close to her—she's not bad-looking in a chunky sort of way. No dice, though. Doesn't have a close friend in the whole orchestra."

"She happens to be a dedicated musician," Beanie retorted, "who puts her art first. I think she'll win this audition."

"Really?" said Jacobus. "But didn't I hear she's filing a grievance against Herza?"

"That's neither here nor there," said Beanie. "She just wanted to make a point—an unfounded one, in my opinion. In the end, Maestro will discount personal issues and choose the best candidate."

"You want to lay me odds on that?" asked Cappy.

Beanie balked.

Scott the server came with the bill and wished them a good day.

"Twenty dollars for a Cobb salad?" Beanie remarked. "That's outrageous!"

"If she wins," Cappy said, "I'll pay for lunch next time."

"You're on," said Beanie.

TEN

In a rare display of equanimity, Cappy and Beanie split the cost of Jacobus's lunch and departed arguing over whether the tip should have been based upon the cost of the meal before or after the tax. Tired of the badgering, Jacobus remained to decompress and finish his coffee, which was better than his home-boiled Folger's. He was counting out single dollar bills from his wallet to add to the tip when he heard two people walk past his table. One of them, an authoritative female, said to Scott the server, "Over there. There in the corner."

The acerbic voice was unfamiliar, but the distinctive asymmetric gait of the second person that dragged by his table was not, so when Jacobus heard the hurried footsteps of Scott the server pass his table on the return trip, he asked for a refill on his coffee.

Pretending to be lost in thought, Jacobus directed his finely honed hearing toward the conversation taking place right behind him. As he had painstakingly trained himself to do, he blocked out that which he did not want to hear: the clatter of silverware, the chatter of extraneous voices momentarily silenced with mouthfuls of pulled elk slider, and piped-in Barry Manilow singing about someone named Lola that provided an extra and unwanted challenge to his concentration. If they're going to ruin a perfectly decent meal with that crap, Jacobus thought, at least they should hire some poor slob to perform live and let him earn a living.

"The BSO is playing hardball," said the woman. Her voice, like her perfume, emanated from a spot immediately behind Jacobus's back. "If we cancel, we lose the eighty-thousand-dollar concert fee."

"That doesn't interest me," said Vaclav Herza, from the far side of the table. "Tell them it was an act of God."

"An act of God is when a damn tornado plows through the Berkshires and rips the shit out of the hillside. It's not when a conductor throws a tantrum. That may be an act, Vaclav, but whatever you may think, you're not God."

"So I should sell my art, my soul, for a pittance?" asked Vaclav Herza.

"Hello, I'm Scott and I'll be your—"

"Leave!" said Herza.

"Hey, no problem. I'll just give you a few moments to decide on your dining choice."

"Wait," said Adrianne Vickers. "Just bring us some hot tea."

"We have a choice of—"

"It doesn't matter. Just go."

"When you're running a two-million-dollar deficit," Vickers continued, "eighty thousand dollars is not a pittance, Vaclav. That's the fee we lose if we don't play. And as CEO it's *my* ass on the line for that, not yours.

"And it's not selling your soul, either. It's just playing a concert with one less rehearsal than you'd like, which is still more than any other conductor gets."

"By canceling," replied Herza, "I am teaching the bean counters that artistic integrity will not be compromised, regardless of the bottom line, as you managers like so much to say. The bottom line is music, not dollar signs. If they have to suffer by informing their

patrons that Herza will not perform due to their mercenary philosophy, then perhaps the patrons will rise up and demand quality. If I
were to capitulate on my ideals now, what message do you think that
would send?"

"What planet are you on, Vaclav? The BSO would love nothing
more than for you to stick to your guns. They're going to get ten
thousand people on the fucking Tanglewood lawn for tonight's James
Taylor concert. It's been sold out for so long that he just agreed
to give another performance in our slot tomorrow and donate the
profits to the Tanglewood student program if we pull out, so they're
only too happy to get out of this. It's a PR and financial disaster for
us, and—"

"It is too late. Herza has spoken."

"Then what are we going to do with the commission? We've already
paid Fouk thirty thousand, and we owe him another thirty."

"We'll play it another time. Anyway, it is a piece of shit."

"Vaclav."

"I said, no more about this. If you want to talk, tell me about the
hall. Is the hall finished?"

"The hall is almost finished." Her voice was petulant, like a scolded
child.

"Almost! What does this mean? Is there a stage to play on? Are there
seats for an audience? When Herza conducts, is he 'almost' ready?"

"Keep your pants on, Vaclav. It will be ready. They're just finishing the details—light fixtures, carpet, painting, making sure the toilets flush. Feel free to test them at your convenience. The auditorium
is totally done. You, for one, will have nothing to worry about."

"Have the acoustics been tested?"

"Over and over again. Everything according to your specifications. They say it's even better than the halls in Boston and Vienna,
that it will make Avery Fischer sound like a subway station."

"A subway station makes Avery Fischer sound like a subway station."

"You know what I mean. Now we just have to pay for it."

"I'm not interested in that."

"No, you wouldn't be. But we've got a deficit. We've got contract negotiations with the musicians, and we've got a capital campaign that depends on the hall being ready to go."

"Just pay the musicians what they want and get that over with."

"That's easy for you to say."

"Not as easy as you think. If I could, I would pay the vultures nothing. They don't know what real work is. Their lives are one long paid vacation, and yet they complain continuously that they are being mistreated."

"Like that O'Brien?"

Jacobus's ears perked up even more. He congratulated himself on the one thing in his life for which he was still disciplined—his daily listening regimen.

"How dare that young hussy have the audacity to bite the hand that feeds her?"

"Don't get all hot and bothered, Vaclav. Her grievance—if she ever files it—will get nowhere. You should make an example out of her. A warning for the rest of them."

Herza did not respond. Maybe he was mulling. Maybe he decided the conversation was over. Jacobus froze, his coffee cup poised in his hand. Then, from deep within Herza's gut arose a long, slow belch.

"They're all the same," Herza continued, to Jacobus's relief. He resumed sipping his coffee. "A distasteful necessity, like the toilets, but a necessity nevertheless, and I must have the best ones if I am to achieve what Brahms and Mozart have instructed me to achieve.

"You look at me as if I were insane, Adrianne. Yes, they have been dead for a hundred, two hundred years, yet they instruct me. Through their music. And it is my responsibility for the world today to know their genius. If I do not, who will?

"It is your responsibility to provide me with the tools. And since these so-called musicians only understand money and nothing else, you must pay them what they ask for."

"In order to do that we have plans to diversify our activities."

"I don't care what your plans are. Pay them what they want and get it over with. They must not be permitted to hold the opening of the hall hostage for their pettiness."

"I don't think they have the balls to strike. We would lock them out first."

"If they strike, or if you lock them out, it's the same disaster. And if either of those things happens, I'll make sure you pay the price."

"Don't you dare threaten me, Vaclav. It doesn't become your charming self."

"Doesn't it? Just be careful."

"I think it's time to leave," said Vickers. "Even the tea wouldn't help."

"Help what?"

"My stomach. You make me sick to my stomach."

Jacobus's coffee had long since turned cold. He heard Vickers and Herza get up from their table and walk past him on their way out of the diner, Vickers striding briskly, Herza lumbering behind. He picked up his mug and pretended to drink.

Knuckles lightly rapped on his table. He had been sitting there a long time, too long, perhaps. Scott the server was impatient for his tip, or to seat the next customers.

"I'll be leaving in a jiff," Jacobus said, imitating Scott's perky tone.

"Watch your step," said a distressingly familiar voice, very close to his ear, very quietly. The voice of a partially disabled, aged East European. "Blind people sometimes have a way of encountering accidents. They can fall down and never get up again."

ELEVEN
SUNDAY

Jacobus fumed even more than the decrepit taxi that shuttled him back to his house. He arrived home with a tightness in his stomach. Herza might not be Ayatollah Khomeini or Mohammar Ghadafi, but he was one first-rate schmuck. Jacobus should have guessed as much. No conductor that good could be otherwise, Tiny Parsley's TAC notwithstanding. But whether it was worth trying to take him down a notch—as O'Brien had pleaded for him to do—even if he could, was another matter.

The pain in his gut hadn't subsided, and he ended up spending a good part of the night wearing down a path to the toilet. Trotsky had even stopped following him down the stairs to the one antiquated bathroom in the house, having finally concluded that they were not in fact about to embark upon a new adventure. Was it the meat loaf, Jacobus asked himself, or was it Herza that made him sick? He hoped it was Herza because he had really liked the meat loaf. Maybe he should've ordered the pulled elk sliders. This thought had prompted another visit to the toilet.

By Sunday morning Jacobus was exhausted, but determined not to be a bedridden invalid he made his way downstairs and, after dragging his brute of a dog off the couch by the collar, became a sofa-ridden invalid, resting his head on its threadbare arm. He tried making himself a cup of coffee but could not keep even that life-giving necessity down without wrenching opposition. At one point Trotsky had come snorting, wagging his stubby tail, and dropped his drool-soaked, heavy-duty, rubber-bone dog toy directly on Jacobus's stomach, presuming that all his master needed was a playful diversion to rouse him from his languor. He did not quite construe Jacobus's response, which was to take the toy and thump the dog on the top of his head. Trotsky thought it was a wonderful new game and barked for more, finally giving up only when Jacobus turned on his side with his back to his loyal friend and played dead.

Throughout his physical torment, one question dogged Jacobus. Herza had clearly gotten the better of him. His shrewdness and perceptiveness were undulled by infirmity and should not be underestimated. Jacobus had learned that lesson, and it was a good one, if only to have taught him a little humility. The question was: Why? Yes, Jacobus admitted, it might be rude to eavesdrop on someone's conversation. But to elicit an unmistakable death threat? Toward a total stranger from someone already in a position of power? Of all that he overheard, was there one thing in particular that Herza wanted to protect from prying ears? That would prompt Herza to take the extreme measure of confronting him? Though the entire conversation between Herza and Vickers was distasteful, it was typical of the ones that had caused Jacobus to flee from the world of classical music decades ago.

Jacobus rolled onto his back. Locking his arm over the top of the couch, he managed to leverage himself into a sitting position. Taking advantage of a full-phase swivet before it subsided into mere heartburn, he picked up the telephone sitting next to the overflowing ashtray on the corner table beside the couch and dialed information for Martin Lilburn's number. Who better than a reporter doing a story on Herza to have valuable information? Jacobus was fairly certain that his participation in this tussle between O'Brien and Herza, which was of no personal consequence to him, would be a futile exercise of wheel spinning, but it clung to him as tenaciously as his stomach bug. What was it about their standoff that persevered in needling him? He tried to banish the thought that his interest might be altruistic, that he was trying to help someone in need. Maybe he was merely bored with his own directionless life, trying to get himself high on the quick fix of trumped-up intrigue. As usual, when Jacobus began to engage in personal introspection, he changed the subject.

Holding the phone to his ear, Jacobus remembered that Lilburn might well still be in the Berkshire area and so he had no way of contacting him. Even if Lilburn had a cell phone, how does one find out someone's cell phone number? Damn, worthless contraptions! He could call the *New York Times* office in the city and try to get them to give the number to him, but it was Sunday. It might take him the whole day. The hell with it. He decided to wait for a more opportune time and was about to return to his prone position when he had another idea. The Tanglewood switchboard put him through to the personnel office.

"Parsley Mortuary," answered the now-familiar drawl. "You kill 'em, we chill 'em."

"I suppose someone in your position needs a little gallows humor," said Jacobus, "but don't you even ask first who it is?"

"Ah, Mr. Jacobus, is it? And a happy Sunday to you, sir. I figure if someone gets offended by that, they'll be offended by me sooner or later anyway, so why not find out right away? You're lucky to find me at the office today."

"I'm just a lucky kind of guy."

"We should all be so fortunate. What can I do for you?"

"What's your policy on showing personnel files?"

"The policy is no."

"Then who gets to look at them?"

"Me and my special friend, Ludwig, who only I can see. And sometimes the CEO."

"Herza?"

"He's never asked."

"What about the musician himself?"

"If there's a compelling reason. Now it's my turn to play Twenty Questions. Animal, vegetable, or Sherry O'Brien?"

"That obvious, huh?"

"Well, you did ask about her when you were in the office."

"I was just wondering if she had a leg to stand on with her grievance. Seeing what's in her file would help."

"No doubt. But even if I wanted to share the goodies, there are all kinds of laws that tell me I can't. As far as her grievance, I'm not saying it's not justified, and maybe if she were in some stock brokerage office or other normal business, she'd have a case, but in the looking-glass world of the symphony orchestra I have to say it's a long shot."

"That's kind of what I've been hearing, anyway. But thanks for nothing."

"My pleasure, sir," said Tiny Parsley. "My door is always open to you. And now I'm off to the big powwow in the sky, which is why you were able to find me here."

"What's up?"

"Contract meeting. The nitty is getting gritty. I wish you could be there with us."

"Why?" asked Jacobus, surprised.

"You said you were a lucky guy. We'll need all the luck that we can get."

TWELVE

With the afternoon concert officially canceled, the meeting had been hastily arranged and both sides were prepared for a long day at the bargaining table. Sunday mornings were generally off-limits for the orchestra's business activities, but with scant time until the expiration of the contract and pressure building for a settlement before the opening of the new concert hall, a negotiation session between the Harmonium Symphonic Society, led by CEO Adrianne Vickers, and the musicians' negotiating team, chaired by Junior Parsley, had been agreed upon to take place at Seranak, the hillside mansion owned by the Boston Symphony overlooking Tanglewood and Mahkeenac Lake behind it. Unlike the name of the lake, however, Seranak is not of Native American derivation. Rather, as the summer residence of Sergei Koussevitzky, the great Russian conductor who brought the Boston Symphony to perhaps its pinnacle of artistic achievement, it is an affectionate contraction of Serge and his wife, Ana, with the *k* for Koussevitzky.

The choice of Seranak was intended to take the edge off the belligerence, if not the intensity, of the moment, to create an atmosphere conducive to a cooperative dialogue and, if the planets were properly aligned, to an agreement. At management's expense, bagels and coffee were provided for both parties by K&J's, and the negotiation table was turned perpendicular to the picture window so that both sides had equal access to the scenic view of the lake surrounded by the Berkshire Hills.

Formal negotiations had commenced more than two months earlier with the musicians' proposal that included a substantial increase in salary and other compensation like pension, seniority, and health insurance; for two additional paid vacation weeks, an increase in paid sick leave, and requests for changes in rehearsal and concert scheduling, overtime provisions, and audition procedures. The prevailing principle was that in order for Harmonium to remain the best orchestra, the musicians needed to have the best contract in the industry. Along with their proposal, the musicians provided charts of comparisons with the other orchestras in their category, a time-consuming effort, in order to demonstrate the fairness and justification of their requests. According to their research, the thirty-eight-page package they offered kept them one step ahead of the Big Five orchestras: Chicago, Boston, New York, Philadelphia, and Cleveland.

Management received the proposal with poker-faced solemnity, let it gather dust for two weeks, then called for a meeting with the musicians, where they presented a two-page response basically calling for cuts in all categories of compensation and an expanded workload.

The musicians, disheartened by the quality and substance of the offer—a reaction that fit management's game plan—had an all-night meeting, and the next day they responded with a counterproposal that incorporated some of management's language but under any degree of scrutiny was essentially a rehashing of their original package.

Adrianne Vickers had then called Junior Parsley and asked for a late-night one-on-one meeting, a request that Parsley found highly irregular and risky, especially as at that point in time they were not yet close to a deadline. Because it could potentially require him to make concessions on big-ticket items, Parsley consulted the rest of his committee. After long and often contentious discussion, the committee gave him an ambivalent go-ahead to meet with Vickers, reasoning that any agreement he would arrive at with her would only be tentative; it would still require the committee's support and then official ratification by a two-thirds majority of the orchestra.

———

Parsley traversed the flagstone walkway that wound through the rho-
dodendron garden and stood at the doorstep of the Scarsdale home
of Robert Vogelman, armed with arguments to support the musicians' proposals but also with a mental list of potential concessions if
the resultant package could still be interpreted as tops in the business. If Vickers would agree to that principle, the numbers could be
ironed out. Nothing was etched in stone.

Surely, Parsley thought, she wouldn't have called this off-the-record
meeting unless she were willing to talk more freely, to explore ave-
nues of mutual interest. He knew the musicians had the upper hand:
Not only was their proposal fair, reasonable, and achievable, the timing
of the concert hall opening gave them huge leverage. Even though
she might not give a damn about the musicians or the music, Vickers
would never jeopardize the big event. If she screwed that up, she'd be
toast. The pressure was clearly on her and this meeting was an opportunity to come to a verbal agreement. She could then go back to being
tough guy at the bargaining table in order to convince the board that
she had done the best job possible. Though Parsley cautioned himself not to be overly optimistic, visions of sugar daddies danced in his
head.

Parsley rang the Big Ben doorbell and took a step back to admire
the architectural lines of the sprawling postmodern house, wondering if he should have gone into a different profession. Vogelman, a
retired anesthesiologist who had once studied viola at Juilliard, was
one of the few truly nonpartisan symphony supporters. He answered
the door and greeted Parsley warmly. They passed an entertainment
room from which he heard a recording of Berlioz that he identified
as a recent Harmonium release on EMI. Parsley shook his head at the
irony, then politely asked after Vogelman's family. Yes, everyone was
fine, said Vogelman, and the girls were all doing well in college.

Vogelman led him to the great room where Vickers was already waiting, and offered him a drink. Unlike his usual self, Parsley declined. Robert patted him on the back, said to both of them, "You need anything, just holler," and left, closing the door behind him.

Vickers, dressed informally in jeans, sneakers, and a University of Michigan sweatshirt, rose from the couch. She had abandoned her makeup—at least most of it—in favor of a fresh-scrubbed appearance. Parsley had never seen her other than in her standard business pantsuit and approved of the transformation.

"Junior," she said, smiling. She extended her hand.

"Adrianne," replied Parsley, enveloping it in his.

"Thanks for coming," she said. "Let's get to work."

Parsley eased himself into the spare modern Scandinavian couch, carefully distributing his weight to avoid splintering it under his bulk, which would have put a damper on the meeting.

"So, what have you got?" he asked.

"If there's one thing we *can* agree on," Vickers said, "it's that we're at loggerheads. I want to break this nasty impasse. You and me. I think we can do it."

"Impasse?" said Parsley. "That's pretty loaded terminology. You haven't even responded to our counterproposal yet."

"Legally, you're right," said Vickers. "Maybe 'impasse' is too strong a word. But unless we can be honest with each other, really honest, that's where I see things ending up. Which would be unfortunate."

"Well," said Parsley, "you asked for this meeting, and here is yours truly. What have you got?"

"It's nothing specific. But I think there's a better way. A way forward. A principle. After that, we can leave the numbers to the bean counters."

Parsley didn't say anything, but he was hoping the next words out of Vickers's mouth would be, "We recognize that the musicians of

Harmonium must continue to have the best contract in the orchestra industry."

He leaned forward. "I'm all ears."

Vickers leaned forward too. With her fingers, she brushed the hair out of her eyes. Their foreheads almost touched.

"Faith-based bargaining," she said.

"Come again," he said.

"It's a new method of negotiating. Both parties agree to put their specific demands to the side and appeal to a higher order for a non-zero-sum outcome. Don't worry, it's not born-again religious or anything. More like a greater good, though I'm told when it really works it's almost spiritual. Both sides agree to do what's best, not just for management, not just for the musicians, and not even for the organization—but what's best for the industry as a whole, for humanity. It's win-win all around."

"I'm not sure I'm following you. Sometimes I can be a little slow on the uptake."

Vickers gave Parsley a sympathetic I-felt-the-same-way-when-I-first-heard-about-this smile and patted his hand.

"I don't know all specific techniques," she said, "but there's this company, Facilitations, that gave a presentation at our professional development retreat in Southampton. They showed us how, if you just sit next to each other instead of having that darn table in between the two sides, it already removes one of the barriers. And if instead of having this group of musicians and that group of management"—she gestured emphatically with her hands—"you pair up one of each, reading from the same documents, you create a sense of camaraderie that leads to agreement. It's amazing what can happen when you put little things like that together. Facilitations provides an intermediary to attend our negotiations. He keeps things on what they call the Plane of

Principles, or POP, and gets the two sides to agree to stick to a few overarching goals—"

"Like world peace and bringing the NHL back to network TV?"

Vickers laughed. "Maybe POP's not quite that lofty."

"Then such as?"

"Such as that our primary commitment is to the continued health of the organization; that we'll do anything, within the realm of fiscal responsibility, to provide great classical music to the community. Things like that. Facilitations doesn't come cheap. They charge fifty thousand dollars per contract negotiation because they have a seventy-six percent success rate, but we've met with the board and they're willing to pay for it. They never guarantee results, but so far they've got a great track record. We're ready to get started. What do you think?"

Vickers put her hand on Parsley's fat knee.

Parsley looked at the hand, then at the smiling face, and said, "I'm outta here."

"You're leaving?" Vickers seemed genuinely shocked. Parsley almost laughed. "Why?" she asked.

"Because this is what you're thinking, Adrianne. You hire this company, Felicitators—"

"Facilitations."

"Whatever. By offering to pay these guys, that means they're in your pocket. They become management shills. 'The realm of fiscal responsibility' is code for you don't plan on raising another cent more than you have to. So, even before we sit down to bargain, you get the musicians to basically agree to cut our own throats by committing us publicly to Fibrillation's—"

"Facilitations."

"To Facilitation's Plane of Principles—to do whatever has to be done to enable management to balance the budget, namely, cut our salaries, pensions, and anything else you can put your hands on. If we agree to that so-called lofty POP, we're dead in the water. And if we balk at joining in, or agree to it and then have second thoughts, you tell the world that management has taken the moral high road, and the musicians are lazy, greedy, two-faced bastards."

"But as we move forward into the twenty-first century—"

"Save that for the board, Adrianne," said Parsley. "See you at the bargaining table."

Robert Vogelman intercepted him before he got to the door. "Leaving so soon?"

"Want to beat the traffic," said Parsley.

"There's never any traffic at this hour."

"Never say never, Rob, though I did have a premonition things were going to get rocky tonight."

"How so?"

"You know the Berlioz you were playing when I showed up?"

"*Symphonie Fantastique.*"

"Yeah, the fourth movement."

"Which one is that?" Vogelman asked.

"'March to the Scaffold.' I think I just got my head chopped off. Anyway, thanks for your hospitality," Parsley added, calculating that he would need a friendly board member when the orchestra went on strike.

Today's meeting at Seranak was management's official response to the musicians' counterproposal. No member of Facilitations was present, but the feeling of do-or-die was.

"Over the past three months we've heard the musicians loud and clear," Vickers began, "and with the proposal you find in front of you you'll see that we've been listening. We believe we've addressed all your major concerns. That's not to say that we can't tweak some details, and though we're not calling this our last and best offer, we're all aware the clock is ticking and we're running out of wiggle room. We'd like to wrap this up, today if possible, so we can all focus our energy on a successful opening of Harmonium Hall. What I'd like to do now is to summarize our new offer and would request that you wait until I'm done before asking questions, which we'll be happy to field."

Vickers gathered her thoughts and began her presentation.

"Clearly, this is a historic time for Harmonium, and as we transition from a touring orchestra to one with a home base, we need to be able to retain what has worked for us in the past and to search for a new paradigm for the future.

"One of the major questions that all parties have been seeking the answer to is: How do we structure a full season in our new home? The musicians have proposed an average of eight services per week, comprising four rehearsals and four concerts. As a compromise, we will essentially agree with that as a target to shoot for. Our only qualification is that in the interest of flexibility, or if revenue opportunities arise, we be able to add an extra concert per week, limited to six times a year the first year of the contract, and increasing one per year until reaching a maximum of nine in the last year of the contract.

"Second, we believe it is up to the music director, and the music director alone, to determine the appropriate number of rehearsals he needs to maintain the level of greatest artistic integrity, and if we were to accept your proposed restrictions on overtime, we don't think we also should tie his hands regarding the number of rehearsals. So our proposal today states that while we will make our best efforts to maintain a balance of your four rehearsal/four concert formula, it will ultimately be up to the music director to make that final determination, but that in no case may there be more than a total of eleven services in a given week, and if there is such a week, one of the adjacent weeks may have no more than eight, which is what you say you want.

"Another issue of importance to musicians is time off, and you have convinced us of the need and the value for the musicians to decompress after months of intense music making. Currently you have nine weeks of paid vacation: two during the Christmas/New Year's season, four between the winter season and the summer tour season, two more between the summer and next winter season, and the one so-called floating vacation week, scheduled at the convenience of the musician.

"Today we want to take a step forward in meeting your needs and propose a real increase in free time for each musician by creating a variation of the floating-week concept. We propose two additional weeks of vacation, making a total of an unprecedented eleven weeks' vacation, but those two would be scheduled by the symphony at their discretion and would be unpaid. Now, if you turn to page two—"

"This sounds like a shoot-the-tuba-player clause," Junior Parsley interrupted.

"If you could wait until I'm finished—"

"Actually, I'd like some clarification now. Are you saying that if the orchestra is doing a Mozart program, for which there is no tuba, you'd schedule that as one of his vacations and he'd go a week without pay?"

Vickers turned to Tiny Parsley, a member of the management team.

"Tiny, could you respond to that?"

"That's something we hadn't really considered," said Tiny, avoiding his brother's stare, "but admittedly, the way it's worded, that might be one of management's options."

"Now, if you turn to page two," intoned Vickers, "you'll see our proposal for musician compensation. First off, salary. We recognize the importance of salary as the primary means of rewarding the musicians for their outstanding work, and as a way to attract the best musicians in the future. At the same time, without wanting to repeat myself, this is a transitional time for us and we want to be sure we're on solid footing as we move forward. That is the board's fiduciary obligation. Therefore, we are proposing a ten percent salary reduction the first year, and then incremental increases every six months starting the second year, so that, as you can see, by the last half of the final year of the agreement you will actually be earning more than you are now, and we'll still be in a highly competitive posture in regard to the Big Five orchestras.

"The second major source of musician compensation is pension. Currently, we make an eight percent annual contribution to the American Federation of Musicians pension fund. We propose to maintain that."

"Meaning," said Junior Parsley, "that if we take a salary cut, our pension goes down too."

"I'm glad you mention that, because our generous compensation package also includes seniority. Currently, seniority pay is a percentage of salary. We propose to convert it to a fixed amount, thereby avoiding the very concern you just mentioned. So whereas it has been one percent per week for every year of service, we now propose a flat rate, which we believe to be much fairer because it isn't subject to the vagaries of salary. We propose that after every five years of service, each musician receive an additional thirty dollars per week."

"Do I understand correctly that what you propose is substantially less than we get now?" asked Junior Parsley.

"Comparing a fixed rate to a percentage is apples and oranges," replied Vickers.

"Moving on. The final piece of the puzzle is health care. Health-care expenses are rising anywhere from twenty to forty percent a year, depending on the provider. You can see for yourself on the diagram on page three that premiums have literally gone off the charts. The bad news is, it will no longer be possible for us to provide the kind of plan we've offered in the past at no cost to the musicians. The good news is, recognizing the importance of this issue, we propose establishing a joint management/musician subcommittee to study the possibilities and come up with solutions, which could result in a change of providers, a change in coverage, or musician participation in the plan.

"I guess that's it. Are there any questions?"

"What about the other issues?" asked Junior Parsley.

"Such as?"

"The musicians have made any number of proposals in response to the historic idiosyncrasy of Harmonium under Vaclav Herza: the excessive rate of music-related injury; of depression and stress-related mental illness related to overscheduling, arbitrary overtime, and verbal harassment; the earlier average retirement age as a result, hence the need for greater pension; the extra cost to the organization of hiring substitute musicians because so many tenured musicians are ill; the need for more paid sick leave as a result; the need for greater, not lesser, health benefits; the seemingly arbitrary demotions of musicians, which you call 'reseating' in the contract; the exhausting tour schedules. I can go on and on. I don't see any response to our proposals here."

"Now that we have a home in Harmonium Hall, tour schedules will be less of a factor."

"Is that your response?"

"As for the others, we believe your working conditions to be in accordance with the industry standard and propose continuing them as currently provided for in the CBA. We see no reason to waste paper with old news. We're trying to cut down on office expenses.

"Oh, yes, we did add some language in the grievance clause. Just to clarify management's rights. Nothing substantial."

Junior Parsley looked left, then right, catching the eyes of the other members of the committee.

"May we caucus?" he asked Vickers.

"By all means."

"Where?"

"Why don't you stay here? We can stretch our legs while you enjoy the view."

Ten minutes later the management team was invited back to the table, chatting with affected nonchalance as they leafed through their assortment of papers, as if doing so would produce the hoped-for result.

"That was a quick caucus," said Vickers. "Ready to sign on the dotted line?" she asked, all amiability.

"Since everyone has a busy schedule, Adrianne," said Parsley, "I'll cut to the chase. This new package is worse than the last one you made. After that one, we responded immediately with proposals to bring us closer together, and it took you a month to get back to us. As you said, the clock is ticking, but any time pressure you may have regarding the opening of the hall you've brought upon yourself. It doesn't bother us. Not only have you not addressed many of our counterproposals, every change you've made is more onerous than before, including your idea for a health-care subcommittee, where you're kind enough to allow us to choose how we want to slit our own throats. The committee has unanimously agreed that we see no further need to talk."

This time the musicians' negotiating team stood up.

"If you think you can fucking pressure us," Vickers said, "by holding the opening of the hall over our heads as a negotiating ploy, that works both ways."

"You've got a hundred-million-dollar capital campaign in the works," countered Junior Parsley, "and you expect us to agree to cut our salary and benefits? You better have a quiet chat with your faith-based gurus. And while we're at it, Adrianne, fuck you too."

THIRTEEN

MONDAY

Jacobus woke up with a start and a shout, the remnants of a disturbing dream entombed somewhere in the foggy recesses of his brain. Whether the dream was of lieder or Liederkranz, he couldn't retrieve it, nor did he care to. Except for his excursions to the bathroom and a brief foray to the backyard to listen to a flock of wild turkeys gobble their way through the underbrush, Jacobus had spent the remainder of Sunday splayed on the couch, unable even to drag himself upstairs to bed.

The crick in Jacobus's neck reminded him that he was still on the couch, its frayed fabric arms exposing the inner plywood, but that was nevertheless a step up from the fever, which seemed to have departed in the night without totally incapacitating him. And even if visions of chopped liver and pastrami didn't quite dance in his head, at least they weren't doing a dirge.

His first task—a simple one for most people, who could do it simply by opening their eyes—was to determine whether it was day or night. He could turn on the radio to find out, but that would require his excavating through what Sherry O'Brien had quaintly referred to as his "paraphernalia" to get to it. So Jacobus did it with his ears. An avian chorus was beginning its warm-up exercises in his forest, either heralding the new day or saying good-bye to the sun at dusk. There being no audible traffic from Route 41, it was more likely early morning, but how early? The mockingbird had not yet begun its comic virtuoso imitation act, which it did only after hearing the other birds, so Jacobus decided it must be about 6:30 in the morning, give or take twelve hours.

Jacobus rubbed his face, felt for the cane next to the couch, and hobbled to the bathroom. He turned on the cold tap and stuck his head under the faucet. Reasonably awake now, he let Trotsky out the back door to go fend for himself, reassuring him he would holler when the burnt toast—their preference—was ready. He went into the kitchen sufficiently recovered to make himself a cup of coffee, brewing it weaker than usual but extra hot because he still felt a little under the weather. Nathaniel was always pushing him to drink tea whenever he caught a bug, but the thought of tea almost brought back his nausea.

Jacobus carried his mug to the living room. On one wall was an old floor-to-ceiling pine bookshelf, but since the ceiling was only a little over six feet high, it didn't provide all that much shelf space. That was one reason, but only one, why most of Jacobus's music and records were strewn everywhere. The only things still on his bookshelves, in fact, were his old books, which he no longer had the ability to read but didn't have the heart to discard. He couldn't use his music for himself either, for that matter, but he kept it to provide his students with the fingerings and bowings that he or his teacher and mentor, Dr. Krovney, had penciled in many years ago.

Nathaniel had devised an ingenious filing system for Jacobus to be able to identify all his records and music. He didn't bother with the books because either Jacobus wouldn't be able to read them or, in the case of his books in Braille, he could read them anyway. With everything else Nathaniel had painstakingly punched a series of tiny holes in the top right-hand corner of all the covers, and as long as Jacobus didn't forget the easily fathomable code, all he had to do was feel the holes with his fingertips and he'd know what it was that he was holding in his hands.

Jacobus had thanked Nathaniel, then immediately ignored the system. The codes long since forgotten, he now foraged among the piles of records on the ancient upright Sohmer piano next to the bookshelf. The second pile to the left, the sixth record down, the one with the frayed edge and brittle Scotch tape. That should be his old Harmonium LP of Rimsky-Korsakov's *Scheherazade* with Herza conducting, recorded shortly after Myron Moskowitz became concertmaster of the orchestra. If he was wrong, he'd know as soon as he heard the first note, but he was not.

Loosely based on *A Thousand and One Nights,* the piece begins with a brief but foreboding introduction by the low brass, representing the voice of the Sultan Schariar, followed by the first of a half dozen exquisite violin solos portraying the seductive "once upon a time" voice of Scheherazade. Moskowitz played the solos with the personality of the protagonist clearly in mind, never overly aggressive, just suggestive enough for the Persian princess to keep the sultan salivating for more. By the time Sinbad's ship crashed against the rocks in the last movement and Scheherazade completed her final commentary, tapering into a "happily ever after" cadence, Jacobus was reaffirmed in his affection for the particular performance, by both Herza and Moskowitz, and for Rimsky-Korsakov's skill in creating vivid musical imagery. Jacobus asked himself the same old questions for which he knew he would never have the answers: Why was it that when he listened to a recording for the thousand and first time, when he knew exactly what was going to happen, he was still enthralled by the music? How is it that we can connect certain sounds an orchestra makes with Sinbad's ship crashing against rocks? They really sound nothing like one another, yet we'd swear we can see the damn boat. How is it that musicians who have nothing in common with the composer, nothing in common even with each other, can band together and create something miraculous? Just look at Herza and Sherry O'Brien, ready to kill each other, two maladjusted humans—like himself, he added—but cavorting like lovers as soon as the performance begins. How different in personality, Jacobus thought, Scheherazade O'Brien was from her namesake. Or was she?

Jacobus was roused from his thoughts by the phonograph needle scratching the inner ring of the LP, scolding him to remove the record before it was ruined. He placed it back in its jacket, then picked up the phone and dialed information, requesting a phone number in Sarasota, Florida. Yet another number to be memorized. How many more could he fit into his brain?

"Moscowitz," said the voice after the third ring.

"Ronnie? Jacobus."

"Jake! That you? How goes it?"

He sounded preoccupied, in a hurry. Myron Moskowitz was, or had been before he retired, one of those violinists who could have had a solo career but were either too busy making money or engaging in extracurricular activities, so although he ascended to the cusp of stardom early in his career, winning prizes in the Queen Elizabeth of Brussels and the Montreal competitions, he ultimately settled for the Harmonium concertmaster job. Not that this was a small feat. It was an accomplishment that Jacobus envied—he would have been in a similar position had things literally not turned black for him—but still, it was the lure of the juicy, predictable paycheck with abundant time for golf and girls, as much as the musical challenge, that had lured Moskowitz.

"You busy?" Jacobus asked.

"Just eighteen holes in a little while."

"On a Monday morning?"

"Monday, Shmunday. If it's morning, it's tee time."

Jacobus considered the supreme expertise of the world's great golfers: their years of training, their ability to concentrate and perform under extreme stress, their physical talent in hitting a ball hundreds of yards into a tiny cup. He shook his head in perplexed sadness that so many untold hours of tireless, dedicated work did the world not one iota of good.

"Maybe I'll just call back another time," said Jacobus, already regretting he had gone even this far.

"No problem, Jake," said Moskowitz. "What's up, hearing from you, out of the blue?"

"It's about your former student. O'Brien."

"Sherry? Got a lot of spunk, that kid."

"She seems to want to follow in your footsteps."

"Don't they all, when they're young? Then when they follow your footsteps into the quicksand and have sunk up to their *pupik* in the mire, then they start to have their second thoughts."

"Sounds like you don't regret retirement."

"Regret? Those last years with Herza gave me an ulcer. When I left, I went kicking and screaming because I didn't want to admit it, but you know what? I had had enough and it turns out I really do like golf—I'm down to an eight handicap. I really do like fishing. I really do like warm weather and a gin and tonic. I go for a drive and watch the Yankees play spring training and have a beer and a hot dog with the grandkids. Okay, they have a Coke. I sold my violin, I've got my pension, and I'm enjoying life. Jake, there is life after Mozart."

"Well, O'Brien has just reached the quicksand part," said Jacobus, "but seems determined to wade through it." He recounted his exchange with her, and Herza's demeaning reprimand, and through the telling felt Moskowitz's demeanor darken.

"When's the audition?" Moskowitz asked when Jacobus finished.

"Prelims begin today," he replied.

"Let me tell you a little bit about Sherry," Moskowitz said, "so you'll know what makes her tick, and then I gotta run.

"She studied with me for five, six years, and getting her to unload her story took all that time. You know what serious teaching is. It's half music, half gymnastics, and half psychiatry. That's three halves. What the hell.

"She grew up in Fort Wayne, Indiana. Her father, Mike, worked on an assembly line at a GM plant. Sherry's mother, Beth or Bess, I can't remember, came from a more cultured background and was a music lover. She and Mike had a hard time making babies and Sherry was their one child. The mother died in childbirth—Bessie, that was her name—but before she died, her final request was that Mike name their baby Scheherazade and to see that she became a violinist. The mother used to watch *Night at the Symphony* on PBS—which is where she fell in love with the violin solo in the piece after which Sherry was named—while husband Mike went to Night at the Saloon to down boilermakers with his assembly-line buddies. Then they took *Night at the Symphony* off the air because people decided watching *Charlie's Angels* was more entertaining, at which point Mike had no more excuse to get drunk.

"But Mike had otherwise been a devoted husband, and he kept his promise, to a fault, as you'll hear, and spent a fortune on the kid's training. But the downside was that, with his blue-collar mentality, he forced the kid to practice seven, eight hours a day, every day, six days a week."

"Only six? He have a soft spot?"

"Sunday was a free day. Mike was a churchgoing man, and Sunday was the Sabbath. For six days you can be a carousing bastard, but if you go to church, all is forgiven. Hey, maybe that's not a bad idea. To make a long story short, all the kid had was the violin—no friends, no hobbies, no social life."

"Sounds like you had a problem student on your hands."

"*Oh, contraire,*" said Moskowitz. "Talk about dogged determination! I wish my other students had that kind of stick-to-itiveness. The kid didn't have a helluva lot of natural talent, if you know what I mean, but every time someone would tell her she had no future as a violinist, she just ramped it up a notch. Sometimes at lessons I felt she was a ticking time bomb waiting to explode, but she never did. She never even threw a tantrum, though I'm sure I gave her cause. She's tough. She can take it. The girl wouldn't take no for an answer. You've heard her play. It's flawless."

"She's got a chip on her shoulder, then," said Jacobus.

"You've nailed it," said Moskowitz.

"You suppose that accounts for her bitching about Herza? Her grievance threat?"

"Look. No one knows better than me that Herza is an A-one prick. But the greater the conductor, the more his prickdom is tolerated. You know that. And the thing is, Herza is the best, so he gets away with murder and no one does anything about it. No one *can* do anything about it. And being concertmaster, well, you get the brunt of it."

"It goes with the territory."

"It goes with the territory," Moskowitz repeated, with emphasis. "One time, I remember we were doing Dvořák Eight and I'm playing the violin solo in the slow movement. It sounds fine to me. The same way I played it for thirty years. Herza stops and tells me to do it again. Doesn't say why. Doesn't say what he wants different. I play it again. I try to play it better. Herza stops again. Tells me to play it again. We played patty-cake ten times, all the while the orchestra is just sitting there, and not one damn time does he tell me what he wants."

"So what's the moral of the story?"

"Who the hell knows? After the tenth time he just kept on going. I think he just wanted to let me and the orchestra know who was boss."

"And you think the same is true with O'Brien?"

"Well, of course I wasn't there, so I don't know for sure. And these days, with women in orchestras, you need to be more sensitive, but . . ."

Moskowitz left that to hang in the air.

"Thanks, Ronnie. Sorry to take up your time."

"No problem. Just one question. Does Herza know about this grievance business?"

"I got the feeling that she's collared everyone at Harmonium and their extended families about it. I'm guessing the only way Herza wouldn't know about it is if he were deaf."

"Too bad. She might have hell to pay. Well, nice talking to you, Jake."

"Get a hole in one," he said and hung up.

FOURTEEN

Because the finishing touches on the construction of Harmonium Hall were not yet complete, and because the orchestra had been booked to play a concert at Tanglewood, the audition for concertmaster of Harmonium took place at Tanglewood's Seiji Ozawa Hall, built in 1994 and named after the Boston Symphony's illustrious music director. The Shed concert hall had been deemed unsuitable for the audition, as it was huge, open sided—thus susceptible to distractions and eavesdropping—and acoustically not sensitive enough for the committee to be able to discern subtle but potentially critical differences in sound quality and tone color between one candidate and another. Ozawa Hall, however, could be insulated from external noise and provided sufficiently decent acoustics for the committee's purposes.

As the audition was for the most important position in the orchestra, that of concertmaster—the first chair of the first violin section—the audition committee was larger than usual, with twenty-four members. Normally, it would comprise the principal string players, one other member of each string section, and one woodwind, brass, and percussion player. For this audition, there also would be an additional *tutti* player from each string section, plus every woodwind, brass, and percussion principal player. Ordinarily, the concertmaster would sit on all audition committees, but in this unique situation that role was taken by the associate concertmaster—the second-chair first violinist—Lawrence Nowitsky. With a ready smile that had grown with his waistline over the years, Nowitsky had a reputation as a levelheaded consensus builder. One of the few musicians able to straddle the gulf between the orchestra and Vaclav Herza, he was elected to chair the committee, which made sense. After all, he would be sitting next to the winner of the audition until one of their careers ended. The union shop steward, who was the orchestra's bass clarinetist though not a voting member of the committee, was entrusted to make sure everything proceeded aboveboard, that there would be no discrimination against a candidate and no unfair or inaccurate voting. Vaclav Herza, the music director, would attend the final round, as was standard, and would have the ultimate say in who would be hired. The committee's recommendation, though potentially compelling, was, in the end, no more than advisory. This also was standard.

All told, an even forty candidates showed up for the audition, at least making the exhausting day easy to schedule. They were divided into

four equal groups, A through D, and each candidate, numbered
I through 10, was slotted for ten minutes. Acknowledging the months
of preparation and the expense of traveling to Tanglewood, as a courtesy the committee determined in its ground rules to give all forty
their full time allotment, though it retained the right to dismiss any
candidate at any time who it deemed clearly unqualified. This the
committee would ascertain by a show of hands, at which point, Nowitsky, if he agreed with the overriding sentiment, would say, "Thank
you. The candidate is excused."

Group A was scheduled to start at 9 A.M. After candidate A10 finished, which would be after about one hundred and ten minutes, the
committee would take a ten-minute break to vote on Group A and to
clear their heads and/or their bladders. For the preliminary round it
was agreed the voting procedure would be simple: Yes meant the candidate was advanced to the next round; no meant the candidate was
excused. A simple majority of thirteen yeses would advance a candidate. There would be no discussion before the vote. However, if a
member had a serious objection to the result for or against a certain
candidate, he could voice that opinion afterward, and if he was convincing, the committee would consider revoting for that candidate.

After Group B finished, the committee would take a lunch break
of an hour. After Group C, another ten minutes, and after Group D,
God willing, they would be done for the day. After each group, the
committee would vote, the union steward would notify the personnel
manager, Tyson Parsley, which candidates, if any, would be advanced
to the next round, and Parsley would so inform the candidates.

As had become the standard procedure for the preliminary round
of orchestra auditions, a curtain was placed between the stage on
which the candidates performed and the committee, which sat in the
audience. This was to ensure anonymity and prevent preferential or
discriminatory treatment. In fact, the committee knew the candidates

only by the numbers they had picked out of a University of Kentucky booster's hat provided by Tyson Parsley when they arrived at 8 A.M. for the audition: A1, A2, A3, et cetera, for the first group, and similarly down the line for the other groups.

Once the candidates chose their numbers, all those not in Group A were instructed to return at the appropriate hour. Tiny Parsley escorted Group A to individual practice rooms scattered in and around Ozawa Hall. He provided each candidate with excerpts the committee had chosen from the overall list and cautioned them not to speak once they were onstage. He would be there with them, and if they were unsure of something or had a question, they needed to whisper it to him, and he would ask the committee. He also recommended that the female candidates wear flat shoes or none at all rather than high heels so that the committee would be unaware they were women when they walked on the reverberant wooden stage.

Each member of the committee was given a pad and pen in order to take notes, because after hearing the same excerpts over and over again, all at the same high level, as time wore on, it was otherwise difficult to recall who did what. Many of the committee members also brought a thermos of coffee.

The audition began promptly at nine. Each candidate was asked to play the first page, approximately, of the nineteenth-century Romantic concerto he or she had prepared (all concertos in all rounds were to be performed from memory), the exotically challenging solos from *Scheherazade*, the gallivanting last movement of Mozart Symphony 39 that required expert bow control, and the hyperkinetic virtuosity of the first page of *Don Juan* by Richard Strauss. The committee listened to each candidate for the full ten minutes, including the time it took for the candidate to leave the stage and the next one to arrive.

Shortly after the final candidate finished at 10:50, the committee voted. There was no discussion. Parsley convened Group A.

"I want to sincerely congratulate all of you on a fine audition. In a very real sense, you are all winners and should be proud of the way you played. Unfortunately, however, the committee is required to make oh-so-difficult judgments and choose candidates who in their view they deem from these few minutes of listening to be most suitable for the awesome responsibilities of the concertmaster position. They've decided not to advance anyone from Group A, but I want to say please don't be discouraged and to thank you all for all of your hard work."

Group B finished at 12:50. One committee member objected to candidate B9 not being advanced because he or she had had to start the *Don Juan* excerpt a second time after flubbing it the first time.

"Everyone is entitled to a mistake," he said, "and B9 played the rest of the audition perfectly."

"Yeah, except that there were others who played the rest of the audition perfectly and didn't make a mistake," rejoined another committee member.

"And B9 didn't even get close to a majority," said a third.

"I'm starving," said a fourth.

"Objection overruled," Nowitsky said.

Parsley convened Group B.

"I want to sincerely congratulate all of you on a fine audition. In a very real sense, you are all winners and should be proud of the way you played. Unfortunately, however, the committee is required to make oh-so-difficult judgments and choose candidates who in their view they deem from these few minutes of listening to be most suitable for the awesome responsibilities of the concertmaster position. They've decided to advance candidates B4 and B5, but I want to say to the others, please don't be discouraged and to thank you all for all of your hard work."

After lunch, the committee listened to Group C, then D. One candidate was selected from Group C. By the time candidate D4 played, they were behind schedule, everyone on the committee was becoming brain-dead, and patience was wearing thin. D4 started playing the Mendelssohn concerto. After about ten seconds, Nowitsky interrupted the candidate's performance.

He said, in the direction of the stage, "I thought the concerto list was Beethoven, Brahms, Tchaikovsky, or Sibelius."

"One moment," said Parsley, who then had a hurriedly whispered exchange with D4. "The candidate says he just performed Mendelssohn with an orchestra and didn't have time to prepare a different one."

Nowitsky looked down the row at his colleagues. Some shrugged, others shook their heads. "Go on," Nowitsky said, "but we'll take that into consideration."

D4 completed his Mendelssohn, then began the *Scheherazade* solo. At the end of the first excerpt, he smudged a not particularly difficult shift on the G-string.

"Thank you," Nowitsky pounced, "that will be all." The rest of the committee nodded in agreement.

By the end of the day, five candidates—accomplished violinists from as far away as Berlin and Seoul—were chosen to advance to the semifinal round, to be heard the next morning. They would be joined by the two candidates who were invited to skip the preliminaries based upon their prior experience, wide reputation, and the fact they were known quantities: Yumi Shinagawa, former second violinist of the New Magini String Quartet, and Scheherazade O'Brien, acting concertmaster of Harmonium.

FIFTEEN

The ground rules for the semifinals were somewhat different. Each of the seven candidates would perform a twenty-minute audition. The repertoire included the entire exposition of the nineteenth-century Romantic concerto (plus cadenza); the first movement of Mozart Concerto Three, Four, or Five; the solos from Strauss's *Ein Heldenleben;* the solo, "Erbarme dich," from Bach's *St. Matthew Passion;* and the last movement of Mahler's Fifth Symphony. As in the preliminaries, the contestants would play behind a curtain.

The voting procedure was also different. After all the candidates completed their auditions, each committee member would vote for his or her top three. A first-place vote would equal three points, a second-place vote two points, and a third-place vote one point. The candidates with either the most first-place votes or the most points overall would be advanced to the finals. It was also within the committee's discretionary authority to advance a third, or even a fourth, candidate, or on the other hand, none at all, in which case a totally new audition would be scheduled for sometime in the future. Also, unlike the preliminaries, there would be discussion of the candidates' performances, regardless of the vote, with the option of calling back a candidate to play again if opinion were divided.

Parsley again held out his hat containing numbered slips of paper. This time, however, they were numbered just one through seven.

The round began at 9:30 and was scheduled to finish at about noon. Lunch was provided for the committee because the postaudition discussion and voting would be intense and probably lengthy. The finals were scheduled to start at 4 o'clock, and who knew how long that would take?

The committee took an unscheduled ten-minute break after candidate number four, not to vote or discuss but simply to decompress from the intensity of their concentration on every detail of each candidate's performance. They resumed at 11 A.M. and listened to the remaining candidates, finishing only slightly behind schedule. The committee members penned their votes and exchanged their ballots for a boxed lunch from the union steward.

The steward caucused with Nowitsky and Tiny Parsley, who joined them from backstage to tally the votes. After checking and double-checking, they reconvened the committee, just finishing their chocolate chip cookies.

Nowitsky announced the results, from most votes to fewest. "So if we base our decision on the number of first-place votes, candidate four is clearly the winner. If we base it on the number of total points, candidates four and two are neck and neck. However, if we base it simply on the total number of votes received for any of the first three places, candidate five may be considered in the running as well. None of the remaining candidates are in the ballpark. Opinions?"

"I voted for number five for third place," said one committee member, looking down at his notes to refresh his memory. "I wrote 'great concertos,' but it was clear from his excerpts that he hasn't been around the block with the repertoire. His tempos were fucked-up. We need someone with experience if he doesn't want to be chewed up by Herza."

"How do you know it was a he?" asked one of the women on the committee.

"I don't," said the other. "That's just what we call traditional English. I stand corrected: 'he or she.' "

Before an argument ignited, Nowitsky quickly interceded, "Any other opinions?"

"I don't know a lot about string playing," said the principal bassoon player, "but I thought his/her playing was very strong. I voted for him/her for second place and think he/she should be advanced to the finals. I think his/her playing was stronger, orchestrally, than candidate two's, which to me sounded too much like chamber music, so even if he/she is young, if he/she is that good, he/she might be someone that we'll regret losing in the long run."

"Thank you for your comments—and your diplomacy," Nowitsky said. "I suggest that we have a straight up-or-down vote whether to advance candidate number five to the finals along with the other two."

"I demand a secret ballot," said one of the members.

"You don't have to demand," said Nowitsky. "We've got plenty of paper and pencils."

The vote was thirteen to ten with one abstaining vote, to advance candidate five.

The seven contestants backstage had become increasingly anxious; the discussion among the committee seemed interminable. One of the contestants had resorted to telling viola jokes to dispel the stress: "Why don't violists play hide-and-seek? Because no one will look for them." The nervous laughter was encouraging if not palliative. Before he had time to tell the answer to, "What do a Scud missile and a viola have in common?" he was interrupted by Parsley.

"We have a result," he said.

The contestants gathered around, no longer interested in the punch line.

"There will be three candidates advanced to the finals. To the remaining four I would like to extend my congratulations and appreciation for your fine playing. The candidates to be advanced, please remain for a brief meeting. They are numbers two, four, and five."

Hurried, insincere congratulations and condolences were exchanged, and the four dismissed candidates departed.

By late afternoon, Jacobus was finally peckish again. He put the finishing touches on an extra-thick tongue on corn rye sandwich, fingered around in the Ba-Tampte sour pickle jar until he found a satisfactorily massive example, and had just sat down to listen to a recording of the Mozart Divertimento in D Major, KV 251, when the phone rang.

"Dammit," he cursed, his oral and aural pleasure put on hold. He picked up the receiver. "What?" he snapped.

"It's me," Yumi said. "I made the finals."

"I know."

"How could you know? They just notified us."

"One, because you sound happy. Two, because I know how you play. I wouldn't have expected otherwise," said Jacobus. "Who else?"

"Sherry O'Brien and a young guy from the Bay Area. We play again in a couple of hours. I've got to run."

"Run? With a violin in your hands? You crazy?"

"Any secret tips for the finals?"

"Just one: Whatever else happens, make sure you take your time. Force yourself to take your time."

"Thanks, Jake. I promise. Now get back to your tongue sandwich and Mozart."

"How'd you know that?"

"You think you're the only one who can figure things out?" She laughed and hung up.

He was happy that Yumi had done well, especially now that his stomach was no longer in revolt, but if he were forced to, he'd still put his money on O'Brien. Maybe it would even be better that way. If O'Brien wins the audition, and has any sense, she won't give a shit about that cockamamie grievance of hers, he thought. The odds were more thoroughly stacked against her on that one than on winning the audition; that was certain. Jacobus dropped the needle on the Mozart, sat in his chair, and took as large a bite of his sandwich as his mouth, if not good sense, allowed.

SIXTEEN

The final round would not be behind a curtain. There is some disagreement within the orchestra community whether the potential for bias in this regard is outweighed by the importance of seeing how a candidate plays, for indeed body language attains a heightened level of significance for the leader of a section, even more so for the concertmaster. Visual cues that could be misleading or just plain distracting, things that can turn off an audience or even sink a performance, should be something a committee is aware of. On the other hand, some committee members might have a prejudice against a woman, or an Asian, or an old person, or a young person, or a short person, so the issue isn't clear-cut and different orchestras have different solutions.

The solution Harmonium resorted to was to invite the entire orchestra to attend and witness, though not to vote in, the finals, thereby minimizing the potential for a committee member to engage in discriminatory behavior. And of course, Herza would be there, and if he liked or disliked someone's playing, it didn't matter what anyone else's opinion was.

So there was no curtain. But there was a pianist, hired to accompany the concertos in order to give the committee some inkling of how the candidate meshed with and responded to another musician on scant rehearsal. A poor substitute for an entire orchestra as accompanist, but auditions are universally acknowledged to be an imperfect science, continually tweaked to make them more effective in identifying the true best candidate.

Though the finalists had had a chance to rehearse their concertos with the pianist after the semifinal round, they were not informed in advance which orchestral excerpts they would be asked to play for their forty-minute auditions. One reason for this was to see how innately they knew the music and how they would perform under even greater duress. The other consideration was fairness: to not give the second and third candidates the advantage of having more time to practice. The committee, and Herza, also had the option of asking someone to play an excerpt a second time with specific instructions as to tempo, dynamics, or other nuance, to see whether the candidate was not only a fine player—they had already determined that—but could also respond immediately to instructions.

At the conclusion of the three finalists' performances, a vote would be taken. If the result was obvious, the committee would recommend that Herza hire the winner. If the result was contentious, which was far more likely, there would be discussion, and perhaps another vote. There was the possibility that the committee would recommend that Herza consider two candidates, or none. They could even ask the finalists to play again. In reality, in this round, the discussion was more important than the vote tally, because the vote was almost always nail-bitingly close.

The three candidates pulled yet another little piece of paper out of Tiny Parsley's U.K. hat. Yumi chose number one; Michael Morrell, who had been a student of the legendary Dorothy DeLay at Juilliard and was at present a first violinist in the San Francisco Symphony, was second; Scheherazade O'Brien third and last.

Yumi was encouraged by the order. Her adrenaline was flowing and she was primed. When she walked onstage, though, she was caught off guard by dozens of orchestra members scattered about the hall who had come to watch her audition, and even more so by the ghoulish visage of Vaclav Herza, radiating power and intimidation from his place far back in the audience, surrounded by a sea of empty seats.

She began the Adagio introduction of her Mozart concerto cautiously, feeling out her surroundings, careful to maintain control, making sure not to throw the accompanist a curveball. The last thing she could afford was to play a note out of tune or have her bow shake from nervousness at the very outset. As the music progressed and she began the Allegro aperto, she felt more comfortable, and as her confidence grew so too did the energetic expressiveness of her playing. By the time she played the Brahms concerto, she was in full stride, combining absolute focus on the mechanics of her playing with a warm, flexible interpretation. She finished the movement, including the virtuosic cadenza by Brahms's friend and colleague, Joseph Joachim, with tasteful flair. Then she waited, in silence, for the committee's instructions.

"May we hear the solo from Shostakovich Fifth, please?"

Yumi leafed through her music to find the part. This solo was the aesthetic opposite of the Brahms—a spare, sardonic nursery rhyme, a caricature of a minuet with hints of turning nasty. In her preparations, Yumi had listened to Harmonium's recording of it with Moskowitz playing the solo, and she performed it with character, flawlessly.

"Could we hear that once more, please," asked Nowitsky, "with a little more bite?"

Perhaps she hadn't accurately gauged the acoustics of the hall. Considering this, Yumi assimilated the request, translating it into a need to be more active with the fingers of her bow grip in order to enhance the articulation, and therefore the sarcasm, of the music.

She played the excerpt again and felt she succeeded in addressing Nowitsky's concern.

"Play it again," came another voice. An unmistakable, slurred, accented voice. In command. Herza. No suggestion what to do differently. No one else made a comment.

Yumi played it again, once more to the best of her ability.

"Play it again," said Herza.

This is a test, Yumi said to herself, to see if I can take the pressure. She forced herself to inhale deeply, looked carefully at the music, listening to it again in her head, and then played. She finished for the fourth time and held her breath.

"Play it again," said Herza.

Once more through the gauntlet with this innocuously treacherous little waltz. It was like a Venus flytrap. Sooner or later it would devour her.

This time there was silence. Yumi waited. The committee waited. Time waited.

"Thank you," said Nowitsky, finally. "Prokofiev Fifth, slow movement, please."

This, too, had its famous pitfalls. In addition to requiring the violinist to sustain a very lengthy, inexorably intensifying melody, at its climax there is a dramatic leap up of a minor ninth high up on the E-string. From day one, every violinist practices octaves, an interval so fundamental to classical music, until they're perfectly in tune. But the conspicuously dissonant minor ninth, just a half step higher, had to be nailed, like an Olympic figure skater having to do a triple whatever from a standing position.

Yumi took her time perusing the music before she started, visualizing that single crucial minor ninth, feeling it in her unmoving fingers. She then played the excerpt with the control of the veteran musician that she was, knowing when technique trumped even musical considerations.

"Thank you," said Nowitsky, when she finished. "Beethoven Third, funeral march, beginning, please."

This excerpt was chosen for the audition because it requires expertly sensitive bow control in order to achieve the phrase shaping and sudden but subtle inflection that Beethoven calls for. Keeping in mind years of Jacobus's cautions regarding rhythm, she tried to keep the musical pulse steady without it becoming stagnant, and conscientiously followed Beethoven's markings regarding dynamic levels and accents.

"Thank you," Nowitsky said, after she had played only the first phrase. Yumi was perplexed. Had they planned for her to stop there, or had she done something unconscionable?

"Schumann Scherzo, please," Nowitsky said.

Yumi had practiced this virtuoso perpetual-motion movement, on the repertoire list of every violin audition, until she could play it in her sleep. She knew she would have no problem with it and even gave it some extra bravura flair in the coda, accelerating the tempo into overdrive even a bit more than was traditionally done at most performances, though Schumann himself had not called for a change in speed.

"Thank you," said Nowitsky. "Tiny, please tell Mr. Morrell we're ready."

Yumi left the stage thinking that she had played her best but couldn't gauge anything from the lack of response by the committee. Why hadn't they requested any of the big concertmaster solos? she asked herself, and concluded she had lost the audition.

Morrell also had chosen the Mozart fifth concerto. He took to heart Mozart's unique tempo marking, Allegro aperto—meaning openly energetic and joyous—and played with the impetuous exuberance of the nineteen-year-old composer. It might not have had the smoothness or refinement of Yumi's performance, but it was certainly a statement of youthful confidence bubbling over.

For his Romantic concerto, Morrell chose the Tchaikovsky, and for sheer power and virtuosity, not inappropriate for this concerto, he managed to raise some approving eyebrows from the committee, if not from the accompanist who had to struggle to keep up with him.

"Thank you," Nowitsky said when he finished the concerto. "Thank you very much. Shostakovich Five, please, the solo."

Morrell, buoyed by his promising start and by the positive energy flowing from the committee, jumped on the Shostakovich. This time eyebrows were raised, but for a different reason.

"Could you try that again, please? Perhaps taking a bit off the tempo. And please follow the dynamics."

Morrell played it again a little slower and softer. The result came off a bit stiff, and one committee member drew an empty square next to his penciled SH5.

"Thank you," said Nowitsky. "Prokofiev Five, slow movement, please."

Morrell found the music in the pile on his stand, and without contemplating the particular challenges of the excerpt, started immediately, a miscalculation common to inexperienced musicians seeking to impress. Suddenly the minor ninth was on top of him, sooner than he could wrap his mind around it. He made the shift, and it came out perfectly in tune. Except it was a perfectly in-tune octave— the wrong note, justifying the very reason this excerpt was on the list. Pencils began scrawling in earnest. The square now had an X in the middle. Morrell must have realized he had made a critical blunder, that in fact he might have just lost the audition, so he redoubled his efforts, trying to play with even greater intensity, greater musicianship. The strategy backfired, as it almost always does, and he missed badly on several notes in the rest of the phrase.

"Would you like to hear that excerpt again?" Tiny Parsley, the facilitator, asked the committee.

"Thank you," said Nowitsky. "That won't be necessary. Beethoven funeral march, please."

"Which symphony?" asked Morrell.

There was a momentary silence.

"Third Symphony," Nowitsky said politely. "Beethoven Third Symphony. 'Eroica.' Funeral march." In his notes, however, Nowitsky wrote: 1. candidate spoke out loud; 2. didn't know FM is 3rd symph!? Nerves?

Obviously disconcerted, Morrell started tentatively; by the second measure, the string players on the committee noticed the hint of a tremor in his bow arm that became more audible as the music progressed. Soon, even the wind players on the committee could hear it. "What gives?" wrote the principal flutist on her pad. Morrell pressed down harder on the string, trying to force the shuddering to stop, but succeeded only in making it worse. His bow began sliding over the string, losing contact with it.

His loss of bow control became contagious. The vibrato in his left hand was now going wild. He began clutching the violin between his chin and shoulder, as if in fear of dropping it, and squeezed the neck of the violin with his left hand in such desperation that his fingers were barely able to move, like an engine that had seized.

Nowitsky stopped Morrell in midphrase. "Thank you. That will be all."

"Would you like to hear the Schumann?" asked Parsley.

"Thank you. We're fine," Nowitsky said mercifully. "Please bring Ms. O'Brien."

Parsley assisted a trembling Michael Morrell off the stage, already whispering to him that this was an experience to grow from—"Don't be discouraged. You made the finals of a great orchestra and you've got a fine future ahead of you"—but it appeared that Morrell, hunched and glassy-eyed, hadn't heard a word.

A few moments later, Scheherazade O'Brien made her way onstage, followed by Tiny Parsley. She had chosen to play the fourth Mozart Concerto, the D Major, that begins with a trumpetlike fanfare on the violin, to be followed by the Sibelius Concerto in D Minor, calculating that Herza would be particularly drawn to its brooding darkness. She had performed both concertos with significant orchestras several times and felt supremely confident of her ability to play them under the stress of an audition. Having also played the audition repertoire and all the concertmaster solos over the years in live performance, it was not pressure she felt but great exhilaration. The moment was hers for the taking.

She tuned her violin to the piano A, nodded to the accompanist, and stood in comfortable attention through four bars of introduction to the Mozart concerto. She readied herself and played the first note, a crisp and lustrous D-natural on the E-string.

"That's enough!" It was Herza. O'Brien stopped.

"Excuse me?" said Tiny Parsley, who from the stage hadn't understood the words.

"Are you deaf? I said that's enough. I've heard enough."

"But, Maestro," said Nowitsky. "I must protest."

Herza rose to leave.

"I am the music director. This candidate is dismissed. Her employment is terminated as of this moment. Hire the Oriental girl. If you don't like it, go file a grievance."

The audition was over.

———

Jacobus was listening to his LP of Otto Klemperer conducting Beethoven's Seventh Symphony. He preferred Toscanini's recording, but that one had a scratch on it causing the last chord of the first movement to repeat endlessly. One can take only so many C-sharps, even Beethoven's.

Toward the end of the fugato in the Allegretto, his private concert was interrupted by a car coming down his driveway. At first he was annoyed at being disturbed, but upon recognizing the sound of the particular engine, he became alarmed. Trotsky, excited by the same sound, jumped up barking.

"Shut up," Jacobus said in a murderous undertone. Surprisingly, Trotsky obeyed. Jacobus turned off the record player and went to the door.

"Hi, Jake," said Yumi.

"You've been crying," said Jacobus. In all the years he had known Yumi he had never heard her cry, though she had had plenty of justifiable reasons to do so. She had been a woman of iron even when she was still his teenage student, but now her tears were enough to make her rust.

"How do you know?" asked Yumi.

"Well, it's the first time you've ever come here unannounced, which means you're either very happy or very upset. From the tone of your voice it's clear you're not very happy."

"I've got good news and I've got bad news," said Yumi, trying to gather her composure, laughing and crying simultaneously.

"Go ahead," said Jake. "I'm waiting."

"I won the concertmaster audition for Harmonium."

"And what's the good news?"

"That's not funny."

"No? I thought it was a pretty good one. Congratulations, anyway. You now have a great job."

"The bad news is, I'm not taking it."

"Come on in, O Enigmatic One, and tell me about it. Can I make you a liverwurst sandwich? With mustard and onion?"

Yumi politely declined.

When she finished relating the story of the audition, Jacobus said, "What Herza did was clearly unfair. He should've let O'Brien play, for sure. But have you considered that maybe he had already made up his mind he wanted you because you played a superlative audition? Did you think of that possibility? Look, he's heard O'Brien's playing for two years now, so he already knew how she sounds. Maybe he just didn't want to waste everyone's time. After all, it was the end of a very long and taxing day. Two days, in fact."

"I thought about that possibility and tried to convince myself it was true. But I have to tell you, I heard Sherry warming up before the audition, and Jake, she's a better orchestral player than I am. Hands down. I've never heard such great orchestral playing before. She should have won that audition. What Herza did was out of sheer malice. I'm sure of it. I could never work for someone like that, and after what he did to Sherry, if I were to take the job, all the other violinists would just be stabbing me in the back."

Jacobus tried unsuccessfully to cover up his laugh with a cough.

"Is that funny?" asked Yumi.

"Only that *tutti* players always stab the concertmaster in the back. Comes with the territory."

"Why?"

"Because the concertmaster gets paid twice as much as they do and gets to tell them how to play."

"That seems petty."

"Welcome to the world of symphony orchestras."

"Is that the world you wanted when you auditioned for concertmaster of the Boston Symphony?"

"I'd rather not go into that."

"Please, I know it hurts, but think of it as a lesson for me. It'll help me know where to go from here."

Jacobus had never spoken to anyone about his own audition and now Yumi was prodding him. He had intended to take that experience with him to the grave and was almost there. So close. That and the Grimsley Competition. Separate events, but two of the three tragic pillars of his life. And they were all connected.

"All right," he muttered. "Just no editorializing, okay?"

"Yes. Thank you."

"It wasn't all that different from your audition," he began. "I practiced my ass off until those damn excerpts were coming out of my pores. I had one advantage over you, having played in the orchestra for some years. The repertoire was already under my fingers. I was pretty cocky in those days, cockier than you, even."

"You said no editorializing."

"I meant from you. Anyway, that's not editorial. That's a statement of fact.

"I was confident of myself, but I made the youthful indiscretion of doing a lot of backstage hotdogging. Showing off stuff. Got a lot of sniggers and looks to kill from my colleagues. I got the message damn quick and thereafter kept my practicing to myself. After all, some of those guys were going to be on the committee, and it wouldn't be politic to piss them off in advance.

"I went to an art exhibit the day before, just to calm down, like you did. I saw this painting by Turner." Jacobus stopped in order to keep his voice from choking.

"It was the last art I ever saw. No matter. I went to bed that night but couldn't sleep. Not nervous. Energized. I knew I was ready. Some people *think* they're ready, but that means you're not ready. You have to *know*. I knew.

"I finally fell asleep. Slept like a baby, in fact. The alarm went off in the morning. I woke up, went to turn it off, and couldn't see a damn thing. At first I thought it was just dark in the room, but nothing could be that dark. So I closed my eyes for a minute, hoping it would go away. The alarm kept on ringing. It was driving me nuts. I opened my eyes again. It was still pitch-black, but I couldn't stand the alarm ringing. I felt around for it and threw it against the wall. That stopped it.

"I panicked. I started raving. Incoherent. I wasn't saying words. Just yelling. I got up and started walking into things. After a while I said to myself, 'This isn't doing any good. I've got an audition to take. I have to focus on that.'

"But how the hell am I going to get there? I can't take a damn step without plowing into a wall, let alone drive. So I called my stand partner, Solomon Goldbloom."

"I remember Sol from when I first studied with you."

"I told him what had happened. He said, 'I'll be right over and take you to the emergency room,' but I told him if he did that I'd kill him. He could tell I was serious, so he came over, grabbed me and my fiddle, and drove me to the hall. We didn't tell anyone I was blind as a bat until it was my turn to play. When the personnel manager finally found out, he was in such shock it didn't even occur to him to disqualify me.

"Luckily, the orchestra had just instituted the curtain rule, so the committee couldn't see that I couldn't see. I played the Beethoven Concerto, the Adagio of the Bach G-Minor Sonata, *Scheherazade*, the Tango from 'L'Histoire' by Stravinsky, *St. Matthew Passion*, the Scherzo from *Midsummer Night*, the first page and solo from *Don Juan*, and the Adagio from Beethoven Ninth."

"But how did you do that without music?"

"I told you. I knew I was ready. Yumi, *you* could've played your audition without music. Anyone playing at that level could. At that point in the game, having the music is just a convenience. It was no big deal."

"It *was* a big deal. And you won."

"Yeah, I won. Talk about Pyrrhic victory. Management gave me a week for my eyesight to come back. The doctors called it foveomacular dystrophy, a swanky term for sudden blindness. They always have fancy names for diseases they can't cure. They said, Yeah, it's possible it'll come back. But it didn't. And I had to give back not only the concertmaster position but my job in the orchestra as well."

"What choice did they have? What choice did *you* have? You couldn't be concertmaster and blind. Could you?"

"Why not?"

"Well, I don't want to 'editorialize,' but, for example, how would you know when the conductor was starting a piece?"

"Honey, you played in a string quartet for years. With great musicians, what do you all do when you start a piece?"

"We look at each other to make sure we start together. That's what I'm saying."

"And? What else?"

"We breathe together."

"Aha! When you're blind, you start listening to things. If you really listened, you'd hear each other breathing together. I bet you do, anyway, subliminally, and that was just four of you. Think about a hundred musicians breathing together.

"Sometimes you listen to an old record, before they had all the fancy microphones and digital editing. When a record still sounded something like a live performance and not Madame Tussaud's wax museum. You can hear Toscanini singing. You can hear Pablo Casals grunting like a humpback whale. There is so much you can hear if you listen."

"You could have done it, then," said Yumi. "You could have been a blind concertmaster."

"If Beethoven could compose the Fifth Symphony and be deaf, it shouldn't be so hard to be a blind fiddler, right? But who the hell knows now?"

"How did you feel when they took the job from you?"

"I take the Fifth. Interview is over."

They sat in contemplative silence for a while, separated by different thoughts.

"I'm going to stay here in the Berkshires for a while and decompress," Yumi said finally. "Just to sort things out, but I'm still not going to take the job."

"It's your call. I respect you for it."

Jacobus heard Yumi drive off. Not that he was any good at it, but he had done his best to comfort her. He had withheld his knowledge of the conflict between O'Brien and Herza, of the threatened grievance, and of his prediction that something like this was going to happen. What he could not foretell, though, was how it would all fall out, now that the shit was going to hit the fan.

SEVENTEEN
WEDNESDAY

The strident hammering from the lobby pierced the walls of the new auditorium and would not have been tolerated under normal circumstances, but with the premiere days away, there was little choice. Herza had threatened to cancel the concert unless the arrhythmic pounding came to an immediate halt, but the contractor, with eight different construction unions working on the project, called his bluff, said go ahead and cancel, what do we care, you'll have to pay us anyway. So the work continued.

But it wasn't the noise that was disturbing the musicians this morning. It was the improbable absence of their acting concertmaster, Scheherazade O'Brien. After the audition, Tyson Parsley had the distasteful duty of calling her and telling her officially that not only had she lost the audition, she had lost her job. Not unexpectedly, she hadn't answered her phone, so Parsley left as sympathetic a message as he could muster. Her absence suggested she had received it. One rumor already swirling was that the winner, Yumi Shinagawa of the defunct New Magini String Quartet, had long been a favorite of Herza's—he having been so idolized in Japan—and the audition result was a foregone conclusion, that Herza had merely been waiting for her to leave her string quartet position. But if that were the case, others reasoned, why wasn't Shinagawa here either?

Whatever the truth of the matter, Tiny Parsley instructed the associate concertmaster, Lawrence Nowitsky, to move over to O'Brien's vacated position. The next four first violinists advanced one chair, and according to contractual protocol, the last-chair first violinist moved up into the now empty sixth chair. Before Nowitsky stood to tune the orchestra, Tiny Parsley quieted the anxious musicians, if not the construction crew, which, oblivious, continued its hammering.

"A few announcements, very briefly," Parsley said. "There will be limited reserved parking available in Lot B for any musicians crazy enough to drive to the concert on opening night. There's a sign-up sheet; if your name's on it, I'll give you a pass. Otherwise, you're on your own.

"Second, the musicians are invited to a reception after the opening concert in the second-tier function room—"

"If it's done by then!" Cappy, always the designated tension breaker, hollered from the back of the viola section, to the laughter of some and to the scowl of Beanie, who shook his head in dismay at his stand partner's breach of protocol.

"It's free food and free booze," continued Parsley, "and if you're bringing a significant other, there's a sign-up sheet for that, too.

"Finally, I'm sure you've noticed that Sherry is not with us this morning. I've been trying to contact her. If anyone knows how I can reach her, please see me at intermission."

Parsley then pointed toward Nowitsky, now the acting acting concertmaster, who dutifully signaled to the principal oboist to play the A for the orchestra to tune, first the winds and brass, then the strings.

Responding to this daily cue, Vaclav Herza lumbered onto the stage, to the accompaniment of a taciturn orchestra that had heard all about the audition, and slowly mounted his stool on the podium.

"Dvořák," he said, lifting his baton.

The "New World Symphony" was one of Herza's and, by extension, Harmonium's signature pieces. There was little that needed to be said, and Herza was content to let the orchestra play; they knew exactly what he wanted of them and he refrained from comment, that is, until the first entrance of the trombones, upon which he rapped his baton against his music stand.

"You, first trombone. You are sharp. Are you trying to ruin my rehearsal? Again from the beginning."

Junior Parsley knew that he had played in tune but said nothing.

When they reached the same moment the second time, Herza stopped.

"Perhaps you should try playing," he said to Parsley, raising his voice, "as if you wanted it to sound good."

At any other time, Parsley would have absorbed the barb in silence. Indeed, he had heard a lot worse. But the tension of the moment, the down-to-the-wire contract negotiations, the last-minute construction chaos—that damn hammering—the obvious anxiety swirling around O'Brien's sudden termination and, ultimately, the sarcastic unfairness of the criticism led him to retort, "That's no way to speak to a professional musician."

Herza placed his elbows on the stand, pressed his hands together in prayerful fashion, and stared at Parsley. "On the contrary," he said. "Someone should have spoken to you that way twenty years ago when there was still some hope for redemption.

"Now, we continue. Rehearsal letter F."

The orchestra finished the first movement and began the Largo that was so popular in America after its premiere that it gradually became "common knowledge" that it had been borrowed from a spiritual, "Goin' Home," when in fact the reverse was true. Midway through the famous English horn solo, though, the noise from the welders on the construction crew became so overbearing that Herza threw down his hands in disgust.

"Lubomir!" he shouted with the little power that his weakened lungs and slurred tongue afforded. Yet Butkus was immediately at the edge of the stage.

"Tell them to stop. Now."

"But they're working overtime to finish before the opening."

Herza put his baton on the stand, pushed himself up from the stool, and limped to Lubomir. Herza slapped the taller man in the face.

"Tell them to take it out of their masturbation schedule, then. And don't you dare cross me again."

"Yes, Maestro," said Butkus. He walked quickly out of the auditorium, not looking at the musicians.

Butkus followed his ears down the hallway to the lobby, the source of the hissing of welding and the ratcheted thumping of drill guns. Ignored by hard-hatted, goggled workers, he groped his way around drums of adhesives and drywall compound, and barrels of tape, screws, and other metallic hardware he couldn't identify. The area generating the most noise, inside of which welders were wearing masks and full-body protective uniforms, was cordoned off by yellow tape. Butkus ducked under the tape and passed a small chemical canister on his way to reprimand the workers for doing their job.

"Hey, get away from that stuff, asshole," said the foreman. "A drop of that'll kill you."

"What stuff?"

"Right there," said the foreman, pointing. "Read the label: 'Danger— thorium welding rods.' You breathe that powder, you could be dead as that cute little picture of the skull you're lookin' at. Now get the hell out."

Butkus hastily ducked back under the yellow tape.

"Just keep the racket down," he said over his shoulder, fully aware that no one could hear him.

At intermission, Tiny Parsley met with the orchestra committee, including its chairman, twin brother Junior.

"How is it," Junior asked, "that when we have concerts overseas you know how to get in touch with everyone, but a hundred miles away in the Berkshires you're clueless as an ear of corn in a pig trough where O'Brien is staying?"

"Calm down, bro! When we're on tour, most of the orchestra stays at the official hotel we book for them, and those who choose not to give us their alternative address so I can make sure everyone gets on the bus. For Tanglewood, there aren't any hotels big enough to accommodate the whole group, especially at the last minute, so we just gave everyone a per diem that included lodging and let them find their own. And since we didn't provide any transportation, there wasn't any need to know where anyone was staying."

"So you've tried her apartment, her cell phone?"

"Of course we did. I'm not as dumb as we look. And we called people she knows who might know her whereabouts, like Myron and Daniel Jacobus, who she played for last week. And we've notified the police in Lenox and Stockbridge and the other towns up there. Just as a precaution. But she could just as well be here in the city. Shit, she could be anywhere. Doesn't anyone in the orchestra know where she was staying?"

"No, we asked around," said Junior. "She doesn't have a lot of friends in the orchestra. She hasn't even slept with anyone here, at least that we know of. She's always been kind of a loner—you know that—just holed herself up practicing for the audition. We're going to call an emergency meeting to decide what to do next."

"What do you mean, 'what to do next'?" asked Tiny.

"Bro, what Herza did to her at the finals was blatantly unfair, if not illegal. But that's not the only thing. It makes the musicians' role on the audition committee as superfluous as tits on a bull. Think of all the hours they have to sit there, and for what? To have Maestro come waltzing in and make a call like that? We need to address the issue of the audition, because it wasn't only unfair to her, it was unfair to the orchestra. It undermines the whole contract if we let this one go."

"Herza won't be happy. He's not going to like the musicians meddling with his authority."

"Well, he better learn to live with it."

Before the second half of the rehearsal began, Junior Parsley announced from the podium that there would be an emergency meeting of the musicians to discuss audition procedures as a result of what had transpired the day before. The orchestra then rehearsed *Death and Transfiguration* by Richard Strauss.

As at the Tanglewood rehearsal, Herza conjured up the sound of the hazy gloom of despair, permeated by the stench of impending death. The tympani imitated the feeble heartbeat, about to surrender.

Herza stopped the orchestra. "You sound like you're hitting a golf ball into a dead sheep," he said to the timpanist.

Later, when the principal flutist's solo did not depict the ray of light shining through the darkness with pristine perfection, Herza growled, "Do it again. And this time take your gloves off."

Finally, after the trombones played a passage where the protagonist undergoes paroxysms of affliction, Herza lambasted them, singling out Junior Parsley.

"What is wrong with you?" he shouted. "Must you get drunk so early in the morning?"

Parsley stared into his music.

"I ask, what's wrong with you? Are you ignorant or merely apathetic?" Herza ranted.

"I don't know and I don't care," Parsley shouted back. Most of the orchestra froze in stunned silence, though there were a few stifled snickers. Herza, immobile, stared at Parsley. Parsley stared back.

"Do not forget," Herza intoned, "in *Death and Transfiguration,* before transfiguration, first comes death."

EIGHTEEN

From the outset there was dissent. The Mega-Herzas contended that the emergency meeting itself was illegal. There was nothing in the musicians' bylaws, they claimed, that authorized the chair of the orchestra committee to unilaterally call a meeting. Junior Parsley responded that with the looming contract deadline, it was imperative to address those audition procedure issues that were currently being negotiated with management, and that with their juggled schedule there was no other time to hold a meeting. Feeling he had the majority opinion on this, he suggested that a motion be made then and there whether the meeting should continue. One of the Killa-Herzas made the motion. It was seconded, then opened for debate. A Mega objected, saying the motion was out of order—the chair may not propose a vote on anything—and moved that the meeting be adjourned. Parsley ruled that motion out of order, as there was already a motion on the floor that had been seconded.

For fifteen minutes there was heated discussion whether the meeting should take place. Those in favor pointed to the seriousness of the issue—audition procedure violations struck at the foundation of the orchestra's ability to hire the best musicians. The very fact that they were debating a motion, they added, meant that the meeting was official already, so why not just proceed? Those opposed pointed to inadequate notice for the meeting; with some colleagues not able to attend due to other commitments, there was barely a quorum. Finally, when arguments began to repeat themselves, a Mega-Herza, out of frustration, called for the question. Hands were raised, aye or nay, and a slim majority enabled the motion to pass. The meeting could now take place.

Though the Killas drew first blood, the Megas were not about to give up. They jumped on the fact that Scheherazade O'Brien, contractually only a glorified substitute, would not even have been permitted to attend this meeting. Her rights were not the rights of a tenured staff musician. Some questioned whether her initial hiring two years earlier had even been legal—there had been no audition at all when she was given the temporary position of acting concertmaster. Like "illegal alien," the word "temporary" became a term of indictment among those against her.

The Killas argued that it didn't matter what the conditions of her contract were. The issue was whether a candidate—any candidate, for any audition—should be dismissed at the whim of the music director, especially if that whim were the result of personal vindictiveness. This issue then was not Scheherazade O'Brien but Vaclav Herza.

The Megas retorted that vague terms like "whim" or "vindictiveness" or even "fairness" were not within the musicians' purview to define. Part of the role of music director, in fact the most important role that distinguished a music director from a guest conductor, was the authority to hire and fire. If you start infringing on that authority, they contended, you're diminishing the role and, in the long run, diminishing the orchestra. What's next, telling him how to rehearse? Telling him what music he can program? It's a can of worms, and a slippery slope, and a black hole, and a Pandora's box, and that's why the audition committee's role has always been, and should always be, advisory. No more, no less.

One of the Killas jumped on this statement. How can we be advisory, she asked, if we don't even have a chance to hear the candidate? Herza has undercut our role to advise, she pursued, which is a violation of our contract. That's the heart of the matter.

"Who the hell do you think you are?" shouted a Mega. "You only got tenure last month and now you're lecturing us about the contract?"

Parsley told him he was out of order, but the Megas were outraged. O'Brien's termination was fully justified under the terms of the contract, they said. Li Jian, one of the Chinese violinists who had complained about the heat at Tanglewood, made the point that everyone in the orchestra—everyone—had at one time been hired by Herza, so we all owe something back to him. His political connections had enabled all the Asian musicians to get green cards to work in the United States faster than anywhere else, so that was another debt. Sherry O'Brien, like any responsible musician, should take her lumps and move on. Who hasn't taken lumps from Herza over the years? Yes, he's tough. But look what we've got. The best orchestra in the world, and the highest paying.

"And that's why the public thinks Herza's such hot shit," interrupted a Killa. "We're the ones who make him look good."

"Impossible to do that!" chimed another, to the glee of the Killas but causing an uproar among the Megas.

Junior Parsley used his capacious lungs to shout down the growing melee, ruled the two Killas out of order, and threatened to bodily evict anyone else who interrupted. Inwardly, he was relieved by the tumult; Li Jian's comments could have split the orchestra along ethnic and age lines. He didn't need that.

What he did need, desperately, was sixty-seven votes, a two-thirds majority of eligible musicians, when it came time to vote on the contract package. He had done the math. There were a hundred and four members, but at present there were three vacancies occupied by subs, including O'Brien. The two-thirds requirement was a double-edged sword. Yes, it meant that management had to give them something good enough to do more than squeak through. On the other hand, if a vote on a contract failed while receiving more than a simple majority, management would have a heyday with the media, yowling, "How could the musicians have refused such a wonderful contract that a majority of them wanted? What a disservice to the public! What a shame!" He'd have as much bargaining strength as a steer in a cattle car.

He gave the floor back to the Megas.

What O'Brien's done is unconscionable, rocking the boat with her grievance, and now she's split the orchestra down the middle. What if the orchestra were to make some sort of stupid protest on her behalf? We'd have hell to pay from Herza. All of us. And now, with the contract negotiations at a critical moment, how will it affect that outcome? How will it affect the endowment drive? Tens of millions of dollars were at stake. More! We can end up losing everything. And for what? For someone who's no longer even a member of the orchestra?

The Killas said no. No, you can't nail this on O'Brien. She has the right to file a grievance. She has the right to audition free of harassment. These are things guaranteed not only in our contract but also by law. It was Herza's retribution for the grievance threat that caused this situation. Nothing else. One of the militant Killas then offered a motion, proposing a vote of no confidence in Vaclav Herza. This was shouted down even before the motion was completed. No one, even the Killas, had the nerve to second it.

Another motion was proposed, as a simple statement of fact: "The musicians protest the treatment of Scheherazade O'Brien by the music director at the concertmaster audition." After all, wasn't this precisely what was being discussed? This motion was seconded, then argued for a half hour—with every word of it analyzed and fought over—before debate was closed. One of the Killas requested a secret ballot, but Parsley reluctantly had to deny the request as their bylaws stated that only votes on the collective-bargaining agreement or on requests by management for waivers or amendments to the CBA are taken by secret ballot.

The vote on the motion failed, predictably, because some of those who would have voted for it on a secret ballot were terrified that Herza could now find out. The Megas moved to adjourn the meeting, a nondebatable motion, but surprisingly that too failed. Parsley, at loose ends what to do next, asked if anyone had anything further to say.

Lawrence Nowitsky, one of the few musicians in neither camp, to whom both Megas and Killas could speak freely, sought common ground and proffered the following motion: "The music director and the musicians shall make their best efforts to promote evenhanded treatment of all candidates at all auditions." He knew it was meaningless, ineffective, and unenforceable, but he hoped that it would at least bring the musicians a little closer together and perhaps provide his former stand partner, O'Brien, a modicum of solace that her experience at the audition had not totally been in vain.

The other musicians also understood that the motion was meaningless, ineffective, and unenforceable, but they were exhausted and didn't want to leave having accomplished nothing, so they quietly voted and passed the motion almost unanimously, with only five musicians—three Megas and two Killas—abstaining.

Parsley asked if there was any further business. Relieved there was no response, he asked for a motion to adjourn, which was made, seconded, and approved with a unanimous grunt. The meeting disbanded, and after everyone departed, Lawrence Nowitsky quietly went to the maestro's office.

NINETEEN

Later that afternoon, at the central office of the Stuyvesant Bank, the meeting of the executive committee of the board of trustees of the Harmonium Symphonic Society was called to order by its chairman, J. Comstock Brundage, whose day job as president of the bank made him very well connected indeed. Besides Brundage and those board members who were heads of symphony subcommittees on marketing, development, finance, the capital campaign, and the new concert hall project, the attendees included Music Director Vaclav Herza; CEO Adrianne Vickers; personnel manager Tyson Parsley; Loren Gardiner, a marketing consultant from DynamiCorp; and Lars Symington of Symington, Symington, and Warburg, SSW, as its competitors called it, the architectural firm that assisted Herza in designing Harmonium Hall. The polished mahogany boardroom table was ringed by leather chairs to accommodate the entire assemblage, who were provided with identical place settings of a pad, pen, and a glass of water. Coffee and an assortment of French pastries were on a Chippendale sideboard against the wall.

"First item of new business on the agenda," said Brundage, after they had voted unanimously to accept the minutes of the previous meeting, "is the status of the Harmonium Hall project."

Taking his cue, Alvin Chynoweth, chair of the hall subcommittee, began his report. Chynoweth had made his fortune as a minority owner of King Kone, a company that sold orange traffic cones and barrels to New York City and neighboring municipalities, that were used to cordon off areas of road repair and construction in the greater metropolitan area. He had retired at the age of forty-one to go into a new field, private investing. His one client was himself, and he had done very well for his client, compounding his wealth as he invested in road, bridge, and building projects—including Harmonium Hall— around the region.

"We're still on target for the hall to open as scheduled. The two most important components are essentially done, the auditorium and Freedom Bridge. I'm pleased to report that the engineers have tested the acoustics and have concluded that they are second to none, and the orchestra's artistic advisory committee has also given it their blessing, no mean feat. Freedom Bridge is all done but for the safety rails. There have been some general delays, as anyone walking through the building can see, but we plugged most of those into our timetable back when we first projected the construction schedule. There will still be some unfinished work to be completed after the first concert, but they'll just be minor cosmetic details, and we've got the workers going full tilt until it's done."

"Aren't safety rails of considerable importance," asked Imogene Livenstock, chair of the capital campaign committee, in whose veins ran the bluest of blood of New York's old families, "especially for a pedestrian bridge?"

"I'll let Lars respond to that," said Chynoweth.

"Absolutely," said Symington. "And I guarantee it will be finished by the downbeat of the concert."

"I would hope it would be completed before the downbeat," said Livenstock. "It would create quite a splash if someone fell in the river on the way to the concert."

When the laughter died, Symington repeated his assurance that all would be in order.

The design of Freedom Bridge had been the most contentious aspect of the entire plan. It was conceived as a twin to the Charles Bridge in Prague, which had been pedestrian-only for decades, unable to bear the weight of modern motorized traffic. There had been objections to the notion of moving crowds of two thousand people from the Lower Manhattan mainland to Harmonium Hall and back without the ability to drive on the bridge. SSW had expected that most people would take public transportation to the bridge and then walk across but were told in no uncertain terms their assumption was pie in the sky, and they had also neglected provisions for obvious things like inclement weather and access for the disabled. SSW professed that they had been misunderstood; their plan had been only preliminary, though in reality these contingencies had escaped their "vision." They labored over possible alternatives, delaying the entire construction schedule, but eventually devised a multifaceted solution that supplemented the pedestrian bridge with a subway stop, a bus stop, and a parking lot on the Manhattan side from which concertgoers could be shuttled to the hall by an extensive fleet of water taxis and ferries. To make this plan a reality, they had to strenuously lobby the MTA and City Hall, undertake studies of the shifting currents of the Hudson River, and work with the Port Authority of New York to make sure they were not in violation of any shipping lanes.

"Cost overruns?" asked Brundage.

"Inevitably. But we're only ten percent over budget," said Chynoweth.

"Isn't that troubling? You're talking about a negative variance of five million dollars, more or less, and we've got ongoing contract negotiations with the musicians. 'Only ten percent' might not be easy to paper over. Adrianne, what about that?"

"Yes, we may need to reconsider fixed labor costs in that light, and we'll do what we have to do. Right now the musicians represent about fifty-six percent of our budget, but fifty percent sounds like a nice round number to me."

"Alvin?"

"I didn't mean to minimize the overrun, Comstock, but the crucial thing is to have the hall up and running. We've negotiated with the construction firm and they've cut us some slack on materials, and your bank has agreed to revisit the terms of financing the project. We also have some unrestricted gifts in the endowment that we can play around with and fold into the building fund. But we have to keep our eye on the prize and get it done because the opening is tied to the capital campaign."

"That sounds like a segue to me," Brundage said, pleased to have used musical jargon, though he knew little else about music.

"I suppose that means it's my turn," said Imogene Livenstock. "I'm happy to report that we will be ready to publicly announce the commencement of our one-hundred-million-dollar campaign at the opening concert gala. We have solid commitments for thirty million and estate-planning pledges for another twenty-five, so we're right on target."

"How solid is solid?" asked Brundage. "You're reporting a big jump since the last meeting, if I recall correctly."

"You do recall correctly," said Livenstock. "Since last month I've been able to persuade—"

"You mean twist a few arms?" asked Brundage.

"Who, little ol' me?" asked Livenstock, batting her eyelashes, receiving more laughs from around the table. Good old Imogene.

"I've locked in a five-million-dollar pledge from the Grimsley family," she continued. "They're eager, and now ready, to buy their way back into the good graces of New York society after that fiasco with the Grimsley violin competition. And we've another two and a half from Bedřich Czsonka, a fellow Czech expatriate of Maestro's who has done very well in pharmaceuticals and wants to express his appreciation for what Maestro has done for freedom in their homeland."

"Any strings attached?" asked Brundage, who, on a roll with his musical wit, gave his inflection a jaunty little upward twist.

"Only that the gifts are contingent upon the hall opening," said Livenstock. "Czsonka's will go toward the endowment of the music director position and he wants to be recognized at the gala for it. But as Alvin said, that's a slam dunk."

"Bedřich is good people," added Alvin, "and his firm doubled its dividend last year."

"Do you have any concerns that this is a house of cards?" asked Devlin Forrester, a former CPA and chair of the finance subcommittee. "What if the hall doesn't open on time and some of these gifts fall through? What happens to the capital campaign? The orchestra?"

"We're not going to go there, Devlin," said Brundage. "At this point that's unnecessary speculation. As Imogene says, everything is on target."

"Yes and no," said Forrester. He took a sip of water and looked down at his notes. "Yes, because we are approaching our budgeted goals, but no, because we budgeted in a one-point-eight-million deficit, and our accumulated debt is approaching four million. We may well have a cash flow problem in about seven months—before revenue from the next year's subscribers kicks in—even if everything goes as planned. Artistic considerations aside, we can't have any more concert cancellations like we just had at Tanglewood."

All eyes turned to Vaclav Herza, who until this point had his closed. He leveled his gaze at Forrester and said, "If you think I am going to compromise artistic integrity for your nickels and dimes, think again. The concert was canceled because rehearsal time was stolen from me by the musicians in their so-called collective-bargaining agreement with our management—an agreement with which I was neither participant nor signatory, I might add—and by the Boston Symphony, which feels that it is more profitable to spend my rehearsal time kowtowing to a pop man with a guitar. That they would transport in three truckloads of electronic equipment for a pop man rather than pursue the interests of serious music shows where their interests lie. So don't expect that your stares are going to change me. If not for Herza, we would not be here today. Go find your shekels elsewhere."

"Maestro, we would never ask you to concern yourself about costs," Brundage intervened. "You are the artist and it's our job—the job of the board and management—to support your vision. It is appropriate at this time to turn the meeting over to Adrianne, who has chaired the strategic-planning committee for the past six months. I believe you have a presentation, Adrianne?"

"That's right, Comstock," said Vickers. "But before the presentation, I'd just like to make a few preliminary remarks.

"Symphony orchestras everywhere are at a historical turning point. Studies by ASOL—"

"Asshole, Adrianne?" asked Brundage, perplexed.

"The American Symphony Orchestra League, Comstock. Their recent report indicates that the old, worn-out model of playing orchestral music by DWEMs is no longer sustainable with today's audiences."

"DWEMs?" asked Imogene.

"Dead white European males. Your Mozarts, your Tchaikovskys, your Beethovens."

"Young lady," said Herza, "I don't recall there being more than one Beethoven."

"I'm just making a point, Vaclav. Yes, their music is great. No one questions that. But audiences are tired of it week in and week out in the same traditional format. We need to invent a new paradigm for the twenty-first century.

"Today, Harmonium is at a crossroads. Not only do we face the same challenges as other orchestras, we are transitioning from a tour-based to a home-based organization and need to create artistic efficiencies in our vision as we move forward. At the end of the day, the elephant in the room is the competition we face from the entire entertainment spectrum here in the city, from the New York Philharmonic to the New York Knicks. Picture the total dollars spent on leisure activity as a pie. With everything going on in the city, the entertainment dollar is sliced up more thinly here than any other metropolitan market in the country, maybe the entire world, and in order to compete we have to interface with the community in a more proactive way than ever before.

"Our five-year strategic plan seamlessly integrates these exigencies into our future. Our contract negotiations with the musicians will reflect our new direction and our need to template a full-length concert season in a single venue, so I'd now like to turn the floor over to Loren Gardiner, vice president of DynamiCorp, one of the country's top entertainment-consulting firms, who has been working with us tirelessly as we move forward. Loren, it's all yours."

"Thank you, Adrianne. Ladies and gentlemen, it is my great honor to have partnered with Adrianne and Harmonium. Let me say first that Harmonium is the greatest orchestra in the world. We at DynamiCorp have been hard at work on a PowerPoint presentation that we've individualized especially for you. Our theme is, 'Put the harmony back in Harmonium,' so let's get started!"

Click.

"As Bob Dylan said, 'The times, they are a-changin',' and it's truer today than ever before." In big bold letters, the screen that had been set up on the far wall proclaimed, THE TIMES, THEY ARE A-CHANGIN'.

Click.

"Now that Harmonium has found a home after all these years, it has been our challenge to remodel the organization just as Harmonium Hall is being remodeled, so it can compete for the entertainment dollar against the likes of the Philharmonic, orchestras from around the world that visit Carnegie Hall day in and day out, and like Adrianne said, more people-friendly events like Broadway, the theater and movies, restaurants, and sports." The screen listed some of New York's cultural, entertainment, and recreational activities. With a wink and an engaging smile, Gardiner added, "I was recently strolling past an adult theater marquee in Times Square that was showing an 'art film' called"—Gardiner made air quotes—"*Rex Tremendae*. Not sure it was for the same clientele Harmonium markets to, but you get the idea."

"I don't get it," said Devlin Forrester.

"You know, like in the Mozart Requiem," said Vickers, jumping to Gardiner's aid.

"Oh," said Forrester.

Click.

"We've targeted some of the most successful organizations in the symphonic field in order to emulate what has worked the best and in order to avoid what has not."

"Which organizations?" asked Imogene Livenstock.

"Good question! And here's your answer."

Click.

The screen displayed the names of five orchestras. "The so-called Big Five orchestras: New York Philharmonic, Boston Symphony, Philadelphia Orchestra, Cleveland Orchestra, and Chicago Symphony. We feel we're in their league artistically—"

"They are not in our league," said Herza.

"I stand corrected," said Gardiner with a smile. "Let's put it this way: They were the best we could find."

Everyone laughed but Vaclav Herza.

Click.

Gardiner proceeded to show a series of graphs and charts with lots of colored lines and shapes that analyzed attendance, and gross and net revenue, from different types of concerts over periods of years, and compared them to the Big Five's overall budgets and to what were termed fixed costs, meaning, more or less, how much they had to pay the musicians. *Click, click, click, click.*

More charts indicated the multimillion-dollar impact those orchestras had on local economies, disproportionately large compared to the number of entertainment dollars that went directly into the organizations themselves. Then there were charts of revenue streams for Harmonium: the percentages that came from the endowment, annual giving, government support, and ticket sales. The board understood the gist after five minutes and was relatively engaged for the first half hour, but after more clicks than they could count, their interest waned.

In the middle of Gardiner's presentation about their aggressive marketing campaign—"there's no such thing as bad publicity"— Brundage said, "I also recall Mr. Dylan saying something about 'blowing in the wind'" and asked if Gardiner would kindly proceed to his conclusions.

"I'd like to turn the floor back over to Adrianne for that," said Gardiner. "DynamiCorp simply collected the data and made the suggestions, but it was up to her subcommittee to make the tough calls. So I thank you for your time. It has truly been an honor working with your fine organization." Gardiner sat down.

Without missing a beat, Vickers handed out a thick, handsomely bound report titled "Saving the Symphony: A Global Strategy" to each executive committee member.

"I am very excited," she said, "to announce the basics of our four-part vision for the future of Harmonium. All the details are in the report and I hope you'll take the time to read them at your convenience.

"Basically, as we move into the future, we see the need to reach out to New York's unique demographic mix, and we think we've come up with a novel, balanced, and, most important, *successful* strategy.

"First, we recognize that the core of our existence is classical music and we will continue with a 'Long Hair' series devoted to the great classics masterpieces.

"Second, within three years we will gradually transition into a full-blown pops calendar, called 'Tops in Pops,' including ten Christmas shows and eight other pairs of concerts throughout the year. We already have Doc Severinsen, Skitch Henderson, Mitch Miller, and Marvin Hamlisch lined up as headliners.

"Third, we will immediately begin planning a four-concert family series of light classical and film music called 'Hip, Hip, Bourrée!'"

"Could we get John Williams for that?" asked Chynoweth, a question that set the rest of the gathering aflutter.

"Great idea, Alvin," said Vickers, having gauged the high level of interest. "If we can pry him from the Boston Pops for an evening, who knows?

"Finally, in order to develop the audience of the future, we are partnering with targeted New York City public schools to create an education program called 'Bach to the Future.' It has been statistically proved that classical music improves test scores, and I'm especially excited that 'BTTF' will offer combined programs of classical, popular, and ethnic music. Starting next year—"

"This is no strategy," interrupted Herza, who had declined an invitation to participate on the strategic-planning committee. "This is obscenity. All of it! We will play what I say. Only what I say.

"Concerts for children?" Herza continued, incredulous. "Why? Do you take six-year-olds to see *King Lear*? Do you read them *War and*

Peace for their bedtime story? For children to listen to Mahler is an absurdity beyond comprehension."

"Schools are no longer providing music education, so someone has to step in," said Vickers. "We need to build young audiences for the future."

"Do you suggest we teach them Strauss's *Salome,* eh? Let them watch the naked young nymphomaniac slipping her tongue between the lips of John the Baptist as his head sits on a silver platter?"

"Maestro, surely you see the need to build young audiences," Loren Gardiner said, jumping to the rescue, "for the future."

"Let me tell you something, fool. The audiences that have supported classical music for the past three hundred years have been, are, and always will be predominantly white-haired, affluent Caucasians. White haired because classical music requires years to acquire good taste; affluent because fine concerts, like fine wine, are necessarily expensive; and Caucasian because the music was composed in Europe by whites for whites. If there are other kinds of music for other races, let them play it, but it will not be the symphony orchestra. *My* symphony orchestra! Do we expect the boogie-woogie man to play Brahms? If the schools want to teach music, let them teach music. If they don't, that is their problem. We play concerts for adults."

"Then how do you suggest we employ the musicians for an entire season?" asked Vickers.

"I am astounded that someone in your position as managing director of a symphony orchestra would dare ask such a question!" said Herza. "The answer does not take an Einstein, only someone with more than a sixth-grade intelligence. We will have a subscription season of twenty-nine weeks. The summer will be for touring—Lucerne, Edinburgh, Salzburg, where people understand music. You have but to call them and say Herza wishes it, and it will be done. You then find

corporate sponsors for the tours. Sony, UBS, American Express—
they line up for Herza. The rest of the year will be the vacation weeks
that the musicians say they need and are already in their contract.
This will give the public their opportunity to go to their more
'people-friendly' activities."

"And how do you suggest we fill the seats at Harmonium Hall with
twenty-nine weeks of programs?"

"I note to the members of the executive committee, Miss Vickers,
that you are asking a question that for six months you have sought to
answer with your so-called strategic committee and have failed mis-
erably.

"Harmonium Hall seats one thousand nine hundred sixteen people.
What is your advance subscription sale for this year?"

"About sixty percent."

"Ah, so you do know something. That means that over eleven hundred seats are already sold for each concert, leaving fewer than eight
hundred remaining. If you multiply that by twenty-nine weeks, and
again by three because we play each concert three times, you need to
sell a total of about seventy thousand additional tickets. In a year.
In a metropolitan area of twenty million people. I think a chimpanzee could accomplish that. Do you not feel capable of being able to
achieve that? Should we hire a chimpanzee to replace you, perhaps?"

Vickers did not respond.

"Should we?" Herza pursued. "Answer me." He pounded the table
so violently that the glasses of water threatened to spill. "Should we
hire a chimpanzee to replace you?"

"No."

"Then stop this talk of 'Pops Tops' and 'Hip Bourrée' and children's
concerts. Because if the talk does not stop immediately, I will resign
immediately, right this minute! Now, you will pay the musicians what

they ask for and you will find the money to pay them, not the least amount necessary but the most amount possible."

"May I interject something here?" asked Alvin Chynoweth. "Just for my own understanding."

"Go ahead," said Brundage. "The floor's yours."

"I've taken a look at the musicians' contract," he said, "and it appears to me that during any given week, they're under the baton of the maestro twenty, maybe twenty-five hours tops. Some of them don't even have to play, like when there's a Mozart symphony, for example. We know they're good, but it seems to me they're getting paid an awful lot for very little work."

"At least," responded Herza, "they are doing *something*. You receive millions from your stocks and your bonds, from your trust funds and your offshore accounts, yet you do absolutely *nothing*. You make no contribution to society whatsoever. So who is the parasite here, Mr. Chynoweth?

"You say the musicians are paid too much. Look at those baseball players," he continued, "who stand out in a field of grass and run around in a circle for three hours, four times a week, for half a year and get paid millions. What they do is meaningless, but Mr. George Steinbrenner knows that if he pays his men the most they will win. Whatever a Yankee is, they are paid to win, and they win. So maybe Mr. George Steinbrenner should replace you on the board.

"It is my job to conduct. It is the musicians' job to play. And it is your job to find the money. Is that understood?"

"Are you taking the musicians' side in this?" asked Brundage.

"Let me tell you clearly," said Herza. "It is not the responsibility of this organization to provide a livelihood for a gaggle of pampered prima donnas. I don't care about their personal lives and I don't care whether they are happy or whether they have liver cancer. If any musicians cannot maintain my standard, they can be replaced by those who can. But I must have the best musicians to make the best music. The only way to get the best is to pay the best."

"However," Vickers said, "in order to pay those musicians, I firmly believe that if we are to move the symphony orchestra successfully into the twenty-first century, number one, orchestra CEOs must work together to realign the market expectations of the musicians; and number two, we absolutely must envision a new paradigm, one in which the organization becomes community based and consumer friendly. People have gotten tired of seeing dinosaurs in a museum."

"Dinosaurs in a museum?" asked Herza. "Is that what the CEO of a symphony orchestra thinks of her organization? A concert hall is a temple. It is not a museum and it is not a Sunday school for children. If you want to teach Sunday school, start a different organization. That is not what symphony orchestras do. Symphony orchestras play symphonies. Others can teach, but no one can play symphonies except symphony orchestras. If your so-called new paradigm takes root, it will spread like a disease, because the public, which has no basis for a standard, will accept anything that is given them. I, Vaclav Herza, have the highest standard. You, the lowest. Yes, you will move the organization into the next century. And then, after fifteen, twenty years, after your successful surgery, you and your ilk will have absolutely killed the patient. Madam, if you order shit at a fine French restaurant, no doubt they will serve it on a silver platter. Nevertheless, it is still shit.

"You and your consultant have wasted this organization's money on your strategic plan that is neither strategic nor a plan. Here is *my* strategic plan: I will conduct what I want, when I want, until the day I die. That is my plan. It is your job to pay the musicians more than anyone. More than Chicago. More than Boston. More than the

New York Philharmonic. Our 'competition,' as you call it. I do not compete. With anybody. I will conduct great music. If anybody wishes to compete with that, that is their decision.

"Now, I make you a very simple proposition. You, our devoted board of trustees, you decide which vision you wish to see instituted for Harmonium: hers or Herza's. Whoever you choose will stay. The other will resign. Immediately."

After a moment's shocked silence, Brundage said, "We will take your suggestion under advisement, Maestro, and give it careful consideration, but," he added, stumbling through, "I don't think there isn't a way we shouldn't be able to work this all out. For now, may we table your proposition and move forward with any other new business? Parsley, anything to report?" he asked in a voice that clearly suggested *let's get the hell out of here.*

Parsley, who had not spoken at the meeting, fumbled momentarily for the glass of water to clear his throat.

Herza eyed Parsley with interest.

"I'll be brief," Parsley said. "The major news is that yesterday the orchestra selected a new, permanent concertmaster for Harmonium, Yumi Shinagawa, former second violinist of the New Magini String Quartet and a very accomplished musician. We're very fortunate to have someone of her caliber in such a significant position."

Congratulations were offered.

Forrester said, "That's great, but other than shake the conductor's hand and point to the oboe to play the A at the beginning of the concert, is this a big deal?"

Alvin Chynoweth said, "Wait a second. I'm a little confused. I thought Maestro Herza was the concertmaster."

Parsley looked down at his hands that he had placed on his notebook and took a deep breath before replying. "An easy enough mistake to make. Maestro Herza is the music director. He is a conductor.

The concertmaster of an orchestra is the first-chair first violinist. Are you a football fan by any chance, Mr. Chynoweth?"

"Go, Columbia Lions!" he replied with a big smile.

"Good. See, the music director is like the coach, and the concertmaster is like the quarterback. The concertmaster gets the signals from the music director and communicates them, either by gesture or verbally, to the musicians. It's also the concertmaster's responsibility to put all the bowings in the string players' parts, like calling the plays in the huddle, so that when you see them playing, they're all moving in the same direction. This of course is not just a visual thing. It affects the way the whole string section plays together. And like the quarterback, the concertmaster is the public face of the whole orchestra." Parsley quickly amended that. "Except for the music director, of course."

"Will this Yumi Shina-whosey-whats begin tomorrow?" asked Devlin Forrester. "It would be perfect for the opening of the hall to have a permanent concertmaster."

"We're currently in negotiations with Ms. Shinagawa regarding her contract, which we may or may not conclude in time. However, we have an able replacement in Lawrence Nowitsky, our backup quarterback, until such time as Ms. Shinagawa is available."

"I heard that Sherry O'Brien has disappeared," said Imogene Livenstock, whose ear was always to the ground, even though the ground for her was far, far below.

"Disappeared?" said Herza. "I would hardly say disappeared. Pouting is more like it. She did not win the concertmaster audition, and so she is telling us by her petulance that she is unhappy. She is a spoiled child. Life will go on."

TWENTY
THURSDAY

Jacobus sat alone on a leather-cushioned bench in the middle of the main gallery at the Clark Art Institute in Williamstown. The curator had explained that he was facing Joseph Mallord William Turner's massively breathtaking oil on canvas seascape *The fighting Temeraire tugged to her last Berth to be broken up,* painted in 1839. "Turner is without doubt the greatest seascape painter ever," said the curator to Jacobus, who was hardly listening. "What's unusual about this one is here we have a royal ship, but instead of being portrayed in customary naval splendor, the *Temeraire* is little more than a floating hulk on its final voyage to the scrap heap, yet it's still bathed in that glorious sky, as if God himself were giving thanks for the ship's dedicated service." When Jacobus didn't respond, the curator wished him a pleasant stay at the museum and then wisely left him alone.

His hands, no longer trembling, were on his knees. He had removed his dark glasses, indifferent whether onlookers were horrified at his glazed eyes, and had leaned forward in supreme concentration, intent on somehow sensing the painting. Except for his vague recollection of the painting's swirling power, he could see it no better now than when he had begun staring at it a motionless half hour earlier. If only he could concentrate harder, maybe . . .

Turner—rather, Turner versus Gainsborough—had been instructive to him in understanding the difference between playing in an orchestra and playing chamber music. Turner's monumental vision, the broad swaths of light and color, colliding in breathtaking explosion as they grappled for ascendancy, was like an orchestral score of Ravel or

Debussy. The overall composition might have an easily definable program, but any given moment was a whirlwind of pure color.

Gainsborough, on the other hand, was definition, detail, control, proportion, balance. A richly refined and polished blend that worked perfectly as a string quartet but in an orchestra would be beside the point. Jacobus respected Gainsborough, but he revered Turner. He continued to stare at the masterpiece, seeking guidance, for it wasn't his current objective to describe to Yumi the difference between orchestral and chamber music playing that had brought him here. It was his visit to Sherry O'Brien.

He had received a phone call first from Tiny Parsley, then Yumi, then one from Moskowitz, and then came the personal visit from his friend, full-time plumber and part-time town police force Roy Miller, wearing his part-time police uniform.

On Tuesday evening, O'Brien had been found lying in bed in a pool of her own blood in Room 226 at the Berkshire View Motel by Sophie Johnstone, the housekeeper who, presuming that O'Brien had already checked out on schedule, had entered to clean the room. Hysterical, she managed to call 911, babbling almost incoherently that she would have cleaned the room sooner except that no one else had booked it for the night because it was midweek and they don't get as many guests in midweek and . . . O'Brien, her pulse barely detectable, was rushed by ambulance to the Berkshire Medical Center in Pittsfield. Johnstone herself was taken to the emergency room, in a state of shock from the unanticipated carnage, and was later given the rest of the week off, with pay, by her employer.

"She lost a lot of blood, Jake," Miller said. He took a sip of the Folger's spiked with Jack Daniel's that Jacobus had provided. "It was bad. Wrists. The doctors aren't sure she's going to make it."

Jacobus did not respond, except to shake his head and slide his mug back and forth aimlessly on the table.

"Why do you suppose someone would do that to herself?" Miller asked. "Someone with that kind of talent. I don't get it. Never have."

"What the hell kind of question is that? Why the fuck are you asking me?" spat Jacobus. "What do you think? That because I'm blind, I'm some damn guru with some kind of paranormal insight?"

"Sorry, Jake. I was just sort of talking out loud to myself. I didn't mean any offense. It's just hard to figure what goes on in someone's mind that would lead them to do that kind of thing.

"Whew. This is too heavy. Like me. Annie says I need to lighten up. In more ways than one, I guess. What have you been up to the last few days? How's Nathaniel?"

"How the hell do I know? He's in Europe with the literati, paparazzi, and hoity-toity at some stinking music festival."

"Jealous, huh? Have any other visitors lately?"

"Take one guess."

"Did you have a chance to talk to her at all? Sherry O'Brien, I mean, in the last day or so?"

"No. Why? And what's with the third degree?"

"Just want to figure out why she'd slit her wrists."

"When she played for me the other day she said she didn't know what she'd do if she lost her audition. I assume she was distraught."

"That sounds right. On the other hand, if she didn't . . ." Miller let the sentence trail away.

Jacobus's antennae went up. Was it not clear-cut? He regretted that choice of words, even unspoken. "If she didn't *what*? You said it was self-inflicted."

"That's what the Pittsfield police say, and every indication says it was."

"But?"

"Well, she was still semiconscious but kind of delirious when they took her in, and the only intelligible thing they could decipher her saying was, 'Jacobus.' She whispered your name over and over."

Jacobus put his thumbs on his temples and fingers on his forehead and pressed hard, trying to stop his head from its involuntary shaking.

"That's all she said?" he asked.

"She's been unconscious since then."

"So if she were to die, that makes me a murder suspect?"

"No, I'm not saying that at all."

"Then just what are you saying, Roy?"

"Only that we want to understand what was going on in her mind. Maybe she was calling for you. Maybe she needed your help. That's all I'm saying."

He found Room 421L, a semiprivate room in the intensive care unit at the Berkshire Medical Center, only after walking around in circles for an hour and going up the wrong elevator. At the desk, they had pinned a visitor's tag on his shirt, so no one bothered him. On the other hand, no one helped him, either. When he found the room, the nurse told him to keep the visit brief, that O'Brien had not yet regained consciousness. Was she dying? She's resting.

The other patient in the room was snoring, but it sounded ugly. Jacobus found a chair on wheels and rolled it to the bedside where he could listen to O'Brien breathing. He wanted to tell her he was sorry he hadn't taken her seriously, that he had shunned her plea for help, and that he was offended by the way she had been abused by Herza. But he was incapable of saying out loud the words that were in his head, even though she was unconscious and the other patient unaware. So he sat there, not knowing what to say, wrestling against introspection, trying to work out the scenario.

If she were awake, she would ask, "Why are you here?"

And what would he say? "Why did you do it? After all . . ." He didn't know how to finish the sentence.

He knew how she felt. He should have known from the outset. He, too, had been there once. So close, crossing the last hurdle, the last bridge, and nothing to stop you. Clear sailing and once you get to the other side, all your troubles will be over. And maybe they would have been, but there's always a Herza to push you over the side of the bridge.

"Still, you should never have done that," Jacobus was now telling her, out loud. "No one should."

But who decides "should"? Him? Least of all, him. He hadn't helped when he could have. No one had helped. Herza won. What was left to do?

There are other orchestras. Other jobs, thought Jacobus. But what was it she had said to him? "I guess you don't understand humiliation."

Jacobus fought against nausea and the urge to flee.

Why had she whispered his name? Was it a plea for help, as Roy Miller had intimated? Or was it an indictment? Was she consigning him to hell for having stood idly by, by uttering that one word, "Jacobus"?

"Excuse me," said a voice from behind him.

"Yeah?"

"I'm Dr. Brexton."

Jacobus didn't respond.

"Are you family?" Dr. Brexton continued.

"If only family members are allowed to visit, then I am."

"No, that's not why I ask. It's because she needs blood. Badly."

"I've got about a pint and a half left in me. She can have it."

"That's kind of you, but we need to get it from a family member, if possible, a parent. She's got a rare blood type."

"Mine's red. Hers a different color?"

"A complete blood type," Dr. Brexton explained patiently, "describes a full set of thirty substances on the surface of RBCs—"

"What the hell are RBCs?"

"Sorry, red blood cells. An individual's blood type is one of the many possible combinations of blood-group antigens. Across the thirty blood groups, over six hundred different blood-group antigens have been found, but many of these are very rare."

"Cut to the chase, Doc."

"I'll try to put it in plain English. If a unit of incompatible blood is transfused between a donor and recipient, a severe acute hemolytic reaction with hemolysis, renal failure, and shock is probable, and death is a possibility. Antibodies can be highly active and can attack RBCs and bind components of the complement system to cause massive hemolysis of the transfused blood."

"In other words, she's in trouble."

"Unless we can find a compatible donor, yes."

"What about the wrists? Will she ever be able to play again? Can you put that in plain English, too?"

"Certainly. Flexion and grip are controlled by the flexor tendons. Extension is controlled by the extensor tendons. The insult at the wrist flexion crease, caused by the razor incisions, where the carpal tunnel starts, also severed the nerve that runs from her neck down through her arms, disrupting her ability to move fingers in either hand to the point of paralysis, and will require extensive surgery for her to regain manual dexterity. How much surgery is still too early to determine."

"She plays the violin."

"She played the violin. But manipulative function is not my main concern."

"There's more?"

"Acute blood loss/critical hemorrhage usually results in death if one is not resuscitated rapidly. Loss of consciousness from the hemorrhage insult would be a result of hypoperfusion—from hypovolemia—and hypo-oxygenation from severe anemia of the brain. One would have to have prolonged hypoperfusion of the brain—hypotension and/or hypoxemia—followed by successful physiologic resuscitation, not necessarily back to a functional state, to be rendered unconscious for days. Different than the unconsciousness that occurs with major head trauma or stroke, systemic hypoperfusion would really rule the day."

"Doctor, are you trying to tell me she could be a vegetable?"

"I'm concerned that she lost so much blood that even if we're able to locate a blood donor, it may well be too late for cognitive recovery."

Jacobus turned his head this way and that, hoping that if he found the proper angle a productive thought would enter it. None did.

"Sorry for the bad news," said Dr. Brexton. "But she's a fighter. She's lucky to be alive."

"How lucky can you get?"

The doctor left. Jacobus sat for a while, then left too, troubled not only by the prognosis but by something—though he couldn't put his finger on it—the doctor had said.

He was spinning around in the revolving exit of the hospital, the point of his cane against the glass enclosure, waiting for the moment when it would find no resistance, indicating it was time to jump off the carousel, when he realized he hadn't made arrangements for getting home. So he completed the three-sixty, reentered the hospital, and asked anyone he heard passing or he bumped into where there might be a public phone he could use. One orderly testily asked, "Don't you have a cell phone?" to which he responded, "If had a cell-o-phone, would I be wasting my time talking to you?" Finally, a helpful nurse told him to make a right, walk through two doorways, and then another right, and "you can't miss it, it will be right there on your left."

When he finally found the phone, he was struck by another idea. He dialed information for Fort Wayne, Indiana, and, as luck would have it, there was indeed a Michael O'Brien listed. The bad luck was that there were four.

He dialed the first and got an answering machine, but the voice sounded too young to be the father of Sherry O'Brien, so he didn't leave a message. The second number was busy. The third was answered after the second ring.

"Hello?" said a woman, her speech slightly slurred.

"Maybe I have the wrong number. Is this Mrs. O'Brien?"

"Yeah. What of it?"

"It's just that I thought Mrs. O'Brien died in childbirth."

"She did. This is Mrs. O'Brien the fourth." She giggled.

To Jacobus, it sounded like she was wed to the fifth.

"May I speak to Mr. O'Brien, please?"

"Hold on.

"Mikey!" she hollered. "Mikey! Someone to talk to you! . . . How the hell do I know? . . . Some guy! . . . Wait a minute," she said to Jacobus. "He's just zipping up." She giggled again and dropped the receiver on a highly reverberant table. Jacobus waited, holding the phone farther from his ear.

"Yeah," said a coarse, guttural voice. Jacobus recognized the cause—a chain smoker—because he had the same symptom.

"My name is Daniel Jacobus. I'm a violin teacher. I'm calling from Massachusetts about your daughter."

"What she get herself into this time?"

"She's had an accident. She's lost a lot of blood, and apparently it's difficult to find a donor."

Jacobus waited for a reply, but there being none, continued. "Since her mother is deceased, I thought you might want to talk to the doctors. Maybe your blood would match what she needs."

"Massachusetts?"

"That's right."

"Who's going to pay for me to fly out to Massachusetts? The government?"

"I'm sure that can be worked out."

"Look, Mr. Jacobs, why don't you just stick to violin teaching and leave well enough alone."

"I just thought that if you love your daughter—"

"I never fucking touched her! You hear that? No one proved nothing. I never touched her!" O'Brien said, and slammed down the receiver.

So Jacobus stared and stared at *The fighting Temeraire tugged to her last Berth to be broken up,* but no matter how hard he concentrated, no glimmer of light or shade or color penetrated his darkness. Yet he continued to stare, and to try, though he had no hope.

TWENTY-ONE

Alone with his abandoned chess game, Jacobus replayed the moves in his head, hoping it would take his mind off his misery. He mulled yet again over his failure to predict the latent danger of Nathaniel's pawn. He picked it up and again felt its form. Nothing had changed. It felt like every other pawn, milled in the same conventional way—same shape, same size, same weight, same ridges. He rotated it in his fingers as he had every day since his defeat. This time, though, he found himself holding it against his cheek. Tears welled up in his sightless eyes and streamed down his unshaven, furrowed cheeks, over his quivering lips, and into his mouth, where he tasted their salt.

He placed the pawn in his mouth between his molars and, with churning jaws, clamped down on it as hard as he could. He bit again, and again, but could not break it, could not destroy it, could not even dent it. He spat it out, saliva covered, into his hand and hurled it against the wall. In a sudden rage, with his forearm he swept all the chess pieces off the board and kicked over the coffee table on which it sat. He grabbed his cane, and in a rampage bulled his way into the kitchen, cracking his head on the doorframe, leaving a bloody mark. He swung the cane wildly, intent on breaking everything within its destructive arc. Glass shattered and he shouted in desperate triumph. He swung again and missed everything and almost fell over, and careened into the refrigerator, bruising his shoulder. Ranting, "I'll kill you! I'll kill you!" he tried to topple the refrigerator, but his strength was insufficient, so he kicked at it until his foot was bruised and swollen, until his leg was too tired to kick anymore.

Jacobus gasped for air, suffocating in his prison, his prison of blackness. Out! He needed to get out! He shouldered the screen door, which exploded open and slapped repeatedly against the side of the house. Air! Where was the air?

Heedless of direction, Jacobus fled the house, tripping over the front steps and into the yard, and spilled over the rusted iron lawn rocking chair, sprawling on the ground as the chair continued to rock. He lay panting, disinclined by pain and fatigue and despair to move.

This is what I deserve, he thought. Alone, facedown in the dirt.

His mind was blank and he struggled to keep it that way forever, devoid of thoughts, devoid of memories. He felt no impulse to respond when an indifferent spider navigated across his brow and down his neck. Slowly, against his will, a tide of thought flooded inexorably onto the foggy shore of his consciousness. He fought to push it back, push it down, but still it came. The same thoughts that had haunted him since childhood, that he had sought to exorcise in his frenzy, were swarming back relentlessly now, a plague of locusts. There was no escape from them. Jacobus reached out for the arm of the chair and dragged himself up out of the dirt, first to his knees and then into the chair, where he breathed as deeply as his smoke-charred lungs would allow. Time passed. He then began to speak aloud into the darkness, though it was not yet dusk, with words that no other human would ever hear.

My name is Daniel Jacobus. I was born December 11, 1920, in Regensburg, Germany. On my seventh birthday, my parents, Isidore and Alicia, gave me a three-quarter-sized violin. It was much too big for me. My first teacher was Max Frenkel. My parents didn't play an instrument, but music was always part of our family. My older brother, Eli, played the piano, much better than I ever played the violin. For Frenkel it was always musician-ship over technique—"what do you want to be, an automobile mechanic?"—even when I was a beginner. He got that philosophy from his own teacher, the great Joseph Joachim. I made good progress.

In 1931, they sent me to New York to participate in the Grimsley Violin Competition on Frenkel's recommendation. By rule, all the contestants were under the age of thirteen. Children. He had high hopes for me. I know he was sincere, but I think he also hoped that if I won, it would enhance his reputation. My parents had mixed feelings about letting me go, and their concerns were borne out, but not in the way they thought.

The winner of the competition would get a Carnegie Hall recital, a solo performance with a specially hired orchestra, and some money. A lot of money, I suppose, for that time. But mainly, the winner would get to play on the so-called Piccolino Stradivarius, the mag-nificent three-quarter-sized instrument that Stradivari had made for the legendary star-crossed midget violinist, Matteo Cherubino, nicknamed "Il Piccolino." I grew to hate that violin.

It was my first time away from Regensburg, let alone my first time overseas. My parents couldn't go with me; they worked and they had Eli to take care of, and they already felt the trouble brewing in Germany, but the organizers of the competition assured them I'd be well taken care of. We—all the contestants—stayed in what was called a hotel, though looking back, it was no more than a dingy boardinghouse. We had our own rooms, not because the sponsors wanted us to be comfortable, only so we each had a space to practice and to isolate us from one another. There were chaperones who enforced the rules. We met for meals in a dining hall, where we were not allowed to speak. At least we had the meals. The people outside, the people still out of work, had nothing; the soup kitchens if they were lucky. It was the Depression. The days of the dance marathons. That's what our violin competition was like. The last one standing. We had one hour in the evening during which we could speak to each other. Other than that, we practiced.

I got sick. I was a skinny kid, and I wasn't used to the food—it wasn't anything like my mother's—or being away from home. I threw up a lot, yet somehow I made it through the first round. I played better in the second round. There were three judges. The head judge was Feodor Malinkovsky, who at that time was the most famous violin teacher in the world. All I can remember about what he looked like was that he looked like a pig. He was round. His bald head was round, his hands were round—you couldn't see any knuckles—his body was round, he had no hair on his head or his face or his arms, and all of him was coated with a thin layer of grease. His eyes squinted and his smile looked like he had to practice it in front of a mirror. His nose and ears were too big for his face and hair came out of them. Instead of a chin, there was a flap of fatty skin that connected his head to his chest. He might have had a tail, but I can't prove it. After the second round, one of the chaperones told me Malinkovsky wanted to see me. He escorted me to Malinkovsky's office, where he knocked on the door and left me. I'll never forgive him.

The great Malinkovsky invited me in. I didn't know much English at the time, so he spoke to me in German, in which he was fluent, but nasal and whiny. He told me how much he liked my playing. He told me that I was exceptionally creative, especially for such a little boy. I thanked him.

"You have a good imagination," he said.

"Thank you."

"And so polite! Someone who plays so well, has such an imagination, and is so polite has a chance to win this competition. A good chance! Would you like to win this competition?"

"Yes, sir."

"Good. Then come closer. Don't be shy. Come closer."

When I stood right in front of him, he said, "Good boy. Now close your eyes and use your wonderful imagination." At which point he took my hand and pressed it on his crotch.

"Now, how does that feel?" he asked.

"I don't know."

"You don't know?" he said, chuckling. "Well, let me show you."

He unzipped my pants and pulled them down.

I told him I thought I should go.

"But don't you want to win a prize, son? This will help stimulate your imagination."

Malinkovsky put his hand inside my underpants and began squeezing.

"Squeeze me just like this," he said, beginning to sweat and to pant.

I did as he said. Then he stood up in front of me, unzipped his pants, and held his penis in front of me with one hand and caressed my head with his other.

"Now just put this in your mouth like a good boy. A good boy."

I told him I couldn't.

"You can't?" he exclaimed. "Someone who can manage the difficulties of the violin so well says he can't do something so simple? Come now! Of course you can do it. Just try. I think you'll like it."

So I did. But I didn't like it. In fact, I gagged and threw up on Malinkovsky's penis, on his legs, and all over his pants that were down around his ankles. He didn't like that.

"What have you done?" he yelled. "I try to help you and you defile me. Get out!"

I pulled up my pants and left. Sherry O'Brien, you were wrong. I know humiliation.

I was not advanced to the final round. I received a certificate of appreciation. A talented boy named Kowolski from Poland won. I don't know what Malinkovsky made him do. He played well, though, I remember. I'm not jealous of that. He died ten years later, in the war. That I'm jealous of. Kate Padgett came in second, and by not winning, her whole life was changed. Then again, if she had won, I would never have met her. But that's another story.

I went home. Of course I didn't say a word about Malinkovsky, who later fled back to Russia to escape growing accusations of pedophilia, which I didn't hear about until much later. He disappeared during a Stalinist purge.

My parents said they were proud of me.

I returned to the U.S. in 1938 to study with Dr. Krovney at Juilliard. My parents told me it would be a wonderful opportunity, but in hindsight I'm sure they knew what was up in Germany and sent me as much for my protection as for my violin playing. I did not know at that time that I would never see my parents or my brother again.

I prospered under Krovney. I learned how to understand what I was doing on the violin, both mechanically and aesthetically, instead of just imitating or randomly trying to play "with feeling." He made me study the music without the violin in my hands. This later helped me as a teacher. He also had some bizarre mechanical exercises. These did not help me as much.

When the war broke out, most of the male students at Juilliard—the American male students—were drafted and went overseas to serve. That left us, a handful of foreigners, overwhelmed by an overabundance of eager, lusty girls searching for nocturnal inspiration after spending the day in the practice room. During those years I devoted almost as much time practicing sex as practicing the violin. Maybe more time. They didn't care that I was a German, or even that I was a Jew, as long as I was available.

And while with relentless efficiency I was seducing an endless stream of anonymous, insignificant others in the dark whose names I hardly knew and whose faces I can't remember, my parents, Isidore and Alicia, were herded into the Auschwitz death camp, and Eli vanished from the face of the earth. My blindness is appropriate punishment, though hardly adequate. Along with my conscience, it is with me forever. I will never forgive myself. I have failed my family and I have failed Scheherazade O'Brien. My very survival proves my atheism. If there were a God, I'd be dead by now.

Jacobus sat unmoving in his chair for he didn't know how long. Thoughts neither of music nor of food entered his head. He was surprised, in fact, with how few thoughts he had at all. He had anticipated that after unburdening himself of the detritus of his life, a flood of energy would rush in to occupy the vacuum. No such event occurred. There was no catharsis, no turning point, only a certain mild lassitude. An acknowledgment, not a victory.

He was still Jacobus; that had not changed. No one would say to him, "Jacobus, look at you! You're a new man!" Maybe they'd say, in hushed tones, "Is it just me, or did you notice Jacobus isn't as crotchety as he used to be?" "Yeah, are you sure he's okay?" Whichever, Jacobus didn't care. He floated in an emotional limbo; the concerns of his own life were past. He did care for the future of Sherry O'Brien and for setting that house in order. He had failed in his effort to see the damn Turner at the museum, but he was able to see with stunning clarity how things were going to turn out with Herza. Though he would do his best to alter the chain of events, the end was now inevitable. After that, he would rest.

Jacobus felt a nudge against his thigh.

"Go away," he said to Trotsky.

Again Trotsky pressed his muzzleless bulldog face into his thigh.

"Go away."

Trotsky backed off but returned moments later with his ball and dropped it, coated in slobber, onto Jacobus's lap. Solid rubber, the ball was a notch bigger than a tennis ball but could still be held in one hand. Jacobus had given up on tennis balls because Trotsky had made a game of piercing and ensnaring them with his lower canines and then growling and madly shaking his head in triumph. Trotsky treated the new variety of balls with inexplicable deference.

When Jacobus still didn't respond, Trotsky, grunting, embedded the ball on Jacobus's lap into his crotch.

"Goddammit," Jacobus said and stood up. Trotsky began to spin in circles.

With the ball in one hand, Jacobus found his cane and headed to the lawn, an acre or so of grass that Roy Miller mowed every week during the summer for cash under the table.

Jacobus felt the weight of the ball, balancing it in his left hand. He tossed it in the air, counted a quick "One, two," swung the cane that he held in his right hand, and made solid contact. The ball, with Trotsky in hot pursuit, rolled about twenty yards. Jacobus knew that if he hit it any harder it would go into the woods. Trotsky was back within seconds. Jacobus held out his left hand, into which Trotsky deposited the slimy ball, then backed up, grunting for more. Jacobus hit the ball again, and again, and again, with a batting average the Boston Red Sox would envy, until Trotsky, panting, gave up and went to the pond for a drink.

Taking the dog's example, Jacobus retreated to the kitchen for a glass of water. O'Brien's whispered "Jacobus" echoed in his ears, and unless he answered her call it would continue to reverberate until the day he died. He was now determined to act, but his chessmen were in disarray. It was time for him to move them into position and put them into play. If he, like Lear, would be a sightless king, it would be the compassionate, decisive Lear, not the Lear of doddering senility.

Never again would he stand idly by.

TRANSFIGURATION

TWENTY-TWO

"You claim to be a reporter?" Jacobus asked.

"That's a leading question," said Martin Lilburn, "and, coming from you, it sounds suspiciously ominous."

"I want to help you with your story."

"Help me with my . . . Now I'm truly alarmed. What is it you are proposing?"

"Ah, now we're getting down to brass tacks. To your knowledge, has Vaclav Herza ever fallen afoul of the law?"

"Herza? Not that I know of. Why?"

"Anything that came close? Rumors that could've, should've been followed up?"

"Of course rumors. There are always rumors. What conductor hasn't had rumors?"

"Such as?"

"The usual. Drugs, affairs, homosexuality, heterosexuality. But nothing ever substantiated. Conductors like him have a legion of handlers who generally do a bang-up job of keeping their charges a long arm's length from prying eyes."

"Like politicians."

"Except politicians get caught a lot more with their hand in the cookie jar. From what I've found out about Herza, his lifestyle would be the envy of the priesthood—in the most saintly sense, that is. Again I ask, why do you want to know?"

"I'll tell you if you agree to research this question for me. And why not? If you find anything out, it would only make your story more of a blockbuster."

"I'm not sure if 'blockbuster' falls within the purview of the *New York Times*, but, yes, I have no problem looking into this. Now, why?"

Jacobus related the story of his encounter with Scheherazade O'Brien from bitter beginning to even more bitter end. "I want to see Herza get his just deserts."

"You're aware that if anything could be proved it could destroy his legacy, his career."

"I'd be willing to let those chips fall where they may, especially if his legacy includes ruined lives."

"And that if I were to print something about him that was ultimately proved false, it would be the end of mine."

"You're a music critic, so you should be used to that by now."

"Please let me know the next time you give a concert, Mr. Jacobus. I'll be there in the front row, with tomatoes aplenty."

"I want you to agree to one more thing."

"You want me to prove Al Capone's innocence?"

"So you do have a sense of humor after all," said Jacobus. "No, I want you to leave O'Brien's name and my name out of your story, wherever it leads."

"That may prove to be impossible."

"In which case the deal is off."

"I take exception to your dictates, telling me what I can or can't write. No journalist would agree to that."

"You won't need to worry about my dictates, Lilburn, if you can prove Herza's dick tastes."

"Your wit astounds as it offends." Lilburn laughed. "I'll take your request under advisement, and if I find anything I'll do what I can to keep your names out, but I will make no guarantee. If that's not good enough, no hard feelings. It's up to you. Why not do your own investigating? It wouldn't be the first time."

"I have no contacts in the city anymore. None that would be of any help, anyway."

"What about Malachi?"

"Lieutenant Alan Malachi, NYPD? If I ever called him about this, first he'd tell me I'm full of shit and then he'd figure out some way to lock me up. No, I've had more than enough run-ins with that Yiddish Eliot Ness. But I think you should call him," Jacobus said, molding his voice into a high-pitched wheeze, "because I'm just a feeble, old, blind coot shutaway."

"And the most dangerous man on earth."

Jacobus inserted the cassette into his portable Kmart recorder, felt for the second button from the left, and pressed it. A few seconds later he heard Nathaniel's voice—rather, a vague facsimile of it—reciting the complete itinerary of his European jaunt, including dates, hotels, and phone numbers. Considerate as always, Nathaniel dictated the phone numbers with progressively longer silences as the digits ascended from 1 to 9 to account for the increase in time it would require dialing them on a rotary telephone.

This Jacobus now did, and though it took almost two minutes to complete the damn number, the phone was answered after only a few brisk European-sounding rings.

"*Bitte,*" said a cultured voice. "*Hotel Wilden Mann.*"

"*Zimmer zwei zwei drei, bitte. Herr Villiams, bitte,*" said Jacobus.

"One moment please," said the voice in precise English. "I'll put you through to his room."

Jacobus wondered whether the origin of "smug" might be Swiss.

"Hello," said a distant voice.

"You just finish dinner?" asked Jacobus, accustomed to Nathaniel's biorhythms.

"Jake! What's up?"

"What'd you have? Chopped liver?"

"You mean foie gras? Not this time. I started with homemade egg noodles with a cheese and lemon zest sauce. Then I had the calves liver with—"

"Enough small talk. I need you to go to Prague."

"Prague? But I just got to Lucerne."

"You'll love Prague. A cup of coffee's only *ten* dollars there."

"When do you need me to go? And why, for pity's sake?"

"Tomorrow."

"Tomorrow? You can't be serious. I just spent a hundred and fifty dollars for a festival ticket to hear the BSO play *Damnation of Faust* tomorrow night."

"Faust, eh? The hell with it. The story's passé. You'll enjoy *Don Giovanni* in Prague."

"How do you know *Don Giovanni*'s playing in Prague?"

"*Don Giovanni*'s *always* playing in Prague."

"So, is there a particular reason you need me to go there, or are you just being my tour director?"

"I need you to find out why Vaclav Herza left Prague."

"Herza? Vaclav Herza left Prague forty years ago to escape the Communist crackdown! Everyone knows that!"

"I want you to find out specifically. What pushed him at that particular moment to leave. Something specific, not generalities."

"May I ask the reason for this? I've really been enjoying this vacation—up till now, anyway."

Jacobus mulled his response.

"Jake, are you there?" asked Nathaniel after the extended silence. "Hello? Hello?"

"Yeah," said Jacobus, finally. "There's someone I didn't take seriously, and now she may be dying, partly because of me. But if we can find something in Herza's past—something that would validate her claims of illegal behavior—maybe that'll restore her will to live."

"Jake, I've known you a long time, and I've never heard you so sentimental or . . . It doesn't even make any sense!"

"You're saying I'm senile?"

"No, I'm not saying that. Not yet, anyway. I'm just saying you have some 'splainin' to do."

"But this is an international call! It's expensive."

"Go for it."

Jacobus spent the next several minutes, speaking as quickly as he could, relating what had transpired between Herza and Scheherazade O'Brien, and how he had dismissed her complaint out of hand, and then the audition and its aftermath.

"Well, I still think it's a needle in a haystack," said Nathaniel. "If I do go to Prague, what can you give me to go on?"

"Your peerless investigative skills, gleaned from being the world's number-one consultant for art and instrument fraud, who has been so successful in his endeavors that he can take annual junkets to international music festivals and buy chopped liver in Lucerne."

"That's it?"

"And your innate good nature. I left that out."

"And how much time do I have, a year?"

"How 'bout a few days?"

"Piece of cake."

"Do I detect a note of sarcasm?"

"Of course not! While I'm at it, would you also like me to find out why Rome was built in more than a day? Was there anything else?"

"Yeah. Is there any way to reverse the charge on this call?"

Jacobus winced as the phone slammed down at the other end.

Jacobus had his reasons for not asking Yumi for the phone number, so he called 411, which put him through to the international operator for an extended conversation, during which he found himself explaining, inadequately, that the person whose number he sought might be listed as either Kate Padgett or Cato Hashimoto. This confused the operator, who asked if he was seeking two parties, in which case he would have to call back to make the second inquiry since she could give him only one number at a time. No, he tried to explain, even though the person whose number he was seeking was English, she had once been married to a Japanese man, and she could be listed either way.

"So this is a Japanese person from England?"

"No, it's an Englishwoman who had been married to a Japanese man."

Why any of this mattered was beyond him, and his mind was still scattered when he was finally given the phone number to a home in the mountain hamlet of Nishiyama in Kyushu, Japan's southern island. His request to the operator to connect him was not-so-politely declined, so he had her repeat the number since he wasn't able to write it down. He hoped the dozen mnemonic devices he employed enabled him to remember it correctly. The phone rang, and continued to ring until Jacobus was about to hang up.

"*Moshi-moshi,*" said a semianesthetized voice.

"Kate, are you all right?" asked Jacobus, alarmed.

"Nothing that a good night's sleep wouldn't cure. Who's this?"

"It's Jacobus. Shit, I forgot it's the middle of the night there in—"

"Jake! What a pleasure to hear from you! I was just getting up anyway. No, no, no. I always rise at three-thirty in the morning. It has been so long. And to what do I owe the pleasure of this call?"

"I just wanted to tell you that your granddaughter won the concertmaster audition for Harmonium."

Jacobus expected Kate to express delight, but instead there was silence. Had she fallen asleep? They were both old, certainly, but was she getting that feeble? He held on to the receiver and listened for some sign of recognition.

"Kate, are you still there?" Jacobus finally asked.

"Yes, I'm still here," said Kate. "I haven't nodded off, if that's what you were thinking."

"Of course not. It's just that I thought you'd be excited."

"If there's one thing I learned from you, the hard way, it's that things aren't always as they seem. And, as you like to say, there are two things."

"What?"

"First, the tone of your voice isn't particularly ebullient, to say the least, and you'd never have made the mistake of calling me in the wee hours unless something was troubling you."

"And second?"

"Yumi is a big girl, a grown woman, in fact. If she were happy with the results of the audition, Keiko or I would have heard from her immediately. After all, here in Japan one honors one's mother and grandmother."

"So you're not senile."

"Always the flatterer."

Jacobus found himself blushing.

"Now, tell me the real reason you called," she continued.

"Well, it's true that Yumi won the audition," he said, "and she should be proud of herself, but the circumstances are lousy, and I'm partly to blame."

"Go ahead and get it off your chest, Jake. I've got plenty of time. There are still several hours until our famous rising sun shows its face."

Jacobus explained everything, how he had tossed off Scheherazade O'Brien's concerns as inconsequential. How, as well as Yumi played, he knew that O'Brien was a shoo-in for the job. How Herza had stabbed O'Brien in the back by making a mockery of the audition, resulting in O'Brien's attempted suicide. Maybe if he had known that she had been abused by her father. But that shouldn't have mattered. He had stepped off the tracks as O'Brien was being railroaded.

"Horrific," Kate said when he had concluded. "Absolutely horrific. And if I might be permitted to read between the lines, Jake, you are now feeling personally guilty and responsible for this tragedy because you failed to read signs in O'Brien's story that were reminiscent of what went on when we were child participants in the Grimsley Competition in 1931."

"Yes, Kate. You read me like an old book. I could have prevented this if I had taken her seriously in the beginning."

"That's where you're wrong, Jake. Yes, we were force-fed Paganini and Wieniawski and Sarasate; and yes, we were prostituted, figuratively, anyway, and abused during that competition, paraded in front of the masses like cherubic dressed-up dolls, and made to publicly perform musical acts unnatural to toddlers. But what O'Brien was dealing with was something different entirely. She's an adult, Jake, and even though she's an extremely frustrated one who came up against one dead end after another, she made her choices to pursue her grievance in the face of almost guaranteed retribution.

"I think you know this, too, Jake. I think what you're really trying to do is change your own history. But you can't do that. You can't change the past. You can only make the future better. You've got to let the past go."

This time it was Jacobus who didn't respond. Sure, she could wax poetic about their competition experience as minigladiators, dueling it out onstage until only one received the thumbs-up, but she had no idea—could have no idea—what had happened to him behind closed doors.

"I didn't mean to sound so harsh," said Kate. "I can be a bitch before I put on my makeup."

"Nah," said Jacobus. "That's not it. As far as I'm concerned, you can be a bitch whenever you want to."

"Ah, you've always had a knack of knowing what a girl yearns to hear."

"I need your help, Kate," Jacobus confessed.

"Now, that's true flattery," Kate said in earnest. "I'm all yours. What can I do?"

"Psychoanalysis aside, I want to honor O'Brien's request. She wanted me to find out if there's been a pattern of abusive behavior by Herza. Not just a conductor being an asshole, which goes without saying, but something that would hold up in court. In my mind, it's one thing for a conductor to insult a musician; it's another to pre-meditatedly rig an audition in order to effectively terminate someone's career."

"A worthy endeavor, no doubt," said Kate, "but conductors are generally immune from retribution, especially the great ones like Herza. They can say whatever they want and the musicians still have to 'kiss my arse, if you please.' "

"You sound like me."

"Not a good sign. In any event, how do I fit in, the dowager violin teacher of the rice paddy?"

"Like you say, Herza's a demigod in Japan, and is almost as revered in China and Korea. Well, I don't know anyone in China and Korea, so I thought I'd start with Japan. I'd like to ask you to find out if there's anything . . ."

"Unsavory?"

"Yes, unsavory, in Herza's history in Japan. From what I've been told, he's been there with his own orchestra and as a guest conductor more often than anywhere else."

"Jake, I would love to help, truly. But I don't know if I'm up for this. I'd have to go to Tokyo, and I haven't been there in decades. I find even the prospect of shopping on the Ginza overwhelming. I don't know anyone there and wouldn't know where to start."

"Yeah, you're right," said Jacobus. "Maybe it was a stupid idea to begin with."

"But wait!" she responded. "Why don't you come here and we could investigate together?"

Jacobus's face reddened as he considered the implications of the invitation.

"Maybe when this is all over," he said, "I could come for a visit. But right now, I've got stuff to do here as well."

"Well, Jake, I hate to disappoint you, but . . . Wait, here's another brilliant idea! I could ask Max to do it."

Makoto Furukawa, the preeminent violin teacher on Kyushu before his retirement about a decade earlier, had befriended Jacobus during a long-ago Boston Symphony tour to Japan. Shortly after the formal introductions and polite bows, the two violinists dropped the cultural pretensions and became drinking buddies. Though neither spoke the other's language, a mixture of music and Suntory whiskey brought them together. Yumi, in fact, had been Max's student before he sent her off to the United States for advanced studies with Jacobus.

"Yes, that might work," said Jacobus. "He could do the legwork, and you could translate back to me whatever he comes up with. But do you think he'd go for it? The last I heard, he was loving his retirement."

"I have a feeling," said Kate, "that Max will be happy to take a break from pruning his fruit trees and singing karaoke to himself."

———

Jacobus made one more call, to the Berkshire Medical Center, and asked about Sherry O'Brien's condition. "Are we family members?" the receptionist asked, and he made the mistake of answering honestly rather than correctly. He was told that the patient was unavailable "at this time." Jacobus hung up, suddenly very tired, not from age itself but from the effort of living.

TWENTY-THREE

Lilburn had discovered that in order to successfully stop drinking, an issue of some urgency, he desperately needed something to replace it, something equally tempting but more user-friendly. At first the chocolates seemed harmless enough—weren't they even now touting their salubrious qualities? Oxidants or antioxidants, one of those, whatever they were. But he found that the more anxious he was, the more chocolate he consumed. Now, as he sat at his desk attempting to finish his story before the deadline while simultaneously helping Jacobus, he saw that there were only three Godiva truffles left in the box. The thought of yet another twelve-step program depressed him.

Blast it! Lilburn thought. How did that gadfly Jacobus talk me into this fool's errand? His desk overflowing with material for his own story, he had wasted hours rummaging through the *New York Times* archives seeking dirt on Vaclav Herza. And among the hundreds of articles written about Herza over the decades—including dozens by Lilburn himself—what had been the result? Nothing.

For a while, he thought he had discovered a thread. He researched the car accident that almost cost Herza his life. Celebrating after the final concert of his first year at the helm of Harmonium, Herza had drunk too much and was driving wildly in his Alfa Romeo convertible when he lost control around a mountain curve in the Lago di Garda region of northern Italy. The car slammed into a tree and burst into flames. It was the era before mandatory seat belts, which probably saved Herza's life because he was ejected from the car, landing in a bed of moss that dampened his burning clothes. The other passenger, Zerlina DiFiori, a famous international model and his fiancée, was trapped in the car that plummeted three hundred feet down the mountainside.

Why did Lilburn go to the trouble of spending hours to track down the family of Zerlina DiFiori when he had more pressing work to do? Maybe because this might have been Herza's Chappaquiddick moment. Or maybe Jacobus pegged him correctly as a sucker for a story. But he finally did get hold of DiFiori's sister, Paola, in a suburb of Milan, and to Lilburn's relief she spoke passable English, though what she had to say was not music to his ears. Paola, the younger sister, now in her sixties, scolded him for stoking the coals of a family tragedy that they had spent most of their lives trying to forget. She called him an ass and some things in Italian that he didn't need a translation to understand but that seemed to make reference to certain pork products. When he tried to ask if the family retained hard feelings toward Herza, Paola hung up on him. Ah, the life of a journalist!

If there had been other reasons for the accident, they were buried with Zerlina. What was certainly true, however, was that Herza's jet-set lifestyle ended with his accident. He never married. As far as anyone knew, he never even socialized. And he never drove again.

The next call Lilburn made was to Lieutenant Alan Malachi of the NYPD. Over the years, he and Malachi had crossed paths on several crimes involving the arts, each investigating in his own way. There was the slaying of violin teacher Victoria Jablonski that followed upon the heels of the theft of the Piccolino Stradivarius. There was the murder of legendary violinist René Allard. Most recently was the brutal dismantling, a mass assassination, really, of the New Magini String Quartet. When Lilburn thought about it, which he tried not to, it occurred to him that somehow Daniel Jacobus had ended up at the center of all those investigations.

Lilburn also knew Malachi's parents, Bernard and Lillian, who were on the boards of any number of art museums in the city. From time to time, they and Lilburn bumped into each other at wine-and-cheese receptions for an exhibit opening or fund-raiser. On each occasion they conversed, the elder Malachis lamented that their child—"our only son!"—went into law enforcement rather than the rabbinate, their first choice, or classical music, their second. "What did we send him to Yeshiva for? To be a narcolept?" Lilburn shook his head along with them, commiserating but understanding exactly why young Alan took the path he did.

But young Alan did not commiserate with Lilburn when he heard his request to research police records to dig into Vaclav Herza's past. In fact, his first question was, "Did Daniel Jacobus put you up to this?" Lilburn did not want to lie to a policeman, at least to such an astute one, so he responded with a neutral, "Why should I do something as stupid as that?" and did manage to twist Malachi's arm to have a rookie patrolman do the homework.

Lilburn rummaged through the bottom drawer of his desk and extracted the ICSOM Directory. The International Conference of Symphony and Opera Musicians annually publishes the contact information for every major American orchestra's members. It was a handy resource for Lilburn, who occasionally had to go straight to the horse's mouth to get accurate information.

"Is this Sigurd Larsen?" he asked, after dialing the first number. After the way Larsen had been treated by Herza, Lilburn was hopeful he would be talkative.

"Who is this, please?"

"This is Martin Lilburn of the *New York Times.* I'm doing a story on Harmonium. I was at the rehearsal at Tanglewood the—"

"I have nothing to say."

"But—"

"I refer you to Junior Parsley, our orchestra committee chairman."

"But it's not about the contract negotiations."

The line went dead.

Lilburn decided to try another tack.

"Casper Lulich?"

"Yes?"

"I'm a friend of Daniel Jacobus."

"Oh, hi! What can I do for you?"

"I'm Martin Lilburn from the *Times,* and—"

"I refer you to Junior Parsley, our orchestra committee chairman."

Lulich hung up.

Lilburn quickly dialed Ebeneezer Frumkin's number. He knew from experience that once the musicians caught on that a reporter was on the trail of a story, they'd circle the wagons. Not that he blamed them. They didn't have a PR budget, while management had paid professionals on their staff who knew how to spin the media. Having only one representative from among the musicians to speak to the press kept the message unified, and it prevented individual musicians from incurring retribution from the likes of Vaclav Herza. It wasn't a bad idea. It was just frustrating.

A woman answered.

"Hello, Mrs. Frumkin? This is—"

"Mr. Lilburn, hello!" she said, with a welcoming Midwestern voice chock-full of "sit here and rest a bit while I bring you a slice of warm apple pie." But that's not what she said.

"Beanie says to refer you to—"

"Junior Parsley, the committee chairman."

"That's right," Mrs. Frumkin said cheerily. "Have a nice day, now. Good-bye!"

Lilburn dialed Junior Parsley and not unexpectedly got his answering machine. He hung up, ate a chocolate truffle, opened his notebook, and had a severe case of writer's block.

TWENTY-FOUR
FRIDAY

"Dress rehearsal" is a bit of a misnomer. Though it is indeed the last rehearsal, concert attire is not required. The term simply suggests something of a hybrid: There can be stopping and starting as in a regular rehearsal, but more often than not it is a straight run-through, like a concert. The conductor makes few, if any, comments, preferring to let the orchestra acclimate to the flow of the music, rather than nitpick his way from one detail to another. If the rehearsal is on the morning of the concert, and particularly if the main work on the program is exceptionally taxing, the conductor, if he has a degree of humanity, will permit the musicians to play on reduced throttle, reserving their energy for the performance.

On the occasion of the dress rehearsal for Harmonium Hall, Vaclav Herza concedes not one inch and browbeats the musicians mercilessly. In the middle of the magnificent tone poem *The Moldau* by Bedřich Smetana is an episode in which the river cascades tumultuously over the rocks of the St. John Rapids. When played by the entire orchestra, the overall effect is impressively staggering; when played individually, especially by the string players, it is also staggering but in a very different way, as the fast tempo and awkwardness of Smetana's part writing make it as perilous to navigate as the rapids themselves.

Vaclav Herza lowers his arms and the orchestra comes to a grinding halt. He peers at the back of the viola section and points to one of the musicians.

"If you are going to fake, my dear friend, at least move your fingers."

Casper Lulich, still holding his viola to his chin, whispers to his stand partner, "Beanie, who's he talking to?"

"Who is talking?" demands Herza. "I want to know who is talking."

Cappy has fallen into a trap and knows it. Since the first year of his tenure as music director, Herza made it clear, via a memo to the personnel manager that has remained posted on the bulletin board, that no one may speak at rehearsals unless directly spoken to. If Lulich confesses, he will be admitting violating that draconian stricture. If he doesn't, Maestro will go on a tirade. In either case, there will be hell to pay.

"Maestro, I just wanted to know to whom you were referring," says Lulich.

"Why? Are there others who are faking as well?"

"I wasn't faking, Maestro." This comment silences whatever other sound there is in the hall. Not accustomed to being contradicted, especially by a *tutti* player, even Herza is caught short. He believes his authority hinges on his reply.

"Well, then," he says, "perhaps you will be kind enough to prove that to us. Please stand up and play from the beginning of the passage."

Another catch-22. Smetana, like Wagner and other nineteenth-century Romantic composers, knew perfectly well the difference between writing a string part for the orchestra, where the mass of orchestral sound occasionally preempted individual accuracy, and one for a quartet, where every note is heard with crystal clarity. Lulich also knows that it is not permitted for a conductor to ask a string player to either stand up or to play alone. Furthermore, he knows that Herza knows both of these things, and also that this unwieldy passage had just been approximated not only by him but by all the string players. But of course he cannot say any of that because it would indict his colleagues. To contradict the music director in front of the orchestra could mean the end of his career.

Lulich, the wounded wildebeest surrounded by hyenas, stares at his music, immobilized with fear.

"I said stand up."

Lulich continues to stare at his music, psychologically anesthetized, waiting to be eviscerated alive.

"Maestro, that's not done in this country," says a voice. To Lulich, it sounds miles away, but it comes from the unlikely person of his stand partner, Ebeneezer Frumkin.

"Not done?" replies Herza. "Herza decides what is done and what is not done, in this country or any other. Now you may join your friend in a duet. Stand up, now."

"I will not," says Frumkin.

"He's right," Junior Parsley shouts.

"And who are you?" asks Herza, suddenly under siege. It isn't clear whether Herza truly does not recognize the principal trombone player who is also chairman of the orchestra committee, or simply considers Parsley's statement to be out of order.

"What do you mean?" asks Parsley.

"I asked who you are. Is that such a difficult question? What is your name?"

"Junior Parsley."

"May I say, Mr. Junior Parsley, hearing your playing is even worse than your voice. Even a deaf person would know you were out of tune, and your sound sickens me."

"No more than looking at you."

"How long have you been in this orchestra, Mr. Junior Parsley?"

"Twenty-two years."

"Twenty-two. That is twenty-one too many. Leave!"

Parsley carefully hands his instrument to the second trombonist, then lunges forward, knocking over stands, sending music flying. Fortunately for him and for Herza, there are four rows of musicians between them, just enough to restrain the enraged and powerful trombonist. Tiny is immediately by his twin brother's side and seizes him by the arm.

"Get him off this stage!" Herza orders. "He has no business among serious musicians."

"You little prick," Junior yells as Tiny tows him off. "You'll get yours."

Herza laughs. "It's too late to apologize."

Herza turns back to the violas. "And you. All of you. You play like cattle. This rehearsal is over." He places his baton on the podium and limps off the stage.

Lubomir is waiting for him in his dressing room with a towel in one hand and an iced tea in the other.

Herza swats at the tea and sends it shattering against the wall.

"Get me Parsley—Tiny Parsley—now. And clean that up."

Herza paces until Lubomir returns with Tiny.

Without preamble, Herza says to Parsley, "I want him fired."

"Who?" asks Parsley. "Who do you want fired?"

"You know, you idiot," says Herza. "The trombonist."

"But he's my brother. I can't fire him."

"He was insubordinate and you will fire him in the next hour or you'll both be fired."

"Junior will file a grievance, and your decision will be overturned. Do you want that to happen, Maestro?"

"They will not overturn it."

"And how can you be so sure?"

"After I inform the grievance committee that your brother disguised himself as you with your eye patch in order to spy on a confidential meeting of the executive board, their sympathies will no doubt change."

"How do you know he did that?" Tiny Parsley stammers, his voice deflated.

"The fool almost knocked over the glass of water that was six inches from his hand. Clearly he had not developed the ability to compensate for lack of depth perception with one eye. Any child could have seen that. Now get out.

"Where's Donaghue?" Herza asks Lubomir after Parsley leaves. "I am tired."

"At the end of the bridge. Waiting in the car."

Donaghue has the engine purring and the air conditioner on full blast. He gives no indication of having just exchanged pleasantries with Tyson Parsley, nor would it ever have occurred to Herza to ask. Once the doors of the Lincoln are closed, the summer heat is held at bay, as are, it seems, the assaults that have been thrust upon Herza's sovereignty.

"Insolent bastard twins," Herza comments as the car heads north on the West Side Highway.

"These contract negotiations," says Lubomir from the front seat. "They're fraying everyone's nerves."

"They're not fraying *my* nerves. I haven't spoken impudently, out of turn."

"No, Maestro."

"I haven't slashed my wrists like that hussy."

"No, Maestro."

"Well, there you have it. There will be no more of this nonsense. I won't tolerate it."

"No, Maestro."

"Oh, shut up."

The first several miles are spent in silence contemplating the heavy traffic. As they approach the merge with the Henry Hudson Parkway, they become increasingly bogged down. The cause of the bottleneck, an overheated Cadillac Eldorado that blocks the left lane of traffic, is being attended to by a large man in shorts and a Hawaiian shirt while his wife shouts deprecating comments about his sexual prowess from the sanctuary of the car's interior. It is at that point that Donaghue, the former security guard, again spies the gray Ford Taurus in his rearview mirror that has been several cars behind them for some time. There is nothing suspicious about this as there are thousands of cars going in the same direction.

"Do something about this traffic," demands Herza from the backseat. "I don't have time to waste."

"Yes, sir. Right away, sir," says Donaghue. He picks up the communication device that has been installed in the car, pretends to push some buttons, and speaks something unintelligible into it.

"They're taking care of it right now, sir."

As soon as they pass the stalled Cadillac and the rubberneckers who are the real impediments, traffic begins to flow. Herza sits back, satisfied that his demands have been promptly met.

Donaghue maintains his speed and so does the Taurus. He exits the parkway and drives toward Herza's Riverdale neighborhood, an oasis in the big city that almost feels like the countryside. He turns in to Herza's tree-lined one-way street and pulls up to the curb. It is a high curb and, the street being narrow, Donaghue has to park close to it to allow other cars to pass, making the door of the Town Car impossible to open on his side, so by practice Lubomir gets out and opens the street-side back door to help Herza out. Donaghue glances in his rearview mirror. The Taurus is in the middle of the road behind them, not moving. When Herza is halfway out of the car, the Taurus suddenly springs to life, heading directly for the Lincoln. "Jesus and Mary, at least let me out first," Donaghue mutters and braces himself in a fetal position.

Lubomir, in the act of extracting Herza from the car, has his hands under Maestro's shoulders. He, too, finally sees the Taurus accelerating toward them. Instantaneously, he pushes Herza back into the car and throws himself on top of him. The Taurus rips off the Lincoln's open door, careens against its front fender, and then, tires screeching, races away.

Herza is up like a cat.

"Who was it?" Herza commands. "Tell me who it was."

"I have no idea, sir," says Donaghue. "It all happened so fast."

By the time the police arrive, Herza has already gone to his bedroom and has left Lubomir with instructions that his nap is not to be disturbed under any circumstances. Since Herza hasn't seen anything, anyway, the police are temporarily content to honor his request. Instead, they take pictures of the damage and scrape some paint shards left by the other car from the right front panel of the Lincoln. They also interview Butkus and Donaghue, from whom they glean conflicting stories.

Butkus is convinced the collision was intentional with the goal of killing the maestro, a plan that he miraculously foiled. Donaghue, on the other hand, says he believes it was simply an impatient New York driver who misgauged the width of the narrow street and did not anticipate the door of the Lincoln opening at the last second. He tacitly blames Butkus for not seeing the Taurus bearing down upon them.

When the police ask Donaghue who he believes might have been bent on killing Vaclav Herza, he claims ignorance. "God's plan," he says, "is beyond me to understand." Yet when they ask the same question of Butkus, his reply is, "Only about a hundred people."

TWENTY-FIVE

Nathaniel had been able to book a couchette for the overnight train from Lucerne to Prague. After making his reservation, he called the office of Sinfonia Prague.

Nathaniel asked the man who answered the phone, "Pardon me, do you speak English?"

"Yes, yes. Of course. What do you want?" he asked impatiently.

"I'm an American author," Nathaniel lied. "I'm doing a biography of Vaclav Herza. I was wondering if I could do some research."

"He hasn't been here for forty years. Why don't you just talk to him?"

"Oh, I certainly will," Nathaniel extemporized. "I just need to do some background to know what questions to ask him. He's not a very patient guy, as you may know."

"I am the orchestra manager, not a historian. I am busy."

"If I came to your office, could you show me your archives?"

"When?"

"Tomorrow morning?"

"Okay, ten o'clock, but I am busy. What is your name? I must know to let you in."

"Nathaniel Williams. And what's yours?"

"Jan Hus."

"Like the religious reformist who was burned at the stake?"

"Yes, like that." Hus hung up.

The three other bunk beds in Nathaniel's train compartment were occupied by travelers who stared at him with inexplicable disapproval. Was it because he was American, black, very large, or simply a stranger? He could have predicted he would be assigned a top bed. In attempting to ascend it he managed to step on the arm of the lower occupant, which didn't help his popularity. Nor did his snoring, exacerbated by the discomfort of an unsupportive, undersized mattress. He arrived in Prague sleep deprived and uncharacteristically crabby, but at least the Swiss-run train was precisely on time, giving him the whole day to make headway on his detective work.

He took a cab to the Old Town Square, the Staroměstské náměstí. Most of the cafés had not yet opened, but he did find an information kiosk and purchased a tourist map of the city. He ambled about the square to orient himself and stretch his cramped legs before going to the office of Sinfonia Prague. Impressed by the Old World charm of the plaza in general, he was particularly engrossed by the fifteenth-century astronomical clock at the edge of the square, a magnificent combination of science and art that no one could dare attempt to reproduce in this day and age. One of Nathaniel's previous professional assignments had been to track down and retrieve an early-nineteenth-century Limoges table clock that had been stolen from an art museum in Cleveland. That piece had been valued at several hundred thousand dollars, so he could only wonder what the Prague clock was worth. There was little danger that a clock the size of a small apartment building would be stolen, but damage? As Nathaniel gazed upon it, admiring its aesthetic qualities, he suddenly realized that the clock, as a functional tool, was telling him it was almost 9:30. Finding an outdoor café nearby that had just opened for business, he quickly downed a boiled egg, muesli with yogurt and berries, toast, and several cups of strong coffee. He twisted the map around to align the clock in front of him with its location on the map and set off on his adventure, going across the square and making a right turn at a street called Železná. After a few more turns he found himself at the office of Sinfonia Prague and rang the bell—one of those old-fashioned ones you wind clockwise—in the middle of the locked door.

"Who is it?"

"Nathaniel Williams, to see Jan Hus," he said and was buzzed in. He ascended a half flight of stairs and followed an arrow to the left on which were scrawled the handwritten initials SP, and found himself at a small, spare office. The only person in the office was a young person—probably a man—sporting a spiky blue Mohawk haircut, nose and tongue rings connected with a gold chain, coin-sized plugs in his earlobes, a swastika tattoo on his forehead, and a cutoff black T-shirt with the enigmatic logo EGG PROJECT on it. He was leaning back in a swivel chair, with eyes that would have been staring at the ceiling had they been open. Czech punk rock blared angrily.

"Excuse me," said Nathaniel, loud enough so he could be heard over the din, "I'm looking for Jan Hus."

"I am Hus," said the young man, opening his eyes but otherwise not changing his position.

"The orchestra manager?"

"Orchestra manager, stage manager, business manager. I do everything around here."

"Well, thank you for letting me do this research. If you could just show me your archives . . ."

"This way," said Hus, snapping himself up from his chair. Nathaniel followed him into a windowless, poorly lit back room of chipped plaster walls and undulating wooden flooring. Unlabeled gray metal file cabinets lined two of the walls. Faded posters of past orchestra events in cheap frames with cracked glass were propped carelessly against the walls. The Formica table in the middle of the room had a carton on it with dust obscuring whatever was written on it.

"I go to lunch at one," said Hus.

"What's in the file cabinets?" asked Nathaniel.

Hus shrugged. "Who knows? I am not a librarian," he said, and left.

What now? Nathaniel asked himself. It was still possible he could make it back to Lucerne for the Mahler Second conducted by Claudio Abbado, a performance he was certain he would treasure. In order to tell Jacobus he had made an effort, he would take a cursory glance at the contents of the file cabinets, then hastily retrace his dusty footprints out the door.

Starting from the left wall and working clockwise, he quickly opened one drawer after another to get an overview of what was inside. There seemed to be no particular organizational rhyme or reason to the files, neither of chronology nor subject matter. Compounded with the fact that it was all in Czech whether written by hand or typewriter, Nathaniel didn't see anything that could be any help at all. Some drawers were so badly warped he was unable to yank them open.

The second-to-last cabinet proved to have something Nathaniel at least could understand: old concert programs. They weren't in folders, merely piled into the drawer. He pulled out a handful and quickly dismissed the hope that they had been stacked chronologically.

Nathaniel gathered up an armful of programs and, spilling some along the way, laid them upon the dusty tabletop. After retrieving a second load, he nosed around the remaining cabinets and, finding no others, spent the next hour organizing them, hoping something might be gained from that exercise. Herza had conducted the orchestra from its founding in 1945 until his departure in 1956, so Nathaniel decided that after 1957 there probably wouldn't be anything of value, but since the programs had been in disarray he examined all of them.

Many of the earliest programs were one-page affairs printed on cheap paper, containing only the barest information: the date, the music to be played, the name of the conductor—always Herza—and the soloists. As time passed, the number of annual concerts increased from a handful to over eighty, and the programs became more opulent, in booklet form on glossy paper with black-and-white photos. In 1951, the names of the orchestra musicians began to be listed, then names of sponsors—most prominently the Communist government, since orchestras in Soviet bloc countries were generally fully subsidized by the state—the history of the orchestra, and professional bios of the soloists and conductor.

It was this last that interested Nathaniel. Though he couldn't read Czech, he saw that all the later bios of Herza were identical, so he took one of them into the office. Jan Hus had resumed his catatonic pose, though the din of the rock music had disappeared.

Nathaniel cleared his throat. "Excuse me," he said, but there was no response.

"Excuse me," he said again, in a louder but still polite voice. Again, no response.

Nathaniel looked closer and saw that Hus was wearing miniheadphones. There was less than an hour left before Hus was going to take a break from his hard work and go to lunch, so Nathaniel approached him and lightly tapped him on the shoulder. Still nothing. Finally, Nathaniel shook him, if not vigorously, at least with definite purpose.

Hus's eyes slowly opened. He looked around, as if unfamiliar with his surroundings, and removed his headphones.

"What do you want?" he asked.

"Sorry to disturb you," said Nathaniel, "but I just wanted to ask you a question."

"What is it?"

"Could you translate this bio of Vaclav Herza for me?"

"I'm not an interpreter," he said. He reinserted his headphones and leaned back, closing his eyes. "I am the manager."

Nathaniel returned to the archives and sat down with the last few programs that Herza conducted, hoping he would be able to find something he could understand that might also be helpful.

The music on the programs included mostly standard, traditional repertoire, with extra-heavy doses of the big three Czech composers, Bedřich Smetana, Antonín Dvořák, and Leoš Janáček, and a formidable representation of Richard Strauss's five greatest tone poems, *Don Juan, Till Eulenspiegel's Merry Pranks, Death and Transfiguration, Also Sprach Zarathustra,* and *Ein Heldenleben.* There was a smattering of contemporary music of Czech composers whose names Nathaniel didn't recognize, and some Soviet composers whose names—Shostakovich, Khachaturian, Kabalevsky—he could, even when written in the Cyrillic alphabet. But all in all, nothing productive.

He looked at the roster of Herza's last few concerts, about seventy-five musicians all told, just enough to get by for all those Strauss works. He wasn't surprised that none of the musicians' names meant anything to him. Most of them were Slavic, with a good helping of German, who might also be Czech citizens, considering the long history of Teutonic domination of the country. His final exercise before packing up was to run his finger down the musicians' roster from concert to concert and try to glean something from that information. There was only one notable personnel change. In Herza's last concert, on November 17, 1956, the principal trumpet player of Sinfonia Prague was one Petru Mihaescu. Before that it had been someone named Klaus Jürgens. Nathaniel looked at earlier programs. Jürgens. Jürgens. Jürgens. As far back as he could find, it was Jürgens. It struck Nathaniel as odd that a conductor would change principal trumpets at his last concert. It was possible this Jürgens had simply gone on vacation, but typically in such a case the program would still have listed him. Maybe Jürgens had decided to retire when Herza left.

He went back into the office and with some trepidation roused Hus again, he hoped for the last time.

"What do you want now?" Hus asked.

"Do you know this Klaus Jürgens," Nathaniel asked, pointing to the name on the program, "or this Petru Mihaescu?"

"I am not a historian. I am the orchestra—"

"I know, you're very busy," said Nathaniel, holding out a ten-dollar bill that was expeditiously, if not graciously, pocketed by Hus. "But do you recognize either of the names?"

"Jürgens, no."

"But Mihaescu?"

"Old Petru. He still plays."

"In the orchestra? After forty years?"

"No, he is retired from orchestra. He plays in a café. Café Espoire."

"Do you know the address of the café?"

"I am not a secretary."

"Could you show me on my map?" Nathaniel pulled out his tourist map and a pen before Hus could say no. Hus scrawled an **X** on one of the side streets on the other side of the square.

"There. That is all I know."

"Thank you," said Nathaniel on his way out. He wondered how an orchestra with this kind of management could continue to exist. "You've been very helpful."

"I didn't expect a Negro," said Hus.

"And I didn't expect an . . ." Nathaniel left the rest unsaid. "Good-bye."

Nathaniel took a bus to the next stop on his agenda, the office of the newspaper *Pravo*. One of the main daily papers in the country, it had grown out of the earlier newspaper *Rude Pravo*, at one time a propaganda arm of the Communist regime that dominated Czechoslovakia from the end of the Second World War until the Velvet Revolution. After his meeting with Jan Hus, he had no illusions about making earthshaking progress.

He entered a no-frills, nondescript building that bore the company's name and found himself in a no-frills, nondescript newsroom. A lot of people appeared to be engaged with one thing or another, and possibly as a result of their preoccupation Nathaniel's presence went unheeded.

He was about to leave when a diminutive, ramrod-backed elderly woman approached him with tiny, piercing eyes, her bun of hair tightly bound and so white it was almost iridescent. Nathaniel would have described her as petite but she radiated too much of an aura of strength. The woman eyed him with what Nathaniel presumed was suspicion.

"Excuse me," he said, "do you speak English?"

"Of course," said the woman.

Here we go again, thought Nathaniel.

"My name is Nathaniel Williams."

"American."

"Yes."

"I am Elena Garnisova," she said, holding out her hand.

"I'm doing research on Vaclav Herza," he said. "I'm particularly interested in the period of time right before he left the country."

"In 1956?"

"Yes."

"Politics or music?"

"Both, I suppose."

"I imagine you don't read Czech."

"That's right."

"Then we have a problem."

"Oh?" asked Nathaniel, already resigned to this prospect. This assignment, this country, had been nothing but problems.

"I wouldn't be able to have translations for what you're looking for until five o'clock. Can you wait that long?"

TWENTY-SIX

Since retiring, Makoto Furukawa had alternated three outfits: there was the breezy comfort of his lightweight cotton *yukata* robe, perfect for the semitropical climate of Kyushu; the gardening outfit that somehow managed to remain spotlessly clean while he cultivated his plot and pruned his fruit trees; and his multipocketed khaki garb that, accompanied by his state-of-the-art equipment, he wore for fly-fishing on the stream that ran along the perimeter of his property.

He had not worn his blue suit, however, since his final day of teaching, when he had it cleaned and pressed before hanging it in his closet. Though he never planned to wear his suit again, a sense of loyalty prevented him from disposing of it. As soon as Cato Hashimoto had called him at the behest of Daniel Jacobus with his assignment, he knew there was a reason he had kept it. There was no question that he would honor his old friend's request, though the reasons for the task puzzled him. So he took the suit off the hanger and had it cleaned and pressed again. He was gratified that it still fit him, though now a little snugly. Walking down the dark side alley, puddled and dirty, in the notorious Roppongi district of Tokyo, he took special care that it remained immaculate.

Furukawa had taken the overnight, high-speed Shinkansen train from Nishi-Kagoshima Station to Tokyo, changing in Fukuoka when it arrived on the main Japanese island of Honshu. He slept well and comfortably, and had a leisurely, traditional breakfast of rice, *nori*, raw egg, grilled salmon, *nattō*—a fermented soybean mush—and green tea, before the train arrived at Tokyo Station.

His older brother, Daizaburo, met him at the station. The last time Furukawa had been in Tokyo was six years earlier, on the occasion of Daizaburo's retirement from his position as a cello professor at the Toho Music School. Upon seeing each other now, they bowed many times in sincere pleasure of their reunion, Makoto bowing slightly more deeply in deference to the elder brother.

They went to their favorite soba shop, Yamazen, that was older than both of them combined and where the noodles were still made by hand and the broth from scratch. In between their slurping and personal reminiscences, Makoto asked his brother about the object of Jacobus's inquiry, the maestro, Erutsa-sama, who had conducted many memorable concerts at the music school. Good manners prevented Daizaburo from inquiring about the reasons for his younger brother's curiosity. Makoto knew this would be the case and was grateful for it, because he did not want to involve his brother in a troubling enterprise in which important people could lose face.

Makoto learned little out of the ordinary. Erutsa-sama had been stern with the student orchestra, directing it with a firm hand, and produced remarkable results. The public always filled Suntory Hall and NHK Hall to hear him conduct the young musicians, a rare accomplishment in a city that boasted eight professional orchestras. When the maestro was in Japan conducting Harmonium, Toho students were given preferential treatment for tickets. There was nothing Daizaburo had to offer that suggested ill treatment by Erutsa-sama. No affairs, no rumors, and, thankfully, no suicides. Perhaps, he suggested, it was that the Japanese were more accustomed to authoritarian treatment and viewed harsh criticism more as an honor than a shame. Makoto shrugged. He didn't agree with Daizaburo on severe methods—even with a student as willful as Yumi Shinagawa had occasionally been, he recalled with a smile—but his brother might not be far off base in the characterization of the Japanese persona.

There was only one thing Daizaburo had to offer that was surprising. Erutsa-sama was enthralled with sumo wrestling. Makoto paused from his enjoyment of the cold sake that had been refreshing him on this hot, humid day and shook his head slowly, considering the possible ramifications of this revelation. He wondered aloud at the dichotomy between the diminutive musician, shorter even than the students he had conducted, and the huge Goliaths who wrestled.

Maybe that's the very reason, Daizaburo had replied. Maybe Erutsa-sama sees himself as a sumo in spirit. Makoto found this interesting—his brother had always been the perceptive one—but not helpful in any direct way. He asked if there was anything more he could find out about this.

"He always went to the tournaments with one of the pianists on the faculty."

"Maybe he can help me, then," Makoto said. "What's his name?"

"It's a she. Nagako Shimidzu," said Daizaburo, and, removing from the inner pocket of his suit jacket an electronic address book in the form of a smiling pink kitten that he had just purchased at the high-tech market in Asakusa, gave his younger brother Shimidzu-san's phone number.

And so Makoto had called Nagako Shimidzu, explained who he was, and invited her to tea. She thanked him profusely, the more so because she had to decline; she was busy with students all day until 9 P.M. She would be happy, though, to talk to him now, at least until her next student arrived.

Shimidzu-san had been a sumo fan since her childhood. She couldn't really explain why. She just found it an exciting change from the humdrum of teaching sixty students a week. But although she, too, was at first surprised at Erutsa-sama's interest in the sport, she was proud that a Westerner, and so famous a Westerner, would actually want to go to a tournament, so she was always more than happy to escort him to Kokugikan, Tokyo's national sumo stadium. Though she always offered, he never allowed her to pay for tickets, and that was good, too, considering the meager salary she received compared to the astronomical rent she had to pay for her fifteen-by-twenty-foot apartment that she shared with her piano and two cats in a suburb of Tokyo an hour away by train on the Ikebukuro Line.

Furukawa asked if there was anything in particular that Erutsa-sama found intriguing about the sport. She replied with one word, a name, actually: Chiyonofuji. Erutsa-sama was a fan, in the true meaning—a fanatic follower—of Chiyonofuji.

Furukawa understood the connection immediately. Chiyonofuji, the Babe Ruth of sumo, was also one of the shortest and lightest among all the wrestlers—only about two hundred forty pounds—but built of sheer muscle. Before a match started, it appeared inconceivable that he would be able to triumph against giants almost twice his size. But

Chiyonofuji used quickness, amazing strength, and astounding guile to push his opponents out of the ring, or even throw them to the ground. Most of all, he conveyed a sense of assurance and confidence that appeared to intimidate even other *yokozunas*.

Now Furukawa had some new insight into Erutsa-sama's personality, but to him it seemed that this trait would be a strength, not the thing that his friend Jacobus wanted to hear about.

Furukawa knew it would be impossible to meet Chiyonofuji himself but asked Shimidzu-san if there was a tournament going on in Tokyo. Unfortunately not, she replied. The last tournament had recently finished, and that one was in Kyoto. She then excused herself. Her break was over and her next student was arriving. Furukawa asked one final question. Sumo matches were all-day affairs. Did she and Erutsa-sama ever dine or seek any other entertainment together after the matches?

Erutsa-sama always went to the same club, she answered. On a side alley in the Roppongi. A high-class geisha house called Cin-Cin, Chéri. Of course, she had never gone there. It was for men only.

TWENTY-SEVEN

Jacobus lowered his violin from his shoulder. He had become listless being a puppet master, manipulating his friends to do the nasty work while he sat alone in the dark, waiting. Though he knew it was too soon, he hadn't heard a word from them and was becoming impatient. Repeated calls to the Berkshire Medical Center were deflected. On one occasion he was able to wrest from the bureaucracy the tantalizing but amorphous statement that O'Brien had shown signs of consciousness. What signs? he asked. Does that mean she'll recover? Whether he asked politely or abrasively, as was his inclination, they told him, "It's still too soon to tell." He asked whether she had spoken, but then they went back to their deflection. "Jacobus," she had said. Why?

To soothe his unsettled mind, he had turned to his most trusted antidote to a lifetime of anxiety, the violin. On this occasion, though, even the Adagio from Bach's G-Minor Sonata failed him. It was immaterial that Jacobus's technique was no longer what it used to be; the music usually poured straight from his soul. Was it his very vexation that led him unwittingly back to G Minor? Could even Bach fail to wrest his troubled mind from its preoccupations?

Before placing his violin back in its case, he cradled it to his ear. Though this eighteenth-century, rosin-encrusted violin made by Joseph Gagliano of Naples had borne witness to more than two hundred years of tears and torment, without Jacobus pulling his bow along its strings it remained mute, wholly incapable of communicating its wisdom and soul. Holding the violin, he felt its accumulated imperfections, like the wrinkles on his brow, and wondered at their cause. Was this jagged scratch on its back the result of simple carelessness, or was its owner an opera musician hurriedly finding his place in the pit before the curtain went up? The premiere of *Don Giovanni*, perhaps, in Prague? It would have been a brand-new fiddle then, and its owner might have cursed his coachman for getting stuck in traffic in front of the opera house and, in his distraction, ruined the glossy perfection of his new prize.

And what about that curious wear and tear that smoothed the edges along the right side of the scroll? That was not a one-shot deal. That would have taken years of placing the violin back in the same, slightly-too-small and off-center wooden case, maybe made by the violinist himself. That meant its owner was both dedicated and poor. Dedicated because he took the violin out, day after day, for years on end; poor because he knew it was a good instrument but couldn't afford a better case. How did this guy provide for his family? Was he a professional violinist back in the day? The village musician who played at weddings and harvest festivals? That would account for the poverty, at least. Or was he an amateur? A tailor who relieved the tedium of his life by playing Bach in the middle of the night? Was he Italian? German? Was he a he?

Too many questions. The violin knew all the answers but was not talking. At this moment, Jacobus felt a great kinship with the Gagliano, and for that reason, hated it. He needed revelations, not more mysteries. He deposited the instrument back in its prison and roughly latched the case shut.

Jacobus shuffled off to his bookshelf. With his cane in his left hand he used his right foot to clear a path among the piles of old music and records in his way. Though it had been years since he had thought about the book, he had a general idea of its location. It was one of the smallest and thinnest, and with age had also acquired the comforting odor of moldy leather. It wouldn't be difficult to distinguish it from the others.

He felt along the top shelf, just a little above his head. Yes, here it was, Nathaniel's gift to him. He removed it from its perch and inhaled to corroborate, erasing any doubt: *The Life and Death of Matteo Cherubino, "Il Piccolino," by Luca Pallottelli (ca. 1785), translated by Jonathan Gardner (1846)*, if he recalled the pretentious title correctly. It was the rare tome Nathaniel had unearthed that helped them solve the mystery of the cursed and stolen "Piccolino" Stradivarius back in 1983. Whether the legendary dwarf violinist, Matteo Cherubino, ever actually existed was still the subject of ongoing musicological debate, but there was no question that the book itself was a one-of-a-kind collector's item. Hell, Jacobus thought, I'm not being sentimental. This book's not doing me any good. Why keep the damn thing?

Jacobus blew some of the dust off the cover and wiped more of it away with his sleeve. He traced his newly blazed trail into the kitchen and recovered the piece of discarded butcher paper from the pastrami that Yumi had brought him. Luckily, it still had an edge of freezer tape on it. Jacobus wrapped the precious book in the paper and sealed it as best he could. Then he rummaged through a drawer containing a lifetime of assorted implements whose functions he could not recall, until he found a pencil, not a pen because he was not able to determine if a pen still wrote. He pondered what to inscribe on the package, then decided even if he could think of something appropriate it would most likely be illegible anyway, so he jammed the pencil back in the drawer and called a cab to take him to the Berkshire Medical Center.

Jacobus arrived at the front desk holding his small treasure in one hand and his cane in his other, and asked to see Scheherazade O'Brien in Room 421L. He knew how to get there, he told the receptionist, hoping that would tip the scales in his favor.

"Are we family?" she asked.

"Nah," he grunted. Then, "Yes!" he almost shouted. "Yes. We are family."

"We're not sure, though?"

"Extended family," Jacobus said. "We're the mother's father-in-law."

"In other words, we're the grandfather."

"Well, yes, in a manner of speaking."

"Okay. In a manner of speaking I'll find out if we're permitting her visitors, family or otherwise. Go have a seat against the wall to your left and we'll let you know. Do we require assistance?"

"No, we don't. How long will we take?" asked Jacobus, already impatient.

"A few minutes. Now go sit down, please."

Jacobus made his way to a bank of connected plastic chairs, and could discern which ones were occupied from the mutters he received. He came to one that sounded empty and with his hand felt that it was cushioned. When he sat down, however, the cushion began to jiggle. The laughter of the obese woman, on whose lap Jacobus quickly but not quickly enough realized he was sitting, was joined by the other patients sitting along the row.

Jacobus jumped up, cursing, and as he made his retreat, the woman's jocular voice bellowed after him, "Haven't had a man that close since my Milton kicked the bucket!"

Jacobus returned to the front desk.

"Goddammit, now can I go see her?" he asked.

"We're on the phone, sir, with a patient. Please be patient."

"What's your name?" Jacobus demanded.

"Waconah, sir."

"Well, Waconah, I'm going to file a complaint with your supervisor."

"Yes, sir. Here's the form. Just fill it out and pop it in the mail. No stamp necessary. And we'll let you know as soon as we can about visiting your granddaughter."

Jacobus walked in the opposite direction from the chairs until he reached the wall, and stood next to a watercooler. He thought about what he would say to Sherry when he saw her. He wouldn't be maudlin. He would be straightforward. Look, he would say, I want you to get better. Soon. Here's a book. If she wanted to talk to him, fine. If not, he would leave the book by her bedside and make his exit. Short and sweet. He just wanted her to understand.

"Sir," came the sound of Waconah's voice. Maybe she was calling to him. He tapped his cane in front of him like a Geiger counter that had found the mother lode and made his way to the desk.

"Yeah," he said.

"Ms. O'Brien's condition still hasn't stabilized. No visitors. None at all. We're sorry about that."

Back in his living room chair, Jacobus merely sat, having eschewed his violin in fear of being jilted a second time by the inability of music to assuage his angst. With little appetite for music or food, what else was left for him to do? Trotsky, sensing Jacobus's malaise, gave him a wide berth, tiptoeing the perimeter of the room as he panted his way to the water bowl in the kitchen.

Jacobus had anointed himself king of the chessboard, but now he felt powerless as a pawn cavalierly traded for the off chance of some future positional advantage, and which sat, an impotent spectator, at the side of the board. He ran his fingers through unwashed, tangled gray hair. He hadn't changed his clothes for days, and his sunken cheeks were rough with thickening stubble. He supposed he should attend to his hygiene. A shower, a shave, fresh clothing, would probably make him feel better, but he shuddered at the thought of shaving with that antiquated electric razor that buzzed raucously and hacked at his skin like a lawn mower with pitted blades, and so his inertia reigned. Oh, to be able to see, if only in order to shave with a real razor! But no, if there was one feat even he, the great Daniel Jacobus, would dare not attempt, it was shaving with a real razor.

He rubbed his steel-wool cheek, this time with some purpose. What thought had just flashed through his mind? Jacobus tried to dredge it up from the border of his awareness, like the theme from the second movement of an obscure Boccherini string quintet. Was it important? How could he know unless he retrieved it? He kept rubbing, hoping by that action to bring the thought to the surface. *Why is the thought of shaving hounding me?*

Jacobus dialed a familiar phone number.

"Roy," he said, "Sherry O'Brien didn't try to kill herself. She couldn't have. Someone else did it to her."

"Slow down, Jake," Roy Miller said. "I hope this isn't one of your famous hunches that can't be proved."

"Up yours, Roy! She couldn't have done it because the doctor said her wrists were so badly slashed that she couldn't move her fingers. That means once the first wrist was cut, it would have been impossible for her to cut the other."

The line was silent for a moment. "You might be on to something there, Jake."

"Check the blade that was found next to her. I'll lay odds it doesn't match the other razors she had in her hotel room. Then check to find where it might have been bought and see if a salesperson can ID—"

"I know what you're saying, Jake. Don't worry. We'll do the police work. Do you know who this someone might be, if your theory pans out?"

"I don't know for sure, but I have a famous hunch."

Jacobus dialed New York City information, but with the city's bucketful of new area codes was momentarily stymied until at length he was informed that Herza's was 718; this victory was offset by the additional notification that the number itself was unlisted. So Jacobus called information for the Harmonium office and after several sidetracks was put through to an administrative intern. By contriving a gruff accent of unidentifiable origin, Jacobus convinced her he was an official from the upper echelons of the Czech government requiring an urgent consultation with the maestro.

The phone rang. Even if O'Brien had cut herself, Herza had held the psychological scalpel in his hand and Jacobus had done nothing to prevent him from wielding it. But, he was convinced, Herza had been there, or at least his surrogate. Jacobus had second thoughts. Was he up to the task? Five times the phone rang. Answer the damn phone. She had called his name. Jacobus. She was right. He was responsible. Six times. Could Herza be away?

"Hello?" answered a voice.

"Who are you?" Jacobus asked.

"I am Lubomir Butkus, Maestro Vaclav Herza's personal assistant. Who are you?"

"I am Daniel Jacobus. I would have had my personal assistant call you but I gave him the day off."

"I have no days off."

"In that case, may I ask, Lubomir, where you were on Tuesday evening?"

"At my master's side. As always."

"And where, may I ask, was your master's side on Tuesday evening?"

"That is none of your concern. Or your business."

"May I have a word with Maestro, please?"

"I'm sorry. He only speaks to those he has requested. He's very busy."

"This is very important."

"Really, now. Maestro is resting. He's had an exhausting day of rehearsals and meetings."

"It's a matter of life and death. Really."

"Life and death? I hardly think so," said Butkus with a pretended chuckle.

"Look, you asshole," said Jacobus, tired of the toying, "the concertmaster of Maestro's orchestra may very well die because of Maestro. So I'm sorry if Maestro is inconvenienced, but if she should die because Maestro was too busy, you can be sure that Mr. Lilburn at the *New York Times* will be the first to hear about it."

"Please hold for a moment. I'll explain your issue to Maestro."

Jacobus heard conversation, but it was too soft and Jacobus could not make out the exchange. Butkus returned to the phone.

"Maestro says he is too busy. But," Butkus continued, suddenly whispering.

"But what?" snapped Jacobus.

"I have a favor to ask of you. I've heard of your reputation among musicians."

"What kind of favor?"

"I believe there is a plot against Maestro," said Butkus. "A conspiracy by the musicians."

"To do what? Throw him a surprise party?" asked Jacobus.

"To humiliate him. I don't know what they are planning, but I can tell there's something going on. A whispering campaign to do something at the opening of Harmonium Hall—to sabotage it—and I implore you to intervene and stop it."

Have I not spelled out my suspicions? Jacobus asked himself. Could this lackey be so delusional? Or, worse, could he in fact be innocent?

"Well, I hate to let you down, Lubomir, but if a little humiliation doesn't kill him, maybe someone else will." Jacobus slammed down the receiver, not for the first time.

TWENTY-EIGHT

In contrast to its bustling activity, the lights in Prague's Staroměstské náměstí were dim, and those that shone reflected in confused profusion off the puddles that had accumulated between the cobblestones during the day's drizzle. Nathaniel, standing in the middle of the square, turned his tourist map every which way. At night, nothing looked as it was supposed to. Whoever came up with name "square" for this asymmetric, multisided plaza must have had a rare form of dyslexia, he thought.

Again, he aligned the astronomical clock to his left with its enlarged facsimile on the tourist map. He then looked at the X that Jan Hus had scrawled for the Café Espoire, which was now to the upper left at the end of one winding street, and traced it back to an intersection with another that should theoretically empty onto the opposite side of the square from where he stood. He looked again in that direction; according to the map, the street he was seeking should be there, but all he saw was the obstructive side of a building—a church or museum, perhaps. He headed toward it anyway, hoping that his confidence, false though it might be, would be rewarded.

Nathaniel circumnavigated the church, for that was what it was, and came back to his starting point without finding the street he sought. He tried it one more time and halfway around came to an unlit alleyway, obscured by the evening mist. This must be it, he thought, though it could hardly be called a street. He followed it nevertheless, and within a few echoey steps was the only person in sight, a sudden and disconcerting transformation from the busy square. A few minutes later he came to an unmarked intersection, and on faith he turned left and hoped for the best. Most of the buildings—whether residences or businesses he couldn't tell—were devoid of activity and luminescence. Clearly this was not a part of town frequented by the tourist crowd.

The small lit sign two blocks away encouraged Nathaniel to quicken his pace. Café Espoire. Thank you, Jesus! As he approached the entrance, men's conversation emerged from within.

Nathaniel was greeted by the entrenched stink of beer, cigarette smoke, and urine, and took one step back. It was even worse than the Circle of Fifths, the bar that he and Jacobus were once invited to in New York City. There, at least, the aroma of garlic overpowered the less appealing smells. Visions of the clear blue waters of Lake Lucerne beckoned. He forced his feet to advance. Encroaching upon territory grudgingly ceded by two of the bar's bleary patrons, who viewed him with unabashed disapproval, he approached the bartender.

"Excuse me, do you speak English?"

"Speak English, speak Spanish, speak Italian, speak German, speak Czech, speak—"

"Is there a gentleman named Mihaescu that works here? A musician?"

"Petru? Yes, he is here, but I wouldn't say he works." The two boozers responded with a low rumble that Nathaniel interpreted as laughter.

"Can you tell me which one of these gentlemen he is?"

"Well, you see, I say he is here, but right now he is not here."

More rumbling.

"When do you expect him?"

"He is supposed to play at ten, so come back at eleven. Maybe he'll be here by then."

Nathaniel looked at his watch. He had almost two hours to kill until ten.

"What do you recommend I do between now and then?"

"Sit. I bring you a Pils."

"Maybe I'll put a hold on that for when I come back," Nathaniel said, convinced by the stale air and stale company of the prudence of going elsewhere. "What about in the meantime?"

"What do you like? Girls, shopping, sightseeing, girls, music, clubs, art—"

"Music. I'm a music lover." Thinking back upon his earlier meeting with Jan Hus, he asked, "Is Sinfonia Prague performing tonight?"

"Why them?" The bartender sounded dismissive. "They don't start until October, anyway."

Nathaniel thought for a moment. "Would there be a production of *Don Giovanni* going on by any chance?"

"Sure! There is always *Don Giovanni* in Prague. First performance of *Don Giovanni* was here in 1787. Mozart loved Prague. Was his second home. There is an estate—"

"Could you show me on the map where the performance is?"

Nathaniel produced the map from his back pocket. It had already become frayed, soggy, and bent to the contour of his imposing buttocks, but he didn't think it was in all that bad condition for the time it took the bartender to find the venue.

"There!" he finally said, pointing to a spot on the other side of the square. "*Don Giovanni,* every night. The tourists love it."

Nathaniel thanked him and left quickly, only in part because the performance started in less than a half hour. He hoped tickets were available.

Fifteen minutes later, Nathaniel was among the approximately one hundred patrons squirming in cramped seats in an auditorium whose shabbiness was not totally cloaked by poor lighting. Before the remaining light was extinguished, he opened the file that Garnisova had given him at the *Pravo* office. There was surprisingly little from

1956, which Nathaniel chalked up to the vagaries of time; the file thickened as it plodded toward the present. Garnisova, bless her heart, had also included recent articles relating to the negotiations among the Prague government—which had donated the funds for the construction of Freedom Bridge—New York City, and the builders of Harmonium Hall. Though everything Nathaniel browsed through was interesting, it shed as little light on the assignment with which Jacobus had entrusted him as the feeble house lights that shone on the meager results of his day's labor. Closing the file, Nathaniel readied himself for the world-famous Prague production of *Don Giovanni*. Performed by puppets.

The overture began, played not by a live orchestra but by a recording. The recording was old and worn and the amplification questionable. Nathaniel sighed and looked at his watch. The curtain went up, revealing a wooden Leporello, Don Giovanni's right-hand man, lamenting his station in life and wishing he were a real gentleman. The comic lightness of the short aria, sung by a marionette backed by a miniature set of a grand palazzo, brought a few amused chuckles from the audience. Then suddenly, Don Giovanni and Donna Anna, who has just been assaulted by Don Giovanni, rush out in a frenzy. Donna Anna's father, Il Commendatore, appears, seeking revenge, and, in a one-sided sword fight, is slain forthwith by Don Giovanni. It all happened so fast, with such tumult, that Nathaniel forgot he was watching string-manipulated dolls. They seemed to have come to life with personalities of their own, and the torment was palpable. This was no lighthearted children's adaptation. Donna Anna's plight aroused a striking degree of pathos; Nathaniel sat back in his seat, intrigued, and watched with rapt attention. So adept were the puppeteers, it seemed that the marionettes were able to change their facial expressions. Nathaniel could easily recall much more wooden acting at the Met.

By intermission, however, he had had enough. His bulk threatened to overwhelm his flimsy chair's ability to support him, and as much as he appreciated the creativity of the production, the actions of the characters on stage had become repetitious. Nathaniel decided that the ghost of Il Commendatore would have to drag Don Giovanni into hell's abyss without his moral support.

Nathaniel had no difficulty finding his way back to the Café Espoire, partly because he was familiar with the route, but also because he now had Mihaescu's music floating on the night air to guide him. He checked his watch. The band was actually ahead of schedule.

He took a corner seat, ordered a pilsner, and observed Mihaescu and his trio. The traditional folk music that formed the core of their repertoire was punctuated with arrangements of the Largo from Dvořák's "New World" Symphony and Mozart's *Don Giovanni,* and of international plums like "Condor Pasa" and "Raindrops Keep Fallin' on My Head," which prompted Nathaniel to request another beer. One of the musicians, a skinny young man hidden behind baggy, tattered clothing and a halfhearted beard, switched from string bass to drums to keyboard, while an older, stocky gentleman wearing a red vest, red fez, and red face alternated on clarinet, accordion, and panpipes. Mihaescu, eagle nosed, in an old wool jacket with elbow patches and sporting a black beret on his wavy graying hair, had an assortment of trumpets, cornets, and flügelhorns at his disposal. Nathaniel, a former musician, noted how cleverly the aging trumpeter allowed his two cohorts to do the heavy lifting while he preserved his embouchure, playing short, easily executed midregister phrases and taking frequent breaks to moisten his chops with a glass of beer, scrupulously monitored by the bartender to make sure it was never empty. Mihaescu's sound had a light, pleasing clarity, relieving any doubt Nathaniel had that he was the classically trained musician he was seeking.

"Petru?" Nathaniel asked, as the group took a cigarette break after a rousing rendition of "Climb Ev'ry Mountain." "Petru Mihaescu?"

"Yes?" asked the trumpeter.

"I've really enjoyed listening to you," Nathaniel said truthfully. "Can I buy you a beer?"

"Why not?" Mihaescu said, taking a seat opposite Nathaniel. "Mind if I smoke?"

"Go right ahead," said Nathaniel. Though he did mind, what difference would the smoke of one more cigarette make to the omnipresent haze? He signaled the bartender for a beer.

"Tourist?" Mihaescu said, sizing up Nathaniel.

"Sort of. I was just at the Lucerne Festival, and this is my first time to Prague."

"No doubt, then, you've seen the puppet *Giovanni* and are now taking in our internationally celebrated nightlife." Mihaescu gestured grandiloquently to his shabby surroundings.

Nathaniel laughed. "I guess you know the routine."

"I happen to be on that recording. Of the puppet production."

"Really?" Nathaniel was surprised to hear that. It also saved him ten minutes of finding an entrée to get Mihaescu to talk about his orchestra experience.

"A fine orchestra. You're a man of many talents, Mr. Mihaescu," he added.

"Hmm, yes I am. Call me Petru." Mihaescu took a long drag of his cigarette, blew the smoke up to the ceiling, and followed it with his eyes. "Yes. Sinfonia Prague, that record. When they were still good, back in the sixties."

"May I ask why you left the orchestra to play . . ."

"In a smelly club, you mean?"

"I didn't mean that in a bad way," said Nathaniel.

Mihaescu shrugged. The beer arrived. Mihaescu lifted the glass and effortlessly downed its entire contents. He wiped the foam from his mouth with his sleeve.

"The real story is how I came to play in that orchestra in the first place." Mihaescu left that morsel dangling and concentrated on his cigarette, holding it vertically in front of him and peering intensely at it, as if it held some unspoken secret.

"And?" Nathaniel prompted.

"And now I have said enough," said Mihaescu. "My cigarette is finished, which means it is time for me to go back to work."

"When's your next break?"

"When I need another cigarette."

"Would you like another pilsner to go with that?"

"If that's how you want to spend your night in Prague, who am I to argue?"

For forty-five minutes, Nathaniel listened to the music with one ear while studying the clientele. Business wasn't exactly brisk, but there were enough customers to sustain the café's existence. Most, he gathered, were local. A few touristy-looking types seeking adventure off the beaten track stuck their heads in and, quickly sizing up the unlikelihood of a Kodak moment, retreated back to the main square.

Nathaniel hadn't eaten much during the day, so while Mihaescu was doing his late shift he took the opportunity to order the *knedlo, zelo,* and *vepřo* that he had seen on the menu of virtually every restaurant he passed. In a few minutes he was served a large dish of bread dumplings, sauerkraut, and roast pork. Though Nathaniel was full when he finished the meal, he was only half satisfied. The food had been appetizing in concept, but like the music, it was somewhat bland, slightly greasy, and, like many good things repeated ad infinitum, uninspired. He decided against ordering the warm apple strudel, even though it came highly recommended in the trio's performance of "My

Favorite Things." Maybe he should have ordered the schnitzel with noodles.

Scattered applause acknowledged Mihaescu's group when it finished its final set with a *Phantom of the Opera* medley and woke Nathaniel, who had had a long two days, too much beer, and a leaden dinner. Not wanting to appear ungrateful, he quickly joined the applause.

Mihaescu arrived at Nathaniel's table with two half liters of pilsner in his hands.

"Since you are buying," he said, "I have saved you the trouble of having to order."

"Thanks for your thoughtfulness," Nathaniel said. Mihaescu returned to his previous chair as if it had been reserved for him.

"Not at all. I will tell you the story of how I got into Sinfonia Prague, and I promise every word is true."

"No doubt."

Mihaescu lit another cigarette, sat back in his chair, and took a long draft of his beer.

"I am from Romania, you know. I was born there, grew up there, studied the trumpet there. In those days it was all government control. Everything. You couldn't breathe without government knowing. With music, if someone heard a kid with talent, government would say, 'Kid, you have talent, you go study with x, y, z. You will make Romania great.' You didn't argue because maybe in the end you could get a better job than cleaning streets. Kids who could play string instruments they sent to conservatories in cities. Kids who played trumpet like me, or horn or trombone, they send to schools out in the country. You guess why?"

"I don't have a clue."

"Noise! Just imagine a school full of kids blowing their brains out playing lousy brass instruments eight hours a day! They figured, 'Put

them out in the countryside where only the cows can hear them.' So
I spend ten years—no family, no friends—making Romania great."

"Did you get a job?" Nathaniel asked.

"Job?" Mihaescu made the gestures of laughing, but no sound
emerged. "There were no jobs! There were no jobs because people
couldn't afford to buy a ticket to a concert, because *they* had no jobs.
But, you see, you weren't allowed to say that, because if you said that,
you would be shot."

"Surely you're exaggerating."

"Okay, I am exaggerating," Mihaescu said. He slammed down his
glass, which was empty, and stood up.

"Sorry," Nathaniel said. "I didn't mean to offend you. How about
another beer? Are you hungry?"

A bowl of goulash and potato dumplings and a plate of stale rolls
arrived with the pilsner. Mihaescu ate in silence, dipping the bread
into the goulash and ignoring Nathaniel until he was almost finished. He dropped his spoon onto the table, splashing gravy onto its
grimy surface, and downed half his beer.

"I crossed the border—don't ask me how because I won't tell you—
because I hear that in Prague you can find work. I play in this club, that
club," he continued. "Finally they hire me here, Café Espoire, with
two other guys, one Czech, one Hungarian. The work is steady. I don't
mind it doesn't pay so well. The food is free. The beer is free. We can
talk to each other, even about politics, but not too much. Compared to
Romania, this is heaven. Maybe not heaven compared to heaven, but
it's okay."

"But you needed something more? Is that why you joined the orchestra?"

"No and no." He finished his beer. "Would you be kind enough to
order me another?" he asked. "It's a long story and you see I get dry."

When Mihaescu had fortified himself, he continued.

"It happened like this. One night, some tall, ugly guy comes in and asks if I want to be principal trumpet player of Sinfonia Prague."

"Just like that?" asked Nathaniel. His waning attention was suddenly aroused. He leaned forward.

"Just like that," said Mihaescu, who, as if on cue, suddenly became more animated. "I get in his car and he drives me to the conductor, Vaclav Herza. You heard of him?"

Nathaniel nodded emphatically.

"I go to his apartment. Herza says to play, so I play what do I know from student days, the Haydn trumpet concerto—what else am I going to play, 'Never on a Sunday'?—and after a few measures, Herza, who is reading the newspaper the whole time, says, 'Very well. You'll do.' When now I look back, I think Herza already knew he was leaving Prague."

"And when was that? When did he leave?" Nathaniel asked, his fatigue a thing of the past.

"Two weeks later. It was big surprise."

Nathaniel felt he was on to something. "Why? Why was it a surprise? Did he give any reason?" He tried to keep the flow of conversation free and easy, and mask his greater interest in Herza.

Suddenly Mihaescu began to fidget. He wiped his face with his hand. He ran his fingers through his hair. He looked in every direction except at Nathaniel.

Nathaniel rephrased the question. "Do you think it had anything to do with Klaus Jürgens leaving the orchestra?"

"I need another beer. Then I talk," said Mihaescu.

Nathaniel shelved his growing impatience. The beer was cheap. He had time to spare. And he was on the verge. Possibly. He just needed to get Mihaescu to open up.

When the old trumpeter again appeared sated, Nathaniel assured him that anything he had to say would be held in strictest confidence, and to level the playing field he told Mihaescu, in general terms, why he was inquiring after Jürgens and Herza.

Mihaescu's probing eyes, seemingly unglazed by drink, looked directly into Nathaniel's. "Vaclav Herza was a Soviet informer," he said, his voice level.

"Tell me more," Nathaniel said, trying to remain calm.

"You see, in 1956 the Soviets invaded Hungary. That was the time of the freedom movement, but then the tanks came to Budapest, and the hope ended. Everywhere."

Mihaescu paused. Nathaniel nodded, conveying sympathy and understanding, silently urging him to continue.

"Maybe you wonder what that has to do with Prague," Mihaescu continued, picking up Nathaniel's unspoken cue. "You see, Soviets knew if freedom could break out in Budapest, it could break out in Prague. Then who knows where? So they form a network. A network of informants."

"But," Nathaniel interrupted, "Vaclav Herza was known for just the opposite. He fought for Czech independence."

Mihaescu looked at his beer for a moment.

"Exactly!" he said, slapping the table. "Who better to have as a spy? Herza mixed with the intelligentsia, the liberals, the artists. There used to be a club, called . . . called . . . Sonja's Bar, on the other side of Charles Bridge. That's where they all met. Not for music, for political. That's where Herza would go to get his information and then pass it on to his masters."

"Did Klaus Jürgens go to this bar also?"

"Sure! Klaus liked to drink, like all trumpet players."

"So if Herza was a valuable informant, why did he flee?"

"Because Jürgens was one of his targets. Jürgens tried to organize the musicians to form a collective. A union. So they would be paid a

living wage. So they would be treated with respect and not like crim-
inals, the way Herza treated them. Jürgens was a true Communist!
Not a Soviet Fascist Communist. Herza would not tolerate Jürgens
organizing the musicians of his orchestra, so he betrayed him to the
KGB."

"You still haven't answered my question."

"It happened so long ago. Some parts of it are hard to remember.
Ah! Now I remember. One night, at Sonja's, Jürgens overheard Herza
passing information to his contact, and he suddenly realized what
Herza had been doing all along. He also realized he now had power
over his boss. He threatened Herza to expose him but made him offer: I keep my mouth shut, you give better treatment for musicians.
But he played his card wrong. Herza fired Jürgens instead, telling the
world that Jürgens was a drunk and couldn't play no more. But he also
still worried he would be exposed, so he runs."

Something didn't sound right to Nathaniel. There was certainly
nothing in the file from the newspaper to suggest Herza was a traitor.
Quite the contrary. He sat back and tapped his fingers on the table.

"That's an amazing story. Can you corroborate this?" he asked.

"I AM NO CORROBORATOR!" roared Mihaescu.

"No, no, no," said Nathaniel. "Calm down. I just mean, is there
someone else who can verify this information? After all, you joined
the orchestra after Jürgens had already left, and Herza was gone shortly
after that. Is there anyone still in Prague, still alive, who was actually
in the orchestra when all this was going on?"

Mihaescu stared blankly at the wall.

"Would you like another beer?" asked Nathaniel.

"That's very kind. There's Geitz," said Mihaescu calmly.

"Geitz?"

"Victor Geitz. He's still alive. He played clarinet. Bass clarinet and
E-flat clarinet. Sometimes saxophone, for *Pictures at an Exhibition* or

Rachmaninov 'Symphonic Dances.' He joined in the forties, retired in seventies."

"Do you have his address? Phone number?"

"I don't. Ask Sinfonia Prague."

Nathaniel didn't relish another conversation with Jan Hus but resigned himself to its likelihood.

"And why did *you* leave the orchestra?" he asked Mihaescu.

"Because of look in eyes."

"Look-in eyes?"

"A lot of orchestra musicians, they don't want to admit when they're finished. I was one of them. But then, after the concerts, I see the look in their eyes—my colleagues' eyes. They were good colleagues—they never say a word. But I look at myself in mirror, and I say, 'Petru, you are getting old. Your lip is going. Your pitch is sagging. You cannot hit the high C in *Zarathustra*. You're not sounding the way you used to.' So I tell my friends and my boss, 'It is time.' They give me a big party and a small pension, and now I'am back in the café."

Nathaniel reached across the table and shook the musician's hand.

"Well, thank you for your time," Nathaniel said. "I appreciate the information."

"Yes, we had a wonderful time fishing together," Mihaescu said brightly.

Nathaniel was a little confused. Perhaps Mihaescu was speaking metaphorically. Maybe it was a poorly translated Czech idiom.

"Yes, we did," Nathaniel said, smiling. He pulled his wallet out of his pocket to get a credit card to pay for the food and all the beer.

"Yes, when you hooked that bass! I never saw a bass fight like that before!"

"No?" asked Nathaniel.

"Never. He tugged that skiff ten, fifteen minutes, at least! But you stuck with it. You landed him. How many did you catch that day? I caught some little ones, some cod, some mackerel, and a John Dory, but you got the big ones!"

"You sure you're not mistaking me for someone else, brother?" Nathaniel asked. Perhaps there was another overweight, overage American black man he had fished with.

"Mistake? I don't think so. I remember it like yesterday. The tide was going out and the sun was just coming up. You brought the coffee, and I brought the beer, as usual. We headed out. The skipper said we were going for grouper, but we didn't have a bite for an hour, so then . . ."

So that he wouldn't have to wait any longer, Nathaniel put his credit card back in his wallet and left cash on the table. He uttered a polite good night to Mihaescu, still reminiscing with bleary eyes over the big one that got away, and left in haste.

TWENTY-NINE

The multicolored flashing neon lights were reflected by puddles, which Makoto Furukawa, in his polished dress shoes, judiciously circumvented. The rain had stopped, but the torpid night remained intensely humid and clammy. The back alley in the Roppongi district of Tokyo, which, like many streets of its type in this endless city, had no name, was so narrow that a single car could hardly manage its way through. "Sidewalks" demarked by a painted white line were ignored by the congestion of revelers and automobiles alike. Nevertheless, the serpentine alley was unnaturally bright with signs of hundreds of nightclubs, stacked one on top of the other in nondescript three- and four-story buildings, keeping the night at bay. Navigating his way through the multitudes, Furukawa kept on the lookout for the rice shop with an antique brass scale in the window that Shimidzu-san told him was the landmark, above which, on the third floor, was his destination. It was no small feat searching for a brass scale at night while dodging drunken businessmen careening toward him, street vendors hawking their goods, and the puddles. Furukawa felt like a character in one of the arcade games at the pachinko parlor he had just passed.

Distracted by a small crowd surrounding a street vendor, an ancient woman selling freshly grilled seafood at a kiosk lit by a single bulb enclosed by a white paper lantern, Furukawa almost walked right past the darkened rice shop. It was only when he stopped to smell the rich aroma of the fish that he spied the brass scale in the window. He looked up and spotted the small red neon sign for Cin-Cin, Chéri among countless others. Finding the door to the club was no problem because as soon as he looked up, a hawker beckoned him to enter.

Furukawa ascended a clean but utilitarian stairway to the third floor and knocked on an unmarked door. It was opened by an elegantly adorned geisha, whose inviting smile said *We have been looking forward to your arrival for so long* even though he was an unexpected stranger. He entered a small, tastefully furnished, incense-infused room with a half dozen or so small round tables, each occupied by one or two businessmen obviously enjoying themselves, catered to by at least as many solicitous kimono-clad geishas. The extravagant design and brilliant colors of the kimonos flowed in the room's discreet lighting as smoothly and continuously as the whiskey being poured at the tables. The geishas' physical beauty was enhanced by their complex makeup, their graceful motions, and their velvety voices.

Furukawa had not been to a geisha parlor for many years. Kagoshima was the closest city to his village, and though they had clubs there, none were on a par with something like this. He knew that nothing overtly sexual was to be expected at a geisha parlor. It was a highly respectable, if highly sensuous, form of refined entertainment, but standing in the foyer, he felt like a fish out of water, like one of the trout he'd caught in his stream that lay flapping in his creel.

A lovely young thing approached him, welcoming him to Cin-Cin, Chéri, and asked him if he would like a seat. The geisha touched his forearm, melting him instantly, and he followed, powerless, to the one remaining empty table.

Within moments, Furukawa was joined by two other geishas, bearing small delicacies and a large bottle. One wore a golden kimono with an intricate floral design and green obi. The other's was sky blue with suggestions of clouds. They, too, welcomed him, their hero, and as they sat by his side, attentive to his every need, he shortly found himself comfortably boasting to them of his greatest accomplishments, divulging to them his most intimate secrets, as if his new partners had been his closest, lifelong confidantes. They listened on tenterhooks to his every word and asked just the right questions, and though he knew it was all a façade, he felt happy to play the role. The one on his left, in the sky-blue kimono, sat close, and from time to time suggestively made contact against his thigh with hers, as if by accident. He knew otherwise. As the one to his right, in the golden kimono, reached across the table for the bottle, she gently placed her hand on his other thigh, and as she poured whiskey into his glass, she "inadvertently" exposed the bare nape of her neck. Furukawa, who couldn't recall the last time he was so aroused, almost forgot why he had come.

Little by little, Furukawa told the tale he had rehearsed on his way to the Roppongi, a narrative about his relationship with Erutsa-sama that combined fact with fiction. It was, he said, upon Erutsa-sama's recommendation that he had come to Cin-Cin, Chéri. The geishas were delighted. Did any of the young ladies know him? he asked. The geishas looked at him quizzically. Did Furukawa detect a sense they were making fun of him? They responded that they themselves could not remember him—this surprised Furukawa, because he had described Erutsa-sama's disfiguration, and there were few enough Westerners who would know of this club, anyway—but they offered to bring their boss to talk to him.

One of the geishas peeled herself from the group without Furukawa even being aware of it. The remaining geisha continued to entertain him. That Western notion of geishas being prostitutes, thought Furukawa, was so wrong. So . . . Western. These women exhibited no skin, hardly touched him, and were not there for sex. They simply made men feel wanted and admired. What more could one ask for?

A man in a very expensive suit approached, and the geishas wordlessly departed. Furukawa was surprised, having expected the boss to be another woman, an elder "graduate" of the program.

"I understand you're interested in this Erutsa," said the man. Furukawa found this stranger's informal directness impolite and off-putting.

"Yes. Erutsa-sama highly recommended your club—I assume you're the boss—and since this is my first time here, I was just wondering if there was anyone, in particular, that he liked." Furukawa let the innuendo linger.

"I see," said the boss. "He did have his favorites. Pussy Willow, but Pussy Willow died."

"Died! And so young?"

"If you're beaten to death, you can die young. A horrible thing. Then there was Lotus Bud. Yes. I'd say Lotus Bud was his favorite. But that was years ago."

"Does Lotus Bud still work here?" Furukawa asked. Perhaps she was a link to some of the unsavory behavior Jacobus was seeking proof of.

"Not anymore. They come and they go. Most of them are from the Philippines or Southeast Asia. It's harder and harder to get them in Japan these days, believe it or not."

Furukawa didn't know whether to believe it or not and couldn't think of a productive way to proceed. He would have offered a bribe for more information, but that might offend such a wealthy-looking man.

"Do you have an address for Lotus Bud? Do you have her phone number?"

"Her?" said the boss, wide-eyed. His face tightened. Then he looked away. His body began to convulse, and, though he attempted mightily to contain it, he started laughing out loud.

Furukawa was highly offended, especially after being treated so royally by this boor's employees. When he had been a teacher, his usually docile demeanor could change on a dime at the first hint of disrespect, and he would let the student know in no uncertain terms that such behavior was unworthy of anyone he was willing to teach and reflected poorly on the student's entire family for having been brought up to act so thoughtlessly. He had never encountered such loutish behavior from any student even in private as he was now confronted with in public.

"May I ask what's so funny?" he asked.

"Don't you know?" He saw the look on Furukawa's face, a combination of anger and utter bewilderment that made him laugh even harder. "You don't know! Lotus Bud is a boy! All these geishas are boys!" His laughter, unrestrainable, burst into a raucous bawl, attracting the attention of all the customers.

Furukawa threw some money down on the table, a lot of money. Racing out, his face burned red, while his erstwhile companions covered their mouths with hands and fans, partly out of politeness to disguise their tittering, but at the same time letting Furukawa know that was precisely what they were concealing.

Furukawa exited the building and glanced in each direction to make sure no one recognized him. He took several deep breaths, wondering what to do next. The limit of his obligation to his friend Daniel Jacobus had been reached, if not exceeded. Was there anything else, within reason, that he could or should do in this wild-goose chase? He looked around him, into the bustling underworld of late-night Tokyo, seeking direction.

THIRTY

Was that a ray of light through the fog of my depression? Lilburn asked himself. For the first time in his career he had missed his deadline, so irrationally obsessed with Jacobus's narrative that he had lost his own. After throwing a silent, personal tantrum, he came to the cathartic realization that not all was necessarily lost; he now had an additional day to find the anchor to his story that might, in the end, enable him to write with a natural fluidity that was currently forced and artificial.

"Hello, Mr. Nowitsky? This is Martin Lilburn from the *New York Times*, and before you hang up, I am not writing a story on the contract negotiations."

"Then I don't have to decline to comment."

"I am writing a story on the history of Harmonium to run tomorrow, for the opening of Harmonium Hall. Let's see, you've been associate concertmaster—"

"Twenty-three years."

Information offered! thought Lilburn. The ice was thawing. "Yes, thank you. And I thought you could give me some perspective on the changes that have taken place."

"I suppose. Give me a f'rinstance."

"Well, I understand that since your longtime stand partner, My-ron Moskowitz, retired, there had been an ongoing search for a new concertmaster."

"Yes, and we have found one. Miss Yumi Shinagawa."

"Can you tell me about the process that resulted in her selection, please?"

"Sorry, I can't comment on that."

"Even in a broad perspective?"

"Mr. Lilburn, you must know very well that in order to avoid com-promising the fairness of auditions, everything about them has to remain confidential. If it got out how candidates played—and let's face facts, all but one of them loses—we'd never get anyone to show up. It's even our policy to not tell the candidates themselves how they played, let alone the media. And if the committee's opinions were leaked, ev-eryone on it would clam up. So while I respect your desire as a re-porter to find things out, I can't comment any more about that."

"Even though I've heard through the grapevine that Sherry O'Brien's audition was given short shrift by Maestro Herza? What if that got around to violinists in the orchestral community?"

"The music director has the authority to hire and fire. It's in our contract. I invite you to read it."

"And that O'Brien is in the hospital with self-inflicted wounds?"

"Sherry's a respected colleague and we wish her all the best."

"How do you get along with Sherry O'Brien?"

"What does this have to do with the history of Harmonium?"

"Human interest. Musicians are people, not just performers. They play tennis, garden, cook Italian food, go to the bathroom, like other humans. Who they really are is something that would be of interest to the reading public."

"Sherry and I get along very well. She's a very private person. Not outgoing, which you wouldn't expect from her playing."

"Did you meet with her socially, outside the orchestra?"

"I don't know what you mean by that. I'm a married man. I have grandchildren."

"My apologies. No innuendo intended. I was just wondering if you spoke of subjects other than music."

"She opened up to me from time to time."

"About?"

"I can't comment on that."

"Of course. What's her current condition?"

"I don't know, and if I did I wouldn't tell you."

"Have things like this ever happened with members of Harmonium before?"

"Things like what?"

The interview was going backward quickly. Pretty soon he would be out the door again and it would close. Lilburn changed the subject.

"As associate concertmaster, no doubt you've been on many audition committees for string players. When I attend concerts, I see there are a growing number of Asian musicians in Harmonium."

"That's true of every orchestra these days. Even in Europe."

"It seems more in Harmonium than elsewhere. How do you account for that?"

"They play very well and their preparation for auditions is unexcelled."

"Yes, I'm sure, but could Vaclav Herza's connection with Japan and the Toho School have something to do with it?"

"No doubt."

Maybe this would lead somewhere. "Could you elaborate?"

"If you were a student at Toho and had Maestro Herza guest-conduct you, wouldn't it be your dream to become a member of Harmonium?"

"Is there nothing more than that, do you think?"

"Of course there is. We're the highest-paid orchestra. Who wouldn't want to come?"

"I was thinking of something rather more personal, perhaps."

"Then you'd have to ask the Asian musicians themselves."

"Perhaps I shall, then, at some point," said Lilburn. "Thank you."

"Think nothing of it," said Nowitsky. "I look forward to reading your story."

Lilburn hung up and then dialed the number for Vaclav Herza he had obtained when he had set up the bungled Tanglewood interview, finagled out of one of Harmonium's innocent management interns, a soprano who, upon graduating from Wesleyan, suddenly realized she had no career in music. The line was busy. On a hunch, he quickly redialed Nowitsky's number. That, too, was busy. Lilburn spent a few minutes considering the implications of that unlikely coincidence and what it portended for getting anything more out of Herza. He dialed Herza's number again.

"Yes?" came the instantly pugnacious voice of Lubomir Butkus.

"This is Martin Lilburn of the *New York Times*."

"Maestro has no intention of speaking to you further."

"Oh, but it's not Maestro to whom I wish to speak."

"No? Then whom?"

"You." Make him come to me, thought Lilburn. Curiosity will get the better of him. And ego. Lilburn stayed mum, against his natural inclination.

"Me? Why?"

"For my story on Harmonium."

"What could I have to say of any value?"

"You've been Maestro's personal assistant for decades."

"I have no comment about my work for Maestro."

"No, and I wouldn't seek to impose. It just seems to me that without you, Lubomir Butkus, Harmonium could never have existed."

"What do you mean?"

"Well, how could it have functioned? I've been following the orchestra since its inception, and who else has been there since day one other than Maestro? You. Only you. You have seen to Maestro's every need. I can give you the list of everyone who has said so." Lilburn hoped Butkus would not ask for the nonexistent list. "You have been the battery that makes the clock tick. If you hadn't been there, day in, day out, everything would have stopped. Your story is the perspective I've been seeking for mine: Harmonium seen through the eyes of the one person who has seen it all."

"I never thought of it like that."

"You have been on all the tours, have witnessed the great triumphs."

"Yes, I have."

"When Harmonium hired you, had you ever met Maestro?"

"I don't understand."

"Let me rephrase: Did you have an idea of your demanding obligations when you first started working for Harmonium?"

"It wasn't like that at all. You are all wrong."

"Enlighten me, then."

"I worked for Maestro long before Harmonium. Many years. I was with him in Prague. Even before. He chose me from the others because he knew I would never betray him."

"He 'chose' you?" Lilburn scolded himself for interrupting a source on a roll, a rookie mistake. Who were "the others," though?

"Never mind. In those days I did everything for him. Even more than now. I was his secretary, his manager, his valet, his driver."

"Yet you weren't with him on the occasion of his car accident." Lilburn slapped himself on the forehead. What an idiotic comment. How could he expect someone to respond to that other than to say, "Fuck you"? No wonder the *Times* had put him out to pasture.

"With that whore?"

"DiFiori? His fiancée?"

"She wanted his money, his fame. He was smart to get rid of her."

"Are you suggesting—"

"Never mind. It was an accident. End of story."

Lilburn needed to keep the stream flowing. "You no longer drive for Maestro. Why did you stop?"

"He had other needs that only I could attend to. Harmonium found the driver sixteen years ago."

"Donaghue."

"Yes."

"It sounds like you don't approve of him."

"I am in no position either to approve or disapprove. Maestro finds him satisfactory. Whatever satisfies Maestro, satisfies me."

Lilburn had what he wanted but kept the conversation going to be sure Butkus stayed in the dark.

"If I may ask, how do you view the current contract negotiations between Harmonium and the musicians? Do you think it jeopardizes the opening of the new concert hall?"

"Maestro has had many enemies, because they had no vision, and Maestro has always prevailed. This time will be no different. It will be his greatest triumph."

"May I quote you on that?"

"What if I say no?"

"I still might."

Butkus hung up.

———

An hour later, Lilburn found himself at the last place he wanted to be, a bar, but he was meeting the person he most wanted to speak to. Paddy Donaghue was now walking through the door, so it was worth the trade-off. Shea's Lounge on Spring Street was one on a list Donaghue had proposed, his familiarity with the place evident from the mumbled greetings he received from patrons and tavernkeeper alike. Though Donaghue was off duty he was always on call, and because his pager might go off at any time with a command to attend to Maestro's needs, Lilburn had bought Donaghue his pint of Murphy's in advance. He disregarded the bartender's smirk when he ordered sparkling water with lime for himself, fondling a Butterfinger in his pocket and congratulating himself for the strength to abstain from stronger libation.

Over the years Lilburn had seen Donaghue a few times, assisting Herza in or out of a limo by the artists' entrance to Carnegie or Avery Fischer. Now he saw the man out of uniform for the first time. Unlike the stereotypical image of an aging blue-collar Irishman, Donaghue had maintained an athletic build and had well-trimmed short hair and alert, probing eyes, ready to do business. He had already informed Donaghue what the subject of discussion would be when he had phoned him earlier.

"How many years have you driven for Herza?"

"Sixteen."

"And before that?"

"I was a security guard. You could check it out."

"That's okay, I believe you." Lilburn had already checked it out. "How would you characterize your relationship with Herza?"

"I drive him where he wants to go. Harmonium pays me."

"That's it?"

"That's it."

"It sounds to me like there's no love lost between the two of you."

"If I may say so, it sounds to me that you're being a wee bit ungrateful."

"Ungrateful? How so?"

"He keeps the likes of you stiffs in business, writin' your reviews and all, and here you are, trying to nail the man to the cross."

Sitting in this seedy bar with his deadline approaching, Lilburn was losing his patience. He rued the moment he vouched for Daniel Jacobus at the Tanglewood rehearsal. Next time, if there is a next time, he'll tiptoe surreptitiously around Jacobus and the old curmudgeon will be none the wiser.

"I do what reporters do. Ask questions. I know not where a story leads until I get there. If *you* want to compare Vaclav Herza to the Messiah, it's on your conscience, not mine."

Donaghue laughed. "You've got the tongue of the Irish, have you now? My dear mother couldn't have put me in my place better than that. Okay, I'll tell you. If you want to be treated like dirt, you'll have no better employer than Vaclav Herza."

"The musicians have been saying that for years. There's nothing new there."

"Ah, the musicians!" Donaghue shook his head and sucked on his beer for fortification. "For a bunch of poofters and wankers, they're not a bad lot, those lads."

"Meaning?"

"All bark and no bite. Most of them, anyway. If they had it in them, they could stand up to the man."

"But should they? Herza is an insufferable ass. Everyone knows that. It's hardly an indictable offense."

Donaghue drained the remainder of his pint.

"Maybe, but someone just tried to kill him for it and almost saved me the trouble."

This was more than Lilburn had hoped for, or even wanted to know. He was supposed to be writing a story about a symphony orchestra, for Christ's sake!

Donaghue related the incident of the charging Taurus without sharing who was behind the wheel. Lilburn took down the name of the officer on the scene, but otherwise Donaghue stonewalled. After all, no one was injured, and Harmonium replaced the Lincoln with a newer model.

"Well," Lilburn reflected, "regardless of his extraordinary level of hubris, this could make Herza out to be a would-be martyr, couldn't it?"

"And that doesn't please you. You've got your own personal ax to grind with the man and you're going for the jugular, then, are you?"

Lilburn considered his motives but, as a journalist, did not want to lay them all on the table for public consumption. "Another beer?" Lilburn nodded in the direction of Donaghue's empty glass.

"No, thank you. One's enough. I never know when I'll receive the calling."

Lilburn smiled in response. "You tell me, then. What's the elephant in the room I'm not seeing?"

"You see, I'm Herza's *official* driver. Butkus is Herza's *unofficial* driver. I take him to rehearsals, concerts, meetings, appointments . . . wherever he needs to go . . ."

"And Butkus takes him to places where he doesn't need to go."

"You catch on fast, laddie."

"Such as?"

"The sluts. Such as."

"Prostitutes, you mean?"

"The worst of the lot. They don't even have pimps. That's why I call them sluts."

"Why, do you suppose? He's got the money for the best."

"It's what suits him. He goes for the filth and doesn't always make nice to them."

"Have you seen any of these girls?"

"Not just girls."

"I stand corrected. Have you seen—"

"No. I haven't seen anything. That's Butkus's terrain, as I said. He finds them, sets up the time and the place, and then does the driving. Neither party gives their real name, and it's never the same lay twice. They clean up well after themselves, those two. I'll grant them that."

"How do you know all this?"

"As I said, I've been by Maestro's side for many a day, and before that I was in security. My dear mother taught me to keep my eyes and ears open, and not even Marcel Marceau could keep a secret like that from me for long."

"Anyone else in on the little secret?"

"The boys who work at Herza's apartment building. They wouldn't be heartbroken to see the maestro get his comeuppance."

"I don't have time right now for all the gory details," Lilburn said, sliding an envelope across the table, "but how much of this can be proved?"

Donaghue didn't even glance at the envelope. A real pro.

"Not a word, at least by me. Not a word. I've told you what you wanted to know, and it's Christ's honest truth, but what you do with it is out of my hands."

Donaghue rose, followed by Lilburn. Donaghue slipped the envelope into a pocket and shook Lilburn's hand.

"Yes, that was the deal," said Lilburn. "But what I find baffling is why, for a man of his station, of his renown, Herza would go to such lengths just for sex."

"It's not about the sex, man. Don't you see that? It's about the power."

Back in his office, Lilburn popped the last Godiva into his mouth and decided he had reached an appropriate terminus for his efforts on Jacobus's behalf. A for effort. A-plus maybe. So what if the results would never stand up in a court of law? He at least had gleaned some nuggets of information he could polish and use for his story, so it wasn't a total wash, was it? He dropped the empty candy box into the waste bin and began to write, when the phone rang. It was Lieutenant Malachi.

"Is it about the car accident?" Lilburn asked.

"Oh, I heard about that accident. Hit-and-run up in Riverdale. That's penny-ante stuff. Minor damage. No charges filed. What I've got for you is the scoop of the century, Lilburn. Are you ready for this?"

"Hold on." Lilburn threw his notepad onto the desk and clicked his pen open. "Go ahead."

"In 1964, Vaclav Herza was cited for possession of marijuana."

"That's it?"

"That's it."

"Was he at least convicted?"

"His lawyer convinced the case officer, one Michael T. Washington, that it was only to relieve the pain resulting from his car accident injuries. It appears from the report that it didn't take much convincing. Washington didn't even fine him. You want his phone number?"

"Never mind. And thank you for trying, anyway."

"It was nothing. Literally. And say hi to Jacobus for me."

THIRTY-ONE

The group of drunken businessmen that earlier surrounded the ancient woman's kiosk had departed and Furukawa was now able to take a closer look at her. Shrunken and hunched over, she needed to look up in order to see straight ahead. She was toothless, and her translucent skin had so many wrinkles they obscured her facial features. With random gossamer strands of white hair doing little to disguise an otherwise bald head, she was the living embodiment of the tiny antique ivory netsuke ornaments that Furukawa had begun collecting when he retired. He caught himself staring and, realizing that the woman was aware of his scrutiny, approached her food stand.

"I'll have the scallop, *oba-san,* please," he said, though he had no appetite.

"*Hai, dōzo!*" said the woman, bowing so low that her nose almost touched her knees. Her bow flowed uninterrupted into a bend toward the cooler, out of which she scooped a live scallop. The mollusk was larger than the left hand in which she held it; with a knife in her right, she deftly pried open the resisting bivalve's shell. Discarding the top shell into the trash, with a pair of tongs she held the other that contained the still-living scallop over a Bunsen burner. With a small ladle in her free hand, she poured a few drops of homemade broth onto the scallop until the sauce began to bubble. She removed the shell from the fire and handed it to Furukawa along with a pair of chopsticks.

Furukawa devoured the scallop almost as quickly as it had been prepared. He removed his handkerchief from his suit pocket and wiped his lips.

"This is one of the greatest delicacies I have ever eaten," he said, almost forgetting his dreadful experience at Cin-Cin, Chéri.

The old woman bowed and smiled.

"I have been in this very spot for more than fifty years," she said, "and have had many customers whose grandchildren now visit here. If I may ask, you are from Kyushu?"

"Yes. How do you know?"

"Your accent. My family home is also Kyushu. Near Kagoshima. But I have not seen my home for many years."

"I, too, live near Kagoshima! My name is Furukawa. Makoto Furukawa." He handed her his business card, which she examined with appropriate thoroughness.

"Ah, Furukawa-san! The violin teacher?"

"Yes, I am."

"Ah, sensei," the old woman exclaimed and began bowing deeply and repeatedly. Furukawa responded in kind. "My daughter," she continued, "Mariko Taniguchi, she studied violin with you many, many years ago! Do you remember her, please?"

Furukawa had no recollection of the name. He had taught hundreds, perhaps thousands, of students over the years, many of little talent, and concentrate as he might, he could not remember a Mariko Taniguchi.

He didn't have the heart to be honest, so he said, "Ah, yes, she played the Beethoven Romance in F Major so beautifully!" Having required almost all his students of even modest ability to study that piece until they could play it reasonably well, he felt he was on pretty firm ground. "What is she doing now?" he asked, to change the subject.

"She is a grandmother! She has two sons and a daughter. The eldest son . . ."

Furukawa listened to the life story of the former student he couldn't remember with great attentiveness, not once looking at his watch, even though late-night subway service would terminate any moment now and he'd have to spend ten times the subway fare to take a cab to his hotel.

Finally, after discussing the possible future prospects for her sixth, and youngest, granddaughter, Furukawa said, "I am honored to have heard about your remarkable family," and acted as if he were preparing to leave.

"You have been to Cin-Cin, Chéri, I see," said the old lady.

"Yes, I have," said Furukawa, unprepared for such a direct statement, but relieved that it would save twenty more minutes of polite conversation before it would be appropriate to bring up the subject.

"I was looking for a man, a foreigner with a disfigured face and who walks lopsided."

"Ah!" said the old woman. "Erutsa-sama! He went to Cin-Cin, Chéri, every time he came to Tokyo."

"And how would you know?" Furukawa asked, immediately regretting the rude tone of his question.

"Because," she said, pretending not to notice the affront, "my daughter went to all of his concerts, and he is a hard person not to recognize."

"Did he usually go to the club alone, do you remember?"

"Not alone. Always with his own driver, another gaijin, who waited in his car and blocked traffic and hurt my business. Gaijin can be so impolite. Just because they won the war—"

"And when Erutsa-sama left the club, was he alone?"

"No, he always left with a geisha, who he would bundle into his car and drive off. Not once did he buy my scallops."

"Was it always the same geisha?"

"Yes, it was the same. Named Lotus Bud."

"Do you know this geisha?"

"I know them all. Poor things. But Lotus Bud has been gone for many years. Disappeared, I'm told." She sighed. "Did you know they're all boys?" she offered.

"Of course." He wasn't lying, he told himself. He had known for almost an hour.

"And did you know they're all prostitutes?"

"Of course. Has Erutsa-sama been back here lately? I would be happy to recommend that he visit your stand."

"I am very honored, Furukawa-sensei. But I have not seen him for years, either."

"Well, then, that is his loss. Now, how much do I owe you for your delicious meal?"

"It is my gift." The ancient woman raised her watery eyes and looked directly at Furukawa. "For remembering my daughter among your countless students."

But for a few tottering businessmen caroming into the side of a garbage can or a building, the street was still, and most of the neon signs had been switched off, depriving the puddles of their borrowed light. The old lady stored her wares and folded down the sides of her kiosk to be rolled away to . . . Furukawa had never thought about where the vendors disappeared to during the day, but the moment to ask had passed. It would be something he would probably never know.

A question occurred to him. Had Lotus Bud disappeared after one of his liaisons with Erutsa-sama? He gazed up at the unlit window of Cin-Cin, Chéri. To avoid the further humiliation of returning there to inquire, he convinced himself that it was closed. He looked one way, then the other down the alley, searching for something to do next, but like the path of his search, the alley was dark, revealing nothing.

THIRTY-TWO

It was Lilburn on the phone.

"What have you got?" asked Jacobus.

"I've got bad news, bad news, and bad news. Which do you want to hear first?"

"No wonder the *Times* dumped you. How about starting with the bad news?"

"I thought you'd ask that. I missed my deadline because of all the checking I did for you on Herza."

"So?"

"So it means the story didn't run today. It runs tomorrow."

"Why's that bad?"

"Tomorrow's Saturday, the slowest day of the week, and the hall opening is tomorrow night. The impact of the story will be a mere ripple instead of a tsunami."

Jacobus couldn't have cared less. "What's the bad news, then?"

"The bad news is I couldn't find anything to pin on Herza. Abusive, yes. Shady, yes. I found that out from every source I talked to, and believe me, I talked to everyone. But criminal? No, unless you call paying for sex a crime. I even went to our friend Lieutenant Malachi and persuaded him to back-check police files. Over all these years there was only one formal complaint ever filed against him."

That might be enough, thought Jacobus.

"For what?"

"Smoking a joint."

"Okay," said Jacobus. "You're two for two. Now tell me the bad news."

"The bad news is that I can't include any uncorroborated nastiness about Herza in the article, except for one thing."

"Go on."

"I refer to a high level of stress at Harmonium due to Herza's heavy-handed insistence on perfection, and its effect upon the musicians. I let the readers connect the dots in the hope they'll conclude what you and I already feel about him."

"That sounds good to me. Why's that bad?"

"Because I had to provide concrete evidence. I had to mention Sherry O'Brien's traumatic experience . . ."

Jacobus began to squeeze the receiver as if it were Lilburn's neck.

"And," Lilburn continued, "I made reference to the source of my information. I had no choice."

Jacobus lowered the receiver. That was an improvement. In the past, he would have slammed it down.

The cab pulled up to the entrance of the Berkshire Medical Center.

"That'll be thirty-one dollars and ninety cents."

"What?" asked Jacobus in disbelief. "Last time it was twenty-nine."

"It's after eleven. Night rate's a ten percent surcharge. Regulations."

"You give senior citizen discounts?"

"No. Just frequent flyer miles."

From a wad in his pocket Jacobus counted out thirty-two singles, the only way he knew to make sure he had the correct amount. He counted them a second time—despite the cabbie's growing irritation—to double-check.

"Here," Jacobus said, handing them over to the driver. "Keep the change."

"While you're at a hospital," said the driver, "get an attitudectomy."

"Get a real job," Jacobus said and slammed the door.

Cane in hand, gift in pocket, Jacobus circled his way through the revolving entrance of the medical center, determined to elude the clutches of the medical establishment that had barred his way to Scheherazade O'Brien's bedside. Now that she would be named by Lilburn, there was even greater urgency for him to prepare her for probable media exposure from the *Times* article. If it were at all possible, he would also make his peace with her. He walked directly toward the front desk, ready to do battle with Waconah.

"Oh, so it's you again," came the voice he was hoping to hear.

Jacobus attempted to respond, but no sound emerged. His mouth opened and closed repeatedly, like a fish out of water. His legs began to tremble. He flung his cane to the ground and, panting, clutched his throat. He let out a hoarse moan and crumpled to the floor. Twice his right leg kicked spasmodically, then he lay motionless, save for a moment of vestigial twitching of his fingers.

A security guard was already at his side.

"He has a pulse," the guard called in Waconah's direction. "Get a doctor here fast."

Waconah picked up the intercom. "Calling Dr. Howard, Dr. Fine. Come to the front desk, stat!" She repeated the message with greater urgency but keeping her voice level so as not to alarm any patients.

The two interns rushed into the lobby and had Jacobus, still unresponsive, placed on a gurney and wheeled into the emergency room. A nurse wired him up to monitors. Dr. Howard checked his vital signs, which revealed a weak pulse and reduced breathing capability.

"Jeez, this guy must've done three packs a day for fifty years with lungs like that," said Dr. Howard, placing an oxygen mask over Jacobus's nose and mouth. "I'll be damned that he's still alive."

"No kidding," said Dr. Fine. "You'd need an auger from Roto-Rooter to unclog his arteries."

Dr. Howard removed Jacobus's glasses, and with thumb and fore-finger pried open his eyelids to check for pupillary response.

"Shit! Look at this! The guy's blind as a post!"

"Yichh! What do you suppose? Advanced glaucoma?"

"No, it's just a little eye jam."

"Don't be sarcastic. Is he comatose?"

"I'm not sure. He seems conscious but is totally unresponsive."

"Stroke?"

"Could be. He definitely needs to be kept overnight for observation."

"Yeah, maybe. But check first to see if he's covered."

"Good idea."

Dr. Fine rummaged through Jacobus's pockets and found his wallet with his Medicare card in it.

"Guy's name is *Jac*obus or Jac*obus* or something like that."

"Hey, wait a second. Isn't he that geezer who lives down by Great Barrington?"

"You mean the violin crackpot who solves murders?"

"Yeah, that one. I think it's Jac*obus*."

"Nah, no way this one could be him. This guy's a definite loser."

"Yeah, but we should cover our ass, just in case. I say he's a keeper."

"I guess you're right."

They wheeled Jacobus through the hospital to a semiprivate room, where an orderly removed Jacobus's street clothes and dressed him in a hospital gown. He was then reattached to monitors.

"What do you give him?" the orderly asked. "Twelve hours?"

"I'll lay odds no more than ten, Larry," said Dr. Howard.

"I'm not so sure," said Dr. Fine. "With today's technology, we can keep a stiff like this alive indefinitely, even if he stays a vegetable. But one way or another, I'd say there's as much chance he leaves this hospital alive as his getting his sight back."

The others grunted their assent.

On their way out the door, Dr. Fine asked his colleagues, "Hey, did you hear the one about how Helen Keller burned her hand?"

THIRTY-THREE
SATURDAY

As the night progressed into early morning, the hospital corridors became hauntingly quiet. The good doctors Howard and Fine, having completed their shifts, had long since departed for their new homes in Williamstown and a weekend of golf. It was only when the efficient humming and beeping of Jacobus's monitors was all there was to be heard that Jacobus, who had lain motionless for as long as he could endure, bolted upright and tore the life-sustaining tubes and wires from his body.

"Idiots," he said. He scrambled down from his bed, intent on dressing as quickly as possible and getting to Room 421L. Searching for his clothes, he bumped into a walker and decided it would be better to roam the halls in his drafty hospital gown. After all, hadn't the fair Waconah admonished him to "be patient"? She just left out the article, and if they have to see my hairy ass as a result, that's their problem.

The walker had tubes on it, which he fastened to his arms with strips of tape still sticking to him. As he maneuvered his way out the door, he bumped into a rack upon which his clothes were hanging. He extracted the biography of Matteo Cherubino from his pants pocket and sequestered it under his armpit.

Jacobus entered the vacant hall and forced himself to move slowly, the recuperating patient taking a midnight stroll. An elevator door opened and shut, and as he headed for it, he was approached by the person who had just emerged from it.

"How's it going?" the man asked Jacobus.

"As my father used to say, I'd rather be rich and healthy than poor and sick."

The man laughed. He asked, "You need a hand?"

"Nah!" replied Jacobus. "Doctor says we need to learn to do this on our own."

"Tough love, huh?"

"Yeah. I'm going to try an apple a day and see if I can get rid of him."

"You got the idea. Well, have a good one."

Jacobus found the button for the elevator and pressed it. Inside, he felt for the Braille on the panel and pressed 4L. Leaving the elevator, he fingered the numbers on the doors of the first two rooms he came to in order to determine his direction. Miraculously, no one questioned him. No one noticed him. He arrived at 421L, opened the door, and entered. The same snoring patient confirmed Jacobus's accuracy in locating the correct room. He rolled his walker to Scheherazade O'Brien's bedside and switched to a chair in order to sit close to her. He found a space on her bedside tray table to put the book, which somehow was no longer important to him. He could hear her breathing and leaned forward. He didn't want anyone else to hear what he was going to say. It didn't even matter if she heard him.

"Sherry," he said quietly. "You and me, we're a lot alike. More than you know. We need each other." He stumbled for a moment. "Actually, I need you more than you need me. You need me like a hole in the head. Once you're better you'll see that there's plenty you can do. Look at me, for example. 'Blind as a post,' that stooge of a doctor said. But I'm still here, sawing away. Life in an orchestra ain't all it's cracked up to be, anyway." He took a deep breath. "I'll make it up to you. I'll make it *all* up to you. Don't you worry."

Jacobus found Scheherazade O'Brien's hand. He held it gently because of the wounds. It was bigger than he had remembered, and harder. Swollen, no doubt. Strangely, it wasn't bandaged. Jacobus's touch roused the sleeping form.

"What the fuck?" said the man in the bed.

"What?" asked Jacobus. "Who are you?"

"Who the fuck are you, you fucking pervert?" said the man, his hand still in Jacobus's clutches.

"Nurse!" the man screamed. "Nurse! Get him the hell away from me!"

Jacobus was paralyzed with shock. He felt his arms roughly grabbed from behind.

"What are you doing here?" voices demanded, rousing Jacobus from immobility.

"Where is she?" he yelled. "Where have you taken her?"

"What are you talking about?"

"O'Brien! Scheherazade O'Brien! Where is she?"

"O'Brien?" said a female voice, more calmly. "I'm sorry to say the patient O'Brien died earlier this evening."

THIRTY-FOUR

Not everyone had Internet service, so the musicians of Harmonium relied upon a traditional phone tree to contact each other in the event of a crisis or a breakthrough in the contract negotiations. Each of the eight members of the orchestra committee called four other musicians, who would in turn call two others. The message the musicians were accustomed to hearing at the eleventh hour was that after long and intensive bargaining, the orchestra committee and management had come to a tentative agreement, and there would be a ratification meeting scheduled imminently. What they were told this time, though, was more shocking than they could have imagined. As a result, the meeting on Saturday morning at 10 o'clock in the unfinished musicians' lounge of Harmonium Hall was fully attended. Lawrence Nowitsky, acting chair of the committee, made the announcements.

Number one: Sherry O'Brien was dead. She had not been able to rally from her extensive self-inflicted wounds. An effort was being made to contact the family in order to arrange a memorial service. Those who might want to participate, either to speak or to perform, perhaps the Adagio from the Samuel Barber String Quartet, should let the committee know.

Number two: Tiny Parsley had refused an order from Vaclav Herza to fire his brother, Junior, so at Herza's explicit insistence Adrianne Vickers fired them both for insubordination. According to the terms of the orchestra's CBA, because Junior was fired for cause, he had no recourse to file a grievance. Tiny, as a member of the staff, had no recourse to begin with. Neither was permitted onto the premises, even to remove his belongings.

Number three: Within an hour after firing the Parsley brothers, in a maneuver undoubtedly engineered by Herza, Vickers was informed by J. Comstock Brundage that, after a vote of no-confidence by the board of directors, her services as CEO of Harmonium were no longer required. She was offered the choice of being fired or resigning; if she chose the latter she would receive a generous severance package and a positive reference in her future job applications. She chose the latter. Once the ink was dry, Vickers was permitted to remove her personal belongings but not her files.

Even the Mega-Herzas were outraged by this stunning turn of events. Having lost their committee leader, personnel manager, and CEO in a single Stalinist purge, the equilibrium of the entire organization was shaken to its foundations. Everyone's career was now in jeopardy, and as they discussed the ramifications of all that had transpired from the moment their music director had imperiously pronounced the winner of the concertmaster audition, their rage coalesced onto the one man in whose hands all power now resided: Vaclav Herza.

From out of confused, impassioned dialogue, two basic issues arose: one, what to do about the contract negotiations; two, what to do at the opening concert that night to signal the musicians' discontent and disapproval.

The union's attorney, Cy Rosenthal, suggested that with the loss of bargaining leadership on both sides of the table, the musicians propose to the board that they and the symphony society mutually agree to freeze all provisions of the contract until such time that constructive negotiations could resume. If nothing else, that would at least provide chairman of the board J. Comstock Brundage an opportunity to learn something about symphony orchestras while the trustees searched for a new CEO. Rosenthal felt confident that the board would agree to such a proposal.

Discussion then turned to Herza's treatment of Sherry O'Brien and the need to convey a unified message of the musicians' outrage. One possible protest that gained traction was for the musicians to sit on the stage of the new hall on opening night and, in front of the full house, refuse to play as a demonstration of solidarity for Sherry O'Brien and the Parsley brothers, and maybe even for Adrianne Vickers.

Rosenthal cautioned the musicians that such an action would be a violation of their CBA, which prohibits a work stoppage during the term of the contract, and they could all be legitimately threatened with termination for following through with that plan. He added that, especially after proposing to extend the contract, to violate its very provisions would seem hypocritical.

There was nothing to prevent individual musicians, however, from calling in sick, Rosenthal suggested. Certainly, everyone felt heartsick over the events. Maybe enough empty chairs would send the same message. Maybe the concert couldn't go on if enough musicians called in.

"That's chicken shit!" shouted Cappy. "I say it's time we looked Herza in the eye as a group! I say we sit there. If some of you can't take it, go ahead and play. But I say we show we've got balls and let the audience decide who's got the moral high ground."

Cappy's speech was greeted with cheering and applause, including Beanie's unprecedented agreement. Nowitsky asked Cappy if he would like to reword the the statement in the form of a motion. Rosenthal suggested that, as the action was to be based upon each individual's conscience, no motion or vote was required. In fact, he warned against one. The union should not and would not dictate to the musicians as a bargaining unit a means of violating a legally binding contract. Each musician was on his own, followed by the dictates of his conscience. Nowitsky, as a personal gesture, said he would refuse to sit in the first chair, that it should remain vacant to honor the memory of Scheherazade O'Brien. Again the musicians applauded. Nowitsky called for a motion to adjourn, which was made and seconded, voted upon, and passed unanimously.

THIRTY-FIVE

Nathaniel, unaware of the death of Scheherazade O'Brien, continued his investigation. He had less trouble finding Victor Geitz than he had Petru Mihaescu. After awakening in a hastily booked bed-and-breakfast not far off the square, Nathaniel called Jan Hus. When Hus professed to have no idea how to find Geitz—"What do you think I am, a . . ."—Nathaniel asked for the address where the old clarinetist's pension checks were sent.

Later that morning he arrived at the Prague City Home for Convalescents, an unprepossessing late-nineteenth-century brick edifice that, before being converted into its present incarnation with fire escapes as prominent as flying buttresses, might once have had some charm.

Nathaniel stopped at the unattended reception counter and tapped the little service bell. After a few minutes, a very broad, austere woman—the word "matron" immediately entered Nathaniel's mind—wearing a white uniform and an old-fashioned nurse's cap approached the counter from the other side. She gazed at him from head to foot, sizing him up.

"Good morning," she said in English. "How can I help you?"

"I'm looking for Mr. Victor Geitz," Nathaniel said. "I'd like to talk to him."

When she looked at him questioningly, he added, "Only a few minutes."

"That is not the problem," said the woman. "You obviously do not know him. Mr. Geitz does not understand English."

"Oh. How thoughtless of me not to have assumed that," Nathaniel apologized.

"Perhaps I can help you," said the woman. "Please tell me the nature of your visitation."

Nathaniel explained that he was writing a book about Vaclav Herza and wanted to get a firsthand account from someone who'd actually played with Herza before he left the country.

"I will accompany you," said the woman. "Visitors are required to have supervision in any case. I am Martina. Follow me." Nathaniel caught himself from saluting and saying, "Aye, aye, sir." She pressed a buzzer and lifted up a hinged section of the counter to grant Nathaniel access.

He followed Martina up a wide, sweeping staircase to the second floor, which she called the first floor, then up another, this one narrow and rickety, to the top floor. They entered a large sunlit room occupied by a dozen or so pajamaed elderly men and women, some engaged in quiet activities, others by their own unfathomable thoughts. A few sat in cushioned love seats or in wheelchairs, reading newspapers or magazines. Others maneuvered in walkers with oxygen tanks attached. Two men sat at a table with a pachisi board on it, though neither contestant was moving. No one seemed to take note of Nathaniel's arrival.

Martina pointed to a skinny man lost in baggy striped pajamas, sitting in a plain wooden chair and gazing through one of the large sealed windows upon the inaccessible outside world. Nathaniel could see only the back of the old man's head, his thin white hair combed as well as could be hoped for over a multitude of age spots.

"Victor," Martina said with quiet authority, then continued in Czech.

Geitz responded by tapping his fingers on the arm of the chair.

"I told him he has a guest," said Martina. "He will see you, but he tires easily, so try not to exhaust him. Five minutes."

They arranged their chairs in front of the window so that Geitz could see them. "V. Geitz" was embroidered on the old man's pajama pocket. Martina took his hand in hers and explained to him the unlikely presence of the big, black American who was here to visit him.

Geitz immediately became highly animated, talking in a rush, and clutched at Nathaniel's hand. Nathaniel feared the man was babbling.

Martina smiled. "Victor is excited. He says this is the first time in twenty years someone has asked him about his music. He says that Vaclav Herza was the greatest of all conductors, that the years he played with him, music was raised to the highest level. He was very sad when Herza left the country. He says he felt abandoned—as if someone had taken a part of his soul."

Nathaniel said, "Please ask if he knows why Herza left."

"To flee the Communists—he means the Russians," Martina said. Nathaniel could tell from Geitz's tone, if not the words, that he assumed this to be common knowledge.

"I heard rumors that Herza was a collaborator," said Nathaniel.

Martina relayed the statement to Geitz, hoping that Martina translated with the subtlety he intended.

At first Geitz played possum, pretending to contemplate his navel, but Martina gave his hand a squeeze and repeated the question.

Geitz's response was dismissive.

"Victor says everyone was like that. It all depended on which way the wind was blowing, and the wind was blowing in all directions at the same time. If there was someone you didn't like, he was a collaborator. If you liked the Soviets, he was a hero. The only ones who didn't blow with the wind were Dubček in '68 and Václav Havel."

"How did Herza treat the musicians?" asked Nathaniel.

When he heard the question in Czech, Geitz began to laugh with a wheeze that reminded Nathaniel of Jacobus, except it was about two octaves higher, like air squeezed out of a balloon.

"Victor says Herza was a real tyrant, especially for such a young man. The orchestra was much more frightened of him than of the Russians. Herza believed that if you wilted under his reign of terror then you were no real musician."

"How did he treat the women in the orchestra?"

Geitz looked confused.

"What women?" Martina translated.

"Does Mr. Geitz remember a colleague, a trumpet player, named Klaus Jürgens?"

Geitz spoke for some time, interjecting a light cackle here and there.

"Victor says that Jürgens was one of the great trumpeters of Central Europe, but then he began to drink a lot—Victor says like all brass players—and his playing descended. Jürgens was given special treatment by Herza—and by this I think Victor means harsh treatment—but not only did Jürgens maintain his individuality as a musician, he made much effort to organize the musicians into a union, and that was not tolerated by Herza."

Nathaniel noticed that Geitz had begun to slump, and the grip on Martina's hand had slackened.

Martina said, "It is time we go now. Victor is tired."

"Just one more question please. Please ask Mr. Geitz if he knows where I can find Klaus Jürgens. Did Herza fire him, or did he retire, or go to another orchestra after Sinfonia Prague?"

Martina had to whisper into Geitz's ear. The response was sluggish. Martina repeated the question. Was his nod an affirmation, or was he falling asleep?

"Victor says, you can find Klaus Jürgens at the bottom of the Moldau. He fell over the Charles Bridge two weeks before Vaclav Herza left Prague."

Nathaniel, panting, tried to maintain the pace set by Elena Garnisova's bun of white hair as they ascended the steep slope.

After his meeting with Geitz, Nathaniel had returned to *Pravo*, not to research more news articles about Herza but to find the obituary of Klaus Jürgens. Garnisova translated it for him. For someone who had been an important musician, it was surprisingly curt. A single paragraph recounted Jürgens's career, culminating in his long tenure as principal trumpeter of Sinfonia Prague. It also briefly touched on his efforts, during the era that Czechoslovakia was a Soviet puppet, to attain "dignity for working musicians and security for their families." With academic dryness wanting in detail, the obituary referred to his death only as a tragic accident that occurred late at night as Jürgens returned home from an evening of labor organizing.

Listed were his survivors: his wife and daughter, Eliska and Katerina, respectively, along with their address. Elena looked in the phone book for both, but there was nothing. After all, forty years had passed. This was not unexpected.

Closing the phone book, Garnisova said, "So, we go to the address and see what we will see."

Nathaniel said she needn't go to the trouble.

"Trouble?" she responded. "Am I not a newspaper reporter? This is my job. And would you know how to get to this address on your own? And if you are lucky enough to find it, then what will you say?" She wrapped a maroon shawl around the shoulders of her gray shin-length dress and said, "Let's go."

So now they were on the outskirts of the city, in a neighborhood—if it could be called that—of eight-story soulless concrete apartment blocks that looked like it had been thrown together by the Soviets in one week in the 1930s. If the central square of Prague exuded humanity's artistic soul, then this charmless appendage of the city, only a few miles distant, expressed how that soul could be thoroughly withered. An oppressive vortex seemed to have sapped light from the sky; the only color in sight was the laundry, hung limply on lines between buildings. Not a tree stood, at least not a living one. There was no apparent reason for the small balconies outside some of the apartments—the only feature of the buildings that was not exclusively utilitarian—except to provide a view of other apartments.

By the time Nathaniel lumbered up to the front door, Garnisova had already entered and examined the directory. There was no one named Jürgens in the building, but Garnisova pressed the buzzer of the apartment number listed in the obituary anyway. There followed a brief exchange. It didn't require a knowledge of Czech for Nathaniel to understand the female tenant's tetchy response to being disturbed.

"It seems," Garnisova said, "that the current inhabitant has never heard of anyone named Jürgens. I propose we return to the office and examine census data. We shall also research later obituaries for the wife and daughter."

Nathaniel could not think of a better alternative. They turned their back on the building and had taken only a few steps when a brick landed at their feet.

Turning around, Nathaniel saw an old, barrel-chested man with suspenders and a white wife-beater T-shirt shouting at them from his second-floor balcony. He was red-faced with a heavy, Stalin mustache and a bushy ring of gray hair encircling the top of a shiny bald head, like an egg in a nest. And he was aiming another brick at them.

Garnisova scolded him harshly. Whatever it was she said, he held his fire. A momentary truce.

"What did you say?" asked Nathaniel.

"That he was fortunate you don't understand Czech because you are a former boxing champion and don't take kindly to racial slurs."

"Whatever works."

She began conversing with the old-timer in a stern but less confrontational tone.

"Let's go up," she said to Nathaniel. "He wants some company."

There was a small pot of tea and a large bottle of Becherovka waiting for them. The pot was full, the bottle not nearly so.

The man introduced himself as Jaroslav Svoboda. His domicile was small, tastelessly decorated, dingy, and unkempt but, to Nathaniel, hospitable in an unassuming way. The only art was a severe portrait of the Virgin Mary by the entrance and a calendar over the kitchen table with an action photo of a soccer player on his knees celebrating a goal. Even before he and Garnisova had time to settle into the seats they had been offered, Svoboda was already asking questions.

"He wants to know if you ever fought Muhammad Ali," said Garnisova.

"You can tell him I used to spar with Joe Frazier, but I broke my hand on Frazier's jaw and had to retire," said Nathaniel. He extended a large fist and hoped that Svoboda's imagination, enhanced by the volume of Becherovka missing from the bottle, would illuminate the nonexistent scars in his dark skin. Svoboda examined Nathaniel's hand as if it were a church icon and nodded reverently.

Friends now, Garnisova explained why they were there. Though Nathaniel couldn't understand a word, it sounded similar to what Martina had said to Victor Geitz at the convalescent home.

Svoboda spoke at length, keeping his lips wet with tea and alcohol.

"Eliska Jürgens died years ago," Svoboda related through Garnisova. "He doesn't know what happened to Katerina, the daughter. She left right after the mother died. For what it's worth, he says the daughter was a dog."

"Can you ask him if he knows anything about the accident sur--rounding Jürgens's death?"

Upon hearing the question in his own language, Svoboda's body began to jiggle. Then his face became even redder and his eyes began to tear. Finally, unable to help himself, he put his head in his hands and, convulsed, emitted loud, unintelligible sounds.

"Is he laughing or crying?" Nathaniel asked Garnisova.

"I don't know. Let me find out."

When the shuddering abated, she asked.

"He says if you think it was an accident, then Joe Frazier must have broken your head, too. He says that it was suicide. That every-one knew it was suicide. I will ask him why he's so sure."

Several minutes later, after Svoboda spoke in an uninterrupted stream, replete with hand gestures and chest beating, she continued.

"He says that devil, Vaclav Herza--and I'm quoting him here, this is not my personal opinion, necessarily—drove him to it. He knows this because he heard Jürgens and his wife argue about it every night for years. He says look at the dents in his ceiling where he pounded his broom to get them to shut up. Eliska wanted her husband to quit, to go elsewhere, anywhere. She told him Herza was turning him into an alcoholic, into a depressive. Jürgens told his wife he couldn't live with himself if he gave in, not only for his own pride but for all his colleagues he would be letting down. He said he would die before he would give Herza the satisfaction of seeing him surrender.

"The wife told him she would leave him if he didn't turn his life around. That every night he would come home from some café drunk—"

"Sonja's?" asked Nathaniel, recalling Mihaescu's story.

She asked Svoboda.

"*Ja.* Sonja," he said, nodding with a knowing smile.

Garnisova continued. "One night, he didn't come home. The next morning they found his body floating in the river, a little down-

stream from the Charles Bridge. He had to cross the bridge to get the
bus to go home. It's a wide bridge. No one could fall off it accidentally. I asked Svoboda if Jürgens might have been drunk. Svoboda
said of course he was drunk, but he was always drunk and never fell
off the bridge before. The next morning, the wife said to the daughter that she knew he would do it sooner or later."

"Was there any note?" asked Nathaniel.

Garnisova relayed the question to Svoboda.

Svoboda was indignant in his reply.

"What do you think I am, a busybody?" Garnisova translated.

The rest of the day proved unproductive. There were no more stories
in the archives surrounding the life and death of Klaus Jürgens. If
there ever had been a Sonja's Bar, there wasn't one now, nor any trace
of it in any of the records Garnisova so diligently explored. That
night, after all the merchants on the Charles Bridge had closed up
their stands and the tourists had left for other diversions, Nathaniel
stood alone alongside the railing, looking down into the unfathomable
depths of the Moldau. In it, he saw dark reflections of the statues of the
saints, a phalanx of holy guardians lining the bridge from one end to
the other, who had failed to protect the life of a broken trumpet player.

THIRTY-SIX

Furukawa, scratching his head with indecision in the deserted alley,
was startled when someone cleared his throat behind him. He wheeled
around to find a rather bland-looking young man with closely cropped
hair, wearing a light sport jacket and narrow tie, and standing no
farther than an arm's length from him.

"Who are you?" Furukawa asked, embarrassed at being caught off guard by this unimposing person who could be mistaken for a schoolboy if he carried a knapsack.

"Don't you recognize me?" asked the young man, trying to hide a smile.

"If I did, I wouldn't ask you, would I?" said Furukawa, already bruised by a night of impudent behavior.

"I meant no offense," the young man said, bowing. "My name is Soichi Ono, and I was the geisha in the blue kimono, the one who—"

"You?" Furukawa peered closely at Ono's face. "Yes, now I recognize you. What do you want, now that you've shamed me? Have you come to rob me? Stay away from me, you perverted—"

"I can tell you about Erutsa-sama," Ono said.

"So, is that it, you want money for information? How do I know you will tell the truth when your entire life is a falsehood?"

"I don't want any money," said Ono, his face taut, tears forming in his eyes.

"Then what do you want?" asked Furukawa, repelled by this sniveling hybrid.

"Revenge."

Furukawa did not know how to respond. What was he getting himself into? What was the extent of his obligation to Jacobus? His feet did not know which direction to take him.

Ono, sensing Furukawa's ambivalence, continued. "There's an *izakaya* that's still open around the corner. They have good food there. Come with me. You can hear my story. Then you decide."

Furukawa made a noncommittal grunt and, with their footsteps echoing in the night, followed Ono down the dark street, having no idea where it would lead.

If not for the lit red lantern in front, they would have passed the *izakaya* had they blinked. They had to lower their heads in order to pass through the tavern entrance made of strings of colored beads. Inside, Furukawa saw two clearly delineated groups who had managed to form an invisible boundary even in the tiny space: on one side, young men who all looked like Ono; grim, heavy-faced street cleaners in their overall uniforms on the other.

"Where would you like to sit?" asked Ono.

Furukawa looked first to his left, then to his right.

"Let's sit at the counter."

As far as Furukawa could tell, the squat woman behind the counter, adorned with thick eyeglasses and silver front teeth, was the only employee. She chatted animatedly to herself; Furukawa would have thought her oblivious of their presence had she not tossed hot hand towels and a bowl of pickled vegetables in their general direction.

Ono asked, "What would you like to drink, Furukawa-sensei?"

"If you can interrupt her monologue, ask if they have good *shochu*."

Ono ordered hot sake for himself and the *shochu* for Furukawa. Without asking, he also ordered the chicken liver yakitori and *agedashi tofu*, explaining that they were the specialties of the house. Furukawa grunted in assent. He wasn't hungry, but it would be good to have something in his stomach with the potent *shochu*.

The street cleaners at a table to Furukawa's left, emboldened by bottles of cheap whiskey, had no compunction expressing their opinions of the young men to his right, who seemed accustomed to the verbal abuse and spoke in hushed tones.

"Are those like you?" asked Furukawa, nodding to his right.

"Would you rather I be a street cleaner?" Ono asked.

Their food arrived, served family style in the traditional manner.

"Are you willing to eat out of the same plate," Ono asked, "or do you find that too distasteful?"

Furukawa looked at the food. "You're right. The chicken liver looks good. Why not?"

Ono poured the sake from the carafe into a small cup and lifted it.

"*Kanpai!*"

Furukawa ignored the toast. "What is it you have to say to me?"

Ono quickly drained the cup and a second one before responding.

"Lotus Bud was a friend of mine. His name was Tadamichi Inoue."

"And a friend of Erutsa-sama, I understand."

"No, we're never friends of our clients, even though we make them think so. Erutsa-sama thought Tadamichi loved him."

"Did Erutsa-sama know that Lotus Bud was a man?"

"Of course."

"How can you be so sure?"

"Tadamichi was an innocent, but he also liked possessions and made the mistake of trying to make money after hours. Whenever Erutsa-sama came to Japan, Tadamichi had visions of new clothes, new jewelry, maybe even a vacation at an *onsen* on the coast."

Furukawa sliced a chunk of fried tofu with one of his chopsticks, swirled it in its savory sauce, and looked at it contemplatively before popping it into his mouth. It was better than what he made at home.

"If you were in my business," Ono continued, "you'd know that people usually aren't who they seem to be on the outside. Erutsa-sama was no exception. For such a small, weak man, who would guess that he would be such a sumo fan?"

Furukawa let the tofu slide down his throat. "A lot of people are sumo fans. Even women."

"More than a fan, then. Erutsa-sama's idea of a date was to take

Tadamichi to an abandoned warehouse near the Tsukiji fish market for mock sumo matches."

"Who were the wrestlers?" Furukawa asked, his interest waxing.

"I'm sorry. I wasn't clear. Erutsa-sama and Tadamichi wrestled each other. Naked, except for their *mawashi* loincloths, like in real matches. They went through all the motions—throwing the salt, slapping their chests, bowing. There was a regulation circle drawn on the wooden floor. And even though Tadamichi was three hundred pounds lighter than a real sumo wrestler, he was certainly much stronger than Erutsa-sama, who was an even more vile sight without his clothing."

"So Erutsa-sama was a glutton for punishment? Is that the way it was?"

"No, Tadamichi was told he must never win! He must pretend to try to win, and they must grapple at close quarters, but in the end he must always allow Erutsa-sama to throw him down.

"One night they had had five or six bouts, always with the same result. The warehouse was hot and smelling more than usual of old fish guts. Erutsa-sama was panting for breath but insisted on one more. When the bout began, Erutsa-sama charged with his head down and Tadamichi leaned back to make it easier for Erutsa-sama to push him over, but Erutsa-sama tripped over his own feet and tumbled out of the circle and went sprawling. It was an automatic defeat. It would have been a funny sight if it wasn't so hideous.

"Tadamichi instantly helped him up and apologized profusely, but Erutsa-sama would have none of it. He slapped Tadamichi across the face over and over again. He drew blood. His own face looked red enough to explode, and he yelled incoherently at Tadamichi as he continued to slap him. Finally he stopped. Maybe he was exhausted. Tadamichi was crying and Erutsa-sama told his assistant to take Tadamichi away. That was the last time anyone ever saw him."

Furukawa swallowed the last of his *shochu* and felt its heat flow down his throat. He wiped his mouth with his handkerchief.

"An interesting story," he said. "But if that's the last anyone ever heard of your friend, how do you know this happened?"

"Because," said Ono, "I was the referee."

THIRTY-SEVEN

If the present was the surface of a Turner sea, Jacobus felt like a diver emerging from the depths of the past. By trying to rise too quickly, the bends had almost killed him, but he had survived and was now bobbing on lightly undulating waves, his head still sinking underwater from time to time. If the sea was his past and the sky his future, he was now able to grasp the continuity between the two that was his life. His sense of disembodiment slowly ebbing, he managed to answer the phone halfway through the second ring.

"Yeah?"

"It's me, Yumi."

"Oh."

"You sound disappointed."

"I've been waiting for a few calls."

"That's not like you, waiting by the phone. They must be important. Are you receiving a Good Samaritan award?"

Jacobus smiled. "No, I'm actually hoping for a phone call from Nathaniel, and . . . some others."

"Well, I was going to invite you to go to K&J's. I hear they have a good weekend brunch. All you can eat. Lots of smoked fish. And they serve till noon."

Jacobus was mildly tempted. Though he couldn't recall the last time he had eaten, he had little hunger.

"Do I sense an ulterior motive here?" he asked.

"You're right, as usual. They've been pressuring me to take the Harmonium job. They're offering me lots of money. Four times more than what I made my last year with the quartet. Plus vacation, pension, health, and a concerto with the orchestra every year."

"Don't take it."

"That was easy! Why not?"

"Because if you felt good about it you wouldn't be asking my opinion. You're troubled by what happened to Sherry O'Brien, as you should be, though it wasn't your fault in any way, shape, or form. You feel you'd be a traitor, taking a position away from her that by all rights should have been hers, and for which she's paid with her own life. You feel that by working for Vaclav Herza, you'd be rewarding him for her death. You think that the musicians will hold you accountable for having cheated your way into the position, which also gutted their limited authority to choose their own concertmaster. Finally, you think if Herza could do something like that to O'Brien, there's no reason he couldn't ultimately do it again, to you."

Jacobus finished his spiel and expected Yumi to respond, but all he heard was silence. Had he said something to offend her? Again?

"You still there?" he asked.

"Jake, you make me cry."

"Then take the damn job," he said angrily.

"No, you make me cry because you've thought so much about me. I went to that Turner exhibit. What it taught me is that there are forces—forces of nature, spiritual forces—that are so much bigger than us, so much more powerful and magnificent, swirling around us. Those skies and those seas! Humans seem so insignificant and our actions so petty. In the end, the best we can do is act ethically, with honesty and integrity. Is that what you wanted me to see, Jake?"

He had intended for her to see the difference between chamber music and orchestral playing.

"Exactly," he said.

"And you're so right. I could never take that job. Thank you. I don't know if I could ever pay you back."

"Actually, you could."

"How?"

"Bring me a bagel and lox from K&J's."

The first call he had been waiting for came a little after noon. He let this one ring a few times, hoping not to jinx it.

"It's Kate," came the one voice he would have wanted half a world closer.

"Kate. It must be the middle of the night in Japan."

"You pick these things up so quickly, Jake."

"What's up?" he asked.

"I have news from Max."

"Go ahead."

Kate related what Max Furukawa had told her about his Tokyo investigation. He had made progress but ultimately came to a dead end.

"He even went to the police," she said, "but in Japan there must be overwhelming proof for the authorities to arrest someone, let alone convict, and unless there is no other way, they will do anything to avoid an international scandal. Who would they rather protect, an adored, world-famous conductor, or a missing transvestite?"

Geisha boys, thought Jacobus. Naked sumo wrestling. But like everything else, no proof. All hearsay.

"Max should have guessed from the beginning," Kate said.

"What do you mean? Guessed what?"

"Do you know what *cin-cin* means, Jake?" she asked.

"It's Italian. A toast, like 'cheers.' That's the reason for the name of the club, right?"

"That's just half of it. The name of the club is actually a pun. Do you know what it means in Japanese?"

"Naked sumo wrestling?"

"Not quite. It's colloquial. *Cin-cin* means penis, and in a vulgar way, no less. Max thought it referred to the clientele. He never expected it referred to the employees."

"Shit, he was probably humiliated as hell. There goes another friend."

"He was concerned you would think that and wanted me to reassure you not to worry. He said he will always be your friend, but . . ."

"But what?"

"He wants you to know that he has retired from the detective business."

The next call came a couple of hours later. Roy Miller skipped the chatty preamble and got right to the matter.

"You were right, Jake. The razor blade is suspicious. We found Miss O'Brien's razors—those pink plastic throwaway Lady Schick jobs—in her cosmetics bag. The one found next to her was an old-fashioned Wilkinson Sword double-edged blade, and it matches her wounds. None of the local stores carry them anymore. We tried Rite Aid, CVS, Kmart, you name it. We'll keep trying, but it's possible the owner had it for a long time."

"Did anyone at the motel notice a pair of elderly ghouls, one tall and lumbering, the other short, bald, and scarred, who both talk with an East European accent?"

"None of the above. Sorry, Jake. We interviewed all the guests and hotel staff we could find, but no one mentioned anyone like either of them."

"What's next?"

"Go over the evidence and crime scene yet again. See if there's anything we've missed."

"How are you feeling about finding Mr. Slasher?"

"I've gotta tell you, Jake, I'm not feeling too optimistic right now."

More waiting. When Nathaniel called, Jacobus could tell from his voice, usually so upbeat, that he was tired. It was around midnight in Prague. Nathaniel explained he had just walked back to his bed-and-breakfast from the Charles Bridge and was in need of sleep. So Jacobus refrained from expressing the disappointment he felt when Nathaniel told him that although he believed Vaclav Herza had killed Klaus Jürgens, he had no proof and couldn't think of any way of getting it. Throughout the story, Jacobus simply responded with soft murmurs of acknowledgment, and when it was over he thanked Nathaniel for all his efforts.

"Maybe we'll have another chess game when you get back," Jacobus offered.

"Do you want me to let you win the next one?" Nathaniel asked.

"Fuck you," Jacobus said, and they both tried to laugh.

As Jacobus had not expected further calls, he was tempted to just let the next one ring. With the slim chance there might be some better news at the other end of the line, he finally answered.

"Mr. Jacobus, it's Tiny Parsley."

Jacobus held the receiver away from his ear. Talking to Kate, to Nathaniel, Yumi, and Roy, that was one thing. Parsley, though, was too close to Harmonium. Too close to O'Brien. He felt himself sinking below the surface again. If he opened his mouth, he would drown.

"Mr. Jacobus, are you okay?" Parsley sounded alarmed. "If this is a bad time . . ."

"It's always a bad time," he forced himself to say. "What do you want?"

"I wanted to let you in on something. You know those files—Sherry's files—you asked me about?"

"What about them?"

"Well, they had been stolen. That's one reason I couldn't have shown them to you, even if it wasn't against policy. I think Lubomir took them."

"Why?"

"Sherry had been seeing a psychiatrist for some time, having to do with her childhood. I really can't go into any more detail than that. I found Lubomir lurking around the file cabinet. He gave me a look."

"Did you see him with the file?"

"No."

"But you searched for the file and it was missing?"

"No. What I did is, I went through all the files. They were all there, including hers, but hers wasn't between Nyquist and Okeda like it should've been. I never would've done that. I may look like a mess, but I'm as anal as the IRS on April sixteenth when it comes to my files. I think Lubomir took it to show Herza and was putting it back when he heard me come into the office, so he hurried up and just shoved it in. I wish I could prove it, but I can't."

"Why are you telling me this now?"

"I've been fired. They can't tell me what to do anymore."

"So where does Herza stand on your TAC now?"

"He's off the chart, man."

The reception on Jacobus's radio was lousy. His house was down in a valley and the woods around it were tall, blocking the frequencies.

That was the conventional wisdom, anyway. Nevertheless, he tuned in to WAMC from Albany, which had a decent signal. Not that he was interested in listening to anything. He just wanted to know what time it was and didn't have the energy to analyze the universe. He listened while Alan Chartock peddled a CD by Pete Seeger for their fund drive until *All Things Considered* came on the air and told him the time. After a few minutes of listening through the static of whether Monica Lewinsky or Saddam Hussein was causing more trouble for Bill Clinton, Jacobus turned off the radio.

Only a few hours until the opening concert of Harmonium Hall. Jacobus had played the chess game and lost, again. Maybe he should have stuck with Tiddlywinks. But to have lost to Herza! That thought sickened him. Not that he had had much hope. Not that it mattered now. The game had been stacked against him from the beginning, and he gave it his best effort, didn't he? Fought the good fight. Kate had been right, though: He had to learn to let go of the past. Yet he felt so alone here in his protective cocoon surrounded by trees and not people. He sat there, in silence, in darkness, no different from any other piece of broken-down furniture in his broken-down house, and no more alive.

He heard a car come tentatively down the driveway. People who liked to explore the Berkshires often did that, to his annoyance, thinking his meandering driveway was some quaint country back road. "Honey, maybe there'll be an antiques store!" Then when they came around the bend and out of the woods and saw his junk shop of a house, they'd speed up and go out the other end.

This particular car came to a stop in front of his house and continued to shudder even after the engine was turned off. An old car that had been driven harder and farther than it had wanted to go.

Footsteps came to the front door. There was a knock. Jacobus was disinclined to answer it. Probably someone lost on the way to

Tanglewood. Who was even playing tonight? The BSO was still on its tour to God knows where. Maybe it was one of those rock bands he could hear even through his stuck windows. What's a mere eight miles for Bloody Stool's amplifiers?

Another knock. What the hell!

Jacobus found his cane, slowly got up from his chair, and went to the screen door.

"Yeah?" he asked.

"I am Sonja."

THIRTY-EIGHT

Lubomir awakens Herza from his preconcert nap promptly at 6 o'clock with the usual soft *tap-tap-tap* on the bedroom door. He enters the room, removes a bolster from the closet, then sets it against the bed's headboard and props the maestro into a comfortable upright position.

Lubomir hands Herza his scores and then goes to the kitchen to put the finishing touches on the chicken consommé and pour the four-ounce glass of VORS Amontillado sherry, Herza's unchanging preconcert supper.

Finishing his preparations, Lubomir assists Herza from his bed, removes the maestro's silk pajamas, escorts him to the bathroom where he cleanses the maestro's head and body with a washcloth. He then rubs shaving gel on the maestro's face and neck and commences the maestro's preconcert shave.

"Nervous, Lubomir? Your hands are shaking."

"The opening of the new hall, Maestro."

"Try not to cut my throat, will you? What is a concert hall, anyway? Only empty space. Until it is filled with music. It is the music—only the music—that counts."

"Yes."

Having completed Maestro's ablutions, Lubomir helps him with his underclothes and then into his blue suit with handkerchief, white shirt, and cravat.

Lubomir retrieves the scores from the bedroom and places them in the briefcase. Herza's white tie and tails, as always, have been sent directly from the cleaners to the concert hall, where Lubomir will dress the maestro upon their arrival.

Lubomir helps Herza down the stairs, though on this night it seems that it is Herza who is helping Lubomir.

Lubomir runs ahead to buzz the elevator but is chagrined to see a sign on it: OUT OF ORDER. PLEASE USE STAIRS. When Herza arrives and sees Lubomir standing there, inadvertently blocking the sign, he says, "What are you waiting for? Get me the elevator."

"I'm sorry, Maestro. We'll have to walk."

"What are you talking about? We take the elevator."

"It's not working."

"Press the button."

"But—"

"I said, press the button."

Lubomir follows his instructions, and after they wait in silence for several minutes, Herza says, "You talk to the manager about this. I want that spic fired."

"Yes," says Lubomir and escorts Herza down three painful flights of stairs to the lobby.

When they arrive at the front door, Oscar the doorman is no-where to be found. "Where the hell is he?" Herza rails at Raul, the concierge, at the security desk, who is reading the sports section of the *Daily News*.

"Night off," says Raul.

"Open the door for me," demands Herza.

"Sorry, that's not in my job description." Raul returns to the paper. When the coast is clear, he picks up the phone and dials his cousin, the manager of a small fleet of water taxis.

Lubomir, holding Herza's briefcase in one hand and Herza's arm in his other, pushes open the door with his shoulder. When they are halfway through, it closes upon Herza's left side, pinning him.

"You fool!" he shouts. "Incompetent!"

"I'm sorry, Maestro. I didn't mean—"

"Shut up and get me into the car before you kill me."

But there is no car to be found. Lubomir is nonplussed.

"What have you done now, you imbecile?" demands Herza. "Where is the car?"

"I don't know," says Lubomir in a panic. He takes out his cell phone and drums in Paddy Donaghue's number, getting it right the third time.

"Donaghue," says the voice, bringing temporary reassurance to Lubomir.

"Where are you?" asks Lubomir in as authoritative a voice as he can muster. "Maestro is waiting."

"Ah, and I suppose I should have notified you, shouldn't I have?"

"What do you mean? Notified me of what?"

"The new car. I had to take it back to the shop. She seems to have developed a malfunction of sorts. Could be the manifold, or the differential, or the universal joint. Point is, she's out of commission. Please convey my blessings of the day to the maestro, won't you?" There is a click and Lubomir is disconnected.

"What is it, you idiot?" asks Herza.

"Donaghue's not coming. Engine trouble."

"Well, then, get a cab! What are you waiting for?"

They arrive at the drop-off for Harmonium Hall fifteen minutes behind schedule. Herza tells Lubomir to hire a water taxi to the entrance of the hall rather than the slower passenger ferry.

"Please hurry," Lubomir says to the pilot. "We're late."

"Yes, sir," he says and immediately revs the engine. He also swings the boat into the current, causing a spray of Hudson River water to rain upon Herza, soaking him.

"Fool!" Herza shouts at Lubomir over the din of the boat's engine. "Are you trying to sabotage me?"

Lubomir remains silent.

The water taxi arrives at the Harmonium Hall docking area.

"Ten dollars," says the pilot.

"What?" bellows Herza. "You give me pneumonia and then you charge me? Do you know who I am?"

Lubomir pays the ten dollars. The pilot pockets the soggy cash but makes no effort to help Lubomir or Herza out of the boat, so Lubomir, on unsteady legs, crawls onto the wet concrete dock. He then grabs Herza's extended hands.

"What are you waiting for?" demands Herza. "Pull!"

With one mighty yank, Lubomir manages to extract Herza from the shifting boat, but in the process Lubomir's left foot slips and the two of them go sprawling, Lubomir backward, Herza forward, onto the dock. The pilot calls the security desk at Harmonium Hall on his ship-to-shore and departs. Herza, moaning in anguish, is able to rise to his knees but no farther. Lubomir is first up and assists the maestro to his feet.

"The scores are safe," says Lubomir, brandishing the briefcase.

Herza says nothing.

They hobble to the artists' entrance of the grand new concert hall and approach the security desk. Lubomir waves to the guard.

"ID, please," says the guard.

"What are you talking about?" asks Lubomir.

"Regulations," says the guard.

"Don't you know who this is?" asks Lubomir.

"I can't say that I recognize him. All I know is, he's dressed inappropriately for a concert."

"I am Herza!" Herza says, beating his chest. "I am Herza!"

"May I see some ID, Mr. Herza?" asks the guard. "Regulations."

"Show him," Herza says to Lubomir. "Show him."

"But, Maestro," says Lubomir, "I don't have your ID."

"Driver's license? Passport? Walmart card?" the guard offers, encouraging.

"I don't drive, and I don't have my passport here," says Herza. "Is this a foreign country?"

"Then I'm sorry. I can't let you in," says the guard, ignoring Herza's tirade.

"This is outrageous!" says Herza. "I built this hall! This is *my* hall!"

"Sorry," says the guard, observing Herza's mud-covered clothes.

They are at a loss.

"Get me in," Herza hisses at Lubomir.

Lubomir, showing the guard his own ID, asks if he would let Herza in if he signs some kind of statement taking responsibility for him. The guard says this is highly irregular but generously offers to make an exception and provides Lubomir with paper and pen, then buzzes them through. After Herza and Butkus pass through the security door, the guard glances back over his shoulder. A carefully laundered set of tails that had been delivered moments earlier is hanging wrinkle-free under his protective eye. He then picks up the hall's interoffice phone and punches in the three-digit extension for Randall Brimley, the orchestra librarian.

THIRTY-NINE

Adrianne Vickers continued to peer around the woman on line in front of her. What was taking so long? Just pay for the damn ticket! She heard the box office person say "standing room only." With so many people behind her, the negotiations for one ticket went on far too long. She would have fired that employee, that is, if she still had her job. At least she was next. She clasped her overladen Louis Vuitton shoulder bag as if it were her child who had been lost at Bloomingdale's for an hour.

The woman in front of her finally resigned herself to purchasing the SRO ticket.

Vickers shouldered her way forward to the ticket window.

"Front-row balcony," she said, looking from side to side.

"We're sold out," said the employee.

"Hey, I know the routine. There are always comps set aside for the bigwigs."

"Which balcony did you have in mind?"

"I don't give a damn. First, second, third. Left, right, center. Just make sure it's front row." She pressed her elbow even more firmly against her shoulder bag.

"Let me check."

"Hurry up."

As the employee examined the computer screen, Vickers caught sight of a uniformed security guard patrolling the other side of the lobby and quickly looked the other way.

"I've got something on the second tier right, but it's third row. The view is perfectly—"

"I said front row, dammit. Christ, don't you understand English? Hurry!"

"Sure. Let me just go ask my supervisor to see if we have what you need."

The employee retreated to the office behind the ticket windows. Vickers's palms began to sweat. When the employee did not emerge after more than a minute, and the people on line behind her started to become irritated with the delay, Vickers's fortitude began to falter.

"Excuse me," said a male voice. Vickers whirled around, expecting an argument with a patron, only to find the security guard, looking much bigger than he had appeared from a distance.

"Could you please open your purse, ma'am?" asked the guard.

"What?"

"I asked, could you please open your purse?"

"You have no right," she said. "It's my private property."

"I have to ask you to open your purse."

"No. I won't."

"Then you'll have to come with me." The guard placed his hand under her elbow.

Though she almost collapsed from the trembling of her legs, Vickers was frozen to the spot. Glassy eyed, she stared straight ahead. Three more guards approached.

"Just come this way, please, ma'am."

"No, I won't," she hissed, panicked into action. "I'm leaving. I forgot my wallet." She turned and fled, weaving through the lobby crowd, clinging to her Louis Vuitton bag. The guards pursued, but their size was a disadvantage and she evaded them, vanishing into the throng swirling at crosscurrents toward the box office, the restrooms, the lounges, and the auditorium. One of the guards radioed his colleagues, gave them a description, told them to keep an eye out for a distraught lady with a large handbag, and hoped she had left the building.

Vickers mingled her way to the gleaming, mirrored ladies' room. Seeing herself infinitely reflected, she retreated hyperventilating to a stall and forced herself to breathe deeply. She couldn't wait very long in the ladies' room; as always, there was a line of women waiting their turns. Should she deposit the gun in the stall and walk away? No, the next patron might see her leaving and put two and two together. She was suddenly torn whether to flush or not flush the toilet. She didn't like to waste water, but if she emerged from the stall without flushing, the other women might think . . . Vickers decided flushing was the wiser course. It would seem more natural. Where's the damn handle, though? The toilet had one of those state-of-the-art motion sensors. What to do? Vickers sat on the toilet—should she pull down her underwear in order to activate the flusher? She counted to thirty before standing up. It flushed. Vickers exited the stall, attempting to look normal. She rinsed her face with cold water. Dammit, where were the paper towels? She went to the electric hand dryer. It wasn't working! She pounded on it. Tomorrow, heads would roll. She would make sure. She bit her lip and took a calming breath, pulled back her shoulders, and adopted her composed and professional look. Like someone in control.

Vickers left the ladies' room and shimmied parrotlike along the marble wall, toward the side exit, now well within her sights. Suddenly, someone took hold of her left arm from behind. She tried to break free and run.

"Adrianne!" said Robert Vogelman. "I certainly didn't expect to see—"

"I can't talk now." She tried to pull her arm away, but Vogelman held on.

Vickers yanked her arm free. Trembling, her hand went into her purse.

Vogelman took a step back, following her hand with his eyes. He looked at her as if she were a wounded bird, first with sympathy, then with concern, and ultimately with the irritation of unwanted responsibility.

"Adrianne, do you need help?" he asked, willing to assist but hoping the invitation would be declined.

"Just let me go."

"Certainly, Adrianne. And good luck to you," he added, but she was already too far away to hear him.

At the other end of the building, Lubomir and Herza, caked with Hudson River mud, wordlessly ascend the elevator to the artists' level where the dressing rooms are situated. They are now almost a half hour behind schedule, and there is barely enough time to dress before the concert starts.

Lubomir unlocks the maestro's dressing room door, removes Herza's filthy suit, and runs to the bathroom for towels to dry him. He sits Herza in the chair at the new cherrywood desk made especially for him and hastens to brew a pot of Darjeeling tea.

He places the tea in front of Herza with an unsteady hand. The cup shakes in its saucer and the tea makes dark little waves—the Hudson River in miniature.

"Coumadin. Where's the Coumadin?" Herza asks.

"What?" asks Lubomir, distracted.

"My Coumadin," repeats Herza.

"Oh, I don't know," says Lubomir absently. "Let me get your concert dress."

Lubomir returns a moment later. "It's not here."

"What? My Coumadin?"

"No. Your tails."

"What do you propose I wear, then? My birthday suit?"

Lubomir remains silent.

"Don't just stand there, idiot. Get my tails."

Lubomir calls the dry cleaner. There is no answer.

"It's too late," says Lubomir to Herza. "There must have been some mix-up."

"Then put my suit back on."

"You can't go on like that."

"Can't? There's no such thing as can't. I will."

"Maestro," says Lubomir, rearranging the tea closer to Herza.

"What now?"

"The musicians."

"What are you babbling about?"

"The musicians. They're not going to play."

"Of course they are going to play. It's their job."

"Nowitsky told me. They're not going to play. They will sit there and refuse to play. They will keep Scheherazade O'Brien's seat—"

"It is not *her* seat. It is the concertmaster's seat."

"They will keep the concertmaster's seat vacant, and they will not lift their instruments for you. They intend to humiliate you."

"Remember one thing, Lubomir," says Herza. "Musicians are cowards. They talk big when they are together, but they fear me and they fear losing their paychecks. I have no fear. They will play."

"I can't let you be humiliated," says Lubomir. "I can't let them destroy you. Now drink your tea, please."

Herza looks at his tea and then at Lubomir. Lubomir looks away.

"*You* drink the tea, Lubomir."

"No," Lubomir stammers. "No. It's for you, Maestro. I'll go find your Coumadin."

"Drink the tea, Lubomir. Take it into the bathroom. Close the door. And drink it. Now."

Without another word, Lubomir obeys.

Herza hears the choking gasps slowly dissipate, then dresses himself in his soiled suit and hobbles off to the stage, scores in hand, shaking his head in wonder that Lubomir would not even consider pouring the tea down the toilet. But where will I find someone to shave me now? Herza thinks, *tsk*ing wistfully. Such a virtuoso with a razor.

Vaclav Herza proceeds to the wings of the stage. He is late, the orchestra has already tuned, and the lights have gone to half. The librarian is nowhere to be seen.

"Where's Brimley?" he asks a stagehand.

"You weren't here. He left," replies the stagehand, who turns his back on Herza and walks away.

Herza limps onto the stage. At first, the impatient audience, seeing their beloved maestro, breaks into tumultuous applause. Almost immediately, however, in recognition of his haggard condition, the applause breaks off and is replaced by gasps. Herza takes no heed of their vexation or even of their presence. Without bowing, he proceeds directly to the podium.

There is no baton awaiting him diagonally across his music because there is no stand at all. Neither is there a seat for him to sit in, and his fall on the dock has exacerbated his chronic back pain so that he can hardly stand. Unable to bend, he drops his beloved scores, his bibles, onto the floor.

Herza ponders the empty concertmaster seat. One by one, he looks each musician in the eye, taking his time. Some look down, some look away, some stare at their music. None return the gaze of his hideous visage. His focus returns to Lawrence Nowitsky, and what might be construed as a smile illuminates Herza's countenance, but if Lizzie Borden had smiled before she chopped Mommy and Daddy into pieces it would have been no more laden with cruelty. Like a whipped cur, Nowitsky inconspicuously slouches into the concertmaster seat.

Herza raises his hands in preparation of the downbeat to Mozart's Overture to *Don Giovanni.* One, then another and another, then all the musicians raise their instruments. Herza flings his arms wide apart, ecstasy etched on his scarred face as he raises his eyes to the heavens and casts open the gates of D-minor hell, inviting the musicians to enter. The musicians, all the musicians, follow him in.

The audience perceives something volatile in the air. The intensity generated by the orchestra is incendiary. What chemistry! What unity of purpose! the audience thinks. What more appropriate name for this greatest of orchestras than Harmonium? The response to the performance is explosive.

Because the hall is already overflowing, no patrons are seated after the overture, but in order to perform *The Moldau,* additional musicians are required, and they enter the stage. The orchestra performs flawlessly, even over the unbridled St. John Rapids, and at the culmination of the work, as the majestic river passes through Prague, the audience feels Czech blood coursing through its veins.

The last work on the first half of the concert is *Death and Transfiguration,* the tone poem for which Herza, as interpreter, has no peer.

Herza extends his arms forward. He closes his eyes and his fingers move imperceptibly. The orchestra begins to breathe with almost inaudible sound, perfectly together. The timpani's heartbeat labors, the shadow of death looming. Then, suddenly, Herza's eyes open wide, his fingers splay as if in spasm, and the orchestra whirls into a paroxysm.

What the orchestra does not know is that Vaclav Herza's pain is not only gestural, it is real. And it is not in his back. It is in his chest. He fights against it. He refuses to submit to it. He continues to conduct.

When it is time for the concertmaster solo, a brief moment of repose within the anguished throes of the protagonist, Herza gives

Nowitsky a nod for his cue and all but stops conducting. Nowitsky plays it with earnest pathos but knows he does not, and never could, sound as beautiful as the violinist he is replacing. The orchestra follows Nowitsky in perfect synchronicity, believing this is merely Herza at his best, whose simple presence can invest the musicians with inspiration. Herza recuperates sufficiently during this temporary respite, and with an economy of motion continues without a recurrence of pain.

Near the end of the piece, the music reaches heavenward at the moment of the protagonist's death and fades in an afterglow of orchestral radiance. Herza keeps his arms out, immobile, like Jesus on the cross. The orchestra doesn't move. The audience doesn't move. Herza puts his hands down and the audience erupts into convulsions of purgative applause. More than applause. Screaming bravos and inarticulate shouting. People jumping up and down with tears in their eyes.

Vaclav Herza ignores them and manages to hobble off the stage. It is intermission.

His dressing room is roped off. J. Comstock Brundage is there and informs Herza that Lubomir Butkus is dead.

"Poor Lubomir," says Herza. "He thought he needed to try to save me from myself. He didn't realize how unnecessary that was."

Brundage says, "Of course, knowing how close he was to you for all these years, we will cancel the rest of the concert."

"Don't be absurd. People die every day. What is one more? Herza will only cancel if someone does not make my tea within five minutes! And my pills! Bring me my pills!"

FORTY

The concert has ended. In his spacious dressing room, Herza sits comfortably behind his desk, wearing his green silk smoking jacket, having enjoyed the novel task of dressing himself for the first time in decades, and having taken his time—let them wait—to find his favorite meerschaum pipe and tobacco, which he is now smoking.

"Enter," he commands.

The first to congratulate the maestro, an elderly woman approximately Herza's age, enters the room. Herza catches a quick glimpse of the long line before the door closes behind her. He sighs. One must do what one must do, he thinks charitably. The woman is standing. Herza remains seated.

"Maestro," says the woman, extending her hand. Herza makes no effort to reciprocate. Instead, he raises his palm to silence her. "No one speaks to Herza until Herza speaks first. You have something to say to me. Now, say it."

"I just wanted to say—"

"How much you loved the Dvořák. Next."

Twenty minutes and twice as many well-wishers later, Herza is tired and impatient to leave. Only one remains, a disheveled blind man. After dispensing with him, Herza will stroll along his bridge and truly savor the moment, alone with himself, the way he wants it.

"Maestro," says Jacobus.

"Silence! No one speaks to Herza until Herza speaks first."

"Then we have a problem."

"Really! And why is that?"

"Because no one speaks to Jacobus until Jacobus speaks first."

They both wait in silence. Jacobus contents himself with inhaling the wonderfully aromatic smoke emanating from Herza's pipe—Dunhill De Luxe Navy Rolls, if he's not mistaken—and taking note of the increasing rapidity of Herza's puffs.

"I recognize you," Herza finally says. "You're the blind man in the front row at the rehearsal and at that sorry excuse for a restaurant."

"Yes, that's right."

"And you despise me, don't you?"

"Why do you say that?"

"Because, Jacobus, I have been conducting orchestras for a half century and the look you are giving me now—yes, even the blind have that look—I have seen on the faces of three generations of musicians. The tightening of the jaw, the thinning of the lips, the lowering of the head. Yes, I know that look very well. Yes, they despise me. And they fear me. All of them. But they also respect me because they know I can make them make the best music."

"Yes, I despise you," says Jacobus calmly, "but not for your music."

"And you're here because you wish to do something about it? So then do something! I am but small, shrunken almost, and old, and have little physical strength. The scars have made my face into something vile, and the stroke makes me drool on one side of my mouth and I cannot even walk so well. This is the sad truth. So, go ahead, Mr. Jacobus, I am helpless. I am at your mercy. Do something if you despise me. Who is stopping you?"

Jacobus stands rigid, his left hand clenching, and with the cane in his right, taps the end of it repeatedly on the floor, like a nervous twitch.

"Bah! You waste my time," Herza says. "Get out of my sight, or does such a comment hurt a blind man's feelings?"

Jacobus remains silent.

"I repeat, you are wasting my time." Herza gets up to leave, whether or not the blind man, who also seems now to be deaf, remains. Herza couldn't care less.

"Klaus Jürgens," says Jacobus. "Lotus Bud."

"Who?" asks Herza, but nevertheless he sits back down.

"Jürgens, your first-trumpet player in Prague, way back when. Lotus Bud, your boy-toy in Tokyo who mysteriously disappeared after he burst your Chiyonofuji bubble. You haven't been back to Japan since."

"I don't know what you are talking about. This Lotus . . . is it some kind of joke? And I have had many first-trumpet players over the years. I barely recall the name," he says.

"Let me refresh your memory, then," says Jacobus. "Jürgens tried to organize the other musicians in the orchestra, to get them a little more job security, a little more respect. A little more dignity. In return, you tried to drum him out of the orchestra. You browbeat him, turned him into a depressive alcoholic, criticized his—"

"You astound me, Jacobus! You have been *spying* on me! Is that it? Collecting *intelligence*?"

"Let's say researching your illustrious past."

Herza taps his pipe on the desk, debating how to proceed.

"Jürgens was a depressive alcoholic long before I encountered him," he says. "Don't forget, I was young and he was old. You know these buglers. It is very sad. They can't stand up to the pressure of their calling, so they drink, complain, organize, drink, complain . . . It's a vicious cycle. And you know what happens, Mr. Jacobus? After ten, twenty years, they can't take it anymore. Their lip is dead and they can't perform anymore and refuse to admit it. They are used-up, over-the-hill deadbeats, and it is no one's doing but their own. You say Jürgens tried to organize. You make me laugh. He was an empty shell trying to get protection for his own pitiful career."

"Yet you never fired him. Why was that, if he was so bad? And after his family, friends, and even his doctor pleaded with you to back off, you laid it on even thicker."

"He could have resigned. No one was stopping him."

"But he was too proud, and there being no pension in those days he couldn't afford to quit. Not with a family to support. Even his friends in the orchestra begged him to retire, but he wouldn't and couldn't. So he was trapped, and you relished it. You enjoyed destroying him."

"My only concern is for the music. That is all I have to say. And now I must be going."

Jacobus hears Herza rise, perhaps too quickly, as the chair in which he has been seated skids noisily on the floor.

"Tell me about his suicide," says Jacobus.

"What do you know about his suicide?" asks Herza with alarm.

"There are some gaps. I thought you could fill me in."

"What is your interest here, Jacobus? Why do you persecute me so?"

"Persecute? Hey, I'm just a fan. When I was young I loved Joe DiMaggio. I'd collect a baseball card here, an autographed ball there. So think of me as an acolyte, trying to figure out how you became such a great conductor. I want to know all about you! Like when you fled Prague right after Jürgens died."

"Mere coincidence. It was 1956, after all! The Soviets had invaded Hungary and were converging on Prague. I had been working behind the scenes to free our country. I would have been arrested."

"They said he jumped off the Charles Bridge."

"Yes, yes," Herza says impatiently. "He couldn't accept that he couldn't play anymore, and he was probably drunk, as usual, so he jumped."

"How do you know? Were you there?"

"In Prague?"

"On the bridge."

"Of course not. Don't be absurd."

"By the way, where's your lackey?"

"Lackey?" asks Herza. Then he chuckles. "Ah, Lubomir. He's indisposed at the moment. He drank something that didn't agree with him. How do you know Lubomir?"

"Because I tried, and failed, to get an interview with you when your boy intercepted the phone."

"Interview? For what reason an interview?"

"To quiz you about Scheherazade O'Brien. Where you were on the night her wrists were slashed."

Jacobus hears Herza tap his desk repeatedly with his fingers. He speaks rapidly.

"So this is what it is all about! This interrogation! This . . . third degree! The poor young lady with terminal carpal tunnel syndrome! You think I'm a tyrant, that I am responsible for driving musicians to their deaths? Musicians who contest my authority, when the real issue is that they're no good? Is that it? And now, because I have no sympathy for sniveling suicides, you are going to be the hero, the defender of the meek, and exact retribution. Is that so?"

"Not suicides. Murders. The murder of Tadamichi Inoue. The murder of Klaus Jürgens. The murder of Scheherazade O'Brien."

"You make me laugh, Mr. Jacobus. You make me laugh, not from joy but from pity. You are pitiful, so pitiful you make up fairy tales."

"You were on the bridge that night with Jürgens. You pushed him into the Moldau."

"And how would you know this?"

"From the police report," Jacobus prevaricates, embellishing the theories that Nathaniel had derived from his inquiries. "Jürgens's wife filed a complaint. She convinced the police that Jürgens would never have committed suicide. An investigation was opened. That's why you fled the country. It had nothing to do with politics. You just used that as a cover."

"And you think I did what? Commit murder?"

"If not you, who else?"

Herza is silent for a long time. Finally he exhales a long sigh.

"I might as well come clean, Mr. Jacobus. I have not told anyone, ever, what I am now about to tell you. I have tried to keep this a secret, but obviously you will not rest until you hear the truth."

"Go on."

"It was Lubomir on the bridge. He pushed Jürgens into the river."

"Lubomir?"

"Yes, the poor, misguided fool. He felt he needed to protect me. One time—yes, I admit this—I had an argument with Jürgens. A serious argument. When he walked out on me, I was beside myself. I was angry, perhaps too angry, and I shouted—to no one in particular— 'who will get this meddlesome musician off of my hands?' Or something to that effect. It is difficult to translate exactly from my native language, you see. It was pure frustration, nothing more, as you, a musician, might understand. But loyal Lubomir, he must have misunderstood my ranting—yes, I know, I am prone to do this—and taken me literally, because it was that very night that Jürgens died. When Lubomir told me what had happened, I couldn't believe it. I told him what a terrible thing he did, but what could I do? He was so devoted, and I felt so guilty he had committed a horrible crime on my behalf. I told him not to worry, that Jürgens was on his last legs anyway, and I would never tell a soul. That is the story, Mr. Jacobus. The whole story. There, you have it. To tell you the truth, I feel much relieved to have finally gotten it off my chest after all these years."

"And O'Brien? Was that a 'misunderstanding' too?"

"Now that you raise the possibility in this context, I would not discount it, Mr. Jacobus. You are an astute analyst."

"Well, I suppose we should be getting Lubomir in here to get his confessions."

"Yes, we should, but I'm afraid that won't be possible."

"And why is that?"

"Because Lubomir inconveniently died during the concert, Mr. Jacobus. And now I am leaving. Feel free to stay as long as you wish, but please don't steal the ashtray."

Jacobus is speechless at this unforeseen counterattack. Herza rises and walks past him. Jacobus has one final weapon in reserve on the chessboard, only one more move to play. Herza opens the door. Jacobus hears him gasp.

"And who are you?" Herza asks. "How long have you been listening?"

Getting no response, he asks Jacobus, "Who is this woman? Your wife, perhaps?"

"Take a closer look."

"I don't know this woman," says Herza, but Jacobus hears an undercurrent of doubt. Maybe even fear. The endgame begins.

"You shouldn't have pushed him," says the woman.

Jacobus hears Herza stagger.

"Yes, it's me," she says. "Sonja."

"I think you need to sit down," Jacobus says to Herza.

"What is it you want?" Herza asks.

"It seems," says Jacobus, "that my good friend Sonja has a slightly different version of your fairy tale. The truth is it was you on the bridge with her and Jürgens, not Lubomir. Lubomir was in the car, waiting. He never knew what you did to Jürgens."

"And why would I have killed him if, as you say, all I wanted to do was torture his existence?"

"Because," Sonja intrudes, "he was telling people you were an informer for the KGB and was going to expose you for the swine that you were. That you are. He was going to tell everyone what he knew."

"It was all lies! It was trash."

"Yes, you and I knew it was a lie. Probably even Klaus knew it was a lie, at least when he wasn't drinking. You wouldn't have gone *that* far. But Klaus frightened you, because if the mere rumor of collaboration circulated, your position, your fame, would be jeopardized. It was the only power he had against you—you, who were young and arrogant—and he was only going to use it because of the cruelty you had inflicted upon him, year after year, even when he was old."

"Cruelty? I thought only of the music! And Jürgens would slander me because I was tough? Because I was demanding? I defended my honor!"

"You defended your position. Who would have hired the great Vaclav Herza if they thought you were an informer? Who?" she lashes out at him.

Jacobus has Herza backed into a corner, cut off from any escape route. There is silence. Not a truce. A reassessment.

"Since we seem to be playing a game of questions," says Herza, "now I have a question for you. Who are you? I have never seen you in my life."

"What?" There is alarm in Sonja's voice, sensing that the serpent has not yet been slain. "You deny you were on the bridge with me the night you pushed Jürgens over? You deny you came to my bar every night to talk politics? About changing the world? That is why they all came to Sonja's Bar. But then, you and me, we both fled in different directions. You to become famous and rich, and me to tend a bar in Mount Vernon, New York, where they talk only of football and breasts.

"You, Vaclav Herza, a man of the people! What a joke. Jürgens was the true Socialist, the true idealist! He stood up to you, and you couldn't bear it. You were the tyrant, just like the Russians."

"He was a drunk."

"You made him so. That night, when Klaus got drunk at the bar like he did every night, his tongue got the better of him. He said things he shouldn't have and I gave him even more drink so he would say such ludicrous things that no one would believe a word. That would have been the end of it, but not for you. You feared exposure more than you feared murder, and Jürgens paid the price for his foolishness."

"So, if you are who you say you are, and what happened happened, why then were *you* on the bridge?"

"You know why."

"Why don't you tell us?" says Herza. "In your own words, of course."

"I was there because you and I had been lovers—I choke to use that word for the things you did to me—and I knew what horrors you were capable of. I am not a murderer. I was there to stop you. But there was no stopping you."

"I would say we have an eyewitness to the murder of Klaus Jürgens," says Jacobus, applying the coup de grâce. Life was a game of chess. Check.

"Yes, you are right. This is all very compelling. I think it is time to call the police," says Herza, subdued.

"That's very civil of you," says Jacobus, his victory complete. "Please don't try to run off. It would just make things very messy."

"I have no intention of running off, because when the police arrive, it is my intention to have this woman arrested for the murder of Klaus Jürgens."

"What?" says Jacobus.

"Three people on a bridge. One man is pushed. That leaves two. One is an old hag, the owner of a sleazy bar, a nobody, the detritus washed ashore. The other is me. Between the two of us, who do you think the police will believe, Mr. Jacobus? Who would *you* believe?"

"I have something for you," says Sonja. Jacobus hears the snap of a purse opening.

"My, my! A gun!" says Herza. "You are going to shoot me!" He sounds more amused than alarmed.

"You killed Jürgens, and now you've killed the young woman," says Sonja. "When I read in the newspaper that she had died, I knew you had done the same thing to her as you did to Klaus. Someone has to stop you, you murderer!"

"Don't shoot!" yells Jacobus.

"Go ahead. Shoot!" says Herza, clearly enjoying himself. "Your hands shake like a leaf. Clearly you're no musician. You are a drunken hag. Shoot!"

A shot rings out, deafening Jacobus's left ear.

Herza cackles.

"There! That proves what I am saying. Your paramour Sonja not only missed me, she incriminates herself! She'll have to pay for repairing the armoire, though," Herza says. "Go ahead. Try again! I'll sit still!"

Another shot. Herza continues to laugh uproariously.

Jacobus, deafened by the shots, strains to hear. Footsteps come racing into the room.

"Put down the gun!" hollers a security guard. Jacobus hears a struggle. He doesn't know which way to turn. The world is ending around him and he is powerless.

Sonja screams, "Let me go! Let me go! I must kill the monster!"

Suddenly it's still. Sonja is sobbing.

"Are you all right, Maestro?" the guard asks.

"Fine, fine," says Herza. "The poor thing is delusional. Maybe my *Death and Transfiguration* was too much for her."

"I'll take care of her," says the guard as he drags Sonja, moaning, out of the room.

"Yes. Yes, you do that. And please see that she receives the care she needs. I'm leaving now. You can reach me at home."

FORTY-ONE

Alone in Herza's dressing room, Jacobus heard no sound other than the ticking of a clock. From the moment Herza departed, Jacobus sat, lifeless, in a chair against the wall, his hands stiffly on his knees, his head bowed, his mind blank. The relentless ticking, at first inconspicuous, seemed to get louder second by second, filling the room. When the ticking became deafening, expanding to occupy every space within his universe, Jacobus doubled over and wrapped his arms around his chest in a futile effort to control the unbearable pain that racked him from within. Involuntarily, his mouth opened unnaturally wide, but no sound emerged.

Why me? What have I done? Scheherazade O'Brien, my parents, my brother, dead. All my doing. For what purpose? Where is my redemption? Where is my soul? Empty. Look at me! Doddering. Senile. Worthless. The space I occupy on this earth would be better served by someone else. Anyone else.

Eventually Jacobus's convulsion ebbed from exhaustion, not resolution. Time passed in the deserted hall. Footsteps approached—two people walking quickly and quietly. The door to the dressing room opened, slowly. To cart him off to the asylum, he supposed.

"Jake!"

"Beanie?" said Jacobus, recognizing the voice through his haze. "What are you and Cappy doing here?"

There was an awkward silence.

"Nothing," said Cappy.

"Let's go," said Beanie.

"Sorry to bother you, Jake," said Cappy.

"Yeah," said Beanie. "Good to see you."

Without another word to him, his two old friends hastily re-treated. Jacobus wondered why Cappy hadn't been whistling.

The Parsley twins sat in Tiny's idling car in Section B of Harmonium Hall's brand-new parking lot. Fresh paint gave it a clean, inviting scent, and the lighting, designed for the security of the affluent concertgoer, made it less dingy than a typical New York City lot, but the brothers were not there to admire a parking lot. Their car was the only one remaining in the area reserved for the musicians and was pointed so that they could see pedestrians descending from Freedom Bridge. There hadn't been any for a half hour at least. Usually as garrulous as Chip 'n Dale, on this occasion Tiny and Junior had little to say as they sat and waited. Without altering his forward gaze, Tiny silently passed Junior a half-empty bottle of bourbon. Junior looked at his watch. They wondered why the Lincoln Town Car was nowhere in sight, why neither Donaghue nor Butkus had made an appearance, and especially why Cappy and Beanie hadn't emerged with Herza as planned. And since they couldn't come up with a good answer to any of their questions, they continued to drink and to wait.

A policeman, on foot, turned the corner into their section.

"Maybe he's just patrolling," Tiny said quietly. "Maybe he'll just keep walking."

"Don't say anything," said Junior. He hid the bottle underneath the seat.

The policeman looked at the car, then at the brothers, curiously.

Tiny waved. The policeman waved back but continued to approach.

The cop tapped on the window. Junior rolled it down.

"Good evening, gents," said the cop, who quickly saw he would be no match for the three-hundred-pound twins, if it came to that.

"Evening," said Tiny.

"Waiting for someone?" the cop asked.

"No," said Junior.

"We were just listening to the radio," added Tiny, by way of explanation, though the radio wasn't on.

"Could you step out of the car, sir? Both of you, please."

Tiny shifted into drive, jammed his foot on the gas pedal, and with a screech the car roared out of the parking lot.

The foot patrolman was unable to pursue. Instead, he called headquarters and reported that he had encountered two suspicious characters in a gray Taurus with a dented left front quarter panel.

A gala bouquet of red, white, and blue fireworks celebrates the consecration of Harmonium Hall. They boom like cannon over the Hudson River, simultaneously illuminating the illustrious countenances of the Statue of Liberty and of Vaclav Herza, accentuating his disfigured grin in sporadic bursts of light.

Herza, standing under the protective statue of his hero, Richard Strauss, gazes back at his creation—Harmonium Hall, this monument to a lifetime of hard work, of determination, of genius—as adoringly as a mother upon her newborn child. Alone on the bridge, and with the cannonade of the fireworks preventing anyone from hearing, he indulges in a bout of sentimentality that surprises even himself. He begins to whistle the Largo from the "New World" Symphony.

That buffoon, Lulich, is not the only one who can whistle, Herza thinks. He has rarely resorted to whistling, that simpleminded diversion of the underclasses, but he knows that with a little practice he could easily surpass Lulich's skill. For the moment, the whistle emerges through his teeth and exits the side of his mouth through his reconstructed lips. It sounds more like the hiss of a teakettle than a true whistle, but it is surprisingly loud and, of course, perfectly in tune.

At the mouth of the Hudson, America's symbol of freedom shimmers in ephemeral outline through Herza's tear-brimmed eyes. What a wonderful country, he extols, where one's past can be rewritten, where one can defeat one's enemies with such ease! Like the hero in Strauss's *Ein Heldenleben,* Herza has dispatched his critics and vanquished his adversaries. Herza craftily modulates from Dvořák's Largo to the hero's theme, and then to "the bombs bursting in air." I should have been a composer, he jests to himself.

As he gazes into the night sky, savoring his glory, a tear finds its way down Herza's scarred cheek. So many years, so much struggle, and now the victory is mine. And there is no one left to claim otherwise. No Jürgens, no Inoue, no Lubomir, no Sonja, no Scheherazade O'Brien. No Jacobus, that feeble excuse for a man.

The Hudson's dark current far below flows with calm, inexorable predictability. Like the Moldau. Herza peers down into it, comforted by its depth and power. He sees the reflection of the fireworks floating on its surface like huge, multicolored jellyfish. Then, magically, embers from above descend gently to the water, hissing, dispersing their illusory counterpart.

Herza turns again toward his glistening mecca. Why shouldn't he savor his accomplishment? he asks himself. He deserves everything.

An umbrella of fire ignites the sky. In its fleeting red glare, Herza believes he has spied someone on the bridge! The light quickly ebbs and Herza peers into the darkness. Is it truly another person, or is it my imagination? He blinks and waits a few seconds for his eyes to adjust to the darkness, but the next eruption makes the world day again. Yes, there is indeed someone else on his Freedom Bridge. A man. A man with a cane, hunched, freeze-framed like a life-sized, two-dimensional cutout of that Charles Chaplin hobo.

That blind cockroach, Jacobus! Herza stares in the direction of the shadowy form, even as the darkness returns.

Jacobus, in the same submissive poster pose, moves progressively closer. The alternation between darkness and brilliant light makes it seem as if he has been lifted and repositioned. He is one, two, three statues away—Mozart, Beethoven, Bruckner—though he seems to be moving more toward the railing than forward.

The fool doesn't even seem to be aware I am here, thinks Herza. I will fix that. I will not have this invalid on my bridge, on this night. I am not going to let that pitiful cripple piss on my parade. Herza begins again to whistle, alternating the Largo and "The Star-Spangled Banner" in mocking insolence. He is so clever, and is an even better whistler than he thought! With his newly discovered skill, he takes childish delight in adorning the tunes with birdlike trills and ornaments.

His eyes are fixed upon Jacobus, who, wavering, has placed his cane on the ground and is now standing under Beethoven. He seems to be measuring the distance between the railings, Herza thinks. Yes, he's trying to fit through them! I should have let the damn architects keep them wider apart.

Jacobus now has his hands on the railing, blindly looking out, leaning over. Only the height of it prevents him from toppling into the river. Jacobus tries to find a footing to hoist himself higher.

So it's Davy Jones's locker, is it? Herza realizes. I must find out who this Davy Jones character was. Well, I'll give the cripple an appropriate send-off. Herza crescendos his rendition of "Goin' Home" to an intentionally grating fortissimo, timing it to make sure it isn't obscured by the almost constant barrage of fireworks signaling the grand finale.

Suddenly, the form of Jacobus stiffens. He stands up straight and swings his head toward Herza like a robotic homing device. Under the thunderous sky, the two men remain unnaturally still. Jacobus shakes his head, as if to reboot his thoughts. He slowly begins to move toward Herza, sliding the tip of his cane along the safety railing's metal supports for direction. As the distance narrows, the click of his cane accelerates, the reverse of a spinning wheel of fortune. Jacobus is now under Mozart and continues to gain ground.

Herza softens his whistling. The fireworks are constant now, anyway, and the rolling volleys deafening over the river. There's no way the cripple can hear him. Yet still he comes! Herza looks up to see the last of the fireworks, after which his concert hall will blend into the night and he will go home. Suddenly, the entire sky lights up in blinding white light, brighter than all the previous fireworks combined, rendering all else invisible. What is this? Herza asks himself. A stab of pain shoots through his heart. His knees begin to buckle. Herza wraps his arm around the railing. He will not show weakness. He will not ask the cripple for help, even if it is offered. Unable to support his weight, Herza's grip on the railing begins to fail. He banishes the thought of Jacobus coming to his aid.

I will persevere, as I always have.

Herza, on his knees, raises his eyes heavenward. The face of Strauss, glowing and smiling, is suddenly replaced by the ghostly countenance of the blind man looking down at him. Herza, his breathing shallow, reaches out in desperation to avoid toppling, and with both hands he clutches Jacobus by his trouser legs. Jacobus staggers backward but doesn't fall. Herza's balance abandons him and his torso slumps forward, his head rocking against the inside of Jacobus's thighs.

Jacobus cranes his neck downward, bringing his own face as close as he can to the maestro's.

"Malinkovsky," Jacobus says quietly.

The maestro gazes up at Jacobus's spectral visage. "You have been, and will always be, a *tutti* player," says Vaclav Herza, and harnessing his last ounce of strength, spits in Jacobus's face.

The saliva seems to nourish the crevices of Jacobus's careworn cheeks, which bloom into what appears to be a benign smile.

"Checkmate," Jacobus says.

FORTY-TWO

SUNDAY

The Metro North train from Grand Central arrived at its last stop, Wassaic, nestled in the bucolic agricultural valley of Columbia County, New York, at 11:48 A.M. Jacobus emerged, his face as ashen as the sky that threatened another day of thunderstorms. Yumi was waiting for him on the platform. Because he looked so haggard, she gently wrapped her arm through his, guiding him down the steps to her car. She was going to suggest stopping at K&J's for lunch on the hour-long drive to his house but decided he needed rest more than food.

"Did you hear what happened?" Yumi asked as soon as they were in the car.

"What happened?" he said flatly.

"It's hard to believe, but Vaclav Herza's dead!"

"Oh?"

"It was on *Weekend Edition* on WAMC. Scott Simon interviewed Martin Lilburn of the *Times.* Herza was on Freedom Bridge and fell into the Hudson River. The current would have taken him out to sea, but someone spotted his body just before it passed the Statue of Liberty. Isn't that ironic?"

"Ironic?"

"Well, for him to die on the night of his greatest success."

Jacobus had planned his next words carefully and had practiced subtle nuances for hours, as if he were preparing a Mozart sonata for performance. "So maybe now you can accept the position."

The car swerved.

"What's the matter? Hit a skunk?"

"No," said Yumi. "You just caught me off guard. The thought hadn't even occurred to me."

"Might not be a bad idea. You'd make a good concertmaster. A fine concertmaster. They'd probably welcome some stability at this point in time." He had said it just right. Leave it up to her. Don't lay it on too thick.

"Do you think so? Maybe you're right. I'll think about it. Yes, I'll think about it."

They rode in silence for a while, the car comfortably winding along the embracing curves of Route 23.

"Drowned, did he?" Jacobus asked.

"You'd think. But they're saying that he might've still been alive when he fell in."

"Heart attack, then? Stroke? He always did have a weak ticker."

Jacobus cocked his head to better hear the confirmation.

"No. Someone shot him through the heart. Can you believe it?"

"Impossible!"

"It's true. Shot him from behind. The bullet lodged in his heart. They said he hardly bled externally at all, and then whoever did it somehow managed to push him over the railing."

Yumi suddenly braked the car, bringing it to a stop.

"Jake, where's your cane?"

ACKNOWLEDGMENTS

Part of my enjoyment writing novels is working with a team of real pros to create the best presentation of the book possible. In that way it's like an orchestra with the release date of the book as the "performance," but I cringe at the thought that this analogy would make me the conductor. In any event, there's a lot more collaborative give-and-take, and I have not yet even come close to glaring menacingly at my perspicacious agent, Josh Getzler, and his assistant, Maddie Raffel, of the Hannigan Salky Getzler agency; or the St. Martin's Press team of my thoughtfully critical editor, Michael Homler, musically compassionate production editor, Geraldine Van Dusen, and publicist, Bridget Hartzler, who has since passed the baton to equally tireless Justin Velella; or my new personal publicist, Janice Evans, who has an uncanny nose for finding a story; or my wry, dog-loving copy editor, Cynthia Merman, for whom I almost make mistakes on purpose just to hear her response.

My son, Jacob, an amazingly creative artist and musician, is always a fount of insight when discussing the relationship between the two art forms, and first introduced me to the genius of J.M.W. Turner's visionary land- and seascapes. My crack medical team, comprising my nephew, Dr. Richard Elias, an eminent New York oral surgeon; his wife,